6̶9̶
p95

D0435986

MILES
0 100 200 300 400 500

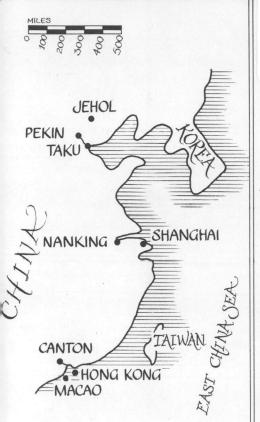

JEHOL
PEKIN
TAKU

KOREA

CHINA

NANKING • — • SHANGHAI

CANTON
• HONG KONG
MACAO

TAIWAN

EAST CHINA SEA

COAST

YANGTSE
VALLEY
&
ESTUARY

NANKING

Kiangyin

Paoshan
Soochow

Tsungming Island

SHANGHAI
Chingpu

TaiHu
Lake

Sungkiang

MILES
0 20 40 60 80 100

Also by George MacDonald Fraser

Flashman
Royal Flash
Flash for Freedom
Flashman at the Charge
Flashman in the Great Game
Flashman's Lady
Flashman and the Redskins
Mr. American
The Pyrates

The Steel Bonnets: The Story of the Anglo-Scottish Border Reivers

Short Stories:
The General Danced at Dawn
McAuslan in the Rough

FLASHMAN
AND THE
DRAGON

FLASHMAN
AND THE
DRAGON

George
MacDonald
Fraser

Alfred A. Knopf   New York 1986

THIS IS A BORZOI BOOK
PUBLISHED BY ALFRED A. KNOPF, INC.

Copyright © 1985 by George MacDonald Fraser

All rights reserved under International and Pan-American Copyright
Conventions. Published in the United States by Alfred A. Knopf, Inc.,
New York. Distributed by Random House, Inc., New York. Originally
published in Great Britain by William Collins Sons & Co. Ltd., London.

LIBRARY OF CONGRESS CATALOGING-IN-PUBLICATION DATA

Fraser, George MacDonald.   Flashman and the dragon.

I. Title.
PR6056.R287F6 1986   823'.914   85-45795
ISBN 0-394-55357-8

Manufactured in the United States of America
FIRST AMERICAN EDITION

For Ka't-lin
a memento of the Pearl River and Tuah Bee

Explanatory Note

It is now twenty years since the Flashman Papers, the memoirs of the notorious Rugby School bully who became a Victorian hero, were found in a Leicestershire saleroom. Of the dozen or so packets of manuscript, seven have so far been published in book form; they have covered four military campaigns (the First Afghan War, Crimea, Indian Mutiny, and Sioux War of 1879), and five episodes of less formal and generally reluctant active service – pirate-hunting with Brooke of Sarawak; as military adviser to Queen Ranavalona of Madagascar; as conspirator with Bismarck in the Schleswig-Holstein affair; in the African slave trade and Underground Railroad; and on the American frontier during the Gold Rush. This eighth volume sees him returning to military service in the Taiping Rebellion and Pekin Expedition of 1860.

Not the least interesting feature of Flashman's recollections, to students of history, is the light they cast on the early years of many famous Victorians, who are seen through the unsparing eyes of one who, while a self-confessed coward, libertine, and scoundrel, was nevertheless a scrupulous reporter. Thus, we have seen him fleeing the murderous wrath of the young politician Bismarck, viewing Congressman Lincoln with wary respect, teaching the infant Crazy Horse how to wink, admiring Lola Montez the aspiring novelty dancer, and toadying to the young Queen Victoria herself. In China he encounters two of the great mercenary captains, a future empress, the founding fathers of the modern British Army and Navy, and those strange, forgotten peasants who changed the face of a great empire. It may be that he provides some new historical insights, while again demonstrating the lengths to which perfidy, impudence, immorality, and poltroonery may be stretched in the enforced pursuit of fame, riches, and above all, survival.

In accordance with the wishes of Mr Paget Morrison, owner of the Flashman manuscripts, I have confined my editing to correcting the old soldier's spelling, checking the accuracy of the narrative (which is exact where matters of verifiable historical fact are concerned) and inserting the usual foot-notes, appendices, and glossary.

G.M.F.

❀ Old Professor Flashy's first law of economics is that the time to beware of a pretty woman is not when you're flush of cash (well, you know what she's after, and what's a bankroll more or less?), but when you're *short* of the scratch, and she offers to set you right. Because that ain't natural, and God knows what she's up to. I learned this when I was fourteen, and one Lady Geraldine, a high-spirited Hebe ten years my senior, lured me out in a punt with the promise of a crown if I minded her clothes while she went bathing. In all innocence, I accepted – and I haven't seen that five bob yet, because the randy baggage had to shell out all her loose change to buy the silence of the grinning water-bailiff who caught us unawares in the reeds, where she was teaching me natural history after her swim. I had the presence of mind even at that tender age to clap my breeches over my face and so avoid recognition as I fled, but you take the point – I had been misled, in my youthful simplicity, by a designing female who played on my natural cupidity.

Ever since, when they've dangled rich rewards before me, I've taken fright. If the case of Mrs Phoebe Carpenter was an exception – well, she was a clergyman's wife, and you don't expect double-dealing from a wide-eyed simperer who sings come-to-Jesus in the choir. I don't know why I bothered with her . . . yes, I do, though; shaped like an Indian nautch-dancer under her muslin, blue-eyed, golden-haired, and with that pouting lower lip that's as good as a beckoning finger to chaps like me – she reminded me rather of my darling wife, whom I hadn't seen in more than three years and was getting uncommon hungry for. So, reading the invitation in Mrs Carpenter's demure smile, and having ten days to loaf in Hong Kong before my ship sailed for Home[1], I decided to have a cast at her; it was a dead-and-alive hole in '60, I can

9

tell you, and how else should a weary soldier pass his time? So I attended morning and evening service, hollering hosannas and nodding stern approval while her drone of a husband sermonised about temptation and the snares that Satan spreads (about which he didn't know the first dam' thing), and gallantly helping her to gather up the hymn-books afterwards. I dined with them, traded a text or two with the Reverend, joined them in evening prayers, squired her along the Queen's Road – she was all for it, of course, but what was middling rum was that he was, too; it ain't every middle-aged vicar who cares to see his young bride escorted by a dashing Lancer with Balaclava whiskers. I put it down to natural toad-eating on his part, for I was the lion of the hour in those days, with my new knighthood and V.C., and all my Mutiny heroics to add to the fame I had undeservedly won in Crimea and Afghanistan. If you've read my earlier memoirs you'll know all about it – and how by shirking, running, diving into cover, and shielding my quaking carcase behind better men, I had emerged after four campaigns with tremendous credit, a tidy sum in loot, and a chestful of tinware. I was a colonel of six years' seniority at 37, big, bluff, handsome Flash Harry, quite a favourite with Queen and Consort, well spoken of by Palmerston and my chiefs, married to the beauteous and wealthy daughter of a peer (and a dead peer, at that) – and only I knew (though I'd a feeling that wily old Colin Campbell suspected) that my fame was all a fraud and a sham.

There had been a time when I was sure it couldn't last, and they were bound to find me out for the poltroon and scoundrel I was – but I'd been devilish lucky, and, d'ye know, there's nothing sticks like a good name, provided you know how to carry your credit with a modest grin and a glad eye. Once let 'em call you a hero, and they'll never leave off worshipping – which is absolute nuts when the worshipper cuts a figure like the adoring Mrs Carpenter's. After three days of my society I reckoned she was ready to melt; all that was needed was a stroll in the garden after dark, a few well-chosen quotations from the Song of Solomon, and she'd play like one of those abandoned Old Testament queens her husband was forever reviling from the pulpit.

As a final rehearsal I took her out to picnic at the Poke

Fullam bungalow, which was the favoured resort in Hong Kong at that time; we found a secluded spot, spread a rug, disposed of the cold prawns and a bottle of Hock, and settled down to exchange my murmured gallantries for her sighs and coy glances – I didn't intend to board her that afternoon, you understand; too public, and she wasn't even part-drunk. As it happened, I'd have been wasting my time, for the innocent Mrs Carpenter had been working to a fixed end just as purposefully as I. And such an end; when I think back on it, words fail me.

She led up to it by talking of her husband's ambition to build a church and hall over at Kowloong; even in those days it was the fashionable place, so he would be quite top dog among the local gospel-wallopers. The difficulty, says she sighing, was money – although even that would not have been insurmountable had it not been for the impending war.

"When Sir Hope Grant begins his campaign, you see, it is certain that there will be a cessation of all China trade, even with Canton," says she. "And when that happens – why, there will be an end to all Josiah's hopes. And mine." And she choked back what sounded like a little sob.

I'd been paying no heed, content to stroke her hand, brotherly-like, while she prattled, but hearing her gulp I perked up. Get 'em weeping, and you're halfway to climbing all over them. I feigned concern, and squeezed her hand, begging her to explain what Grant's campaign could have to do with dear Josiah's church-building. I knew, as all the world did, that Grant was due in Hong Kong shortly with a fleet and army whose purpose would be to go up-country and force our latest treaty down the Chinese Emperor's throat, but it wasn't liable to be much of a war: show the flag to the Chinks, kick a few yellow backsides, and home again with hardly a shot fired – the kind of campaign that would have suited me, if I'd been looking for one, which I wasn't. I could thank God I'd be homeward bound before Grant arrived, for he knew me from India and would certainly dragoon me into service if I were silly enough to be on hand. You don't pass up the chance of employing the gallant Flashy. And *he* don't pass up the chance of making himself scarce.

"But even a *little* war will put an end to traffic with the

Chinese merchants," she lamented. "Oh, it is so hard, when Josiah and his friends have invested so wisely! To be robbed of the deserved profit that would have fulfilled his dream! It is too bad!" And she looked at me with trembling mouth and great blue eyes – Gad, she was like Elspeth, even to the imbecile parting of those crimson lips, and the quivering of her top hamper. Feeling slightly fogged, I asked, what investment had dear Josiah made?

"Why, opium, of course! He was so clever, laying out Papa's legacy in two thousand chests of the very choicest Patna," says this fair flower of the vicarage. "And it would have fetched ever so much money at Canton – more than enough to build our dear little church! But if war comes, and he cannot sell his cargo . . .' She sniffed and looked woebegone.

"D'you mean to tell me," says I, astonished, "that Josiah is smuggling poppy?" I know the Church is game for anything, as a rule, and Hong Kong only existed for the opium trade; most everyone was in it. But it don't go with dog-collars and Sunday schools, exactly.

"Gracious, no! Dear Sir Harry, how could you suppose such a thing? Why, it is not *smuggling* at all nowadays!" She was all lovely earnestness as she explained – and so help me, these were her very words: "Josiah says that the fifth supplementary clause of the new treaty removes *all* restrictions on the trade in opium, cash, pulse, grain, saltpetre . . . oh, I forget all the things, but one of them is spelter, whatever that may be; it sounds very horrid. It is true," she admitted gravely, "that the treaty is not yet *ratified*, but Sir Hope Grant will see to that, and Josiah says there can be no illegality in profiting by anticipation." So there.

Josiah'll end up in Lambeth Palace or Dartmoor, at this rate, thinks I. Imagine – a clergyman peddling the black smoke. Purely out of curiosity, I asked didn't he have moral qualms? She twitched her tits in impatience.

"Oh, Josiah says that is Nonconformist missionary talk, and that it is well-known the natives of China use opium as a sedative, rather than as a narcotic, and that it does not one-tenth of the harm that strong waters cause among our poorer classes at home. Gin, and such things." Then she sighed again, and they quivered in dejection. "But it is all by the way now. If he cannot sell the cargo . . . and he could have built our church and to spare, too!"

With enough over to start a couple of brothels, no doubt, the way Josiah did business. "Hold on," says I. "*Why* can't he sell it – where is it, by the way?"

"At Macao. Josiah is gone over today to see it put aboard the fast crabs and scrambling dragons." Not two years out of the schoolroom, sink me, and she was talking like a taipan.*

"Well, there you are – he can send it up Pearl River to the Canton factories tomorrow, and sell it to the Hongs."

"Oh, if it were so simple! But you see, Sir Harry, with all the war talk there is word that the Chinese merchants have been *forbidden* to buy from our people . . . and . . . and Josiah and his friends have no influence to persuade them."

"Then get Dent or Jardine to run it in – they'll persuade anybody – and get a better price than Josiah could, I dare say."

"And take all our profit in commission! They are the greediest persons, you know," says this tender child. "Besides, the price is settled. Josiah vows to take no less than eight pounds a chest."

"Jesus – I mean, dear me!" says I. "Two thousand chests – why, that's near a ton, isn't it? Sixteen thousand quid!" I was no expert, but you couldn't be in Hong Kong five minutes without knowing the going figures. "Phew! Well, my dear, he'd better get it to Canton somehow before the war starts – stay, though: can't he put it in bond until things are more settled?"

"It is prepared chandoo, not raw cake," says the Opium Queen pathetically. "Unless it goes directly, it must spoil. Oh, is it not wretchedly unlucky? Those who *could* run it will do so only on extortionate terms; those who *would*, for a fair consideration, are not people who could deal with the Chinese officials and merchants. Josiah has a skipper, a Mr Ward, but he cannot speak Chinese, even!"

* Fast crabs and scrambling dragons were opium-running craft.

13

And it was then, with another superb sigh, that she turned those great misty eyes on me in undoubted appeal, and said in a little voice: "It would be so easy . . . for the *right* person, you see." She looked away, downcast. "Josiah says he would pay him ten per cent."

Lady Geraldine had been rather more subtle . . . but she hadn't been offering sixteen hundred quid. Handsome pocket money, if you like – and easier to earn than falling off a log, for whatever the Pekin government said, the Hong merchants would cut Confucius's throat to buy a ton of chandoo, whoever offered it. And she was right – all that was needed was someone with bold front and bearing who could brush aside inconvenient officials on the run up-river, stick out his jaw at any Chink jack-in-the-office who threatened confiscation, and see that Josiah's ignorant skipper found his way safe to Jackass Point. Nothing in that.

Mind you, she had a hard bark, asking a British Army colonel to nursemaid her shipload of puggle – yet why not? Here was I, friendly disposed, officer and gentleman, knew the ropes, spoke the lingo (well, I could understand a Mandarin, and make myself enough understood in turn; with the coolies I had to use pigeon and my boots), and just the chap to stare down any yellow office-wallahs. A week till my ship sailed, ample time . . . sixteen hundred . . . Mrs Carpenter swooning with gratitude . . . h'm . . .

You must remember that these thoughts ran through my mind with those innocent-wanton eyes fixed on mine, and that excellent bosom heaving between us. And if you think she was a froward piece, or that I should have smelled a battalion of rats . . . well, it was a plausible tale, and not even a scent of risk. With our garrison at Canton, the Pearl was as safe as the Avon, and there was no stigma – well, not to signify. It was "trade", not "opium", that would have raised an eyebrow at Horse Guards. And sixteen hundred . . . for a jolly sail on the river?

"We . . . I . . . should be *so* grateful," she murmured, and gave me a quick slantendicular.

"You little goose!" says I indulgently, "if you want *me* to do it . . . why not say so?" I gave her my sad Flashy smile. "Don't you know I'd do anything for you?" And with a light

14

laugh I kissed her masterfully, munching away, and I dare say we might have done the business there and then if a gaggle of brats with a governess hadn't hove in view, causing us to break clean and remark on the splendid view, such a perfect day for picnicking.

We settled the details in the tonga back to town, myself making light of it and pinching her palm, she all flushed confusion and breathless gratitude. How could she and dear Josiah ever thank me? Well, Josiah could stump up the rhino on my return, and she would certainly do the rest, if I could judge by the light in her eye and the way she shivered when I squeezed her knee. They're all alike, you know.

Aye. I should have remembered Lady Geraldine.

* * *

I don't know who ran the first chest of opium into China, but he was a great man in his way. It was as though some imaginary trader had put into the Forth with a cargo of Glenlivet to discover that the Scots had never heard of whisky. There was a natural appetite, as you may say. And while the Chinks had been puffing themselves half-witted long before the first foreign trader put his nose into the Pearl River, there's no doubt that our own John Company had developed their taste for the drug, back in the earlies, and before long they couldn't get enough of it.

This didn't suit the ruling Manchoos, for while they were as partial to a pipe as the next heathen, they saw that it was ruining the commonalty, and who would hew the wood and draw the water then? These Manchoos, you see, were fierce warriors who had swept in from the north centuries earlier, and dealt with China much as our English forebears did with Ireland (not that we ever forced the Paddies to wear pigtails as a badge of serfdom). They established a Manchoo ruling class, took all the plum posts, ran the country with a sloth, inefficiency, and waste that would have shocked a Bengali babu, treated the conquered Chinese like dirt – and sat back in complacent luxury, growing their finger-nails long, cultivating the more rarefied arts, galloping their concubines, developing a taste for putrefied food, preaching pure philosophy and practising abominable cruelties, exalting the trivial and neglecting the essential, having another romp at the concubines, and generally priding themselves on being lords of creation. Which, since they hardly admitted the existence of the world outside China, is what they were.

So you can see they resented white interlopers who bade fair to undermine their Empire with poppy drug, and did their damnedest to stop the trade, but couldn't. To their chagrin they discovered that their God-given superiority, their highly-refined taste in eggshell pottery, and their limitless lines of ancestors, availed nothing against any Dundee pirate with a pistol on his hip and a six-pounder in his bows who was determined to run his opium in. Which made the Manchoo Mandarins wild with outraged pride, and more high-handed towards foreigners than ever, with the result that war broke out in 1840. Being Chinese and useless, they lost, and had to cede Hong Kong to us and open up Treaty Ports to European trade. And the poppy-running went on as before, only more so.

You'd have thought that would teach 'em manners, but not a bit of it. Instead of realising that foreign trade had come to stay, they convinced themselves that we were only there on sufferance, and they could treat our traders and emissaries as dirt, evil-smelling foreign savages that we were. They *knew* China was the centre and master of the world, and that everyone else was barbarian filth, lurking on their outskirts plotting mischief, and needing to be brought to heel like untrained curs. What, admit us as equals? Trade freely with us? Receive our ambassadors at Pekin? (The Chinese for "ambassador" is "tribute-bearer", which gives you some notion of their conceit.) It was unthinkable.

You have to understand this Chinese pride – they truly believe they have dominion over us, and that our rulers are mere slaves to their Emperor. Haven't I heard a red-button Mandarin, a greasy old profligate so damned cultivated that his concubines had to feed him and even carry him to the commode to do his business, because he'd never learned how – haven't I heard him lisping about "the barbarian vassal Victoria"? As for the American President – a mere coolie. (And you won't teach John Chinaman different by blowing his cities apart with artillery, or trampling his country underfoot. Well, if a footpad knocks *you* down, or a cannibal eats you, it don't follow that he's your superior, does it? Fiercer and stronger, perhaps, but infinitely lower in the scale of creation. That's how the Chinese think of us – and damn the facts that stare 'em in the face.)

So, even after we'd licked them, and gained a trade foothold in the Treaty Ports, they continued as arrogant as ever, and finally over-stepped the mark in '56, boarding the British ship *Arrow* (though whether she was entitled to fly the Union Flag was debatable) and arresting her Chink crew because one of 'em was believed to be a pirate (which some said he wasn't, but one of his relatives might be). The usual Chinese confusion, you see, and before you could say "Snooks!" we had bombarded Canton, and the local Mandarin was offering thirty dollars for British heads.

I believe it might have blown over if the clown Cobden, abetted by Gladstone and D'Israeli (there's an unholy alliance, if you like), hadn't worked himself into a sweat in Parliament, saying it was all our fault, and it was a scandal the way our opium-traffickers abused the Chinese, who were the most saintly folk on record, while British bounce and arrogance were a byword, and we were just picking a quarrel, more shame to us. This had Palmerston spitting his false teeth all over the shop; he damned Cobden and the Chinks for rascals both, said our honour had been flouted, and anyway we had only bombarded Canton with the "utmost forbearance" (good old Pam!), and was Cobden aware that the Manchoos had beheaded 70,000 folk at Canton in the past year, and were guilty of vices that were a disgrace to human nature, hey?

Fine Parliamentary stuff, you see, and when Pam lost the vote and had to go to the country, he won a thumping majority (which was what the old scoundrel had been playing for all along) and the Chinese war was on with a vengeance. It was a scrappy business, but after we took Canton the Chinks had to climb down and agree to a new treaty, admitting us to *inland* trade, with Ambassadors at Pekin. But being still as arrogant as ever, they dragged their heels about signing, and when we sent a fleet up the Peiho to persuade 'em, damned if they didn't have a sudden burst of martial valour, and handed us a splendid licking at the Taku Forts. So now, in the spring of '60, with an uneasy truce between Britain and China, Hope Grant was coming with an army of British and Frogs, to convoy our ambassador to Pekin, and make the Emperor sign.[2]

You must bear with my historical lecture, for I have to show you how things stood if you are to understand my tale. For all the official coolness between Pekin and ourselves, commerce was still going on between our traders and Canton (which we continued to hold) but the Carpenters were right to wonder how long it might continue, with our invasion imminent. Which brings me back to the point where I agreed to escort their cargo of poppy up the Pearl, with the prospect of a jolly river cruise, sixteen hundred sovs, and a fine frolic with dear Phoebe when I got back to Hong Kong.

Mind you, as I leaned on the rail of the lead lorcha bearing up beyond Lintin Island two days after our picnic, with the rising sun rolling the fog-banks up the great estuary, I could honestly say it wasn't either the cash or the lady that had made me turn opium-runner. No, it was the fun of the thing, the lure of sport-without-danger, the seeking for fresh sights and amusements, like this magnificent Pearl River, with that wondrous silver mist that I suppose gave it its name, and its fairy islets beyond the Tiger's Gate, and the dawn breeze rippling the shining water and filling the sails of the stubby junks and lorchas and crazy fisher-craft – and the pug-nosed, grinning Hong Kong boat girl rolling her poonts on the thwart of a sampan and shouting: "Hi-ya, cap'n! Hi-ya! You wanchee jiggee no wanchee jiggee? You payee two hunner' cash, drinkee samshu? Jollee-jollee!"

"Who you, Dragon Empress?" says I. "Come aboard, one hunner' cash, maybe all-same samshu." They're the jolliest wenches, the Hong Kong boaters, plump little sluts who swim like fish and couple like stoats. She squealed with laughter and plunged in, reached the lorcha in a few fast strokes, and was hauled inboard, all wet and shiny and giggling in her little loin-cloth. Anything less like an angel of Providence you never saw, but that's what she was; if I'd guessed, I'd ha' treated her with more respect than I did,

18

slapping her rump and sending her aft for later. For the moment I was content to muse at the rail, enjoying the warm sunshine and the distant green prospect of Lintin, where the coolies could be seen languidly pursuing the only two occupations known to the Chinese peasant: to wit, standing stock-still up to the knees in paddy-water holding a bullock on a rope, or shifting mud very slowly from one point to another. Deny them these employments, and they would simply lie down and die, which a good many of them seemed to do anyway. I'm told that Napoleon once said that China was a sleeping giant, and when she awoke the world would be sorry. He didn't say who was going to get the bastards out of bed.

I put this to Ward, the skipper commanding the two lorchas which made up our little convoy. He was a brisk, wiry, bright-eyed little Yankee about ten years my junior, and though he hadn't been in China more than a month or two, you couldn't have wished for a smarter hand at the helm of a lorcha, or a sharper tongue when it came to keeping the Chinese boatmen up to the mark; he was a young terrier, and had learned his trade on American merchantmen, with a mate's ticket, damn-your-eyes, which was fair going at his age. For all that, he had an odd, soft streak; when one of the Chinks was knocked overside by a swinging boom, and we lost way fishing him out, I looked to see Ward lay into him with a rope's end for his clumsiness, or hang him from the rail to dry. But he just laughed and cuffed the Chink's head, with a stream of pigeon, and says to me:

"I fell overboard on *my* first voyage – and what d'ye think I was doing? Chasing a butterfly, so help me, I was! Say, I was a lot greener than that Chink, though! C'mon, ye blushing Chinese cherubs, tailee on makee pull! Pullee, I say! Tell ye what, colonel, it takes an awful lot o' these beggars to do one man's work!"

That was when I observed that the Chinese were the idlest rascals in creation, and he frowned and chuckled all together.

"I reckon," says he. "But they could be a fine people, for all that. Give 'em some one to lead 'em, to drive 'em, to show 'em how. They got the prime country in creation here – when they find out how to use it. Say, and they're smart –

you know they were civilised while we were still running around with paint on? Why, they had paper an' gunpowder centuries before we did!"

"Which they use to make kites and fireworks," says I. It was plain he was an old China hand in the making – and after a few weeks' acquaintance, too. "As for their civilisation, it's getting rottener and more corrupt and decadent by the minute. Look at their ramshackle government –"

"Look at the Taipings, if you like!" cries he. "That's the new China, mark my words! They'll stand this whole country on its head, 'fore they're through, see if they don't!" He took a big breath, smoothing his long black hair with both hands in an odd nervous gesture; his eyes were shining with excitement. "The new China! Boy, I'm going to get me a section of that, though! Know what, colonel? – after this trip, I might just take myself a long slant up the Yangtse and join up with 'em. *Tai'ping tieng-kwow*, eh? The Kingdom of Heavenly Peace – but can't they fight some? I guess so – and you may be sure they're on the look-out for mercenaries – why, a go-ahead white man could go right to the top among 'em, maybe make Prince even, with a button on his hat!" He laughed and slapped his fist, full of ginger.

"You're crazy," says I, "but since they are too, you'll fit right in, I dare say."

"Fred T. Ward fits in anywhere, mister!" cries he, and then he was away along the deck again, chivvying the boatmen to trim the great mainsail, yelling his bastard pigeon and laughing as he tailed on to the rope.

Not only China-struck, but a well-fledged lunatic, I could see. Of course he wasn't alone in having a bee in his bonnet about the Taipings; even the European Powers were keeping an anxious eye on them, wondering how far they might go. In case you haven't heard of them, I must tell you that they were another of those incredible phenomena that made China the topsy-turvy mess it was, like some fantastic land from Gulliver, where everything was upside down and out of kilter. Talk about moonbeams from cucumbers; the Taipings were even dafter than that.

They began back in the '40s, when a Cantonese clerk failed his examinations and fell into a trance, from which he

20

emerged proclaiming that he was Christ's younger brother –
a ploy which, I'm thankful to say, I never tried on old
Arnold after making a hash of my Greek construes at Rugby.
Anyway, this clerk decided he had a God-given mission to
overthrow the Manchoos and establish "the Tai'ping" – the
Kingdom of Eternal Peace or Heavenly Harmony or what
you will. He went about preaching a sort of bastard Christianity which he'd picked up from missionary tracts, and in any
normal country he'd either have been knocked on the head
or given a University Chair. But this being China, his crusade
had caught on, against all sense and reason, and within a few
years he'd built up an enormous army, devastated several
provinces, thrashed various Imperial generals, captured
dozens of cities including the old capital, Nanking, and come
within an ace of Pekin itself. Getting madder by the minute,
mark you, but among the millions of peasants who'd rallied
to him and swallowed his religious moonshine, there were
some likely lads who plotted the campaigns, fought the
battles, and imposed his amazing notions of worship and
discipline on a sizeable slice of the population.

This was the famous Taiping Rebellion*, the bloodiest war
ever fought on earth, and it was still going great guns in '60.
Countless millions had already died in it, but neither the
Imperials nor the rebels looked like winning just yet; the
Imps were besieging Nanking, but not making much of it,
while various Taiping armies were rampaging elsewhere,
spreading the gospel and piling up the corpses, as not in-
frequently happens.

There was some sympathy for the Taipings among those
Europeans (missionaries mostly) who mistakenly thought
they were real Christians, and a few enthusiasts, as well as
rascals and booty-hunters, had enlisted with them. Mean-
while our government, and the other foreign states who had
some trade interest in China (and hoped to have a lot more)
were watching uneasily, afraid to intervene, but devilish
concerned about the outcome.

So there you are: a Manchoo government with an idiot
Emperor who thought the world was square, fighting a

* See Appendix I.

21

lethargic war against rebels led by a lunatic, and preparing to resist a Franco-British invasion which wasn't to be a war, exactly, but rather a great armed procession to escort our Ambassador to Pekin and persuade the Chinks to keep their treaty obligations – which included legalising the opium traffic at that moment personified by H. Flashman and his band of yellow brothers[3]. And in case you think I was incautious, heading up-river at such a time, take a squint at the map, and be aware that all the bloodshed and beastliness was a long way from Canton; you'd not have caught me near the place otherwise.

We were into the Bocca Tigris, where the estuary narrows to a broad river among islands, before I started to earn my corn. Out from Chuenpee Fort comes an Imperial patrol boat with some minor official riff-raff aboard, hollering to us to heave to; Ward cocked an eye at me, but I shook my head, and we swept past them without so much as "good day"; they clamoured in our wake for a while, beating gongs and waving wildly, but gave up when they saw we'd no intention of stopping. Ward, who'd been anxiously scanning the big forts on the high bluffs overlooking the channel, shook his head with relief and grinned at me.

"Is it always so easy?" cries he, and I told him, not quite, we'd meet more determined inquiry farther on, but I would talk our way past. Sure enough, in late afternoon, when we were clearing Tiger Island, up popped a splendid galley, all gold and scarlet, with dragon banners and long ribbons fluttering from her upper works, her twenty oars going like clockwork as she steered to intercept us. She had three or four jingals* in her bows, and fifty men on her deck if there was one; under a little canopy on her poop there was a Mandarin in full fig of button-hat and silk robe, seated in state – and flying a kite, with a little lad to help him with the string. Even the most elderly and dignified Chinese delight in kites, you know, and no city park is complete without a score of sober old buffers pottering about like contented Buddhas with their airy toys fluttering and swooping over-head. This was a fine bird-kite, a great silver stork so lifelike

* Heavy muskets mounted on tripods and worked by two men.

22

you expected it to spread its wings as it hovered hundreds of feet above us.

To complete this idyllic scene, the galley carried on its bows a huge wooden cage, crammed with about twenty wretched coolies so close-packed they could hardly stir – criminals being carried to their place of punishment, probably. Their wailing carried across the water as the galley feathered her oars and an officer bawled across, demanding our business.

"*Ruth* and *Naomi*, lorchas from Hong Kong, carrying opium to the factories," shouts I in my best Mandarin, and he said he must come aboard and examine us. I told Ward to keep way on the lorchas, and on no account to heave to. "If those thieving bastards once get on our deck, they'll have the stoppings out of our teeth," I told him. "But if we keep going, there's nothing they can do about it."

"Suppose they fire on us?" says he, eyeing the jingals.

"And start another war?" I nodded at the Union Jack at our stern, and hollered across the water:

"Our licence is in order, your excellency, and we are in great haste, and must proceed to Canton without delay. So you can bugger off, see?"

This provoked a great screaming of instructions to heave to immediately, but no one moved to the jingals, so I jumped on the rail and pointed to our flag.

"This is a British vessel, and I am a close friend of Pa-hsia-li, who'll have your yellow hide if you get gay with us, d'ye hear?" In fact, I'd never met Harry Parkes, who was our man at Canton – and pretty well lord and master of the place – but I guessed the mention of his name might cause 'em to think. "Sheer off, damn you, or we'll have half the oars out of you!" She was gliding in to head us off, not thirty feet away, and in a moment her oars would be crumpled against our hull; it was a question of who gave way. Suddenly she veered on to a parallel course, with the officer shrieking to us to heave to; I made a rude gesture, and he ran to the Mandarin for instructions.

I was half-expecting what came next. There was a barked order, and a dozen of the galley's crew ran forward and seized on the wooden cage in which the criminals were packed like so many herring. On the order they heaved, sliding the cage until it was poised on the lip of the bow platform; her oars took the water again, keeping her level with us – and then they just looked across at us, and the officer repeated his demand to us to heave to. I turned away and told Ward to keep her going. He was gaping, white-faced; the poor devils in the cage were squealing like things demented and struggling helplessly.

"My God!" cries he. "Are they going to drown them?"

"Undoubtedly," says I. "Unless we heave to and allow ourselves to be boarded and plundered on some trumped-up excuse. In which case they'll certainly drown 'em later, just the same. But they're hoping we don't know that – and that being soft-hearted foreign devils we'll spill our wind and come to. It's a special kind of Chinese blackmail, you see. So just hold your course and pay 'em no heed."

He gulped, once, but he was a cool hand; he turned his back as I had done, and yelled to the helmsman to hold her steady. There was dead silence on our deck; only the creaking of the timbers and the swish of water along our side. Another yell to heave to from the galley . . . silence . . . a shrieked order . . . an awful, heart-rending chorus of wails and screams, and an almighty splash.

"Fine people, with a prime country, as you were saying," says I, and strolled over to the rail again. The galley was still abreast, but in her wake there was a great bubbling and boiling to mark where the cage was sinking to the bottom of the Pearl. Ward came up beside me; his teeth were gritted and there was great beads of sweat on his brow.

"Old China or New China," says I, "it's all the same, young Fred."

"The goddam swine!" cries he. "The cold-blooded yellow bastard – look at him there, with his goddam kite! He hasn't even moved a muscle!" His face was working with rage. "Goddam him! Goddam him to hell!"

"Amen," says I, and watched the galley slowly falling astern before turning back towards the shore, the silver stork-kite hanging in the air far above her. Suddenly a brightly-coloured object went whirling up the string, and then another – gaily-painted paper butterflies which were

24

brought to a sudden halt by a twitch on the kite-string, so that they fluttered in the breeze, glinting and turning, just below the stork.

"Would you have heaved to when they made to drown those poor beggars, Fred?" I asked.

He hesitated. "I guess," says he, and looked at me. "That's why you're aboard, huh?"

I nodded. "You see, they daren't offer us violence – not after the *Arrow* affair. And they've no *real* right to stop an opium boat – but they'll use every trick they know to bluff you, and once they're aboard, and you don't speak Chinese, and they outnumber you ten to one – well, they can sort of confiscate your cargo – oh, and release it later, no doubt, with apologies . . . and lo and behold, your chests of first-rate chandoo have been replaced, hey presto! by a ton of opium dross. See?"

"Bastards!" was all he said. "Him an' his goddam kite!"

"Speaking of which – see those butterflies? Somewhere up near the Second Bar an active little Chink with a spy-glass is taking note of 'em – which means that round about the Six Flats we'll meet another deputation, with a much more important Mandarin on board. It may be politic to present him with a couple of chests, rather than risk any embarrassment."

"How's that?" His voice was sharp. "Give him some of our opium?"

"What's sixteen quid out of sixteen thousand?" I wondered.

He was silent for a moment. "I guess," says he, and then: "Six Flats is up beyond the First Bar, isn't it?"

I said it was, and that we ought to be there tomorrow noon, and after a little more talk he said he'd better take post on the second lorcha for the night, as we had agreed, so that both vessels were under proper control.

"Remember – keep close up, and don't stop for anything," says I, and he swore he wouldn't. He didn't bother with a small boat, but just dropped over the side and trod water until the second lorcha came by, and he scrambled aboard. A good boy that, thinks I; green, but steady. By Gad, I didn't know the half of him, did I?

25

The boatmen were cooking their evening meal forward, but I'd brought cold fowl and beef, and after a capital meal and a bottle of Moselle while the sun went down I was in splendid trim for my Hong Kong girl, who was sitting by the stern-rail, singing high-pitched and combing her long hair. We went down to the tiny cabin, and were buckled to in no time; a fine, fat little romp she was, too, taking a great pleasure in her work and giggling and squealing as we thrashed about, but no great practitioner of the gentle art. But you don't expect Montez or Lily Langtry for sixpence, which was what I was paying her; she was a crude, healthy animal, and when I'd played myself out with her she retired with a flask of the promised samshu and I settled down to my well-earned repose.

She was back at first light, though, crawling in beside me and grunting as she rubbed her boobies across my face, which is better than an alarm clock any day. I laid hold, and was preparing to set about her when I realised that she was trembling violently, and the pretty pug face was working with a strange, ugly tic.

"What the devil's the matter?" says I, still half-asleep, and she twitched and sniffed at me.

"Wantee piecee pipe!" says she, whimpering. "Mass' gimme! Piecee pipe!"

"Oh, lord!" says I. "Get one from the boatmen, can't you?" She wanted her opium, and I could see she'd be no fun until she'd had it. But the boatmen hadn't any, or wouldn't give it, apparently, and she began to blubber and twitch worse than ever, sobbing "Piecee pipe!" and pulling the pipe from her loin-cloth and shoving it at me. I slapped her across the cabin, and she lay there crying and shivering; I'd have let her lie, but her first awakening of me had put me in the mood for a gallop, and it occurred to me that with a few puffs of black smoke inside her she might be stimulated to a more interesting performance than she'd given the previous night. It was only a step under the companion to where half a ton of the best chandoo was to be had; Josiah would never grudge a skewerful in such a good cause, I was sure.

So I growled at her to get her lamp going and bring

her pin, and she came panting as I pushed through the chick-screen to the long main hold which ran the full length of the lorcha under its flush deck. There were the chests, and while she twitched and whined at my elbow I rummaged for a handspike and stuck it under the nearest lid. She had her little lamp lit, and was holding out the skewer in a trembling paw – as I said before, she was a most unlikely-looking guardian angel.

I levered the lid up with a splintering of cheap timber, and pulled back the corner of the oilskin cover beneath. And then, as I recall, I said "Holy God!" and came all over thoughtful as I contemplated the contents of the chest. For if I hadn't had Mrs Phoebe Carpenter's word for it that those contents were high-grade prepared Patna opium, I'd have sworn that they were Sharps carbines. All neatly packed in grease, too.

❁ There was a time, in my callow youth, when the discovery that I was running not opium but guns would have had me bolting frantically for the nearest patch of timber, protesting that it was nothing to do with me, constable, and the chap in charge would be along in a moment. For opium, into China, was a commonplace if not entirely respectable commodity, whereas firearms, into anywhere, are usually highly contraband, and smuggling 'em is as often as not a capital offence. But if twenty years of highly active service had taught me anything, it was that there is a time to flee in blind panic, and a time to stand fast and think. Given the leisure, I daresay I'd have replaced that chest lid, slapped the slut who was staring wildly at me, and taken a turn on deck to reflect, thus:

Had Mrs Carpenter spun me a web of yarn, and were she and dear Josiah aware that their cargo consisted of the very latest repeating weapons? Undoubtedly; Josiah had supervised the loading of the chests, and what he knew his wife knew, too. Very good, to whom should a God-fearing British clergyman and his wife be smuggling guns in China? Not to any British recipient, and certainly not to the Manchoo Imperials – which left the Taiping rebels. Utterly incredible – until one reflected that there were Taiping enthusiasts among our people, and none warmer than those clergy who believed that the "long-haired devils" were devout Christians fighting the good fight against the Imperial heathen. Were Carpenter and his wife sufficiently demented for that? Presumably; if you're religious you can believe anything. Well, then, if they wanted to supply Sharps carbines to the Taipings, why not ship 'em up the Yangtse to Nanking, where the Taipings were in force, instead of to Canton, where there wasn't a Taiping within a hundred miles? Simple: Nanking

28

was under siege, the Yangtse was a damned dangerous river, and they'd have had to run the stuff through Shanghai, where there'd have been a far greater risk of detection.

But, dammit, how could they hope to smuggle guns into Canton, where our garrison and gunboats were thick as fleas, and the chests would have to be opened at the factories? That was plainly impossible – so they didn't intend the lorchas ever to *reach* Canton. No, if their skipper turned eastward into the web of tributaries and creeks short of the First Bar, to some predetermined rendezvous . . . a Taiping mule-train waiting on a deserted river-bank . . . off-load and away up-country . . . why, it could be done as safe as sleep. And poor old Flashy, *whom they'd needed to keep meddling and acquisitive Chinese officials at bay during the run past the forts*, and who had performed that service to admiration – why, he'd be no trouble. Could he, Her Majesty's loyal servant, go running to Parkes at Canton to confess that he'd been instrumental in providing the Taipings with enough small arms to keep 'em going until doomsday? Not half.

And that little snake Ward must be up to the neck in it! Hadn't he announced himself a Taiping-worshipper only yesterday? Wait, though – he'd also admitted that he would have hove to for the Imperial galley, which would have been fatal to him . . . By gum, had that been acting for my benefit? Yes, because later when I'd remarked that we might have to part with a chest or two as "squeeze" to the Mandarins, he'd been taken suddenly aback, until he'd reflected that the lorchas would never get that close to Canton. The lying, dissimulating, Yankee snake . . .

That, I say, is how I *would* have reasoned, given the leisure – and I'd have been dead right, too. As it was, no leisure was afforded me; some of it went through my mind in a flash – the bit about Ward, for instance – but I hadn't had time to slam the chest cover down when I felt the lorcha swing violently off course, her mainsail cracked like a cannon, there was a yelling and scampering of bare feet overhead, and I had flung the wench aside, dived into the cabin, grabbed my Adams from beneath my pillow, and was up the companion like a jack-rabbit.

I emerged just in time to duck beneath the main-sail boom

29

as it came swinging ponderously overhead with a couple of boatmen clinging on, yelling bloody murder as they tried to secure it. The others were at the rail, pigtails flapping and chattering like monkeys, staring forward. By God, the *second* lorcha was now ahead, and there was Ward at her helm; we were close in by the east bank – it must be the east, for there was the sun gleaming dully through the morning mist, the first rays turning the waters to gold around us. But we were running *south*! My lorcha was just completing her turn; I spun round in bewilderment. Two of the boatmen had the tiller jammed over as far as it would go – and a furlong behind us, its oars going like the Cambridge crew as it raced down towards us, was a dandy little launch rowed by fellows in white shirts and straw hats, with a little chap in the sternsheets egging them on. And half a mile beyond *that*, emerging from a creek on the east bank, was an undoubted Navy sloop. She was flying the Union Jack.

There are times, as I said, to run, and times to think – and by God I couldn't do either! I know now that Ward, a stranger to the Pearl, and with only a clown of a boatman as pilot, had missed his turning in the dark, and run slap into one of our Canton patrollers, but in that moment I was aware only that the blue-jackets were upon us, and poor old Flash was sitting on top of the damnedest load of contraband you ever saw. I acted on blind instinct, thank heaven; the launch was closing in, and there was only one thing for it.

"Ward, you toad!" I bellowed. "Take that!" And springing on to the rail to get a clear shot at him, I let blaze with the Adams. He sprang away from the tiller of the other lorcha, and I loosed off another shot which struck splinters from his rail; his boat yawed crazily, and in the crisis he behaved with admirable presence of mind: he was over her rail like a porpoise, taking the water clean and striking out like billyho for the bank, not a hundred yards off. I jumped down, roaring, and was about to send another ball after him when one of my helmsmen whipped out his kampilan and came at me, screaming like a banshee. I shot him point-blank, and the force of it flung him back against the rail, clutching his guts and pouring blood. Before his fellows could move I had my back to the rail, flourishing the Adams, and bawling to them to stand off or I'd blow 'em to blazes. For an instant they hesitated, hands on hilts, the ugly yellow faces contorted with rage and fear; I banged a shot over their heads, and the whole half-dozen scampered across beside their wounded mate. Behind me I heard a young voice, shrill with excitement, yelling "In oars! Follow me!", the launch was bumping against our side, and here was a young snotty, waving a cutlass as big as himself, and half a dozen tars at his heels, jumping on to our deck.

"Come along, you fellows!" cries I heartily. "You're just in time! Careful, now . . . these are desperate villains!" And I gave a final flourish of the Adams at the boatmen, who were crouched, half naked and looking as piratical as sin, beside their leaking comrade, before turning to greet the gaping midshipman.

"Flashman, colonel, army intelligence," says I briskly, and held out my hand. He took it in bewilderment, goggling at me and at the boatmen. "Just have your lads watch out for those rascals, will you? They're gun-runners, you know."

"My stars!" says he, and then gave a little start. "Flashman, did you say – sir?" He was a sturdy, snub-nosed young half-pint with a bulldog chin, and he was staring at me with disbelief. "Not . . . I mean – *Colonel* Flashman?"

Well, I don't suppose there was a soul in England – not in the Services, leastways – who hadn't heard of the gallant Flashy, and no doubt he was recognising me from the illustrations he'd seen in the press. I grinned at him.

"That's right, youngster. Here, you'd best put some of your fellows aboard that other lorcha – why, blast it, the brute's getting clear away!" And I pointed over the rail to the near shore, where the figure of Ward was floundering ashore in the shallows. Even as we watched he disappeared into the tall reeds, and I sighed with inward relief. That was the star witness safely out of the way. I damned him and turned away, laughing ruefully, and the snotty came out of his trance like a good 'un.

"Jenkins, Smith – cover those fellows! Bland – take the launch to that other lorcha and make her safe!" The other lorcha, I was pleased to see, was floundering about with her crew at sixes and sevens. As his tars jumped to it, the snotty

31

turned back to me. "I don't understand, sir. Gun-runners, did you say?"

"As ever was, my son. What's your name?"

"Fisher, sir," says he. "Jack Fisher, midshipman."

"Come along, Jackie," says I, clapping him on the shoulder like the cheery soul I was – no side, you see. "And I'll show you the wickedness of the world."

I took him below, and he gaped at the sight of the Hong Kong girl, who was crouched shivering and bare-titted. But he gaped even wider when I showed him the contents of the "opium" chests.

"My stars!" says he again. "What does it mean?"

"Guns for the Taiping rebels, my boy," says I grimly. "You arrived just in time, you see. Another half-hour and I'd have had to tackle these scoundrels single-handed. Your captain got my message, I suppose?"

"I dunno, sir," says he, owl-eyed. "We saw your lorchas, turning tail, and I was sent to investigate. We'd no notion . . .'

So Ward's guilty conscience had been his undoing – if he'd held his course the Navy would never have looked at him, and if they had, why, he was just carrying opium, and had the famous Flashy to vouch for him. For he wasn't to know I'd sniffed out his real cargo. Gad, though, if that slut hadn't begged for a pipe of chandoo, I'd have been in a pretty fix, with Ward panicking, the Navy's suspicions aroused, and myself flat-footed when they came aboard and started rummaging. Thanks to her, I'd had those few minutes to plot my course.

"Mr Fisher," says I, "I think it's time I had a word with your skipper, what? Perhaps you'd be good enough to take me aboard?"

You see, of course, what I was about. It was the ploy I'd used on the slave-ship *Balliol College* in '48, when the Yankee Navy caught us off Cape San Antonio, and to save my skin I'd welcomed our captors with open arms and let on that I'd only been with the slavers to spy on them*. Then, I'd had Admiralty papers to prove my false identity, but here I had something infinitely better – my fame and reputation. For

* See *Flash for Freedom!*

32

who, boarding a gun-runner and finding valiant old Flashy holding the miscreants at bay single-handed, would suspect that he was one of the gang? Heroes who have led the Light Brigade and braved the heathen hordes at Cawnpore and Kabul, are above suspicion; Master Fisher might well be fogged as to what I was doing there, exactly, but it never crossed his innocent young mind that I was anything but what I'd announced myself – an army officer apprehending villainous foreign smugglers. And since I was from intelligence, no doubt there was some splendid mystery behind it, and explanations would follow. Quite.

Nor did the prospect of explaining trouble me – much. After all, I was Flashy, and it was well-known officially that I'd been up to my ears in secret affairs in India and Central Asia, and here, they would think, was more of the same. Once I'd determined what tale to tell, it was simply a matter of carrying it off with modest assurance (trust me for that) and a pinch of mystery to make 'em feel confidential and cosy, and they'd swallow whatever I told 'em, nem. con. There wouldn't be a soul to give me the lie, and *some* of it would be true, anyway. (I'm proud to say it never occurred to me to tell the real truth, with Mrs Carpenter, etc. They'd never have swallowed *that* – which is ironic. Anyway, it would have made me look an imbecile.)

So when I was aboard the sloop, and its young commander had listened to little Fisher's report and my own terse embellishments, and whistled softly at the sight of the lorchas' cargo, I was perfectly prepared for the inevitable question, asked with respectful bewilderment:

"But . . . how came you to be aboard of them, sir?"

I looked him in the eye with just a touch of tight-lipped smile. "I think, commander," says I, "that I'd best report direct to Mr Parkes at Canton. Least said, what? You received no message from him about . . .?" and I nodded at the lorchas. "Just so. Perhaps he was right. Well, I'll be obliged if you'll carry me to him as soon as may be. In the meantime," I permitted myself a wry grin, "take good care of these Chinese villains, won't you? I've been after 'em too long to want to lose 'em now. Oh, and by the way – that boy Fisher shapes well."[4]

He couldn't get me to Canton fast enough; we were in the Whampoa Channel by noon, and two hours later dropped anchor off Jackass Point, opposite the old factories. Then there was a delay while the lorchas and their crews were taken in charge, and the commander went to make his report to his chief, and to Parkes – I didn't mind, since it gave me time to polish the tale I was going to tell – and it wasn't until the following morning that I was escorted through the English Garden to the office and residence of Harry Parkes, Esq., H.M. Commissioner at Canton and (bar Bruce at Shanghai) our chief man in China. From all I'd heard, he was formidable: he knew the country better than any foreigner living, they said, for though he wasn't thirty he'd been out since childhood, served through the Opium Wars, been on cutting-out expeditions as a schoolboy, done all manner of secret work and diplomatic ruffianing since, and carried things with a high hand against the Chinese – whose language he spoke rather better than the Emperor.

He greeted (I won't say welcomed) me with brisk formality, stiff and upright behind his official desk, not a hair out of place on the sleek dark head. Energy was in every line of him, from the sharp prominent nose to the firm capable hands setting his papers just so; he was all business at once, in a clear, hard voice – and suddenly, convincing him didn't seem quite so easy.

"This is a singular business, Sir Harry! What's behind it?"

"Not much," says I, hoping I was right. Clever and easy, I don't mind – I'm that way myself – but clever and brusque unsettles me. I handed him the "requested and required" note Palmerston had given me when I went to India – the usual secret passport, but pretty faded now. "You had no message from me?"

"I did not know you were in China, until yesterday." He glanced up sharply from the passport. "This is more than three years old."

"When I left England. What I've been doing since will have to stay under the rose, I'm afraid –"

He gave a little barking laugh. "Not altogether, I fancy," says he, with what he probably imagined was a smile. "Your knighthood and Victoria Cross are hardly state secrets."

"I meant since then – this past year. It has nothing to do with this affair, anyway – that's a tale that's soon told." I breathed an inward prayer, meeting the steady grey eyes in that lean lawyer face. "I'm due home on the *Princess Charlotte*, sailing on the eleventh –"

"In three days? Grant is due on the thirteenth. I beg your pardon, pray continue."

"Aye, well, two nights ago I was over in Macao, looking up an old chum from Borneo, when I was with Brooke." No harm in dropping in that glorious acquaintance, I thought. "I needn't mention his name, It's of no importance, but he's a downy bird, Chinese, with an eye in every bush – an old White Lily Society man, you know the sort . . ."

"His name might be valuable," says Parkes, and his hand went ever so casually to a vase of flowers on his desk; he lifted it with three fingers round the stem, and set it down again. Clever bastard.

"Exactly," says I, and ran my thumb over three fingertips[5], just to show him. "Well, we talked shop, and by way of gossip he let fall that a shipment of arms was going up-river to the Taipings – Shih-ta-kai's people, he thought. Which was nothing to me – until he mentioned that they were British bought-and-paid-for, though he didn't know who. Not strictly my *indaba*, you may say, but it struck me that if it got about that British arms were going to the Long-Haired Devils, it might cause us some embarrassment with Pekin, you know?"

I looked for a nod, but he just sat there with his fingers laced on the blotter before him. I'd a feeling that if you'd fired a gun in his ear he wouldn't have taken his eyes from mine.

"So I thought I should have a look. Nothing official to be done on Portuguese territory, of course, but my friend knew where the lorchas were preparing to weigh – and there they were, sure enough, ostensibly loaded with opium, if you please. On the spur of the moment I approached the skipper –"

"That would be Ward."

It was like a kick in the throat. I couldn't help staring, and had to improvise swiftly to explain my obvious astonishment.

"Ward, you say? He told me his name was Foster." The

35

sweat was cold on my spine. "You knew . . . about him, and the shipment?"

"Only his name. My agents in Hong Kong and Macao send notice of all opium shipments, vessels, owners, and skippers." He lifted a list from his desk. "Lorchas *Ruth* and *Naomi*, owned by Yang Fang and Co., Shanghai, commander F. T. Ward. No suggestion, of course, that he carried anything but opium." He laid it down, and waited.

"Well, on impulse, I asked him for a lift to Canton." By gum, he'd shaken me for a second, but if that was the extent of his knowledge I was still safe – but was it? This was a foxy one – and on instinct I did the riskiest thing a liar can do: I decided to change my story. I'd been about to tell him I'd stowed away, full of duty and holy zeal, and come thundering out at the critical moment, to prevent the rascals escaping when our sloop hove in sight. Suddenly I knew it wouldn't do – not with this cold clam. I've been lying all my life, and I know: when in doubt, get as close to the truth as you can, and hang on like grim death.

"I asked him for a lift to Canton – and if you ask what was in my mind, I can't tell you. I knew it was my duty to stop those guns – and placed as I was, without authority in a foreign port, that meant staying with 'em, somehow, and taking whatever chance offered."

"You might," he interrupted, "have informed the Portuguese."

"I might, but I didn't – and I doubt if you would, either." I gave him just a touch of the Colonel, there. "Anyway, he refused me, mighty curt. I offered passage money, but he wouldn't budge – which settled it for me, for any honest trader would have agreed. I was going off, wondering what to do next, when he suddenly called me back, and asked did I know the river, and did I speak Chinese? I said I did, he chewed it over, and then offered to take me if I'd act as interpreter on the voyage. I had only a moment aside to tell my Chinese friend to get word to you, or Hong Kong, of what was forward. But you've had no word from him?"

"None, Sir Harry," and not a flicker of expression – I could have brained the man. There's nothing more discouraging than lying to a poker face, when what you need is gasps

36

and whistles and cries of "I'll be damned!" and "What happened then?" to whet your prevarications.

"Aye, well, I can't say I'm surprised. He'll talk to a pal, but he's leery of official circles, blast him. Well, we sailed, and what I needed, of course, was a squint at the cargo. But they never left me alone for a moment. Foster –" I changed the name just in time "– and the Chinks were always on hand, so I must bide my time. I stayed awake the first night, but no chance offered; the second night, I'm afraid, I just caulked out." A shrug, and rueful Flashy smile, followed by an eager glint in the eye. "But then I had a splendid stroke of luck. Just before dawn, a native girl of the crew – a cook or some such thing, I suppose – woke me, begging for a pipe of opium! Would you believe it? There was no one about – and here was a heaven-sent chance to open a chest, with a ready explanation if I were detected. So I did – and there were the Sharps!"

God, it sounded lame – especially the *true* parts, which I thought was damned hard. I waited; if the man were human, he must say something. He did.

"You must have formed some plan by this time – what did you hope to do, alone, against so many?" He sounded impatient – and downright curious.

"For the life of me, Mr Parkes, I wasn't sure." I grinned him straight in the eye, bluff, honest Harry. "Tackle the crew with my revolver? Try to scuttle her? I don't know, sir. By the grace of God the sloop hove in sight just then . . . and I did tackle 'em! And the rest you know."

He sat for a moment, and I braced myself for the incredulous questions, the outright disbelief – and then he gave his sudden bark of a laugh, and struck the bell at his elbow.

"Some coffee, Sir Harry? I'm sure you deserve it. That, sir," says he, shaking his head, "is the most damned unlikely tale I ever heard – and what I'd say to it if I didn't *know* it for true, I cannot imagine! Well, it *is* unlikely, you'll own?" He chuckled again, and it seemed to me an indignant frown was in order, so I gave one, but it was wasted since he was talking to the bearer with the coffee-tray. Relief and bewilderment filled me; he'd swallowed it . . . he *knew* it was true . . .? What the deuce . . .?

37

"Speaking in my official capacity, I have to say that your actions were entirely irregular," says he, handing me a cup, "and might have had serious results – for yourself. You risked your life, you know – and your honour." He looked hard at me. "A senior officer, found aboard an arms-smuggler, without authority? Even with your distinguished name . . . well . . ." He stirred his own cup, and then smiled – and, d'ye know, I realised he *was* just twenty-nine, and not the fifty-odd he'd sounded. "Between ourselves, it was a damned cool bit of work, and I'm obliged to you. But for you, they might have given us the slip; they'd certainly have made some sort of fight of it. My congratulations, sir. I beg your pardon – more sugar?"

Well, this was Sunday in Brighton all of a sudden, wasn't it, though? I'd hoped for acceptance, with or without the doubtful glances that have followed me round the world for eighty erratic years – but hardly for this. It didn't make sense, even – for it was a damned unlikely tale, as he'd said.

"Saving my poor veracity," says I, "you say you *know* it's true?" Flashy ain't just bluff and manly, you see – he's sharp, too, and I was playing my character. "May I know how?"

"I'd not deny myself the pleasure of enlightening you," says he briskly. "We have known for some time that arms shipments, provided by a syndicate of British and American sympathisers, have been going up the Pearl to the Taipings – Shih-ta-kai, as your Chinese friend said. Who these sympathisers are, we don't know –" that was good news, too, "since the work was entirely overseen by a most skilful Chinese, a former pirate, who brought the arms to Macao, shipped them up the Pearl in lorchas, and passed them to the Taipings . . . where? To be brief, we smoked the pirate out a week ago, and he met with an accident." He set down his cup. "That forced the syndicate's hand – they needed a new man, and they chose Ward, heaven knows why, since he knew nothing of the Pearl, or of China. But he's a good seaman, they say, and from what we know, devoted to the Taiping cause. The idiot. And at the last moment, when he must have been wondering how the deuce he was going to find his way up-river, without a word of Chinese in his head, and rendezvous with the Taipings, you dropped into his lap. We may guess," says he, "what your fate must have been if he had reached his destination. But I'm sure you weighed that."

I gave an offhand shrug, and when we'd picked the shattered remnants of my cup from the floor, he pinged his bell again. "Fortunately, we now had Mr Ward and his convoy under observation at Macao, and our sloops were waiting for him beyond the Second Bar. Come in!" cries he, and the door opened to admit the prettiest little Chinese girl, in a flowered robe and high block shoes; a Manchoo, by her coiled hair and unbound feet. She smiled and bobbed to Parkes, and glanced sidelong in my direction.

"An-yat-heh!" snaps Parkes, and she turned and bobbed at me. I could only nod back, mystified – and then my heart lurched. She was washed and dressed and painted up like a Mandarin's daughter, but there was no mistaking. She was the Hong Kong boat girl.

"Thank you, An-yat-heh!" says Parkes, and she bobbed again, shot me another slantendicular look, and pitti-pittied out.

"An-yat-heh," says Parkes drily, "is a most capable and, I fear, most immoral young woman. She is also the best spy on the Pearl River. For the past week she has been keeping close watch on Frederick Townsend Ward. She saw his lorchas sail from Macao, and followed in a sampan manned by other of our agents. She would have contrived to get aboard the lorchas," he went on impassively, "even if you had not been there, for it was her task to see where the cargo was landed, in the event that Ward had eluded our patrols. She was surprised to learn, from eavesdropping on the crew, that you were apparently unaware of the true nature of the cargo – for of course the smugglers were not to know that you already had their secret, and spoke of you as a dupe, to be disposed of when you had served your purpose. She was pleased, she tells me, to discover that you were not one of the smugglers; in some ways she is a naive, affectionate girl, and seems to have formed an attachment to you."

Whether this was accompanied by a leer, a frown, or nothing at all, I can't say – knowing Parkes, probably the last. I was in too much mental turmoil to notice – by God, the luck! For it fitted – my tale to Parkes corroborated exactly what she must have told him of the voyage. But if I'd given him the stowaway yarn . . . it didn't bear thinking about. I put it by, and listened to the brisk, impersonal voice.

"She is, as I said, a resourceful young woman. When the sloop was sighted, she determined to draw your attention to the cargo, in the hope that when you saw how you had been deceived, you might cause some disturbance, and hinder their escape – as indeed you did. Having no English but pigeon, and doubting her ability to make you understand Cantonese, she hit on the novel plan of persuading you to open a chest by pleading with you for opium."

I sat quiet for a moment – and if you want to know what I was thinking, it wasn't what an almighty narrow shave I'd had, or of prayers of thanksgiving, or anything of that sort. No, I was asking myself when, if ever, I'd been so confoundedly fooled by two different women in the space of four days. Mrs Phoebe Carpenter and An-yat-heh, bless 'em. White or yellow, they were a hazardous breed in China, that was plain. Parkes, with the satisfied air of a rooster who has done crowing, was regarding me expectantly.

"Well, she's a brave girl," says I. "Smart, too. And you, sir, are to be congratulated on the efficiency of your secret service."

"Oh, we get about," says he.

"I'm sorry that rascal Foster – Ward, did you say? – got clear away." I scowled, Flashy-like. "I've a score to settle with that one."

"Not in China, Sir Harry, if you please." He was all commissioner again. "He served you a scurvy trick, no doubt, but the less that is heard of this business the better. I shall require your word on that," and he gave me his stiff-collar look. "It has all been quite unofficial, you see. No British law has been broken. The gun-running offence took place within the Imperial Chinese Government's jurisdiction; we had no legal right to detain or hinder Ward and his fellows. But," he gave another of his sour smiles, "we do have the gunboats. And since Her Majesty's Government is *strictly neutral* as between the Imperials and the Taipings, it is

40

certainly not in our interest that British citizens should be arming the rebels. A thought which prompted your own action, you remember. No." He squared off his pencils in columns of threes. "We must consider the incident happily – and in your case fortunately – concluded."

That, of course, was the main thing. I was clear, by the grace of God and dear little An-yat-heh. There would be no inconvenient inquiries which might have led back to the conniving Mrs Carpenter – who, it occurred to me, might well be blackmailed to bed before I sailed for home. As for Ward, I'd not have gone near the dangerous brute; I gave Parkes my word with feigned reluctance.

"He may not be such a rascal, you know." Parkes frowned, as though it irritated him to admit it. "He has courage, and his devotion to the rebel cause, if misguided, may well be sincere. There are times when I would be glad to be rid of the Manchoos myself. But that is not our concern." He sniffed. "For the moment."

Not my concern at any time, old lad, thinks I. Now that I was apparently out from under, I was in a fret to get away from this omniscient satrap while the going was good. So I shuffled, and began to thank him, bluff and manly, and hope that I hadn't been too great a nuisance, eh, to him and his gang of busybodies – when he stopped me with a knowing look, and pulled a Portent of Doom (a blue diplomatic packet, to you) from his desk.

"There is another matter, Sir Harry – one which I fancy you will consider an amend for your recent adventure." Eyeing that packet, I suddenly doubted it. "You recall that I said I was unaware of your presence in China, until yesterday? Listen, if you please." He took a sheet from the packet. "Yes, here we are . . . 'it is thought that Colonel Flashman may be en route through China. In that event, you are to require him to proceed forthwith to Shanghai, and there place himself at the disposal of H.M. Minister and Superintendent of Trade.' "

I'd known that packet was damned bad news as soon as I saw it. What the hell did they want me for – and on the eve of my sailing for Home, too? Whatever it was, by God, they weren't coming between me and my well-earned idleness!

41

I'd send in my papers first, I'd . . . Parkes was speaking, with that sharp, smug smile on his infernal face.

"I was at a loss to know how to comply, when the sloop brought you here so unexpectedly opportune. Indeed, we should thank Mr Ward – for had you remained in Hong Kong it is odds that you would have sailed for England before I had time to inquire for you there. Our Chinese despatches can be infernally slow . . ."

In other words, if that bitch Carpenter hadn't hocussed me up the Pearl with her lies, I'd have been safe and away. And now the Army had me again. Well, we'd see about that – but for the moment I must choke back my fury until I knew what was what.

"How extraordinary!" says I. "Well, what a fortunate chance! What can it mean?"

"Why, they want you for the Pekin business to be sure!" cries the bloody know-all. "The despatch is confidential, of course, but I think I may be forgiven if I tell you that Lord Elgin – whose Embassy to China will be made public shortly – has asked that you be attached to the intelligence staff. I think, too," and he was positively jocular, rot his boots, "that we may see the hand of Lord Palmerston here. My dear Sir Harry, allow me to congratulate you."

❀ At the beginning of this memoir I gave you my first Law of Economics; if I have one for Adversity it is that once your essentials are properly trapped in the mangle there's nothing for it but to holler with a good grace and wait until they roll you out again. Not that hollering does any good, but it relieves the feelings, and mine were in sore need of release after my interview with Parkes. I vented them in a two-day spree in Canton, taking out my evil temper on tarts and underlings, and sleeping off the effects on the mail-boat down to Hong Kong.

For there was nothing to be done, you see. After three years of truly dreadful service, in which I'd been half-killed, starved, hunted, stretched on a rack, almost eaten by crocodiles, assaulted with shot and sabre, part-strangled by Thugs, and damned near blown from a cannon (oh, and won glorious laurels, for what they were worth), I'd been on the very point of escaping to all that made life worth living – Elspeth, with her superb charms and splendid fortune; ease, comfort, admiration, and debauchery – and through my own folly I'd thrown it away. It was too bad; I ain't a religious man, but if I had been I swear I'd have turned atheist. But there it was, so I must take stock and consider.

There was no question of sending in my papers and going home, although it had passed through my mind. My future content rested too much on the enjoyment of my heroic reputation, which would have been dimmed, just a trifle, if I'd been seen to be shirking my duty. A lesser man could have done it, and naught said, but not Sir Harry Flashman, V.C., K.B.; people would have talked, the Queen would have been *astonished*, Palmerston would have damned my eyes – and done me dirt, too. And when all was said, it wasn't liable to be much of a campaign; two or three months,

43

perhaps, in which I'd be well clear of any danger that was going, boozing on the staff, frowning at maps, looking tired and interesting, and moving paper about with my hair becomingly ruffled – oh, I knew my intelligence work, never fear.

So I rolled down to Hong Kong, savouring the revenge I would take on La Belle Phoebe – and what d'you think? She and the gun-running Josiah had cleared out to Singapore, ostensibly to join some missionary society at short notice. A likely tale; give 'em three months and they'd be running the Tongs. But their sudden departure was hardly noticed in a new sensation – Sir Hope Grant had arrived with the advance guard of the fleet and army which was to go up-country, defend Old England's rights and honour, and teach the Chinks to sing "Rule, Britannia". From Pittan's Wharf you could see the little white lines of tents where the camp was being laid out on Kowloong, so I decided to tool over and let them see how dam' lucky they were going to be in their intelligence department.

There were advance parties from all the regiments; the first thing I saw was Sikh riders in the red puggarees of Fane's Horse and the blue of Probyn's, tent-pegging on the beach, with white troopers cheering 'em on – and to my astonishment they were Dragoon Guards. God help you if it rains, my lads, thinks I, for with twenty-one stone in each saddle you'll be up to your bellies in the paddy-mud in no time. It was first-rate mixed cavalry for all that; I watched a bearded, grey-coated *sowar*, eyes glaring, whip out a peg and wheel away to yells and cheering, and was glad I wasn't a Manchoo Tartar.

It was the infantry coats I wanted to see, though, for (and I'm a horse-soldier as says it) I know what matters. When the guns haven't come up, and your cavalry's checked by close country or *tutti-putti*, and you're waiting in the hot, dusty hush for the faint rumble of *impi* or *harka* over the skyline and *know* they're twenty to your one – well, that's when you realise that it all hangs on that double line of yokels and town scruff with their fifty rounds a man and an Enfield bayonet. Kitchener himself may have placed 'em just so, with D'Israeli's sanction, *The Times*' blessing, and the Queen

44

waving 'em good-bye – but now it's *their* grip on the stock, and *their* eye at the backsight, and if *they* break, you're done. Haven't I stood shivering behind 'em often enough, wishing I could steal a horse from somewhere? Aye, and if I'm still here it's because they seldom broke in my time.

So it was with some satisfaction that I noted facings and markers – the old 60th Royal Americans, the Buffs, a fatigue party of the 44th – I felt a cold shudder at the memory of the bloody snow by Gandamack, the starved handful of survivors, and Soutar with the Colours of this same 44th wrapped round his waist as the Ghazis closed in for the kill. Well, we'd have a few Ghazis on our side this time; there were whiskered Pathans chattering round a camp-kettle, so I took a chapatti and a handful of chilis, gave the time of day to a *naik* with the Sobraon medal, and passed on, drawn by the distant pig-squeal of pipes which always makes my dear wife burst into tears – ah, we've our own home-grown savages in tow, have we, thinks I. But they weren't Highlanders, just the Royals.

Theirs wasn't the only music on Kowloong, neither. I loafed up to the big tent with the flag, whence came the most hideous, droning, booming din; there was a staff-walloper climbing aboard his Waler, a couple of Maharatta sentries on the fly, and a slim young fellow with a fair moustache sitting on a camp-stool, sketching. I came up on his blind side, just for devilment, and he started round angrily.

"How often have I told you never to –" he was beginning, and then his good eye opened wide in amazement. "Flashman! My dear fellow! Wherever did you spring from?"

"Here and there, Joe," says I. "The Mad Musician is within?"

"What? Here, I say! You can't go in just now, you know – he's composing!"

"Decomposing, by the sound of it," says I, and stuck my head in at the fly. Sure enough, there was the lean, gaunt figure, in its shirt-sleeves, sawing away like a thing demented at a great bull fiddle, glaring at a sheet of music which he was marking between scrapes, and tugging at his bristling grey whiskers, to stimulate the muse, no doubt. I flipped a coin into a glass on the table.

45

"Move on to the next street, my good man, will you?" says I. "You're disturbing the peace."

Being a sensitive artist – and a major-general – he should have gone up three feet and come down spluttering. But this one had no nerves to begin with, and more mastery of himself than a Yogi. He didn't so much as twitch – for a second I wondered if he hadn't heard me – and then he played another chord, jotted it on his manuscript, and spoke without turning his head.

"Flashman." Another chord, and he put his fiddle by and turned to fix me with those wild, pale eyes that I hadn't seen since Allahabad, when Campbell pinned the Cross on me. "Very good, Wolseley," says he to Joe, who was fidgetting behind me. He took my hand in his bony grip, nodded me to a stool – and then he stood and looked at me for two solid minutes *without saying a word*.

Now, I tell you that in detail to show you what kind of a man was Major-General Sir James Hope Grant. You don't hear much of him nowadays; Wolseley, the boy who was sketching at the door, has ten times the name and fame[6] – but in my time Grant was a man apart. He wasn't much of a general; it was notorious he'd never read a line outside the Bible; he was so inarticulate he could barely utter any order but "Charge!"; his notions of discipline were to flog anything that moved; the only genius he possessed was for his bull fiddle; he could barely read a map, and the only spark of originality he'd ever shown was to get himself six months in close tack for calling his colonel a drunkard. But none of this mattered in the least because, you see, Hope Grant was the best fighting man in the world.

I'm no hero-worshipper, as you may have gathered, and my view of the military virtues is that the best thing you can do with 'em is to hang them on the wall in Bedlam – but I know cold fact when I see it. With sword, lance, or any kind of side-arm he was the most expert, deadly practitioner that ever breathed; as a leader of irregular cavalry he left Stuart, Hodson, Custer, and the rest at the gate; in the Mutiny he had simply *fought* the whole damned time with a continuous fury that was the talk of an army containing the likes of Sam Browne, John Nicholson, and (dare I say it?) my vaunted but

46

unworthy self. Worshipped by the rank and file, naturally; he was a kindly soul, for all they called him the "Provost-Marshal", and even charming if you don't mind ten-minute silences. But as a hand-to-hand blood-spiller it was Eclipse first and the rest nowhere.[7]

He thought I was another of the same, never having seen me in action but believing what he was told, and we'd got on pretty well, considering my natural levity and insolence. He couldn't make this out at all, and I'd been told on good authority that he thought I was insane – the pot calling the kettle "Grimy arse", if you ask me. But it meant that he treated me as a wild, half-witted child, and grinned at my jokes in a wary sort of way.

So now he asked me how I did, pushed coffee and biscuits at me (no booze for maniacs, you see), and without any preamble gave me his views on the forthcoming campaign. This was what I'd come for: twenty words from Grant (and you were lucky if you got that many) were worth twenty thousand from another. I knew the rough of it – twelve thousand of ourselves and five thousand French to escort Elgin and the Frog envoy, Gros, to Pekin, in the teeth of frenzied Chinese diplomatic (and possibly military) opposition. Grant was fairly garrulous, for him.

"Shared command. Montauban and I. Day about. Lamentable." Pause. "Supply difficult. Forage all imported. No horses to be had. Brought our own from India. Not the French. Have to buy 'em. Japan ponies. Vicious beasts. Die like flies." Another pause. "French disturb me. No experience. Great campaigns, Peninsula, Crimea. Deplorable. No small wars. Delays. Cross purposes. Better by ourselves. Hope Montauban speaks English."

That would make one of you, thinks I. Would the Chinese fight, I asked, and a long silence fell.

"Possibly." Pause. "Once."

Believe it or not, I could see he was in capital spirits, in his careful way – no nonsense about beating these fellows out of sight or being in Pekin next week, which you'd have got from some of our firebrand commanders. His doubts – about the French, and supply transport – were small ones. He would get Elgin and Gros to Pekin, without a shot fired

47

if he could contrive it – but God help the Manchoos if they showed fight. Bar Campbell, there wasn't a general I'd have chosen in his place. I asked him, what was the worst of it.

"Delay," says he. "Chinese talk. Can't have it. Drive on. Don't give 'em time to scheme. Treacherous fellows."

I asked him the best of it, too, and he grinned.

"Elgin. Couldn't be better. Clever, good sense. Good-bye, Flashman. God bless you."

Perhaps he said more than that, but d'ye know, I doubt it – I can see him yet, bolt upright on his camp-stool, the lean, muscular arms folded across his long body, the grizzled whiskers like a furze-bush, chewing each word slowly before he let it out, the light eyes straying ever and anon to his beloved bull fiddle. As Wolseley strolled with me down to the jetty, we heard it again, like a ruptured frog calling to its mate.

"The Paddy-field Concerto, with Armstrong gun accompaniment," says he, grinning. "Perhaps he'll have it finished by the time we get to Pekin."

I had learned all they could tell me, and since Hong Kong is a splendid place to get out of, I caught the packet up to Shanghai to present myself to Bruce, as directed. It was like going into another world – not that Shanghai was much less of a hell-hole than Hong Kong, but it was *China*, you understand. Down in the colony it was England peopled by yellow faces, and British law, and the opium trade, and all thoughts turning to the campaign. Shanghai was the great Treaty Port, where the Foreign Devil Trade Missions were – British, French, German, American, Scowegian, Russian, and all, but it was still the Emperor's city, where we were tolerated and detested (except for what could be got out of us), and once you poked your nose out of the consulate gate you realised you were living on the dragon's lip, with his fiery eyes staring down on you, and even the fog that hung over the great sprawling native city was like smoke from his spiky nostrils.

The Model Settlement was much finer than Hong Kong, with the splendid houses of the taipans, and the Bund with its carriages and strollers, and consulate buildings that might have come from Delhi or Singapore, with gardens high-walled to keep out the view – and then you ventured into the native town, stinking and filthy and gorged with humanity (with Chinese, anyhow), with its choked alleys and dung-heaps, and baskets of human heads hung at street-corners to remind you that this was a barbarous, perilous land of abominable cruelty, where if they haven't got manacles or cords to secure a suspected petty thief, why, they'll *nail* his hands together, you see, until they get him to the hoosegow, where they'll keep him safe by hanging him up by his wrists behind his back. And that is if he's merely *suspected* – once he's convicted (which don't mean for a moment that he's guilty), then his head goes into the basket – if he's lucky. If the magistrate feels liverish, they may flog him to death, or put the wire jacket on him, or fry him on a bed of red-hot chains, or dismember him, or let him crawl about the streets with a huge wooden collar on his neck, until he starves, or *tattoo* him to death.

This may surprise you, if you've heard about the fiendish ingenuity of Chinese punishment. The fact is that it's fiendish, but not at all ingenious; just beastly, like the penal code of my dear old friends in Madagascar. And for all their vaunted civilisation, they could teach Queen Ranavalona some tricks of judicial procedure which she never heard of. In Mada-gascar, one way of determining guilt is to poison you, and see if you spew – I can taste that vile *tanguin* yet. In China, I witnessed the trial of a fellow who'd caught his wife perform-ing with the lodger, and done for them both with an axe. They tried him for murder by throwing the victims' heads into a tub of water and stirring it; the two heads ended up floating face to face, which *proved* the adulterers' affection, so the prisoner was acquitted and given a reward for being a virtuous husband. That was, as I recall, the only Chinese trial I attended where the magistrate and witnesses had not been bribed.

So much for the lighter side of Chinese life, which I'm far from exaggerating – indeed, it was commonplace; after a while you hardly noticed the dead beggars in the gutters and cesspits, or the caged criminals left to starve and rot, or even the endless flow of headless corpses into the *chow-chow*

49

water of the Yangtse estuary off Paoshan – a perpetual reminder that only a short way up-river, no farther than Liverpool is from London, the Imperials and Taipings were tearing each other (and most of the local populace) to pieces in the great struggle for Nanking. Imp gunboats were blockading the Yangtse within fifty miles, and Shanghai was full of rumours that soon the dreaded Chang-Maos, the Long-Haired Taiping Devils, would be marching on the Treaty Port itself. They'd sacked it once, years ago, and now the Chinese merchants were in terror, sending away their goods and families, and our consular people were wondering what the deuce to do, for trade would soon be in a desperate fix – and trade profit was all we were in China for. They could only wait, and wonder what was happening beyond the misty wooded flats and waterways of the Yangtse valley, in that huge, rich, squalid, war-torn empire, sinking in a welter of rebellion, banditry, corruption and wholesale slaughter, while the Manchoo Emperor and his governing nobles luxuriated in blissful oblivion in the Summer Palace far away at Pekin.

"The chief hope must be that our army can reach Pekin in time to bring the Emperor to his senses," Bruce told me when I reported at his office in the consulate. "Once the treaty's ratified, trade revived, and our position secure, the country can be made stable soon enough. The rebellion will be ended, one way or t'other. But if, before then, the rebels were to take Shanghai – well, it might be the last straw that brought down the Manchoo Empire. Our position would be . . . delicate. And it would hardly be worth going to Pekin, through a country in chaos, to treat with a government that no longer existed."

He was a cool, knowledgeable hand, was Bruce, for all the smooth cheeks and fluffy hair that made him look like a half-witted cherub; he might have been discussing Sayers's chances against Heenan rather than the possible slaughter of himself and every white soul on the peninsula. He was brother to Elgin, who was coming out as ambassador, but unlike most younger sons he didn't feel bound to stand on his dignity.[8] He was easy and pleasant, and when I asked him if there was a serious possibility that the Taipings might

50

attack Shanghai, he shrugged and said there was no way of telling.

"They've always wanted a major port," says he. "It would strengthen their cause immensely to have access to the outside world. But they don't want to attack Shanghai if they can help it, for fear of offending us and the other Powers – so Loyal Prince Lee, the ablest of the rebel generals, writes me a letter urging us to *admit* his armies peacefully to Shanghai and then join him in toppling the Manchoos. He argues that the Taipings are Christians, like ourselves, and that the British people are famous for their sympathy to popular risings against tyrannical rulers – where he got that singular notion I can't think. Maybe he's been reading Byron. What about that, Slater – think he reads Byron?"

"Not in the original, certainly," says the secretary.

"No, well – he also extols the enlightened nature of Taiping democracy, and assures us of the close friendship of the Taiping government when (and if) it comes to power." Bruce sighed. "It's a dam' good letter. I daren't even acknowledge it."

For the life of me I couldn't see why not. A Taiping China couldn't help but be better than the rotten Manchoo Empire, whose friendship was doubtful, to say the least. And if we backed them, they'd whip the Manchoos in no time – which would mean the Pekin expedition was unnecessary, and Hope Grant and Flashy and the lads could all go home. But Bruce shook his head.

"You don't lightly overthrow an Empire that's lasted since the Flood, to let in an untried and damned unpromising rabble of peasants. God knows the Manchoos are awkward, treacherous brutes, but at least they're the devil we know. Oh, I know the Bishop of Victoria sees the finger of divine providence in the Taiping Rebellion, and our missionaries call them co-religionists – which I strongly suspect they're not. Even if they were, I've known some damned odd Christians, eh, Slater?"

"South America, what?" says Slater, looking glum.

"Besides, could such people govern? They're led by a visionary, and their chief men are pawnbrokers, clerks, and blacksmiths! Talk about Jack Cade and Wat Tyler! Lee's the best of 'em, and Hung Jen-kan's civilised, by all accounts – but the rest are bloody-minded savages who rule their conquered provinces by terror and enslavement. Which is no way to win a war, I'd say. They'd be entirely unpredictable, with their lunatic king liable to have a divine revelation telling him to pitch out all foreign devils, or declare war on Japan!"

"But suppose," I ventured, "the Taipings win, in the end?"

"You mean," says Bruce, looking more cherubic than ever, "suppose they look *likely* to win. Well, H.M.G. would no doubt wish to review the position. But while it's all to play for, we remain entirely neutral, respecting the Celestial Emperor as the established government of China."

I saw that, but wondered if, in view of the possible Taiping threat to Shanghai, it mightn't be politic to jolly along this General Lee with fair words – lie to him, like.

"No. The Powers agree that all such overtures as Lee's letter must be ignored. If I acknowledged it, and word reached Pekin, heaven knows what might happen to our forthcoming negotiations with the Imperial Government. They might assume we were treating with the rebels, and Grant might even have a real war on his hands. We may have to talk to the Taipings sometime – unofficially," says he, thoughtfully, "but it will be at a time and place of our choosing, not theirs."

All of which was of passing interest to me; what mattered was that Elgin wasn't due out until June, and as his personal intelligence aide I could kick my heels pleasantly until then, sampling the delights of Shanghai diplomatic society and the more robust amusements to be found in the better class native sing-songs and haunts of ill-repute. Which I did – and all the time China was stropping its dragon claws and eyeing me hungrily.

Pleasuring apart, the time hung heavy enough for me to do some light work with the politicals of the consulate, for we maintained an extensive intelligence-gathering *bandobast*, and it behoved me to know about it. It consisted mostly of strange little coolies coming to the back door at night with bits of bazaar gossip, or itinerant bagmen with news from

52

up-river, the occasional missionary's helper who'd been through the lines at Nanking, and endless numbers of young Chinese, who might have been students or clerks or pimps – all reporting briefly or at length to swell the files of the intelligence department. It was the most trivial, wearisome rubbish for the most part – there wasn't, alas, an An-yat-heh among the spies to cheer things up – and devilish dull for the collators, who passed it on for sifting and summary by the two Chinese supervisors whose names, I swear to God, were Mr Fat and Mr Lin. By the time they'd pieced and deduced and remembered – well, it's surprising what can emerge from even the most mundane scraps of information.

For example, it was the strangest thing that enabled us to foresee the end of the great siege of Nanking in April '60. The Imperialists had huge entrenchments circling the city, and the river blockaded on both sides, but couldn't breach the rebel defences. The Taipings, hemmed within the city, had various forces loose in the countryside, but nothing apparently strong enough to raise the siege. It was such a stalemate that a great fair had actually been established between the Imp lines and the city walls, where both sides used to meet and fraternise, and the Imps sold all manner of goods to the Taipings! They brought food, opium, women, even arms and powder, which the Taipings bought with the silver they'd found in Nanking when they captured it back in '53.

A ludicrous state of affairs, even for China; it took my fancy, and when one of our spies sent down particulars of the market trading, I happened to glance through it – and noted an item which seemed a trifle odd. I ain't given to browsing over such things, you may be sure, and I wish to heaven I'd never seen this one, for what I noticed proved to be a vital clue, and set Bruce thinking earlier than he need have done, with the most ghastly consequences to myself.

"Here's a rum thing, Mr Fat," says I. "Why should the Taipings be buying bolts of black silk? Dammit, they spent 500 taels* on it this week – more than they spent on cartridge. Are they expecting funerals?"

* About £160 at that time.

"Most singular," says he. "Mr Lin, have the goodness to examine the return for last week."

So they did – and the Taipings had bought even more black silk then. They clucked over it, and burrowed into their records, and came to an astonishing conclusion.

Whenever the Taipings undertook any desperate military action, they invariably raised black silk flags in every company, which their soldiers were bound to follow on pain of death – they even had executioners posted in the ranks to behead any shirkers, which must have done wonders for their recruiting, I'd have thought. And when we learned presently that the black silk had been sent *out* of the city to two of the Taiping armies in the field – the Golden Lions of the famous Loyal Prince Lee, and the Celestial Singers under Chen Yu-cheng – it was fairly obvious that Lee and Chen were about to fall on the Imp besiegers. Which, in due course, they did, and our knowing about it in advance enabled the Hon. F. W. A. Bruce to plan and scheme most infernally, as I said. (If you wonder that the Imps didn't realise the significance of the black silk they were selling the Taipings – why, that's the Imperial Chinese Army for you. Even if they had, they'd likely just have yawned, or deserted.)

I was fool enough to be mildly pleased at spotting the item – Fat and Lin regarded me with awe for days – but I wasn't much interested, having discovered far more important matter in the secret files, which enabled me to bring off a splendid coup, thus:

It appeared that Countess H——, wife of a senior attaché at the Russian mission, paid weekly visits to a Chinese hairdresser, and, under the pretext of being beautified, regularly entertained four(!) stalwart Manchoo Bannermen in a room above the shop, later driving home with a new coiffure and a smug expression.

[Official conclusion by Fat and Lin: the subject is vulnerable, and may be coerced if access should be required to her husband's papers. Action: none.]

[Unofficial conclusion by Flashy: the subject is a slim, vicious-looking piece who smokes brown cigarettes and drinks like a fish at diplomatic bunfights, but has hitherto been invulnerable by reason of her chilly disdain. Action:

advise subject by anonymous note that if she doesn't change her hairdresser, her husband will learn something to her disadvantage. Supply her with address of alternative establishment, and arrange to drop in during her appointments.]

So you see, you can't overestimate the importance of good intelligence work. Fascinating woman; d'you know, she smoked those damned brown cigarettes *all* the time, even when . . . *And* kept a tumbler of vodka on the bedside table. But I digress. Bruce was preparing his bombshell, and it was on my return from an exhausting afternoon at the hairdresser's that he informed me, out of the blue, that he was sending me to Nanking.

There was a time when the notion of intruding on the mutual slaughter of millions of Chinese would have had me squawking like an agitated hen, but I knew better now. I nodded judiciously, while my face went crimson (which it does out of sheer funk, often mistaken for rage and resolution) and my liver turned its accustomed white. Aloud I wondered, frowning, if I were the best man to send . . . a clever Chinese might do it better . . . one didn't know how long it would take . . . have to be on hand when Elgin arrived . . . might our policy not be compromised if a senior British officer were seen near rebel headquarters . . . strict neutrality . . . of course, Bruce knew best . . .

"It can't be helped," says he briskly. "It would be folly not to employ your special talents in this emergency. The battle is fully joined before Nanking, and there's no doubt the Taipings will crush the Imps utterly in the Yangtse valley, which will alter the whole balance in China; at a stroke the rebels become masters of everything between Kwangsi and the Yellow Sea." He swept his hand across the southern half of China on his wall map.

"I said some weeks ago that a time might come when we must talk to the Taipings," says he, and for once the cherub face was set and heavy. "Well, it is now. After this battle, Lee's hands will be free, and it's my belief that he will march on Shanghai. If he does, then we and France and America and Russia can ignore the Taipings no longer; we'll be bound to choose once and for all between them and the Manchoos." He rubbed a hand across his jaw. "And that's a perilous

55

choice. We've avoided it for ten years, and I'm damned if I want to see it made now, in haste."

I said nothing; I was too busy recalling, with my innards dissolving, that at the last great battle for Nanking, when the Taipings took it in '53, the carnage had been frightful beyond contemplation. Every Manchoo in the garrison had been massacred, 20,000 dead in a single day, all the women burned alive – and it would be infinitely worse now, with both Taipings and Imp fugitives joining in an orgy of slaughter and pillage, raping, burning, and butchering everything in sight. Just the place to send poor Flashy, with his little white flag, crying: "Please, sir – may I have a word . . .?"

"We can only maintain a de facto neutrality by keeping 'em at a distance," Bruce was saying. "If they advance on Shanghai, we're bound either to fight – and God help us – or come to terms with them, which the Manchoos would regard as a flagrant betrayal – and God help our Pekin expedition. So it is our task to see that the Taipings don't come to Shanghai."

"How the deuce d'you do that?" I demanded. "If they beat the Imps at Nanking, and have blood in their eye, they won't stand still!"

"You don't know the Taipings, Sir Harry," says he. "None of us does – except to know that with them anything is possible. I *think* they'll come to Shanghai – but this crazy king of theirs is capable of declaring a Seven Year Tranquillity, or some such stuff! Or launching his armies west to Yunnan. It is possible they may do nothing at all. That's why you must go to Nanking."

"What can I hope to accomplish?" I protested, and he took a turn round the room, fingered a few papers, sat down, and stared at the floor. Devising some novel means of plunging me into the soup, no doubt.

"I don't know, Sir Harry," says he at last. "You must persuade 'em not to march on Shanghai – at least for a few months – but how you're to do it . . ." He lifted his head and looked me in the eye. "The devil of it is, I can't send you with any authority. I've not replied to Lee's letter, but I'm having a verbal hint discreetly conveyed to him that he may expect a . . . an English visitor. No one official, of

56

course; simply a gentleman from the London Missionary Society who wishes to visit the Heavenly Kingdom and present his compliments. Lee will understand . . . just as he will understand what is meant when the gentleman expresses the opinion – merely the opinion, mind you – that while a Taiping attack on Shanghai would destroy any hope of British co-operation, restraint now would certainly not incline us to a less favourable view of their overtures in the future."

"I can see myself putting that in fluent Mandarin!" says I, and he had the grace to shrug helplessly.

"It is the most I can authorise you to convey. This is the most damned ticklish business. We have to let them see where we stand – but without provoking 'em into action, or offending 'em mortally (dammit, they may be the next government of China!), or, above all, being seen to treat with them in any official way whatsoever. That's why your presence is a gift from God – you've done this kind of business in India, with considerable success, as I recall." Well, that was so much rot; my diplomatic excursions had invariably ended in battle and beastliness on the grand scale, with my perspiring self barely a length ahead of the field. He got up and glowered at the map, chewing his lip.

"You see how difficult it is for me to give you guidance," says he. "We do not even know what kind of folk they truly *are*. The Heavenly King himself has hardly been seen for years – he keeps himself secluded in a great palace, surrounded by a thousand female attendants, thinking wonderful thoughts!" I was willing to bet he didn't spend all his time thinking. "If he could be persuaded to inaction . . . to hold Lee in check . . ." He shrugged. "But who is to say if he is even rational, or if you will be allowed near him? If not, you must do what you can with Loyal Prince Lee."

A splendid choice, you'll agree, between a recluse who thought he was Christ's brother, and a war-lord who'd done more murder than Genghiz Khan.

"The only other who may be open to reason is the Prime Minister, Hung Jen-kan. He's the wisest – or at least the sanest – of the Taiping Wangs. Mission educated and speaks English. The rest are ignorant, superstitious zealots, drunk on blood and power, and entirely under the sway of the

57

Heavenly King." He shook his head. "You must use such tactful persuasions as seem best; you will know, better than I could tell you, how to speak when you are face to face with them."

In a high-pitched shriek, probably. Of all the hopeless, dangerous fool's errands . . . supposing I even got there.

"How do I reach Nanking? Aren't the Imps blockading the river?"

"A passage has been booked on Dent's steamer *Yangtse*. She got through to Nanking last week – the Imps give our vessels passage, and the river will be clear as far as Kiangyin still. If she's stopped there you must go on as seems best; one of our people, a missionary called Prosser, will be looking out for you – you'll have papers from the London Missionary Society, in the name of Mr Fleming, but the Taipings will know precisely who and what you really are, although neither they nor you will acknowledge it."

So it was settled; I was for the high jump again, and not a damned thing to be done about it. He went over it all a second time, impressing on me the delicacy of the task, how H.M.G. must be in no way compromised, that every week of delay would be a godsend – but the main thing was to convince this crew of homicidal madmen that, whoever they killed next, it shouldn't be done at Shanghai.

"Well, sir," says I, all noble and put-upon, "I'll be honest; I'll try, but I don't think there's a hope of success."

"Another man might say that out of reluctance to go, for his safety's sake," says he solemnly. "I know that with you, the thought of danger has not crossed your mind." He was right there; it had stayed rooted. "God bless you, Sir Harry." And with the angels choiring above us, we shook hands, and I marched out, and bolted for the lavatory.

*   *   *

I had my Adams in my armpit, a Colt in my valise, a hundred rounds, a knife in my boot, and a bulky notebook containing every known fact about the Taipings, courtesy of Messrs Fat and Lin, when I boarded the *Yangtse* on the following evening. It was a good two-day run to Nanking, in ideal conditions; at present, it might take a week. I was too sick and scared and furious to pay much heed to my surroundings, and as I remember the *Yangtse* was like any other river steamboat – half a dozen cabins aft for the Quality, of whom I was one, a couple of saloons below for those who couldn't afford a bunk, and forward a great open steerage for the coolies and the like. Her skipper was one Witherspoon, of Greenock, a lean pessimist with a cast in his eye and a voice like coals being delivered. I've no doubt I spent the time before we cast off brooding fearfully, but I don't recall, because as I leaned on the rail looking down on the quay and the oily water, I saw about the only thing that could have provided any distraction just then.

The steerage gangway was swarming with coolies, and poorer Chinese, and a few white riff-raff – Shanghai was well stocked with poor whites and shabby-genteel half-castes and scourings from half the countries on earth, even in those days. There was lascars, of course, and Dagoes of various descriptions, Filippinos, Greeks, Malay Arabs, and every variety of slant-eye. Some of 'em were half-naked; others carried valises and bundles; the half-dozen Sikh riflemen who acted as boat-guards shepherded 'em aboard none too gently under the great flickering slush-lamps which cast weird shadows on the dockside and the steerage deck.

I was watching with half my mind when I noticed a figure stepping from quay to gangway – and even in that motley assembly it was a figure to take the eye – not only for the outlandish cut of attire, but for style and carriage and . . . animal quality's the only phrase.

I like tall women, of course. Susie Willinck comes to mind, and Cleonie of the willowy height, and the superb Mrs Lade by name and nature, and Cassy, and that German wench in the Haymarket, and even such Gorgons as Narreeman and Queen Ranavalona. Mind you, there's much to be said for the little 'uns, too – such as the Silk One, Ko Dali's daughter, and the little blonde Valla, and Mrs Mandeville the Mad Dwarf, and Whampoa's playmates, and Takes-Away-Clouds-Woman, and that voluptuous half-pint, Yehonala (but we'll come to her presently). On the whole, though, I ain't sure I don't prefer the happy medium – like Elspeth,

59

and Lola, and Irma, and Josette, and Fetnab, and . . .
Elspeth.

It is no disrespect to any of these ladies, all of whom I
loved dearly, to say that when it came to taking the eye, the
female coming up the steerage gangplank was the equal of
any and all. For one thing, she was six feet six if she was an
inch, with the erect carriage of a guardsman, and light on
her feet as a leopard. She was Chinese, beyond a doubt,
perhaps with a touch of something from the Islands; when
she laughed, as she did now, to the squat fellow behind her,
it was with a deep, clear ring, and a flash of teeth in a lean,
lovely face; not Chinese style, at all. She had a handkerchief
bound tight round her head, and for the rest her clothing
consisted of a blouse, cotton breeches ending at the knee,
and heavy sandals. But round her neck she had a deep tight
collar that seemed to be made of steel links, and her arms,
bare to the shoulder, were heavy with bangles. As to the
lines of her figure, Rubens would have bitten his brush in
two.

With the plank crowded ahead of her, she had to wait,
holding the side-rail in one hand and lolling back at full
stretch, carelessly, laughing and talking to her companion.
She chanced to look up, and met my eye; she said something
to the man, and looked at me again, laughing still, and then
she was up the plank like a huge cat and out of sight.

I'm not the most impressionable of men, but I found I was
gripping the rail with both hands, and clenching my jaw in
stern resolve. By gum, I couldn't let that go unattended to.
Built like a Dahomey Amazon, but far taller and incompar-
ably more graceful. And possibly the strongest female I'd
ever seen, which would be an interesting experience. No
common woman, either; how best to coax her up to the
cabin? Probably not money, nor a high hand. Well, the first
thing was to get a closer look at her.

I waited till we had cast off, and the screw was churning
the water, with the lights on Tsungming Island glittering in
the dark distance far ahead. Then I asked the steward where
the ladder was to the steerage; he pointed down the companion, and said I would find the mate by the saloon door,
he'd show me. Sure enough, a fellow in a pilot cap came out

of the saloon and started up the ladder as I started down. He glanced up, smiling, starting to bid me good evening, and then his jaw dropped, and my hand shot under my jacket to the butt of the Adams.

It was Mr Frederick Townsend Ward.

❀ For perhaps five seconds we just stared at each other, and then he laughed, in the pleasantest tone imaginable.

"Well, damn me!" says he. "It's the Colonel! How are you, sir?"

"Keep your hands in front of you – sir," says I. "Now come up, slowly." I stepped back to the cabin deck, and he followed, still grinning, glancing at my hidden hand.

"Say, what's the matter? Look, if that's a piece under your coat – this is a law-abiding boat, you know –"

"You mean she isn't running guns to the Taipings?"

He laughed heartily at this, and shook his head. "I gave that up! Say, and you took a shot at me – two shots! What did you *do* that for? You weren't going to come to any harm, you know. I'd ha' taken you back to Macao when we'd delivered the goods!" He sounded almost aggrieved.

"Oh, forgive me! No one told me that, you see. It must have slipped everyone's mind, along with the trivial fact that you were carrying guns, not opium."

"Listen, Carpenter said the less you knew the better," says he earnestly. "Those were his orders. The damned dummy," he added irritably. "If he'd ha' given me a real Chink pilot, we'd never ha' seen that Limey patrol-boat. Hey, how did you come out of that, though?"

"Perhaps I didn't." I said it on the spur of the moment, and his eyes widened.

"You don't mean they broke you?" He whistled. "Gee, I'm sorry about that! I sure am, though." Absolutely, he sounded shocked. "Over a passel o' guns. Well, I'll be!" He shook his head, and smiled, a mite sheepish. "Say, colonel . . . why don't you let that hog-leg alone, and come on in

62

my berth for a drink? See here, I'm sorry as hell – but t'wasn't my fault. 'Sides, it's over and done with now." He looked at me, half-grinning, half-contrite. "And you're ahead o' me by two shots. No hard feelings. Okay?" And he held out his hand.

Now, I know a rogue when I see one – and I was forming a strange suspicion that Mr Ward wasn't a rogue at all. Oh, I've known charming rascals, bland as be-damned, and the eyes give them away every time. This fellow's were bright and dark and innocent as a babe's – which you might say was all against him. And yet . . . he sounded downright pleased to see me. I couldn't credit he was that good an actor; and why should he trouble to be? There was nothing I could do to him, now; certainly not here.

"I ought to blow your blasted head off!" says I.

"You dam' near did!" cries he cheerily, and when I continued to ignore his hand: "Okay, you've got a right to be sore, I guess. But why don't we go lower a couple, anyway? I'm off watch."

Indeed, why not? I can only say he was a hard man to refuse, and the truth is I was curious about him. He was a rare bird, I felt sure, so I followed him out of the warm night into the stuffy little cabin, where he seated me on the bunk and poured out two stiff tots. "Say, this is fine!" says he, sitting on the locker. "How've you been?" And without letting me reply he rattled off into a recital of his own escape through the paddy, and how he'd smuggled himself back to Macao, and thence up the coast to Shanghai, where he'd flourished his papers at Dent's, and got himself a mate's berth. I watched him like a hawk, but he was easy as old leather, prattling away. Crazy, undoubtedly, but if he was crook, it didn't show.

"It's not a bad berth," says he, "but I won't stick. Fellow called Gough, one of your people, commands a gunboat flotilla for the Imps. He's offered me second place on the *Confucius*; reckon I'll take it."

"What happened to the notion of being a Taiping prince?" I asked, and he grinned and pulled a face.

"No, sir, thank you. I've had a look at 'em, these past few weeks. They're not for Fred T." He shook his head so firmly that, thinking of my own mission, I pressed him for information.

"Well, all this stuff about being Christians – they don't have the first notion! They have a lot o' mumbo-jumbo about Jesus, that they've picked up an' got wrong, but . . . Listen – to give you an idea, when they get a new recruit they give him three weeks to learn the Lord's Prayer, and if he can't – whist!" He chopped his hand against his neck. "No fooling! Now, what kind of Christianity is that, will you tell me? And they treat the people something shameful. Take all their goods – 'cos no one can have property in the Taiping, it's all in common, 'lessn you're one of the top Wangs. And they put 'em to work in companies, like it was the army, and if they're too old or sick to work – whist again! And everybody has to work for the Taiping, see, and obey all their foolish rules about religion, an' learn the proclamations of the Heavenly King by heart – and, boy, they're the wildest stuff, I tell you! The Thousand Correct Things, an' the Book of Celestial Decrees, and nobody understands 'em a little bit!"

I said the missionaries were all for them, and he shook his head again. "Maybe they used to be, but now they've had a good look. You go up-river, into a Taiping province, you see the ruin, the gutted villages, the bodies laying about in thousands – and it ain't as if all their rules and discipline made things better – why, they make it worse! Nobody has land, so nobody can plant 'cept the Taiping tells him, an' the local governors, why, they have to wait for orders from further up, an' the fellow further up . . . well, there's nothing in it for *him*, and he probably used to be a shoemaker, anyway, so what does he know about crops? He knows the rules, though, and learns a new chapter of the Bible each day, and thinks Moses was a Manchoo Mandarin who thought better of it!"

I recalled that the Heavenly King himself had been an educated man, and while he was crazy there must be some Taipings who knew how things should be run; he scoffed me out of court.

"That kind of person – you mean merchants and clerks and fellows with some schooling – they have no time for the Heavenly Kingdom; they're mostly dead, anyway, or made themselves scarce. Why should they truck with a crowd that just robs 'em and says they're no better'n the peasants? 'Sides, they can see the Taipings are only good at killing and stealing and laying waste."

"You seem to have learned a lot in a short time," I said, and he replied that one trip up to Nanking, and a look at the country around, had been enough for him. "They're so mean and *cruel*," he kept saying. "Sure, the Imps are worse – their army's rotten, and they just use the war as an excuse for plundering and killing wherever they go – but at least they've got something behind them, I mean, a real government, even if it doesn't work too well . . . a . . . a . . . sort of like the Constitution. I mean . . . China." He grinned ruefully, and poured me another drink. "I don't make it too clear, I guess. But the Taipings just have this crazy dream – and they're no good at making things work. Well, the Imps aren't much better, maybe, but at least they can read and write."

I asked if he had seen anything of the leading Taipings at Nanking, and he said, no, but he had heard plenty. "They do all right, from what I hear – that's what really got my goat. There's all this fine talk about love and brotherhood and equality – but the Wangs live in palaces and have a high old time, while the people are tret no better'n niggers. You know," says he, all boyish earnestness, "at the beginning, they made the women and men stay apart – there was a special part of Nanking for the girls, and if they and the boys . . . you know . . . why, they just killed 'em. Even now, 'lessn you're married – well, if you . . . you know . . . they just – whist! The poor people are allowed one wife, but the Wangs . . ." He blew out his cheeks. "They have all the girls they want, and aren't there some doings in those palaces? So I heard." I found this quite cheering, and pressed him for further details, but he didn't have any. "It's one law for the rich and another for the poor, I guess," says he philosophically. "Mind, they've done some good things, like not letting girls bind their feet, and don't they come down hard on crooks and shysters, though! Stealing, opium-smoking, girls selling themselves, anything illegal at all – or even just talking out of turn – and off comes the head. I've seen that."

I wondered how long the people would endure a rule quite as despotic as the Manchoos', and even less efficient, and he laughed.

"Wait till you see those Taiping soldiers! One thing *they*'re good at is discipline – putting it on the people, and taking it themselves. That's why they can whip the Imps, easy; they're real good, and so are their generals. I'll tell you something, an' the sooner all our people realise it, the better – this here's going to be a Taiping China, for keeps, unless we – I mean you British and us Americans, and the French maybe, do something about it." He'd become very earnest, rapping his finger on the locker; a serious lad, when he wasn't being crazy. But all his talk about the Wangs and their women had reminded me of what I'd been about in the first place, so presently I left him and strolled down to the steerage. Besides, my chat with him had almost been in the way of duty, and I was due for a spell of vicious recreation.

It was full night now, and we were thumping upstream with the Tsungming lights to starboard and the last warmth dying from the night wind. The great steerage deck, poorly lit, was littered with sleepers, and I was about to turn back, cursing, and wait until daylight, when I heard voices forrard. I picked my way over the bodies and rounded the deckhouse in the bows, and my heart gave a lustful little skip – there was the slim, towering figure at the bow-rail, talking with a couple of Chinese rivermen; they turned to glower at me, and then the girl laughed and said something, and the Chinks melted into the dark, leaving the two of us alone under the bow-lamp. She lounged with her elbows on the rail – Jove, what a height she was, topping me by a good four inches. I stepped up to her, lustfully appraising the play of the superb muscles on the bare bangled arms, the lazy grace of the splendid body, and the sensuous hawk face above the strange chain collar. Aye, she was ready to play; it was in every line of her.

"Hiya, tall girl," says I, and she shot me an insolent, knowing look, like a vain tart.

"Gimme smoke, *yao*," says she, extending a palm. "Yao" is "foreigner", and not at all polite from a Chinese to a white man.

66

"The black smoke, or one of these?" I offered my cheroot case, and the slant eyes flickered.

"A *fan-qui* who speaks Chinese? A cheroot, then." Certainly not a common woman; she spoke Pekin, albeit roughly. I lit her a cheroot, and she held my hand with the match in slender fingers whose grip made me tingle; not a whore's touch, though, just simple strength. She inhaled deeply – and so did I, gloating.

"Come to my cabin," says I, slightly hoarse, "and I'll give you a drink."

She showed her teeth, gripping the cheroot. "There's only one thing you want to give me," says she – and named it, anatomically.

"And right you are," says I, quite delighted. This was something new in Chinese women – coarse, insolent, and to the point – so to show my own delicacy and good breeding I gripped her port tit; under the thin blouse it felt like a large, hard pineapple. She gave a little grunt, and a long, slow, wicked smile at me, drawing on her cheroot.

"How much cash?" says she, narrow-eyed.

"My dear child," says I, gallantly relinquishing her poont, "you don't have to pay me! Oh, I see . . . why, I wouldn't insult you by offering money!" Wouldn't I, though – I was boiling fit to offer her the Bank, but I guessed it wouldn't answer with this one, in spite of her question. She had a damned leery look in her eye, sensual and calculating, but with a glint of amusement, unless I was mistaken.

"No cash, hey? But you expect me to ––––?" Her vocabulary was deplorable, but at least it left no room for misunderstanding.

"That's the ticket," says I heartily, "so instead of further flirtation I suggest that we –"

Suddenly she chuckled, and then laughed outright, with her head back and everything quivering to distraction. I was preparing to spring when she came up off the rail, bangles tinkling, and stood looking down at me, the ogre's missus contemplating a randy Jack-the-Giant-Killer. It's a rum feeling, I can tell you, being surveyed by a beauty half a head taller than you are. Stimulating, though.

"Suppose," says she, in that soft deep voice, "that I *took* payment? I might rob a rich *fan-qui*."

"You might try, Miranda. Now then –"

"Yes, I might. And if you, big clever *fan-qui*, caught me . . ." She put her hands on her hips, with that lazy smile.". . . you might beat a poor girl – would you beat me, *fan-qui*?"

"With pleasure," says I, slavering at the prospect. She nodded, glanced either way, gave me her insolent grin again, drew deep on the cheroot – and pulled the front of her blouse down to her waist.

For a moment I stood rooted, hornily agog before all that magnificent meat, and then, as any gentleman would have done, I seized one in either hand, nearly crying. Which was absolutely as the designing bitch had calculated – she suddenly gripped my elbows, I instinctively jerked them down to my sides, and without stooping, or shoulder movement, or the least exertion at all, she lifted me clean off the deck! I was too dumbfounded to do anything but dangle while she held me (thirteen-stone-odd, bigod!) with only the strength of her forearms under my rigid elbows, grinned up into my face, and spoke quietly past the cheroot:

"Would you really beat a poor girl, *fan-qui*?"

Then before I could reply, or hack her shins, or do anything sensible, she straightened her arms upwards, holding me helpless three feet up in the air, before abruptly letting go. I came down cursing and stumbling, clutching at the deckhouse for support. By the time I'd recovered my balance, she was modestly replacing her blouse, taking a last pull at the cheroot, and flicking it over the rail. She put a hand on her hip, grinning derisively, while I seethed with rage and shame – and awe at the realisation of that appalling strength.

"All right, then, damn you!" I snarled. "Twenty dollars? Fifty if you'll stay the night!"

God, how she laughed, the strutting, arrogant slut – and she'd lifted me like a kitten! I don't know when I've felt so mortified – or so determined to have my way with a woman. Well, it wasn't going to be rape, that was sure – nor money, apparently.

"Fifty dollars?" She laughed. "No, *fan-qui* – nor fifty

thousand, from a weakling. But a strong man, now . . ." She waited, with that taunting, confident smile, daring me, as I fell to raging at her and then to whining, saying it had been a trick, she'd taken an unfair advantage, damn her . . . and then I gave a great gasp, like Billy Bones in apoplexy, rolled my eyes, clutched my heart, and reeled fainting against the deckhouse . . . well, she'd not have been human if she hadn't stepped up for a closer look, would she?

I bar hitting women, except for fun, especially when they're strong enough to uproot the town hall clock, but I was choking with vengeful fury – toss me about like thistledown, would she, the infernal slut? I let out a whimpering groan, and as she advanced, alarmed, I let drive my right into her midriff with all my force; she doubled up like a rag doll, her knees buckling, and I was on her back in an instant, twisting the chain collar like a garotte, flattening her by sheer weight. She clawed back at me over her shoulder, and I shot my left hand under her arm and on to the nape of her neck in a half-nelson. I was blind with rage and fit to murder, and if she'd been less abominably powerful I might have done it. But as she heaved and strained beneath me it was all I could do to hang on, doing my damnedest to choke her with the steel links biting into her throat. We thrashed and rolled about the deck, her long legs flailing; thumping against the bulkhead, then against the rail, my aching fingers twisting the collar ever tighter, her splendid shoulders heaving to break my grip – God, she was strong, and I knew in a few seconds she must break the lock.

I gave one last despairing heave on the collar, and suddenly felt her slacken beneath me; her head gave a little beneath my left hand, and I roared with triumph. Suddenly her free hand was slapping the deck, in the age-old wrestler's submission; I clung to the chain like grim death.

"Had enough, damn you?" I wheezed. "Give over, you bloody monster?" Slap-slap, on the deck, I let the collar slacken an inch – and suddenly she reared up, breaking the headlock and tearing the collar free. I rolled away, preparing to fly for my life, when I realised she was scrambling back, holding her throat, her other hand up to ward her face. Was she beat? Was this the moment to set about her with my belt? – and then I realised that she was poised on one knee, ready for battle . . . and she was absolutely grinning at me, bright-eyed . . . and we were no longer alone.

The unholy row had attracted half Kiangsu Province, by the look of it, certainly every coolie on the steerage deck, and a ragged mob was staring from either side of the deck house, with her Chinese rivermen to the fore, looking mighty truculent. As they pressed forward I put my back to the rail, reaching for the Adams – which I'd forgotten until that moment. The sight of it stopped them dead, the rivermen's hands came away from their knife-hilts – and the girl stood up, her shoulders shuddering and heaving, and grunted something in river dialect. Then she looked at me, gasping and rubbing her throat, and so help me, she was grinning again, positively amiable.

Tuckered as I was, I wondered bemusedly if that murderous struggle had been the usual courting ritual of this female Goliath; lust revived as I observed her fine dishevelment, with one udder peeping provocatively out of her blouse; I put up the Adams, scowled back at the mob, and then jerked my head at her. She grinned broader than ever, taking in great breaths and rubbing her throat, but then she shook her head.

"Good-night . . . *fan-qui*," says she, pretty hoarse, and then she turned and disappeared into the staring rabble behind her. Truth to tell, I didn't much mind; I was bruised and exhausted, and another bout would have carried me off; if that was what she was like merely fighting for her life, God knew how she'd behave in amorous ecstasy. I straightened my coat and pushed through the crowd, marvelling at the minds (and bodies) of women – treat 'em civilised, and they swing you round their heads; strangle 'em, and suddenly they're all for you. Because there was no doubt about it, now; she fancied me. It's all a matter of the proper approach.

*   *   *

I knew better than to seek her out next day, as we steamed up the sluggish Yangtse; the consummation of our wooing would be all the better for keeping. I saw her once, as I

70

paced the upper walk after tiffin; she was standing in the steerage, gazing up, and raised a hand and gave her lazy smile at sight of me. I smiled back, surveying her carefully like a farmer at the stock-ring, then nodded as one satisfied for the moment, and turned away to resume my stroll. Aye, let her wait. I had other matters to occupy me, during the day at least; I chewed the fat with Ward, boned up on my Taiping notebook, wondered when the devil Bruce's agent would turn up, and was first in quest of news at every village landing-place.

The crisis was plainly at hand up-river. Off Tungchow, a down-river boat informed us that the great battle about Nanking had become a rout, with the Taipings everywhere victorious; Chen's Celestial Singers were driving through to relieve the capital, while General Lee was driving the Imps like sheep and breaking their blockade on the river.

"And ye ken what that'll mean," declares Skipper Witherspoon ominously. "Every scoondrel in an Imp uniform'll be castin' awa' his coat and turnin' bandit. It'll be worse than Flodden. Goad help the country! We'll no' see Nanking this trip, I'm thinkin'; we'll dae well if we get the boat's neb twenty miles past Kiangyin."

This was serious, for it meant that the last fifty miles of my journey would be through lawless country scourged by Imp deserters and Taiping fanatics. Well, they could count me out; if there was no sign of Bruce's man, I'd turn back with *Yangtse* when Witherspoon decided he'd reached the safety limit; I couldn't be blamed, if the country was impassable. But I knew Bruce wouldn't care for that, and I was still studying to find a good excuse when we pulled in at Kiangyin late in the afternoon. It was the usual miserable hole of mud buildings and rickety bamboo wharves, with the usual peasants gaping apathetically, and stinking to wake the dead – the peasants and Kiangyin both. Beyond the town, stale paddy stretched away to the misty distance, with a few woods here and there, and the inevitable agriculturists and bullocks standing ankle-deep. A depressing spectacle, in no way redeemed by the appearance of the Rev. Matthew Prosser, B.A., God rest him.

He came aboard like a vessel of wrath, stamping up the

gangway and roaring, a small, round, red-faced cleric with corks hanging from his hat like an Australian swagman, a green veil streaming behind, an enormous dust-coat, and a fly-whisk which he used as a flail on hindering Orientals. Behind him tottered an urchin with his valise, and Prosser was furiously demanding the cabin steward when his eye lit on me, and he started as though he'd been stung. He kept darting furtive glances at me while he hectored the steward, and was no sooner inside his cabin than the door opened again, and his crimson face appeared, crying: "Hist!"

I went over, and he dragged me in and slammed the door. "Not a word!" cries he, and stood, listening intently with his corks bobbing. Then, in a thunderous whisper: "I'm Prosser. How-de-do. We shall be bearing each other company, I believe. Say nothing, sir. Remember Ehud: 'I have a secret errand unto thee, oh King; who said, keep silence'." And he gave an enormous wink, which in that furious red face was positively alarming. "Be seated, sir! There!" He pointed firmly to the bunk, and began rummaging like a terrier in his valise.

As it happened, I remembered Ehud, the Biblical left-hander who was adept at sticking knives in folk, which was a portent if you like. As to Prosser, he seemed such an unlikely agent that I asked him if he knew Bruce in Shanghai, and he rounded on me with bared teeth. "Not another word! Discretion, sir! We must bind our faces in secret. Now where," he snarled, rummaging again, "did I put it? Aha, I have it! The cup was found in Benjamin's sack!" And he lugged out a rum bottle which must have held half a gallon. He beamed, peered at the level (which was marked in pencil), set it on the table, and caught my eye.

"Well, Balshazzar drank wine, did he not?" cries he. "But only after sundown, sir. And then but a small measure, against the evening chill. Yes. Now, sir, attend to me if you please. I believe you speak Mandarin? Good." He seemed vastly relieved. "Then when we have reached our destination, I shall make you known to a certain personage, and leave you to your business." He nodded heavily, glanced at the bottle, and muttered something about the Lord being good to them that wait.

"But you'll be staying with me in . . . where we're going?" says I. He might not be much, but he'd be better than nothing.

He shook his head angrily. "No such thing, sir! I am known, you see, and they watch me, and send forth spies that they may take hold of my words. You will do better without me – indeed, the less we are seen together, the better, even now. And once I have made you known, discreetly, to one who, like Timothy, is faithful in the Lord . . . *faithful*, I say . . . then my task is done. Besides, I have my own work!" And he glared at the bottle again, while I concluded that the faithful one must be the *Loyal* Prince, General Lee Hsiu-chen of the Taipings. Why the devil couldn't he say so, instead of acting like Guy Fawkes?

This was disconcerting. I'd supposed I would be dry-nursed to Nanking by some capable thug who not only knew the Taipings backwards, but could give me all manner of useful tips, and do most of the work, with luck. Instead, here was this bottle-nosed parson, who didn't want to be seen near me, couldn't wait to get shot of me, and daren't even say the simplest thing in plain language.

I said I must have some information, and he said, quite short, that he hadn't any. I pointed out that the boat might not go as far as Nanking, in which case he'd *have* to be seen in my company, probably trudging through bandit-infested country. He didn't take this kindly, but growled that if the hosts of Midian were prowling, the Lord must see us through, and cheered me up no end by producing an ancient muzzle-loader revolver from his valise and jamming rounds into it, twitching towards his bottle the while.

I gave up, and left him with a nasty reminder that sundown wasn't for another half-hour. As soon as the door closed I heard the cork pop. Be not among wine-bibbers, thinks I, and recalling that that verse ended with reference to riotous eaters of flesh, went in search of dinner.

Well, it was all sufficiently hellish. How, I asked myself for the thousandth time in my life, had I got into this? A couple of months earlier I'd been homeward bound, and now I was heading on a secret mission that made my flesh crawl, into the bloodiest civil war ever known, on a rickety steamboat in company with the likes of the Reverend Grogpickle and Frederick Townsend Ward who, between them, probably had as sure a touch for catastrophe as any pair I'd ever struck. Stay, though – there was my wrestling wench down on the steerage deck. A bout with her in my cabin might not disperse the blue-devils entirely, but God knows when I'd have another chance. I finished my dinner quickly, and went out on the upper deck.

We were well up from Kiangyin by now, but what kind of country we were in it was impossible to tell. The sky overhead was clear enough, with a bright silver moon, but the river itself was shrouded with fog, and we were pushing into the fleecy blanket at slow ahead, the siren hooting dismally. Traces of it hung like wraiths on the narrow promenade outside the cabins, with a clammy touch on the skin; the sooner I was snug with my giantess, the better.

Out of curiosity I stuck my head into Prosser's cabin, and he was flat on his back and snoring in an atmosphere you could have cut up and sold in the pubs. And I was just pulling the door to again when a sudden tremendous shock threw me off my feet, the *Yangtse* shuddered like an earthquake, plates shattered in the dining-saloon, and faint cries of alarm sounded from the steerage deck. The boat lurched, and stopped, and began to swing. She was aground.

I pulled myself up, damning Witherspoon or whoever was at the wheel – and in an instant was flat on my face again as a ragged volley of shots came out of the mist to port, smashing a window overhead and splintering woodwork, someone shrieked in pain, the brazen clash of a gong started beating out on the water, and the night was rent by a chorus of infernal yelling from beneath the stern. Shots were cracking out, mingled with the explosion of fire-crackers – one landed within a foot of me, snapping and sending out a shower of sparks – something hit the *Yangtse* a grinding jar on her quarter, and close at hand were racing feet and Ward's voice yelling:

"Pirates! Stand to! Pirates!"

❀ To race into my cabin, seize the Adams, and ram handfuls of loose rounds into my pockets was the work of a few seconds; to guess what had happened took even less time. River bandits, or possibly Imp fugitives turned brigand, had somehow blocked the channel and were about to swarm aboard – that thump under the stern had been a raft or sampan, crowded with Chinese savages who would pour over us in a wild, slashing wave, slaughter and torture most hideously whoever survived the attack, loot and burn the steamer, and be off into the web of side-creeks before the nearest Imperial garrison was any the wiser. I'd seen it in Borneo, and knew precisely what to expect – which is why you now behold the unusual spectacle of Flashy making *towards* the scene of action, and not fleeing for cover – of which there wasn't any.

For I knew that in this kind of ambush the first sixty seconds was the vital time. That wild volley, the ridiculous fire-crackers, the clashing gong and the howling chorus – these were the war-whoop, designed to freeze the victim in terror. Our attackers would have few fire-arms; they'd rely on cold steel – swords, knives, kampilans, axes, Aunt Jemima's hatpin – to hack down opposition, and once they were on our decks in force we were done for. Catch 'em with a brisk fire before they could board, and we stood a fair chance of driving them off.

I pounded along the narrow promenade to the after rail and could have whooped with relief at the sight of two Sikh guards on the wide stern deck ten feet below me, blazing away at the devil's crew who were tumbling over the quarter-rail. About half a dozen had reached the deck, horrible creatures in loin-cloths and pigtails, wielding swords, others in peasant dress with spears and knives, shrieking contorted yellow faces everywhere – and the two Sikhs with their Miniés calmly picked their men and tumbled 'em with well-placed shots.

"Reload! Reload!" I bawled, to let 'em know they were covered, for they'd been about to drop their empty pieces and draw their swords, which would have been suicide. One Sikh heard me, and as I opened fire with the Adams he and his mate were whipping in fresh charges. I knocked over two with five shots, and with four down they wavered at the rail. I was feverishly pushing in fresh loads when I heard another revolver, and there was Witherspoon beside the Sikhs, booming away across the smoke-filled deck.

I heard feet behind me, and there was Ward, pistol in hand. "Get forrard!" I yelled. "They'll come at the bow, too!" He didn't hesitate, but turned and went like a hare – you'll go far if you live through this, thinks I, and in that moment I heard the screams and yells and clash of steel from the steerage forrard, and knew that they were into us with a vengeance. I turned to the rail again – and here was more bad news, for Witherspoon's gun was empty, one of the Sikhs was down, and the other was laying about him with his rifle-butt. A dozen pirates were on the deck, and even as I let fly again I saw Witherspoon cut down by a gross yellow genie with a kampilan. I blazed away into the brown, and now the vicious horde had spotted me, yelling and pointing upwards. A shot whistled overhead and a spear clattered on the bulkhead behind me – and I thought, time to go, Flashy my son.

For it was all up. God knew what was happening at the bow, but the brutes were well established here, and in two minutes they'd be butchering the coolies and cutting down the remaining crew. My plan was already formed: time to reload, down to the saloon deck or even lower, and at the first sight of the enemy, over the side and swim for it. And after that the Lord would provide, God willing. Which reminded me of Prosser, but he was a certain goner, drunk and damned.

I came down the ladder at a race, reloading frantically, and reached the saloon deck. All hell was breaking loose on the steerage forrard; I heard the crash of the Miniés – Ward must have the remaining Sikhs at work. Then down to the main deck – I knew there was no way through from the stern; the pirates there would have to climb up to the saloon deck and come down as I had done. I slipped through the door to the open steerage, and it was like Dante's Inferno.

A battle royal was raging round the deckhouse forrard, but nothing to be seen for smoke. Nearer me, coolies were going over the rail like lemmings, apart from a sizeable group over to starboard who were wailing fearfully and evidently trying to burrow through the deck. For twenty feet in front of me the port side of the deck was almost clear as a result of the coolie migration – by God, here were two of 'em coming *back* over the rail! And then I saw the glittering kampilans and the evil, screaming faces, and I shot the first of them as he touched the deck. The second, a burly thug in embroidered weskit and pantaloons, with an enormous top-knot on his bald skull, sprang down, waving an axe, and I was about to supply him with ballast when a fleeing coolie cannoned blindly into me, I went sprawling – and my Adams clattered away into the scuppers.

No one, not even Elspeth, ever believes this, but my first words were: "Why the hell don't you look where you're going?", followed by a scream of terror as the bald bastard lunged for me, axe aloft. There wasn't time to scramble or strike; I was down and helpless, he took just a split second to pick his target – and someone shouted, high and shrill: "Hiya, Shangi! Nay!" His head whipped round in astonishment, and so did mine. Fifteen feet away, just clear of the smoke obliterating the forward deck, stood the tall girl, looking like Medusa. Her kerchief and blouse were gone; there was blood on her breeches and on the chain collar, and in one hand she carried a bloody kampilan.

The old China Sea trick, in fact – half your pirates come aboard as passengers, and turn on the crew when the attack begins. She and those ugly rivermen . . . It was a fleeting thought, and of small interest just then, as Shangi of the axe held his hand in the act of disembowelling me, and responded with a huge beam:

"Hiya, Szu-Zhan!"

and having observed the courtesies, swung up his axe to

cleave me. I heard her scream something, he shot her an angry look and a curse, took final aim at me, and swung. I shut my eyes, shrieking, there was the sound you hear in a butcher's shop when the cleaver hits the joint, and I thought, how deuced odd, that was his axe in *me* – and I felt no pain at all. I looked again, and he was standing side-on, chin on breast, evidently meditating; then I saw the kampilan hilt protruding from his midriff, and eighteen inches of bloody blade standing out behind him, and he crashed forward on the deck, his axe dropping from his hand.

It had taken five seconds since the coolie barged into me – and now I was scrambling over the deck, grabbing the Adams, aware that she was still poised in the act of throwing – and as I came round, two more pirates were mounting the rail, seeing their fallen pal, and going for her with blood in their eye. I shot one in the back; she caught the second by his sword-arm, and I heard the bone snap. Something hit me a terrific clout on the head, and I was on my knees again, with the deck and the night and the hideous din of battle spinning round me; I tried to crawl, but couldn't; the Adams was like lead in my fist, and I knew I was losing consciousness. A boot smashed into me, steel rang beside my head, voices were screaming and cursing, and suddenly I was whirled up, helpless; I was suspended, floating, and then I was flying, turning over and over for what seemed an age before plunging into warm, silent water, into which I sank down and down forever.

*   *   *

Nowadays, in the split second of uncertainty between sleeping and waking, I sometimes wonder: which is it going to be this time? Am I in the Jalallabad hospital or the Apache wickiup, the royal palace of Strackenz or the bottle dungeon under Gwalior, the down bed at Bent's Fort or the mealie bags at Rorke's Drift? Is this the morning I go before the San Serafino firing-squad, or have I only to roll over to be on top of Lola Montez? On the whole, it's quite a relief to discover it's Berkeley Square.

I mention this, because in all the unconscionable spots I've

78

opened my eyes, I've known within seconds where I was and what was what. The Yangtse Valley, for some reason, was an exception; I lay for a good half hour without the least notion, despite the fact that I could overhear people talking about me, in a strange language which, nevertheless, I understood perfectly. That's the oddest thing; they were talking in a Chinese river dialect (quite unlike Mandarin) *which I haven't learned yet* – but in my awakening, it was as clear as English. Ain't that odd?

One fellow was saying they should cut my throat; another says, no, no, this is an important *fan-qui*, I should be held for ransom. A third thought it was a damned shame that I'd been the cause of their falling out with the Triads, because those Provident Brave Butterflies were likely lads whom it was foolish to offend. A fourth said they could hold their wind, since *she* would do what *she* pleased – guess what? At which they all haw-hawed and fell suddenly silent, and a moment later a hand was raising my head, and strong spirit was being trickled between my lips, and I opened my eyes to see the lean handsome face over the steel chain collar.

Then it came rushing back – the boat, the pirates, that hellish mêlée in the steerage. I struggled up, with my head splitting, staring around – a camp-fire among bushes beside a sluggish stream, half a dozen Chinese thugs squatting in a half-circle, regarding me stonily . . . two of them I recognised as rivermen who'd been talking to the tall girl that first night. And herself, kneeling beside me with a flask in her hand, eyeing me gravely; she'd lost her kerchief, and her hair was coiled up most becomingly on top of her head, which must have made her about seven feet tall. For the rest, she wore a peasant shirt now, and the ragged knee-breeches, complete with blood-stain.

I demanded information, fairly hoarse, and she gave it. The *Yangtse* had been ambushed by members of the Provident Brave Butterfly Triad – once a perfectly respectable criminal fraternity which, in these troubled times, had abandoned its urban haunts and gone rogue in the countryside. She and her associates knew the Butterflies quite well; had, indeed, been on friendly terms –

"Until you had to put your knife through Shangi's guts!" cries one of the lads. "What the hell for? Why?"

He and his friends had spoken their river dialect before; his question now was phrased in a dreadful mixture of bastard Pekinese and pigeon, which I could just make out. Why he used it, I couldn't think, unless out of courtesy to me – which it probably was, in fact. They have the oddest notions of etiquette, and can show great consideration for strangers, even unwelcome prisoners, which I seemed to be.

Anyway, when he wondered why she'd corrected poor old Shangi's exercises for him, she simply said: "Because it pleased me," glanced at me, and then looked away with her lazy smile.

"It'll please you, then, when the Butterflies make feud, and kill us all," says he, or words to that effect. "You'll see. What's more, he –" flicking his finger at me "– shot Ta-lung-ki. We'll get the blame for that, too."

"It saved my life," says she, and looked at him. "Are you complaining, you little ——?"

He hurriedly said, no, of course not, and Shangi and Ta-lung-ki were admittedly a pair of prominent bastards . . . still, it was a pity to provoke the Triads . . . he merely mentioned it.

"Who *are* you?" I interrupted, and she looked slightly surprised.

"Bandits," says she, as one might have said "Conservatives, of course", and added with a lift of the splendid head: "I am Szu-Zhan."

Plainly I was right to look impressed, although I'd never heard the name. I nodded solemnly and said: "I see. You work with the Triads?"

It appeared they didn't; she and the boys were *real* bandits, not townee roughs. Sure enough, they'd been preparing to take the *Yangtse* farther up, but the Triads had got in first, and Szu-Zhan and her gang had been pursuing a neutral policy until (here she looked at me steadily) it had become necessary to intervene. After that, to avoid further embarrassment, they had left, and she'd been considerate enough to throw me over the side first.

"What happened to the others – the passengers and crew?"

"They will be in Kiangyin by now," says she. "From the bank we saw them beat off the Triads; then they refloated the boat and went down-river."

Ward, you son-of-a-bitch! I thought to myself. He'd absolutely fought his way clear – and thanks to the zeal of my protectress I was stuck in the wilderness. Not that I could complain – but for her I'd have been digesting Shangi's axe by now. Which was highly flattering, although I'd known, of course, after our tussle behind the deckhouse, that she had worked up a ravenous appetite for me. It didn't surprise me, for – I say this without conceit, since it ain't my doing – while civilised women have been more than ordinarily partial to me, my most ardent admirers have been the savage females of the species. Take the captain of Gezo's Amazons, for example, who'd ogled me so outrageously during the death-house feast; or Sonsee-array the Apache (my fourth wife, in a manner of speaking); or Queen Ranavalona, who'd once confessed shyly that when I died she intended to have part of me pickled in a bottle, and worshipped; or Lady Caroline Lamb – the Dahomey slave, not the other one, who was before my time. Yes, I've done well among the barbarian ladies. Elspeth, of course, is Scottish.

And here now was Szu-Zhan of the glorious height and colossal thews – when I thought of the strength that could drive a kampilan through a stout human body from fifteen feet, I felt a trifle apprehensive. But at least I was safe with her, and would be most lovingly cared for, until . . .? Aye, the sooner we took order, the better.

"Szu-Zhan," says I gravely, "I am in your debt. I owe you my life. I'm your friend, now and hereafter." I held out my hand, and after a moment she grasped it, giving me her pleased, insolent smile. It was like putting your hand in a mangle. "My name is Harry, I am English, and stand high in the British Army and Government."

"Halli'," says she, in that deep liquid voice – and d'ye know, it never sounded better.

"And I'm indebted to your friends also," says I, and held out my hand again. The six proud walkers looked at each other, and frowned, and scratched, and scowled – and then

81

one by one came forward, and each took my hand, and muttered "Hang" and "Tan-nang" and "Mao" and "Yei" as the case might be. Then they all sat down again and giggled at each other.

"I need to go back to Shanghai, quickly," I went on. "The British Trade Superintendent will pay many taels for my safe return. In silver. I can promise –"

"Not to Shanghai," says she. "Not even to Kiangyin. This is Triad country, so we go west, until we are strong again – thirty, forty swords. Then let the Butterflies feud!" And she sneered at Mao, the argumentative one.

"Then let me go," says I. "I pledge two hundred taels, to be paid to you wherever you wish. I'll make my own way back."

She studied me, leaning back on her elbow – and if you don't think that shirt, bloody breeches, and great clog sandals can look elegant, you're mistaken. The long hungry face was smiling a little, as a cat might smile if it could. "No. You were going to Nanking. We can take you there . . . or farther." And for the first time since I'd met her, she dropped her eyes.

"Hey!" cries Yei, who I learned was the gang idiot, and had just reached a conclusion the others had known long ago. "She wants him to ——!" Obviously they'd all gone to the same elocution class. "That's why she wants to keep him with us! To ——!"

Her response might have been to blush and say, "Really, Yei!" – and perhaps, by Chinese bandit standards, it was. For she was on her feet like a panther, reached him in two great strides, plucked him up wriggling by the neck, and laid into him with a bamboo. He yelled and struggled while she lambasted him mercilessly at arm's length until the stick broke, when she swung him aloft in both hands, dashed him down, and trampled on him.

He came to after about ten minutes, by which time I had lost any inclination to argue with the lady. "Nanking let it be," says I. "As it happens, I have business with the Loyal Prince Lee." That ought to impress even bandits. "You know the Taipings?"

"The Coolie Kings?" She shrugged. "We have marched

82

with them against the Imps, now and then. What is your business with the Chung Wang?"

"Talk," says I. "But first I shall ask him for two hundred taels in silver."

We spent the night where we were, since the crack I'd taken on the head had left me feeling fairly seedy. Next morning I had nothing worse than a bad headache, and we set off north-west through the wooded flats and flood-lands that lie between the great river and the Tai Hu lake to the south. Nanking was about fifty miles ahead, but in the state of the country I reckoned it would take us a good four days, and wary travelling at that.

For we were marching into a battle-field – or rather, a killing-ground that stretched a hundred miles, where the remnants of the Imperial armies were fleeing before the Taipings, with both sides savaging the country as they went. I've seen slaughter and ruin in my time – Gettysburg, and Rio villages where the Mimbreno had passed through, the Ganges valley in the Mutiny time, and the pirate-pillaged coast of Sarawak – but those were single battle-grounds, or a few devastated villages at most. This was a whole country turned into a charnel-house: village after burned village, smoke on every horizon, corpses, many of them hideously mutilated, on every wrecked street and in every paddy and copse – I remember one small town, burning like a beacon, and a pile of bodies of every age and sex outside its shattered gate – that pile was eight feet high and as long as a cricket pitch; they had been herded together, doused with oil, and burned.

"Imps," says Szu-Zhan, and I daresay she was right, for they were worse than the rebels. We saw scattered bands of them every hour, and had to lie up as they passed: mobs of Bannermen, in their half-armour and quilted jacks, Tiger soldiers like grotesque harlequins in their close-fitting suits of diagonal black and yellow, Tartar cavalry in fur-edged conical hats and gaudy coats, dragging wailing women behind their ponies. In one place we saw them driving a crowd of peasants – there must have been a couple of hundred – into an open field, and then they just charged among them, and butchered them with their swords and lances. And

83

everywhere the dead, and the death-smell mingling with the acrid smoke of burning homes.

I don't describe this to harrow you, but to give some notion of what China was like in that summer of '60. And this was one small corner, you understand, after one battle, in a vast empire where rebellion had flamed for ten long years. No one can ever count the dead, or tally the destruction, or imagine the enormity of its blood-stained horror. This was the Taiping – the Kingdom of Heavenly Peace.

After the first day, though, I barely noticed it, any more than you notice fallen leaves in autumn. For one thing, my companions were indifferent to it – they'd lived in it for years. And I had my own skin to think about, which means after a little time that you feel a curious elation; you are alive, and walking free, in the Valley of the Shadow; your luck's holding. And it's easy to turn your thoughts to higher things, like journey's end, and your continued survival, and the next meal, and the slim towering figure ahead, with those muscular buttocks and long legs straining the tight breeches.

The devil of it was, while we were sleeping out there was no privacy, with those six villains never more than a few yards away, and dossing down beside us at night. She was watching me, though, with that knowing smile getting less lazy, and her mouth tightening with growing impatience as the hours and miles passed. I was getting a mite feverish myself; perhaps it was the barbarous conditions, and the frustration of being so near, but I wanted that strapping body as I wanted salvation; once, when we lay up in a wood while a long convoy of Imp stragglers went by, we found ourselves lying flank to flank in long grass, with the others behind the bushes, and I began to play with her until she turned on me, her mouth shaking and searching for mine. We pawed and grappled, grunting like beasts, and I dare say would have done the trick if the clown Yei hadn't come and trodden on us.

By the second afternoon we had struck a patch of country which the war seemed to have passed by; peasants were hard at it standing in the fields, and not far ahead there was a fortified hill-summit, betokening a safe village; we had picked up some baggage and side-arms on our journey, and even a

84

cart to push them in, at which the bandits took complaining turns, and Szu-Zhan said we should stay that night at an inn, because camping out you never knew when you might be molested by prowlers. It's a great thing, property-owning.

We were such an evil-looking gang – especially with myself, a big-nosed, fair-skinned barbarian, which is the height of ugliness to the Chinese – that I doubted if they'd let us through the gate, but there was a little temple just outside the wall, with a vulture-like priest ringing a hand-bell and demanding alms, and once Szu-Zhan had given him a handful of cash he croaked to the gate-keeper to admit us. It was a decent village, for China; the piled filth was below window-level, and the Inn of Mutual Prosperity had its own tea-shop and eating-house – quite the Savoy or Brown's, if you like, a shilling a night, bring your own grub and bedding.

Indeed, I've fared worse at English posting-houses in my schooldays than I have in some rural Chink hotels. This one was walled all round, with a big archway into its central court, and we hadn't stopped the cart before a fat little host was out with the inevitable tea-pot and cups. Szu-Zhan demanded two rooms – one on the side-wall for the six lads, and another de luxe apartment at the top of the yard, away from the street – those are the better, larger rooms, and cost three hundred cash, or eighteenpence. They're big and airy – since the door don't fit and the paper in the windows lets in fine draughts, but they're dry and warm, with a big *kong*, or brick platform bed, taking up half the room. Under the bed there's a flue, for dry grass or dung fuel, so you sleep most comfortably on top of a stove, with the smoke going up a vent in the wall – or rather, not going up, since the chimney's blocked, and you go to bed in dense fog. Privacy is ensured by closing the door and getting mine host to jam your cart up against it.[9]

There wasn't a "best" room available, until Szu-Zhan shrugged back the cloak she'd picked up, and rested her hand on her cleaver-hilt, at which mine host blenched and wondered if the Paddy-field Suite wasn't vacant after all; he signified this by grovelling at our feet, beating his head on the ground in the kow-tow ("knocking head", they call it),

85

pleading with us to wait just a moment, and then scrambling up, grabbing a servant, and getting him to deputise as kow-tow-er while the host scurried off to eject a party who had just booked in. He fairly harried them out, screaming – and they went, too, dumb and docile – while the servant continued to bash his brains out before us, and then we were ushered in, another tea-pot was presented with fawning servility, and we were assured that dinner could be served in the apartment, or in the common-room, where a wide variety of the choicest dishes was available.

It was the usual vile assortment of slimy roots and gristle which the Chinese call food, but I had a whole chicken, roasted, to myself – and it was during the meal that I realised my companions were not "Chinese", but Manchoos. The common Chinks eat out of a communal rice-bowl, but even the lowliest Manchoo will have his separate rice-dish, as Szu-Zhan and her companions did. (Better-class Manchoos, by the way, seldom eat rice at all.)

Other interesting native customs were to be observed after the meal, when the six, gorged to the point of mischief, announced that they were off to the brothel next door. I've never seen prostitution so blatant as in China, and this although it's a hanging offence; all through our meal, shabby tarts with white-painted faces had been becking and giggling in the doorway, calling out and displaying the mutilated feet by which the Chinese set such store, and the lads had been eating faster and faster in anticipation. Now, with the samshu and tea going round, Szu-Zhan, who'd been leaning back against the wall, sipping and eyeing me restively, threw a bag of cash on the table and reminded them that we would be off at dawn. Put money in front of a Chinese, even if he's starving, and he'll gamble for it; they turned out the purse, yelping, and fell to *choi-mooy*, the finger game, in which you whip your hand from behind your back, holding up one or more fingers, and the others have to guess how many, double quick.

In two minutes they were briefly at blows, with the tarts hanging over the table, egging them on; then they settled down and the fingers shot out to a chorus of shouts, followed by groans or laughter, while Szu-Zhan and I sat apart,

86

nibbling a fiery-tasting ginger root which she'd spoke for, and killing the taste with tea and samshu.

I watched her, strong teeth tearing at the ginger root, and saw she was breathing hard, and there was a trickle of sweat down the long jaw; she's on a short fuse now, thinks I, so I took her hand firmly and led her out and quickly across to the room. I had her shirt and breeches away before the door closed, and was just seizing those wonders, yammering with lust, when she spun me round in an iron grip, face to the wall, and disrobed me in turn, with a great rending of linen and thunder of buttons. She held me there with one hand while with the other she drew a long, sharp finger-nail slowly down my back and up again, faster and faster, as she hissed at my ear, biting my neck, and finally slipped her hand round my hips, teasing. I tore free, fit to burst, but she turned, squirming her rump into me, seizing my wrists and forcing my fingers up into her chain collar, panting: "Now, Halli', now – fight! Fight!" and twisting her head and shoulders frenziedly to tighten my grip.

Well, strangulation as an accompaniment to la galop was, I confess, new to me, but anything to oblige the weaker sex (my God!). Besides, the way she was thrashing about it was odds that if I didn't incapacitate her somehow, she'd break my leg. So I hauled away like fury, and the more she choked the wilder she struggled, plunging about the room like a bronco with Flashy clinging on behind for his life, rolling on the floor – it was three falls to a finish, no error, and if I hadn't secured a full nelson and got mounted in the same moment, she'd have done me a mischief. After that it was more tranquil, and we didn't hit the wall above twice; I settled into my stride, which calmed her to a mere frenzy of passion, and by the time we reached the ecstatic finish she was as shuddering clay in my hands. As I lay there, most wonderfully played out, with her gasping exhausted beneath me, I remember thinking: Gad, suppose she and Ranavalona had been joint rulers of Madagascar.

The trouble was that, being so infernally strong, she recovered quickly from athletic exercise, and within the hour we were at it again. But now I insisted that I conduct the orchestra, and by giving of my artistic best, convinced her that grinding is even better fun when you don't try to kill each other. At least she seemed to agree afterwards, when we lay in each other's arms and she kissed me lingeringly, calling me *fan-qui* Halli' and recalling our contortions in terms that made me blush. So I drifted into a blissful sleep, and about four o'clock she was there again, offering and demanding violence, and this time our exertions were such that we crashed through the top of the bed into the fireplace, and completed the capital act among the warm embers and billowing clouds of ash. Well, I reflected, that's the first time you've done it in a Chinese oven. *Semper aliquid novi*.

* * *

A little touch of Flashy in the night goes a long way with some women; then again, there are those who can't wait to play another fixture, and so ad infinitum. I suppose I should be grateful that Szu-Zhan the bandit was one of the latter, since this ensured my safety and also gave me some of the finest rough riding I remember; on the other hand, the way she spun out that journey to Nanking, over another three days and tempestuous nights, it looked long odds that I'd have to be carried the last few miles.

She gave me concern on another, more spiritual score, too. As you know, I've no false modesty about my ability to arouse base passion in the lewder sort of female (and some not so lewd, neither, until I taught 'em how), but I've never deluded myself that I'm the kind who inspires deep lasting affection – except in Elspeth, thank God, but she's an emotional half-wit. Must be; she's stuck by me for sixty years. However, there were one or two, like Duchess Irma and Susie, who truly loved me, and I was beginning to suspect that Szu-Zhan was one of those.

For one thing, she couldn't get enough of my company and conversation on the march, plaguing me to tell her about myself, and England, and my time in the Army, and places I'd visited, and my likes and dislikes . . . and whether I had a wife at home. I hesitated at that, fearful that the truth might displease her, but decided it was best to let her know I was spoke for already. She didn't seem to mind, but

88

confessed that she had five husbands herself, somewhere or other – a happy, battered gang they must have been.

She would listen, intent, to all I said, those slant eyes fixed on my face, and the arch, satisfied smile breaking out whenever I paid her any marked attention. Then on the last lap into Nanking she fell thoughtful, and I knew the poor dear was brooding on journey's end.

On the previous afternoon we had come into Taiping country proper, and I saw for the first time those red jackets and blue trousers, and the long hair coiled in plaits round the head that marked the famous Chang Maos, the Long-haired Devils, the Coolie Kings. What I'd heard was true: they *were* finer-featured than the ordinary Chinks, smarter, more disciplined even in their movements – aye, more austere is the word. Their guard-posts were well-manned, on the march they kept ranks, they were alert, and full of business, holding up their heads . . . and I began to wonder if perhaps Napoleon was right. The greatest rebellion ever known; the most terrible religious force since Islam.

Szu-Zhan proved to be well-known to them, by repute, and now I learned how many professional brigands had joined with the Taipings, out of no ideals, but just for the loot and conversation, only to fall away because they wouldn't take the rigid discipline – quite trivial military crimes were punished by death or savage flogging, and apart from that there was all the rubbish of learning texts and the Heavenly King's "thoughts" and keeping strictly the Sabbath (Saturday, to them, like the Hebrews). So Szu-Zhan took part with them only when she felt like it, which wasn't often.[10]

They treated her with immense respect – mind you, he'd have been a damned odd man who didn't. I've known a fair number of females who were leaders of men, and every time someone has thought fit to remark on the fact of their sex. Not with Szu-Zhan; her leadership was a matter of course, and not only because she was gigantic in stature and strength. She had a quality; put 'em on an outpost together and even Wellington wouldn't have pressed his seniority.

But my own humble presence in the party helped to speed us on our way, too, for they were eager to welcome any outside Christians who might take word home of what splendid chaps they were; they knew, you see, that what their movement needed was the approval of the great Powers: Britain, France and America for preference, but Paraguay would do at a pinch. So we rode the last day, all eight of us, in our cart hauled by forty straining peasants in harness, with Taiping guards flogging 'em on; when one collapsed they kicked him into the ditch and whistled up another.

I'll not forget that ride in a hurry, for it took us not into Nanking, but into the heart of the vast army of Golden Lions, commanded by General Lee Hsiu-chen, the Loyal Prince, and the man I had come to see. I had mixed feelings about meeting him; great men are chancy, and best viewed from a distance as the parade goes by.

And didn't this one have a parade of his own, just! Mile after mile of outposts and lines and bivouacs, swarming with orderly mobs of red coats and white straw coolie hats; parks of artillery, laagers of store-wagons and equipment carts; great encampments for the separate corps – the Youths, the Earths, the Waters, the Women, who are respectively the light infantry and scout battalions, the sappers and builders, the river navy, and the female regiments, who alone were a hundred thousand strong. I looked on those anthills of disciplined humanity, covering the ground into the hazy distance, and thought: Palmerston, you should see this. God knows about their quality, although they look well, but for weight of numbers they'll be bad to beat. Take on the Russians, or the Frogs, or the Yankees, if you like, but don't tangle with this, because you'll never come to the end of them.[11]

Well, I was wrong, as you know. A dreamy young Scot and a crazy American between them brought the Great Kingdom of Heavenly Peace down in bloody wreck in the end. But I wouldn't have bet on it that day below Nanking. And this wasn't the half of them; the rest were still out yonder, murdering Imps.

When we were clearly coming to the centre of the camp, I decided it was time to announce myself as an English gentleman seeking General Lee. That cleared our way to a cluster of head-quarter tents, where I made myself known to an officer outside the biggest marquee of all, with stalwart bowmen in fur caps and steel breastplates standing guard, a golden lion standard at its canopy, and yellow ribbons fluttering from its eaves. He told me to wait, and I turned to Szu-Zhan, asking her to act as my sponsor. She shook her head.

"No. Go in alone. He will not wish to see me."

"He will when I tell him that it's thanks to you I'm here," says I. "Come on, tall girl! I need you to speak up for me."

She shook her head again. "Better you speak to him alone. Don't worry, he will understand what you say." She glanced round at the six wise men, who were studying their orderly surroundings with contempt, and spitting over the edge of the cart. "You'll get no credit from this company, *fan-qui*."

Something in her voice made me look closer – she'd been calling me "Halli'", not "fan-qui" for days now. Her eyes seemed bigger, and suddenly I realised, before she turned her head away sharply, it was because there were tears in them.

"For God's sake!" says I, stepping up. "Here, come down this minute! Come down, I say!"

She slipped over the edge of the cart and leaned against it with that artless elegance that could make me come all over of a heat, and looked sullenly down at me. "What the devil's the matter?" says I. "Why won't you come in?"

"It is not fitting," says she stubbornly, and brushed a hand over her eyes, the bangles tinkling.

"Not fitting? What stuff! Why . . . Here!" A thought struck me. "It's not . . . anything you've done, is it? You're not . . . wanted . . . for being a bandit, I mean?"

She stared, and then laughed her great deep laugh, with her head back, the steel collar shaking above her bosom. Gad, but she was fine to see – so tall and strong and beautiful. "No, Halli', I am not . . . wanted." She shrugged impatiently. "But I would rather stay here. I'll wait."

Well, the darlings have their own reasons, so when the officer returned I went in alone, and was conducted through a long canvas passage ending in a heavy cloth of gold curtain. He drew it back . . . and I stepped from the world into the Kingdom of Heavenly Peace.

It was downright eery. One moment the noise and bustle of the camp, and now the dead silence of a spacious tent that was walled and roofed and even carpeted in yellow silk; filtered light illuminated it in a golden haze; the furniture was gilt, and the young clerk writing at a gold table was all clad in yellow satin. He put down his brush and rose, addressing me in good Pekinese:

"Mr Fleming?" He called it Fremming. "The gentleman from the Missionaries of London?" I said I was, and that I wished to see General Lee Hsiu-chen (whom I was imagining as Timoor the Tartar, all bulk and belly in a fur cloak and huge moustachios).

He indicated a chair and slipped out, returning a moment later in a brilliant scarlet silk jacket – the effect of that glaring splash of colour in the soft golden radiance absolutely made me blink. I rose, waiting to be ushered.

"Please to sit," says he. "This is not ceremonial dress."

He sat down behind the table, folded his hands, and looked at me – and as I stared at the lean, youthful face with its tight lips and stretched skin, and met the gaze of the intent dark eyes, I realised with shock that this slim youngster (I could give him several years, easy) must be the famous Loyal Prince himself. I tried to conceal my astonishment, while he regarded me impassively.

"We are honoured," says he. His voice was soft and high-pitched. "You were expected some days ago. Perhaps you have had a troublesome journey?"

Still taken aback, I told him about the river ambush, and how Szu-Zhan and her friends had brought me across country.

"You were fortunate," says he coolly. "The tall woman and her brigands have been useful auxiliaries in the past, but they are pagans and we prefer not to rely on such people."

Not encouraging, but I told him, slightly embarrassed, that I'd promised her two hundred taels, which I didn't have, and he continued to regard me without expression.

"My treasurer will supply you," says he, and at this point in our happy chat a servant entered with tea and tiny cups. Lee poured in ceremonious silence, and the trickle of the tea sounded like a thundering torrent. For no good reason, I

92

was sweating; there was something not canny about this yellow silken cave with the scarlet-coated young deaths-head asking if I would care for distilled water on the side. Then we sat sipping in the stillness for about a week, and my belly gurgling like the town drains. At last he set down his cup and asked quietly:

"Will the Powers welcome our army at Shanghai?"

I damned near swallowed my cup. If he handled his army as briskly as his diplomacy, it was a wonder there was an Imp soldier left in China by now. He waited until I had done hawking and coughing, and fixed me with those cold dark eyes.

"It is essential that they should." He spoke in the flat, dispassionate tone of a lecturer. "The war in China is foregone. The dragon will die, and we shall have killed it. The will of the people, inspired by God's holy truth, must prevail, and in the place of the old, corrupt China, a new nation will be born – the Taiping. To achieve this, we do not need European help, but European compliance. The Powers in effect control the Treaty Ports; the use of one of them, Shanghai, will enable us to end the war so much the sooner."

Well, that was what Bruce had said, and what we, in our neutrality, were reluctant to grant, because it would put a fire-cracker under Pekin's backside and Grant would have to fight all the way to the capital against an Imperial Government who'd feel (rightly) that we'd betrayed 'em to the Taipings.

"We are aware," he went on, "that Britain has a treaty with the Emperor and recognises his government, while not acknowledging even our existence. Perhaps she should recall the saying of an English poet, that treason cannot prosper because with prosperity it ceases to be treason. The Taiping is prospering, Mr Fleming. Is that not a sound reason why your country should look favourably on our request to come to Shanghai in peace and friendship?"

So much for Oriental diplomacy – long fingernails and long negotiations, my eye! There was his case, stated with veiled menaces, before I'd got a word in, let alone Bruce's "tactful persuasions". One thing was clear: this wasn't the time,

93

exactly, to tell him we didn't want his long-haired gang anywhere near Shanghai.

"But there is more, much more, than mere practical interest to bind our countries." He leaned forward slightly, and I realised that behind the impassive mask he was quivering like a greyhound. The dark eyes were suddenly alight. "We are Christian – as you are. We believe in progress, work, improvement – as you do. We believe in the sacred right of human liberty – as you do. In none of these things – *none!*" his voice rose suddenly "do the Manchoos believe! They respect no human values! Why, for example, do they shuffle and lie and evade, rather than permit your Ambassador to go to Pekin to sign the treaty to which they are pledged? Do you know?"

I supposed, vaguely, that they hoped we'd modify a few clauses here and there, if they put off long enough . . .

"No." His voice was level again. "That is not why. They would sign today – at Canton, or Shanghai, even Hong Kong. But not at Pekin. Why? Because if the ceremony is *there*, in the Hall of Ceremonies in the Imperial City, with your Lord Elgin and the Emperor, the Son of Heaven, face to face . . ." he paused, for emphasis ". . . then all China, All Under the Skies, will see that the Big Barbarian does *not* go down on his knees before the Celestial Throne, does *not* beat his head on the ground before the Solitary Prince. That is why they delay; that is why General Grant must go up with an army – because Lord Elgin will not kow-tow. And that they cannot endure, because it would show the world that the Emperor is no more than any other ruler, like your Queen, or the American President. And that they will not admit, or even believe!"

"Touchy, eh?" says I. "Well, I dare say –"

"Is a government to be taken seriously, that would risk war – conquest, even – rather than forego the kow-tow to that debauched imbecile? Come to a Taiping prince, and he will take your Ambassador's hand like a man. That is the difference between a power blinded by ignorance, pride, and brutality, stumbling to its ruin, and a power enlightened, democratic and benign. Allow me to pour you some more tea."

94

Now you'll have noticed that for all his cold, straight talk, he hadn't said they were coming to Shanghai willy-nilly; he'd urged powerful reasons why we ought to invite them, with a strong hint of the consequences if we didn't. Well, we'd have to wait and see, but it was plain I was going to have the deuce of a job fobbing him off for as long as Bruce wanted. This was the kind of steel-edged young fire-eater who'd want a straight answer, p.d.q., and wouldn't wear any diplomatic nods and winks. By gad, he wasted no time; how long had I been with him – ten minutes? Long enough to feel the force that had brought him in ten years from apprentice charcoal-burner and private soldier to the third place in the Taiping hierarchy behind Hung Jen-kan and the Tien Wang himself. It was there, in the cold soft voice and hard unwinking eyes; he was a fanatic, of course, and a formidable one. I didn't care for him one damned bit.

However, I had a part to play, even if we both knew it was a sham. So I thanked him for his illuminating remarks about his great movement, which I looked forward eagerly to studying while I was in Nanking. "I am only a traveller, as you know, but anxious to learn – and to pass on what I learn to my countrymen who are . . . ah, deeply interested in your splendid cause."

"What you will learn, and pass on," says he, "will include the elementary scientific fact that revolutions do not stand still. Tomorrow I shall conduct you personally to Nanking, where I hope you will do me the honour of being my personal guest for as long as it pleases you to stay."

So that was that, and he must have slipped a quick word to his treasurer, for in the outer tent – and how free and airy it seemed after that golden bath – a little chap was waiting with a bag of silver and a scroll, which I was invited to sign with a paint-brush. When in Rome . . . I painted him a small cat sitting on a wall, he beamed, and I strode out to the cart . . . which wasn't there.

I stopped dead, looking right and left, but there was no sign of it; nothing but the limitless lines of tents, with red-coats swarming everywhere. I turned in astonishment to the officer who had admitted me.

"The woman who was here, with the cart – the very tall woman . . . and six men –"

"They went away," says he, "after you had gone in to the Chung Wang. The woman left that for you."

He jerked his thumb at one of the little flagstaffs planted before the marquee; something was hanging on it, something shining. I went over and was reaching for it in bewilderment, when I made out what it was. Her steel-chain collar.

Wondering, I took it down, weighing it in my hands. Why the devil had she gone off – leaving this?

I stared at the officer. "She left this . . . for me? Did she say why?"

He shook his head, bored. "She told me to give it to the big *fan-qui*. Nothing more."

"But she said she was going to wait!"

"Oh, aye." He stopped in the act of lounging off. "She told me to say . . . that she would always be waiting." He shrugged. "Whatever that may mean."

❀ There's a test which I apply to all my old flames, when I think back sentimentally to moments of parting, and it's this: if she'd been mine to sell, how long would I have kept her? In the case of Szu-Zhan, the answer is: another night or two at most. Aside from the fact that she was wearing me to a shadow, I needed no encumbrances in Taipingdom; by all accounts they were a strait-laced lot who mightn't take kindly to a bandit mistress, and I couldn't afford to lose face. Perhaps she sensed that, and had the good sense to make herself scarce.

Yet as I stood by the dusty camp road with the flags and ribbons fluttering in the evening wind, and the sun going down misty beyond the lines, I confess I felt a moment's pang at the thought that I'd straddled her for the last time. And I still keep the chain collar in my drawer upstairs, with the Silk One's scarf, Lakshmibai's stirrup, Lola's letter, Irma's little glove, and that mysterious red silk garter with "Semper Fidelis" embroidered on it that I'm damned if I can place. Anyway, it shows I still think kindly on Szu-Zhan.

But even she pales in memory when I look back to that time, for now I was entering on one of the strangest episodes of my life, which I wouldn't believe myself if I were to read it in someone else's recollections, but which you may take my word for, because I was there, in the Eternal Kingdom of Heavenly Peace, and you know I ain't about to start stretching at this time of day. I can say I've walked in Nephelococcygia,* as old Arnold would have called it, and when I tell you that it beat even Madagascar for craziness, well . . . you shall judge for yourselves.

There was little sign of it during the two days I was in

* Cuckoo-City-in-the-Clouds (Aristophanes).

Lee's camp, and as I compared the tales I'd heard with what I was now seeing for myself, I wondered if perhaps the Taipings hadn't been grossly misrepresented by Imp and foreign propagandists. That they were savage and blood-thirsty, I knew from the journey up – but what Oriental army is not? They were no mere barbarian horde, though, but a splendidly-disciplined force far more formidable than we had imagined. As for their lunacy, I'd spoken with one of their great men, and found him sane and intelligent enough, if a bit of a zealot. Very well, their Heavenly King might be a barmy recluse with odd notions of Christianity, but it all seemed a far cry from the days when the early Wangs, or princes, had been as crazy as he was, and went about calling themselves Kings of the East, West, North, and South, and murdering each other right and left. The titles of their successors were undoubtedly odd – Shield King, and Assistant King, and Heroic King, and Cock-eyed King (that is true, by the way), but if their Loyal Prince, General Lee, was anything to go by, they were business-like enough. So I reasoned, and the shock was all the more unexpected when it came.

We went into Nanking on the second afternoon. Lee, borne in a chair of state by Taiping stalwarts, was magnificent in yellow robes and satin boots, wearing a gold crown in the shape of a tiger with ruby eyes and pearl teeth, and carrying a jade sceptre; this, he explained, was ceremonial dress for a council of all the Wangs, who would deliberate on what should be done now that the Imps had been driven from the Yangtse Valley. Like marching on Shanghai, no doubt.

We made a brave procession, with a company of red-coat spearmen marching ahead, singing "Who would true valour see" in Chinese, and damnably off-key, and in the rear a squadron of mounted bowmen in backs-and-breasts, mighty smart – I'd noted that the Taipings had comparatively few hand-guns, but artillery by the park. I rode a Tartar pony beside Lee's chair, so that he could point out such objects of interest as the distant Ming Tombs, one of the wonders of ancient China, and the huge siege-works from which the Imps had been expelled two weeks earlier, massive entrenchments bigger than anything I saw later in the Civil War or in France in '70, and filled now with thousands upon thousands of decaying corpses raked together from the battlefields which extended for miles around. The stench was appalling, even with armies of coolies burying for dear life, with quicklime by the cart-load. Lee said it was nothing to '53, when the river was so solid with corpses that boat traffic had had to be suspended.

Nanking lies on the Yangtse bank, girdled by hills, and long before we reached it we could see those famous beetling walls, sixty feet high and forty thick, which enclose the city in a great triangle twenty miles about. It's one of the finest cities in China today, but when we'd passed through the long tunnel at the south gate I was shocked to find myself gazing on a scene of ruin and desolation. The suburb had been razed flat, and was swarming with crowds of miserable-looking serfs labouring at nothing, so far as I could see, under the direction of Taiping troops; starving beggars everywhere, ragged children played among the pot-holed streets and piles of rubble; all was foul, muddy, stinking squalor.

Any doubts I might have had about the social nature of the Taiping revolution were dispelled in the next hour. The Great Kingdom of Heavenly Peace obviously consisted of two classes: the State (the Wangs, the officials, and the army) and the populace, who were the State's slaves. Everyone, you see, must work, according to his capacity, but he ain't paid. How does he feed and clothe himself, you ask? He has no money, since it and all his valuables and property have been confiscated by the State, but there are no shops anyway, since all is rationed and distributed by the State. He is thus free of all care and responsibility, and can give his mind to work and absorbing the precepts, decrees, and heavenly thoughts of the Tien Wang, or Heavenly King. And if the rations are shorter and the work harder and the laws more savage than under the evil Imps – well, there's a good time coming, and he can take comfort in the knowledge that what is happening to him is "correct". The foul old system has given way to Heavenly Peace, and while the baskets of heads are even more numerous than in Shanghai, and there's no lack of malefactors crawling about in wooden collars placarded with their offences (disobeying "celestial commands", mostly), well, there's a certain tranquillity about that, too. At least every man-jack had his wooden token with the Heavenly Seal on it, to prove his existence and to use as a passport in and out of the city – what happened to anyone who lost his token I don't care to think.

But if the folk were ground down in misery, the military were riding high, and no mistake. I recall one splendid figure in crimson coat and hood, marking a subordinate Wang, mounted on a mule and attended by three skinny urchins carrying his sword, his flag (each Taiping officer has a personal flag), and his umbrella; all three, I was informed, aspired to being "ta-jens" (excellencies) some day, like their master, with power of life and death over all despised civilians – such as another urchin sitting naked in the gutter offering *stones* for sale. I was so bemused by this that I bought one (and still have it) amidst the laughter of Lee's retinue; only later did it occur to me that it must be a *State* stone, which the little bugger had no right to be selling, presumably. He probably owns half Nanking by now. It's pleasant to think that I may have founded his commercial career.

Lee didn't seem to notice the filth and poverty of the state he'd been extolling to me two days earlier, but he drew my attention to the incessant drum and gong signals booming across that muddy desolation, and to the fluttering coloured flags on the walls relaying messages to the central watch-tower ahead; all was efficiency and discipline where the military were concerned, with battalions of red-coats chanting at their drill, and there were thousands of off-duty Taipings sauntering among the coolie crowds; I reckon every fourth man was a soldier – which explains why the slave population voiced no audible discontent.

All this was plainly the "progress, work, and improvement", to say nothing of the "sacred right of human liberty", which Lee had described to me. Now I beheld proof of his "benign enlightened democratic" government, as the ruins gave way to the splendid new palaces and offices being built in the city centre for the Wangs and their favoured subordinates. We passed through broad, well-kept streets, flanked by magnificent yellow walls, with lofty minarets and towers beyond, tiled in red and green and lavishly decorated;

extensive gardens were being laid out by coolies hard at it with mattocks and spades, scaffolding clung to the new buildings like spiders' webs, and great loads of brick and paint and timber and tile were everywhere to be seen. The place was humming like a beehive; well, thinks I, if this is the revolution, I'm all for it.

To remind everyone of what a bloody good idea it all was, every other street corner had an official orator reading out His Heavenly Majesty's poems and meditations to rapt crowds of soldiers and officials and a few hang-dog peasants, all no doubt reflecting what fine transcendental stuff the monarch was turning out these days.[12]

"The Grand Palace of Glory and Light," says Lee, as our cavalcade turned a corner, "the earthly residence of the Tien Wang," and I had to admit that it laid over everything we had seen before. There was a forty-foot yellow wall emblazoned with ferocious dragons and hung with yellow silk scrolls of His Majesty's ghastly poems in vermilion ink; a vast gilded gateway guarded by cannon and splendidly-caparisoned sentries with matchlocks; and through the gate you caught a glimpse of the palace itself, a half-completed monstrosity of minarets and peaked roofs, tiled in every conceivable hue, with dragon designs and silken banners and revolting Chinese statuary; it must have covered acres, and was slightly more grandiose than the Taj Mahal, if in more questionable taste. There was even an enormous granite boat to commemorate the Heavenly King's arrival in the city in '53 – the real boat was rotting in a shed round the back.

We dismounted before a low wall dividing the length of the street – the quality use the palace side, and the rabble t'other, and if the latter stray the guards beat 'em to pulp in the name of democracy. Lee led the way through the gate and then through a series of courts and gardens of dwarf shrubs, discoursing as he went – and it was now that I got the unexpected shock I mentioned earlier. For after some commonplace remarks about the building, he suddenly says:

"In describing this as His Majesty's earthly residence, I do not imply any earthly term to his existence. He is, as you know, immortal, but a time will come when he decides to take up permanent abode in Paradise. As it is, he makes

101

frequent visits there, in his Dragon Chariot, for discussions with God. Of late his wife has accompanied him on these excursions to Heaven, and conversed with the Heavenly Father and the Elder Brother Jesus."

I wondered if I'd misheard, or if he was speaking symbolically or even with irony. But he wasn't. He went on, conversationally:

"It is a gratifying demonstration of the ordained equality of the sexes in the Heavenly Kingdom that the Heavenly King's consort enters so fully on his affairs. It was she, you know, who received the divine command that henceforth the Tien Wang should devote himself to meditation – apart from such duties as annotating the Book of Revelation – so that he may be fully prepared to take his place with the Junior Lord, his son, in Paradise, and sit with God and the Elder Brother."

"I see," seemed the best response with which to cover my sheer amazement and alarm. Until now, this apparently normal young man had spoken sanely and rationally, and here, suddenly, without a gleam in his eye or foam on his lips, he was talking the most outrageous balderdash. I knew that from all accounts the Heavenly King was as mad as a senile Sapper, but this was one of his foremost generals! Could he conceivably believe this bilge about dragon chariots and tête-à-têtes with the Almighty, with Mrs Heavenly King going along, presumably to help with the service of tea and ginger biscuits?

Hesitantly, and in the hope of receiving an answer that would restore my faith in Lee's sanity, I inquired how old his Heavenly Majesty might be, and when he could be expected to go aloft permanently, so to speak. I was a fool to ask.

"In earthly terms," says Lee placidly, "he is forty-seven, but in fact he was born out of the belly of God's first wife before Heaven and Earth existed. How else could he have observed all the events of the Old Testament, and Jesus Christ's descent to earth, before deciding to manifest himself in 1813? As to when he will sit with the Heavenly Family permanently, and shine on all lands and oceans, we cannot tell. The Heavenly South Gate will open one day; in the meantime, we must all fight valiantly for eternal glory."

"There's no doubt of that," says I. Was he having me on? Or did he simply repeat this moonshine because it wasn't safe to do otherwise? It's hard enough to read a Chinaman's thoughts, but I had a horrible feeling he meant every word of it. Dear God, were they all non compos mentis?[13]

He left me with these uncomfortable thoughts, in a small outer palace, with an escorting officer, while he went in to the Wang council, and no doubt to hear an account of what they'd had for luncheon in Heaven yesterday. Nor did my surroundings do anything to quiet my fears; we were in a fairly filthy audience chamber, decorated with the crudest kind of drawings, gilded lanterns, and tatty flags and bunting, presided over by a grinning young imbecile who was plainly far gone with opium – which I, remembering that it was a capital offence, thought odd until I learned that he was the acting Prime Minister, "the Son of the Prince of Praise". He wore a filthy silk robe and a big embroidered dragon hat with a little bird on top, and was surrounded by officials; there was also a half-company of troops posted round the hall – filthy, slovenly brutes quite unlike the smart Taipings of Lee's camp.

My guiding officer presented me to this beauty, who giggled vacantly, invited me in a slurred, stuttering voice to pass into the dining-room next door, apologised for having no strong drink to offer me, and at the same time reached under his table and handed me out a bottle of London gin. I declined courteously, and passed the time studying a great wall map of the world – or rather, of "The Entire Territory of the Heavenly Kingdom to Endure for a Myriad Myriad Years". It showed China as a perfect square, with Nanking in the middle, but no sign of Pekin; Japan was a speck, Britain and France small blobs in the top corner, and a smear to one side proved to be the State of the Flowery Flag, or U.S.A. to you. The rest of the world had apparently been suppressed by heavenly decree. (We are the Red-haired State, by the way, and according to a scroll beside the map which my guide translated, we are the most powerful country apart from China, on account of our correct methods, shrewdness, dishonesty, and refusal to be subjugated.)

There was a great inner arch from the chamber, and through it, across an open court, could be glimpsed the gateway to the Inner Palace, with "Sacred Heavenly Door" inscribed above, and two enormous painted dragons, one eating the sun and the other pursuing a shrimp. I was pondering the mystical meaning of this when a most unholy din broke out from the Inner Palace – guns firing, drums rolling, cymbals clashing – and across the courtyard passed a procession of women bearing steaming golden dishes (bad pork and cabbage, by the odour) in at the Sacred Heavenly Door. This, says my escort, was the signal that the Heavenly King was going to dinner, drawn by women in his Dragon Chariot; the guns and drums would continue until he had finished. I asked if we could go in for a peep, and he looked shocked.

"Only the thousand women attending His Heavenly Majesty are permitted in the Inner Palace," says he. "The presence of men – except for the Wangs and certain great ones – would disturb his constant labour of writing decrees, revising the Scriptures, and conceiving new precepts. If we are privileged, we may presently hear the result of his morning's meditation."

Sure enough, he'd barely finished speaking when trumpets blared from the Inner Palace gateway, and across the court came the most stunning Chinese girl, all in green silk and carrying a golden tray with a yellow silk scroll.

"The Bearer of Heavenly Decrees!" cries my chap eagerly, and he and every soul in our audience chamber dropped to his knees yelling "Ten thousand Years! Ten thousand Years!", the only exceptions being the ignorant foreigner Flashy, who stood admiring the approaching beauty, and the deputy Prime Minister, who fell flat on his face and was sick.

The Bearer of Heavenly Decrees sashayed in like the Queen of Sheba, unrolled her scroll, glanced round superciliously (with a brief frown at the leering barbarian), and in a high sing-song voice read out the Heavenly King's last thought before luncheon: it was a decree announcing that since his birthday fell next week (renewed yells of "Ten thousand Years!") all the Senior Wangs might take another ten wives in addition to the eleven they had already, while Lesser Wangs would have their ration increased from six to

104

nine. The public (who had one wife if they were lucky) were not mentioned.

Thunderous applause greeted this announcement (though what they had to cheer about wasn't clear to me), and the Bearer of Heavenly Decrees handed her scroll to a grovelling minion, smiled graciously, shot me another reproving look, and made her stately way back to the palace, twitching her shimmering rump as she went. Observing this, and reflecting on the new decree, which all present were hailing with enthusiasm, I made a mental salute to the Taiping Rebellion – like all revolutionary movements (and for that matter all governments) it was plainly designed to ensure the rulers an abundance of fleshpot, while convincing the ruled that austerity was good for the soul. But barring the Papists, I couldn't think of a regime that had the business so nicely in hand as this one.[14]

Needless to say, I kept the thought to myself, although I couldn't resist trying to draw Lee gently when he came to bear me off to dinner at his own palace, apologising that it wasn't completed yet, in spite of the efforts of a thousand coolies who were slaving like beavers on it. I remarked that it was a fine system where the workers were content to live like pigs while providing their rulers with luxury – and not getting a penny piece for it. He just shrugged, and says: "You English believe in paying for work. We know better – are we not a great empire?" It wasn't even cynical, just a plain philosophy, like his apparently sincere religious lunacy, and left me wondering harder than ever about him.

His was a modest enough spread, a mere gold and white bijou residence set in two or three acres of magnificent garden, with fantastically-dressed boys and girls swarming round us like gilded butterflies and ushering us to a charming little pavilion surrounded by a miniature rock and tree garden. Here a tiny child in yellow silk was waiting on the steps, and I was taken right aback when he bowed, held out a hand to me, and says in perfect English: "Good afternoon, sir."

I recovered enough to say: "Well, hollo yourself, young shaver, and see how you like it," and at that there was

105

a burst of laughter from the pavilion, and out comes a jolly-looking Chinese, all portliness in a rather faded blue dragon robe. He patted the lad on the head and gave me an inclination that was half-nod, half-bow.

"My dear sir," says he, "you remind me that my own English is too correct, and that if my son is to master the language he must go to school to you." He chuckled and lifted the boy up in a muscular arm. "Eh, young shaver?"

This was astonishing, but now Lee came up and presented me, reciting the titles of the stout party, who stood listening with a quizzy grin: ". . . Founder of the Dynasty, Loyal Chief of Staff, Upholder of Heaven, Adjudicator of the Court of Discipline –"

"– and former secretary of the Artisans Christmas Club at Hong Kong!" cries the stout chap merrily.

"– His Excellency Hung Jen-kan, First Minister of the Heavenly Kingdom," concluded Lee, and I realised that this cheery, plump-faced man, bouncing the child on his shoulder, was the power behind the throne, the reputed brain of the Taiping, second only to the Tien Wang himself. They were setting out the best crockery for Flashy, weren't they just? As Lee ushered us into the pavilion, I was trying to remember what I'd heard of Jen-kan – that he'd spent his life mostly in Protestant Missions (which accounted for his excellent English), that he was the Heavenly King's cousin, but had taken no part in the revolution until a year ago, when he'd turned up suddenly at Nanking. Since then he'd risen like a rocket to Supreme Marshal (Generalissimo, they call it); I wondered how Lee and the other Wangs felt about being so suddenly outstripped.

Four little tables, one apiece, had been set out for dinner in the pavilion. The small boy addressed me, airing his English, ceremoniously helped me to my place, and Jen-kan, grinning with proud delight, winked at me – a thing I'd never seen a Chinese do before.

"Forgive my son," says he, "but to speak English to an Englishman is for him a dream come true. I encourage him, for without English how can he hope to reap the benefit of Western education, which is the best in the world? Every child in China must learn English," he added gravely, "if

106

only so that they may understand the jokes in *Punch*." And he roared with laughter, shaking in his chair.

It was extraordinary, from a Chinese – but as I soon learned, Jen-kan was an extraordinary man. He knew the world, and had his feet on the ground; the bright brown eyes, which vanished in the fat, good-natured face when he laughed, were deep and shrewd, and he *thought* more like a Westerner than any Oriental I ever knew. Here's one that matters, I thought, listening as he gassed non-stop, mostly in Chinese for Lee's benefit, but now and then forgetting himself into English, with splutters of mirth. Lee sat impassive, being the perfect host, inviting me to dishes, deprecating the food – which was superb, I may say. It came in nine little petal-shaped dishes to each table, the petals fitting together to form a perfect rose as the meal progressed. No chopsticks, either, but Sheffield knives and silver forks and spoons; several of the dishes were Western, in politeness to me, I fancy. There was wine in gold cups held in enamelled silver cases – sherry, if you please, from bottles with wrapped paper plugs instead of corks. I had thought liquor was forbidden in the Taiping; Jen-kan pealed with mirth.

"So it is! But I told the Tien Wang, if I cannot drink, I cannot eat. So he gave me a special dispensation. Unlike this law-breaker." And he nodded at Lee, who surveyed him in silence and poured more sherry.

When the meal was done, and the servants had brought hot Chinese wine and cheroots, Jen-kan nodded to his son, who rose, bowed to me, and piped: "Sir, I take my leave, charmed by your conversation and by the courtesy with which you have tolerated my clumsy attempts at your glorious language."

"My son," says I, "you speak it a dam – a great deal better than most English boys twice your age." At which he shot his father a delighted glance before composing himself and marching out. Jen-kan proudly watched him go, sighed contentedly, bit a cheroot, glanced at Lee, and then at me. Business, thinks I, and braced myself. Sure enough, Lee asked if I had given thought to what he'd said at our first meeting: what was the likely British reaction to a Taiping march on Shanghai?

107

I was starting to say that as a humble traveller from the London Missionary Society I could only speculate, when Jen-kan broke in.

"We can dispense with that . . . Sir Harry." He chuckled at my expression of dismay. "If Mr Bruce wishes his intelligence chief to pass incognito, he should choose one whose likeness has not appeared so frequently in the picture papers. I acquit him of trying to impose on *us*, but he should remember that the *Illustrated London News* may not be unknown in Pekin. Now, may I say how delighted I am to make your acquaintance? I have been an admirer for years – ever since you dismissed Felix, Pilch and Mynn . . . in '42, was it not?" He beamed jovially on this reminder of how Englified he was, and since there was no use beating about, I shrugged modestly, and he put his elbows on the table, Western fashion.

"Good. Now we can talk plainly. The Loyal Prince has already given you reasons why you should welcome us at Shanghai. This may have led you to suppose that our arrival depends on Britain's attitude. It does not. We shall come when we are ready, in August, with or without British approval." He drew on his cheroot, regarding me benevolently. "Obviously we hope for it, and I am confident that when Mr Bruce realises that our occupation is inevitable, he will decide to welcome it. He will be in no doubt of our invincibility once you have reported to him; you have seen our army, and you will observe it in action when the Loyal Prince goes presently to expel the Imps from Soochow."

That was uncomfortable news, but I didn't let on.

"Mr Bruce will see that our final victory over the Manchoos is only a matter of time, and that opposition from Britain at Shanghai would be not only futile but impolitic. You will also inform him that, as an earnest of good will to Her Majesty's Government, our first act in Shanghai will be to place an order worth one million dollars for twenty armed steamships, which will greatly hasten the destruction of the Imperial forces."

He studied a moment, like a man who wonders if he's left out anything, and gave me his fattest smile. "Well, Sir Harry?"

So there it was, the big stick and a carrot, and my mission dead and buried. For plainly no persuasion of mine was going to keep the Taipings away from Shanghai; all Bruce's diplomatic step-dancing would be wasted on these fellows; they said, and they would do. Unless it was bluff, in which case counter-bluff might be in order . . . I ran cold sweat at the thought, knowing that what I said next might alter the history of China – God, what Napoleon would have given to be in my shoes, and how I wished he was.

"I'm obliged to your excellency," says I. "But do you think it wise to take Britain's reaction for granted?"

"I don't!" cries he cheerfully. "Whether you welcome or oppose us, we shall have Shanghai." Mildly he added: "The Loyal Prince's army will number not fewer than fifty thousand men."

"Fifty thousand men who've never met British or French regulars," says I, equally mildly. Not diplomatic, I agree, but I ain't partial to having the law laid down to me by fat chaps with yellow faces. This one just smiled and shook his head.

"Come, Sir Harry. A mere token garrison. Mr Bruce could not resist us even if he wished – which I am persuaded he does not."

Well, that was God's truth, but I had to play it out for what it was worth. I gave him my true-blue stare. "Possibly, sir. But if you're wrong, there exists a possibility that you'll find yourselves at war with Great Britain." Bruce would have swooned to hear me.

"Why?" This was Lee, sharp and intense, his lean face strained. "Why? What can it profit England to fight against fellow Christians? How can –?"

"Loyal Prince." Jen-kan raised a plump finger. "Our guest knows his people better than you do. So, with respect, do I. And they are the last I should try to . . . persuade, in normal circumstances. But the circumstances are not normal, Sir Harry," he came back to me. "Shanghai is not a British city; it is the Emperor's, and you are," he smiled apologetically, "only his tenants, in an upstairs room. Your lives and property will be safe from us – indeed, your traders will enjoy a freedom unknown under the Manchoos." He grinned a fat

109

man's satisfied grin. "You will welcome us. Britain does not want another war in China – certainly not with a regime that offers million-dollar contracts. When did the Manchoos promise as much? They don't even like your opium!"

I waited until his laughter had subsided. "Well, sir, if that's the message I'm to take to Mr Bruce –"

"Yes, but not yet." He wagged a finger. "In August. In view of what you have said, it may be better if Mr Bruce has short notice of our intention. We don't wish him to have too much time to think, and possibly commit some indiscretion." He beamed shamelessly. "I am quite frank, you see. No, in August you will go back to Shanghai – with a Taiping army two days behind you. That will surely inspire Mr Bruce to a wise decision. And we shall be in good time before Lord Elgin reaches Pekin to conclude a treaty committing him to the losing side. All things considered, he may well decide not to go to Pekin at all."

He sat there, a Chinese Pickwick, smacking his lips over his hot wine, while I weighed the essential point.

"You mean I'm a prisoner here?"

"A guest – until August. Two months, perhaps? It will be a most pleasant holiday; I am selfish enough to look forward to it. Mr Bruce may wonder what has become of you, but he will hardly inquire after a mere traveller from the London Missionary Society." Oh, he was a right twinkling bastard, this one. "And you may take satisfaction that you are performing the duty he laid on you – of keeping the Taipings away from Shanghai for the present." That gave me a horrid start, but he went on amiably. "He will be able to pursue his policy of strict neutrality – until August. Until then, we shall be doing what he wants; he will be doing what we want. It is very satisfactory."

* * *

He was right, of course. If Bruce knew the Taipings were dead set on Shanghai, he'd have time to reinforce, perhaps even send for Grant. Lull him with inaction, and when the blow fell in August he'd have no choice but to submit to Taiping occupation – although whether we'd accept that *quite*

110

as tamely as Jen-kan supposed, I was by no means sure. One thing was plain: there wasn't a ghost of a chance of my escaping to warn Bruce ahead of the fair – not that I had the least inclination, you understand, I knew when I was well off, and would be well content to wallow for a few weeks in the luxuries of the revolution.

Of these there was no shortage at the pavilion to which Lee conducted me after Jen-kan had gone, jovial to the last. It was another bijou palace surrounded by dwarf gardens, and belonged to Lee's brother – a genial nonentity who was learning to write, I remember, labouring away at scrolls with a tutor. The apartments I was given were in exquisite taste; I recall the pink jade writing set and inkwell, the sprig of coral mounted on a silver block with gold pencils thrust through the branches, the tiny crystal paperweights on the gleaming walnut desk. The fact that I remember such things is proof that I was feeling pretty easy at the prospect of my captivity; I should have known better.

Lee hadn't said a word beyond courtesies after our meeting with Jen-kan, but I sensed an unease in him, and wondered why. It was fairly plain that he disliked the Prime Minister jealously, and I'd no doubt that behind the scenes some very pretty clawing went on among the Wangs, in which I might conceivably be a useful pawn. There was no plumbing that, and since Taiping interest seemed to require my health and happiness, I didn't care much. But I could see Lee was anxious, and when he took leave of me that night he finally came out with it.

"In our discussion with his excellency, I sensed – correct me if I am mistaken – that you are not wholly convinced of our ultimate success." We were alone on the verandah, in the warm evening shadows, and as he turned those cold eyes on me I felt a prickle of disquiet. "I do not ask for a political judgment, you understand, but for a military opinion. You have seen the Imps; you have seen us. Do you believe we shall win?"

There was only one politic answer, and since it was what I believed, pretty much, I spoke straight out.

"Barring accidents, you're bound to. I'd not wager on the Imps, that's certain."

He considered this. "But you do not say that victory is assured, beyond all doubt?"

"It never is. But any soldier can see when the odds are in his favour."

"I can see more." The yellow-robed figure seemed to grow more erect, and his voice was hard. "I know we shall win."

"Well, then, it doesn't matter what I think."

"But it does," says he, mighty sharp. "It matters what you tell Mr Bruce."

So that was the pinch. "I'll tell Mr Bruce what I've just told you," I assured him. "I believe he'll have every confidence in your success." I nearly added "provided you leave Shanghai alone, and don't provoke the foreign devils", but decided not to.

"Confidence," says he slowly, "is not faith. I could wish you had . . . absolute faith."

He was a fanatic, of course. "You can put more trust in my confidence," says I lightly. "Faith ain't a matter of counting guns and divisions."

He gave me another keen look, but left it there, and I'd forgotten all about it by the time I turned in. I was pleased to see that Taiping luxury didn't stop short of the bedroom door; they'd given me a cool, spacious chamber with screens onto the garden, and a great soft bed with red silk mattress and pillows – all that was lacking was the Bearer of Heavenly Decrees. I wondered dreamily as I dropped off if Lee's brother, being a lesser Wang, would care to rent out one of the new wives he'd just been awarded . . . or all three, and I could give him confidential reports on endurance, ingenuity, and carnal appetite. Flashy, riding examiner . . . Gold Medal, Nanking Exhibition, 1860 . . . a pretty thought, on which I slid into a delightful dream in which the Bearer of Heavenly Decrees appeared as identical triplets who came gliding into the room in green silk dresses and steel-chain collars, bearing scrolls on golden trays, ranging themselves beside my bed and smiling alluringly down at me. I was just debating whether to tackle 'em one at a time, or all three together, when I realised that I couldn't see their faces any longer, for they were all three wearing black hoods, which

112

seemed deuced odd . . . and the green dresses were gone, too, under black cloaks . . .

I came awake an instant too late to scream. The black figures seemed to swoop down on me, steel fingers were on my mouth and wrists, a heavy cloth was whipped over my head, and I was dragged helpless from the bed by invisible hands.

❀ There's no blind terror to compare with it – being hustled along, lurching and stumbling, by invisible attackers. You're lost, blind, and half-suffocated, you can feel the cruelty in the clutching hands, horrible pain and dissolution await you, and the only thing worse is the moment when the blanket comes off – which mine did before my assailants had taken twenty strides.

There was a yell and a clash of steel, a buffeting shock as my captors staggered, and I was crashing to earth, dragging the blanket away, to find myself rolling in a flowerbed, with one of my kidnappers clawing at me in the dark. I shrieked as I caught the flash of steel in the half-light, and then the knife-point was beneath my chin, and I was shuddering still, whispering entreaties for my life.

It ain't the best position to view a fatal mêlée that is going on a few yards away, with dark figures slashing and swearing in the shadows. I heard one horrid gurgle as a blade went home, caught the glittering arc of a curved sword swinging and the grating ring of the parry, but for the most part they fought in silence. Then the blanket was over my head again, and I was being rushed along, barking my shins and trying to yell for help, until they pulled up, a voice hissed: "Walk!" in Chinese, and I felt the prick of the point again, in my spine this time. I walked.

How far we went, I can't guess, but it must have been a good quarter of a mile before I felt paved stones under my feet, and presently was aware of bright light outside the blanket, and the sound of hushed voices. I was hustled up a few steps, and then there was carpet under my bare soles. We stopped, the knife was removed, and the gripping hands were withdrawn. I didn't stir, but stood shrouded and quaking for a good five minutes, when I was pushed forward

114

again, over tiles and then on to another carpet. The blanket was whipped away, and I stood blinking in bright light. Facing me, breathing with an agitation to equal my own, although my bosom could never have heaved like hers, stood the Bearer of Heavenly Decrees.

Just for a moment I wondered if I was dreaming, but she was fully-clad, so it seemed unlikely. Deuced fetching, for all that, in a blue silk gown such as the Manchoo ladies wear, in which there are three or four skirts of varying lengths, with huge hanging sleeves, and her hair done up in high buns. She was one of your round-faced Chinese beauties, and none the worse for that, but my attention was distracted by the black-cowled figured at my elbow throwing back his hood, and I found myself gaping at General Lee Hsiu-chen.

"I apologise. It was necessary," says he, and I wasted no time in babbled questions. He'd tell me what he wanted me to know. He was breathing hard, and I saw a trickle of blood on the back of his hand. He nodded to the girl, and she walked away to a curtained arch at the end of the short, carpeted passage in which we stood. She waited there, head averted, and Lee spoke rapidly, getting his breath back.

"You are to be granted audience of the Heavenly King. It is a highly unusual honour. Few foreigners have seen him for many years. He understands that you are from the London Missionary Society. Say nothing of how you came here. Listen to him." He smiled, an odd, dreamy smile that sent chills up my back. "Yes. Listen to him. Do not be surprised if he talks all night. He does not tire as mortals do."

He gestured me towards the archway, and as I approached, the Bearer of Heavenly Decrees turned and held out a red silk robe – I was in the sarong I wear in bed – slipping it over my shoulders. Then she pulled back the curtains, beckoning me to follow.

The heavy smell of incense struck my nostrils as I saw we were in a small, low chamber hung round with dragon silks. At the far end was a deep divan caught in a pool of light from two tall candlebranches, and on it reclined a short, stocky figure in white silk embroidered in gold. He was nodding sleepily in that joss-laden air, while a female voice recited high and clear:

"The Heavenly Father, the Elder Brother, the Heavenly King, and the Junior Lord shall be Lords forever. The Heavenly Kingdom is established everywhere, and the effulgence of the Heavenly Family is spread upon all the Earth for all eternity."

The voice stopped, and the Bearer of Heavenly Decrees rustled forward, dropped to her knees half-way to the divan, kow-towed several times, and addressed the chap on the couch. I caught the words ". . . London Missionary Society . . ." and then she was hurrying back to me, motioning me forward, indicating that I too should kow-tow. Well, the hell with him, Heavenly King or not. I walked forward, and got a close look at him as I began to make a half-bow – a tubby little Chink, with long dark hair framing a round, amiable face, a short sandy beard, and great dark eyes that shone in his pasty face like a hypnotist's, but with none of the force of your professional mesmeriser. They were placid, dreamy eyes, friendly and kind . . . and what the devil was I doing, kow-towing? I jumped up, vexed, and the big eyes smiled sleepily, holding mine. So that was his secret; you couldn't help looking at him. With an effort I tore my glance away – and realised that we were not alone. And I can pay no higher tribute to the Tien Wang's magnetic personality than to say that only now did I notice those others present.

One was kneeling on the couch, holding a scroll from which she had been reading. She wore a towering gilt headdress, like a pagoda, and a little fringe of gold threads round her hips. That was all her attire, and out of deference to royalty I modestly lowered my eyes, and found myself contemplating another naked female reclining at my feet – one more step and I'd have trod on her buttocks. I half-started back, afraid to look in case there were more bare houris perched on the candelabra. But there were just the two, twins by the look of them, still as superbly-shaped statues, lovely faces intent on the man on the couch, and apparently unaware of my existence. Reluctantly, I looked back at him, and he smiled vacantly.

"Welcome, in the peace of God," says he, and indicated a silken stool by the couch. It was a deep, liquid voice, with a curious husky quality. I sat, uncomfortably aware that the reclining poppet was only inches from my foot, and that if I looked straight ahead my horizon was voluptuously filled by the charms of the kneeling nymph. It's hell in the Taiping, you know. Not that I bar contemplating the undraped female form, but there's a time and a place, and heaven knew what I'd interrupted. I wondered if these were two of his reputed eighty-eight wives, or if he, too, had been voted a few spares, next week being his birthday and all. Good heavens – was it possible one of them was for me? I didn't like to ask, and I didn't get the chance, for he fixed me with those luminous, empty eyes and his melancholy smile, and began to speak to me. My heart was hammering, what with the knowledge that this was *the* Tien Wang, the Chinese Messiah, one of the most powerful men on earth, and that what passed between us might be vital . . . Bruce's instructions . . . my mission . . . That, and the nearness of those mouth-watering little flesh-traps – d'you wonder I was sweating? It was like a wild dream: the sweet, husky voice, pausing every now and then as though to compel an answer, the blindly shining eyes, the heavy reek of incense, the silk edges of the stool hot under my hands, the satin gleam of bums, bellies and boobies in the candle-shine, the soft lunatic babble which I'd not believe if I didn't remember every word:

Tien Wang: . . . The London Missionary Society. Ah, yes . . . but I do not remember you . . . only Dr Sylvester, my dear old friend . . . (*Long pause*)

Flashy: Ah, yes . . . your majesty. Sylvester. To be sure.

T.W.: Dr Sylvester . . . how long? How long? (*Goes into trance*)

F. (*helping matters along*): Couple of months, perhaps?

T.W. (*reviving vaguely*): You have spoken with Dr Sylvester recently? Then you are greatly blessed. (*Beatific smile*) For you have made the Journey. I felicitate you.

F.: Sorry?

T.W.: The Journey to the Celestial Above. I, too, have spoken with Dr Sylvester in Heaven, since his earthly death in 1841. Soon the portals will open for us all, and we shall rest in the Divine Halls of Eternal Peace. Have you visited Heaven often?

F.: Not to say often. Nothing like your majesty . . . weekends, that sort of thing. Just to see Sylvester, really . . . oh, God . . .

T.W.: How well I recall his discourse . . . illuminating . . . constructive . . . wise . . .

F.: Absolutely. Couldn't get enough of it. (*Long pause, during which F.'s attention wanders*)

T.W.: His humanity was equalled only by his scholarship. Was there a fruit of learning that he had not plucked? Divinity . . . philosophy . . . theology . . . metaphysics . . .

F. (*musing*): Tits. (*in confusion*) No, I mean metaphysics! Geometry, anything . . . he knew it all!

T.W. (*benignly*): Soon we shall join him, when we have made the final Journey, but only after long and laborious struggle. When you first visited Heaven, were you given new bowels?

F.: Eh? Oh . . . no, no, I wasn't. I wasn't considered worthy, you see . . . your majesty. Not then. Not for new bowels.

T.W.: Take heart. I too was rebuked when I first entered the Golden Doors. Jesus, my Elder Brother, was angry because I had not learned my Bible lessons well. He was correct. We must all learn our Bible. (*Long pause*)

F. (*desperate*): Moab is my washpot, over Edom will I cast out my shoe. Er . . . Genesis, Exodus, Leviticus, thing . . .

T.W.: I remember how kind Jesus's wife was . . . and when my heart and entrails had been removed, I was given new ones, of shining red.

F.: Red, eh?

T.W.: And God gave me a sword to exterminate demons . . . and a seal of authority. The demons transformed themselves eighteen times, as they have power to do.

F.: Yes, yes . . . eighteen. Shocking.

T.W.: But I drove them down to Hell, and the Heavenly Mother gave me fruits and sweets. As I ate them, marvelling at their savour, God traced the Devil's misdeeds to errors in Confucius, and rebuked him. But Confucius defended himself vehemently.

F. (*indignant*): He did, did he?

T.W.: Then Jesus and the Angels joined in against Confu-

118

cius, who tried to sneak away to join the Devil, Yen-lo, but he was caught and brought back and beaten. (*Smiling blankly*) But at last God allowed him to sit in Heaven, in recognition of past merits.

F. (*doubtful*): Well . . .

T.W.: Yen-lo is the Serpent-Devil of the Garden of Eden . . .

F.: *Is* he? Ah!

T.W.: . . . and when Eve heeded his words, she was driven forth, and her children were drowned in the Great Rain. But Yen-lo seeks ever to steal men's souls, ensnaring their senses with beautiful temptations . . . there were beautiful hand-maidens in Heaven . . .

This seemed to give him an idea, for the husky voice, which had been droning away as at a lesson learned, trailed off, and he turned to stare at the splendid naked nymph kneeling beside him. It was the first sign of intelligence I'd seen in him, for he was plainly madder than Bedlam; his mouth twitched, and he came up from his reclining position to gape, and then to reach out and fondle her neck and shoulder and arm. She stayed stock-still; he leaned closer, gaping, and I had to strain to hear.

". . . we must strive to discern false beauty from true," he muttered, "and manfully resist Yen-lo, seeking solace only in that which is pure. So we should study the Book of One Hundred Correct Things. Let us hear now how we may resist temptation."

I'd have thought it was the last thing he needed to hear just then, but it was evidently a cue, for the kneeling beauty came to life with a sudden shudder that caused his Heavenly Majesty to grunt alarmingly and gape wider than ever. She lifted her scroll and began to read in a shrill, breathless little voice:

"Temptation must be eradicated from the world, and from the human mind. By sight, by scent, by touch may temptation be aroused. Temptation is caused by the original sin of lust, in the beginning of the world."

Well, no one was going to argue with that, least of all Flashy, grinding his teeth, or the Tien Wang, staring and hanging on every word, so to speak. Then he lay back with

119

a gentle groan, as she leaned forward over him, reading rapturously.

"Temptation results from indecision. As a homeless person wanders, seeking relief, so the unstable mind is always subject to temptation, which beguiles the senses of the unwary, or," her voice sank to a whisper, "those who lack the power of decision."

She sighed convulsively, no doubt at the pathos of the thing, and with difficulty I restrained a sharp cry. The Tien Wang, on the other hand, emitted a low, percolating sound, staring up at them like one who lacked the power of decision but would get round to it presently.

"A mind lured by temptation will deteriorate from day to day," whispers the reading girl soulfully, and shook her pagoda, which tinkled. "Conscience will perish. Ah, beware when conscience perishes, for then . . . then lust will grow."

There was much in what she said, as the veins standing out on my bulging forehead testified. She'd been practically suffocating him, but now she straightened up, rolling her scroll, and his majesty gave a little whimper, and reached up a pawing hand. At the same moment the female at my feet stirred, gliding up to rest her arms on the divan, blast her, her hand straying on to his knee. He gaped vacantly at her, going red in the face and breathing with difficulty, looked back at the reading girl, who was opening another scroll, and began to growl – whether it was possible for his mind to deteriorate any further was doubtful, but plainly conscience was about to perish.

"As lust grows, and conscience dies, the Devil will seize his opportunity," croons the reading hussy, and I contemplated her twin's alabaster bottom, poised within easy reach, and wondered if I dared play the Devil myself. In the nick of time I recalled that this panting idiot on the couch was the monster who had slaughtered millions and took heads off for adultery; God knew what he did to molesters of the Heavenly Harem. I bit my knuckles instead, watching helpless as the reader reached her peroration; the brute was dazedly pawing at her with one hand while the other clutched at her twin, who seemed to be trying to climb into his lap. Suddenly the

120

reading girl flung aside her scroll and lunged down at him, babbling:

"Suppress temptation! Throw out evil! Cleanse the heart! So the felicity of Paradise will be won! Everyone shall conquer temptation, and having thus strengthened himself, will be able to attack the small demons! Universal peace will follow!"

And I've no doubt it did, to judge by the gasps and sobs and rhythmic pagoda tinklings which pursued me as I fled a-tiptoe for the archway. Well, it would have been damned bad form to stay, and I swear to God I couldn't have – not without committing the fearful lèse-majesté of plunging into the mêlée crying "Me, too!" Not that they'd have noticed, probably. The women were ecstatics, and as for that lecherous lunatic with his crimson bowels and visits to heaven – well, aside from being the starkest maniac I'd ever struck, he was also a damned poor host. And *he* had inspired the Taiping rebellion? It passed belief – but he did, and if you doubt one word of his conversation with me, or his concubine's recitation, you'll find every last syllable of them in scholarly works written about him by learned men – all except about Dr Sylvester, for whom I believe I'm the sole authority. And that, you'll allow, was the sanest part of it.[15]

No – he was a raving, dangerous, dreadful madman, and one of the most diabolical powers ever loosed on a suffering world. Hung Hsiu Chu'an, the Coolie King. As to his depravity – in my eyes his one redeeming quality – I've told my tale, and you may put it in the balance between those who claim he was a celibate saint, and t'others who say he was topsides with Tiberius. I'll add only that no one disputes that he lived surrounded by a thousand women, eighty-eight of 'em "wives". And devil a thought for his guests.

I emerged in the corridor panting like the town bull, to find the Bearer of Heavenly Decrees wide-eyed and palpitating anxiously; by George, she'll never know how close she came to being dragged off and ravished. But here was Lee, pale and eager.

"You saw him? He spoke with you? What did he say?" He gripped my arm in his excitement, and I had sense enough to take time to reply.

121

"General Lee," says I, gulping. "I've never seen or heard the like in my life."

He let out a hissing breath, and then smiled slowly. "I knew it. I knew it. He is like God, is he not?"

"He's certainly like nothing on earth," says I, and caught a drift of tantalising perfume from the Bearer of Heavenly Decrees, who had edged up, all eyes and ears. I gritted my teeth and tried not to notice her. "D'ye mind sending her away?" says I hoarsely. "After such an experience I find her presence . . . distracting." He snapped a word and she sped off, undulating in a way which brought sweat to my temples.

"I can see you are much moved," says Lee gently. "It was inevitable, but I am uplifted beyond all expression." He fairly glowed with holy zeal. "For now that you have seen him, you too have . . . faith."

It didn't sink in for a moment. "D'you mean to say," I croaked, ". . . *that* was why you had me brought . . . just to see . . . him?" I gaped at the man. "In God's name! Did you have to kidnap me? I'd have gone willingly if you'd –"

"There was no time to explain. It was necessary to be secret and sudden – as you saw. I had learned that there were those who would have kept you from his presence if they could. Fortunately, they failed."

"But . . . who were they? Why? See here, I might have had my throat cut by those swine, whoever –"

"It does not matter, now. For you have seen him, in his divinity. And now you, too, believe." He studied my face. "For you do believe, do you not?"

"By God, I do!" cries I fervently. What I believed, I wasn't about to tell him, which was that his Heavenly King and the whole kitboodle of them were cracked beyond repair. I'd have a fine report to give Bruce, if ever I got out of their demented clutches. I shook my head like a man awe-struck. "General Lee," says I solemnly, "I am in your debt. You have opened my eyes to the full."

"No. *He* has done that," says he, looking like Joan of Arc. "Now you can tell your people what manner of being leads the Taiping. They will share your faith." He nodded, content. "And I can go to Soochow, and later to Shanghai, with a

122

quiet mind. Whatever my enemies may wish, they cannot undo what has been done for you tonight."

"Amen," says I, and on that he said that henceforth I could stay at his brother's place in perfect safety, for now I'd seen the Heavenly King no one would molest me. I assured him again that it had been the biggest thing in my life, and because I'm cursed with curiosity, I asked him: "General – you have been privileged to see the Heavenly King countless times. Tell me, does he usually receive visitors . . . alone? Or does he have . . . er . . . attendants with him?"

He frowned, and then slowly shook his head. "Whenever I have stood in his divine presence," says he, "I have never been aware of any but him."

Which suggested either that I had caught his majesty off duty, so to speak, or that his faithful followers were so besotted with worship that they didn't notice, or didn't care, when naked trollops climbed all over him. Some damned odd cabinet meetings they must have had. One thing was sure, they didn't call Lee the Loyal Prince for nothing.

*   *   *

Now I've told you plain, at some length, of my first day and night in Nanking, because there's no better way of showing you what the Taiping was like, and in the two long months I was with them everything I saw merely went to confirm that first impression. I saw much of their city, of their crazy laws and crazier religion, of the might and ruthlessness of the military (when I was with Lee at the capture and sack of Soochow), of the blossoming incompetence of their top-heavy administration, of the abyss between the despotic, luxuriating rulers and the miserable slave populace in this glorious revolution dedicated to equality – it's all in my *Dawns and Departures of a Soldier's Life* (one of the volumes D'Israeli's bailiffs never got their hands on), and ain't to the point here. Enough to say that I recognised the Taiping as a power that bade fair to engulf China – and was already mad and rotten at the heart.

Don't mistake me; I don't preach. You know *my* morals and ideals, and you won't find the Archbishop shopping for 'em in a hurry. But I know right from wrong, as perhaps only a scoundrel can, and I'll say that there was great virtue in the *notion* of Taiping – if it hadn't somehow been jarred sideways, and become a perversion, so that the farther it went, the farther it ran off the true. One thing I knew I would tell Bruce: the Manchoos might be a corrupt, unsavoury, awkward crew, but we mustn't touch *this* ship of fools with a bargepole – not even if the alternative was to go to war with them. And that was a daunting thought, for the one thing *right* about the Taiping was its army.

I saw that for myself when Lee took me to Soochow, the last big Imp foothold in the Yangtse valley, about thirty miles south of Nanking and one hundred and fifty from Shanghai. It was a strong place, with heavy fortifications on White Dragon Hill, and as soon as I saw them I put Lee down privately as a bungler who must have been lucky until now, for he'd brought hardly a gun with him. Twenty thousand good infantry, marching like guardsmen and chanting their war-songs, transport and commissariat as fine as you could wish for, the whole advance perfectly conducted – but when I looked at those crenellated walls, with the Imp gunners blazing away long before our vanguard came in range, and the paper tigers and devil banners being waved from ramparts crowded with men . . . well, it's your infantry you'll be wasting, thinks I. How long a siege did he anticipate, I asked him, and he smiled quietly and says:

"My banner will be on White Dragon Hill within three hours."

And it was. He told me later he had close on three hundred infiltrators inside the walls, disguised as Imp soldiers; they'd been at work with friendly citizens, and at the given time two of the gates were blown open from within, and the Taiping infantry just rolled in like a wave. I've never seen the like: those long ranks of red coats simply thundered forward, changing formation as they went, into two hammer-heads that engulfed the gates, up went the black death banners, and heedless of the storm of shot that met them those howling devils surged into the city and carried all before them. The battle lasted perhaps an hour, and then the Imps wisely changed sides, and they and the Taipings

124

sacked the place, slaughtering and looting wholesale. I wasn't inside the walls until next day, by which time it was a smoking, bloodstained ruin; if there was a living citizen left he wasn't walking about, I can tell you.

"Nothing can withstand the might of the Tien Wang," says Lee, and I thought, God help Shanghai. I realised then that my soldiering had been of the genteel, polite variety – well-mannered actions like Cawnpore and Balaclava and the Kabul retreat in which at least the occasional prisoner was taken. In China, the idea of war is to kill everything that stirs and burn everything that don't. Just that.

I was a week at Soochow with Lee, and then he sent me back to Nanking, to ponder and count the weeks till my release. I won't bore you with their passage; I was well housed and cared for at Lee's palace, feeding of the best, but nothing to do except loaf and fret and improve my Chinese, and devil a wench to bless myself with, thanks to their godless laws. Which, when I considered what was going on in the Grand Palace of Glory and Light, was enough to make me bay at the stars.

The only diversion I had while I ate the beansprouts of idleness and brooded lewdly on the Bearer of Heavenly Decrees and the Tien Wang's Heavenly Twins (I was never inside his palace again, by the way) was when Hung Jen-kan would have me over to his house for a prose. The more I saw of him, the better I liked him; he was stout and jolly and full of fun, and was plainly the only dog in the pack with two sane brains to rub together – damned good brains they were, too, as I discovered, and for all his jokes and guffaws he was a dangerous and ambitious man. He had great charm, and when you sat with him in his big cluttered *yamen* (for he kept nothing like the sybaritic state of the other Wangs; rude comfort was his sort) it was like gossiping with a chum in the gunroom: the place was littered with port bottles, full and empty, along with three Colt revolvers on the side-table, boxes of patent matches, a broken telescope, a well-thumbed Bible next to the *Woolwich Manual of Fortification*, a shelf packed with jars of Coward's mixed pickles, bundles of silver ingots tied with red waxed string and thrown carelessly on the bed, an old barometer, piles of French crockery, jade

125

ornaments, tea-cups, a print of the Holy Well in Flintshire propped up against *The Young Cricketer's Companion*, and papers, books, and rubbish spread in dusty confusion.

And in the middle of it all, that laughing fat rascal in his untidy yellow robe, swilling port by the pint and eating steak with a knife and fork, pushing the bottle at me, lighting our cheroots, chortling at his own jokes, and crying thanks after his servants – who were the ugliest old crones imaginable, for Jen-kan of all the Wangs kept no harem, or affected any grand style. Aye, it was easy to forget that in little more than a year he'd climbed within a step of supreme power in this crazy revolution, and held in his podgy fingers all the reins of state.[16]

The other Wangs were a surly crew of peasants beside him – Hung Jen-ta, the Heavenly King's elder brother, who gave himself ridiculous airs and sported silk robes of rainbow colours; Ying Wang, the Heroic King, who bit his nails and stuttered; and the formidable Chen Yu-cheng, who had abetted Lee in the great defeat of the Imps a few weeks before; he was from the same stable as the Loyal Prince, but even younger and more handsome, dressed like a plain soldier, never saying a word beyond a grunt, and staring through you with black snake eyes. They said he was the most ferocious of all the Taiping leaders, and I believed it.

One other I met at Jen-kan's house, a weedy, pathetic little lad of about eleven, tricked out in a gold crown and sceptre and a robe fairly crusted with jewels; everyone fawned on him and knocked head something extravagant, for he was the Tien Kuei, the Junior Lord, son of the Heavenly King – which made him Jesus's nephew, I suppose.

Possibly they all talked sense in the Council, with Hung Jen-kan, though I doubt it; in public their conversation seemed to consist of childish discussion of the Heavenly King's latest decree, or poem, or pronouncement, with misquoted references to the Scriptures every other sentence. It was like listening to a gang of labourers who'd got religious mania; it wasn't real; if I hadn't had Jen-kan to talk to, I believe I'd have lost all hold on common sense.

At least he could give me occasional news of the world outside, which he did very fairly and humorously (although

126

if I'd known the thoughts that were passing behind that genial chubby mask I'd have got precious little sleep of nights). It was a waiting time, that early summer of '60, not only for me, but for all China. Elgin had arrived at last, and sailed north with Grant and the Frogs to the Peiho mouth, whence they would march 15,000 strong to Pekin in August, Jen-kan reckoned, though it was doubtful if they would get there before September. By then Lee would have launched his sudden stroke at Shanghai, forcing Bruce to choose one side or t'other at last; meanwhile Jen-kan was bombarding him with letters to which Bruce didn't reply. So there was a lull through June and July, with Grant and Elgin girding their loins to the north, and Bruce and the Taipings listening for each other at either end of the Yangtse valley. Only one minor portent disturbed the peace, and when Jen-kan told me about it, I couldn't believe my ears. But it was plain, sober, unlikely truth, as follows:

With Shanghai in uncertainty, the China merchants there had got the notion to raise a mercenary force to help defend the city if the Taipings attacked. According to Jen-kan, it was a bit of a joke – a mob of waterfront rowdies, sailors, deserters, and beachcombers, everyone but the town drunk – oh, no, he was there, too, in force. There were Britons, Yankees, Frogs, wogs, wops, Greeks, every sort of dago – and who d'you think was at the head of this band of angels? None other than Mr Frederick Townsend Ward.

It just shows what can happen when your back's turned. How he'd graduated from steamboat mate to this new command, I couldn't imagine, but when they took the field in June it was the biggest farce since Grimaldi retired. For young Fred, not content with guarding Shanghai, led his amazing rabble upriver one fine night to attack a Taiping outpost at Sungkiang. They found the place, for a wonder, but most of 'em were howling drunk by the time they got there, and the Taipings shot the boots off them and they all tumbled back to Shanghai, Ward damning and blinding every step of the way.

But he didn't give up, not he. Inside the month he was back with another crew, sober this time, and most of 'em Filippino bandits, with a few American and British officers.

127

He'd drilled some sense and order into them, God knows how . . . and they *took* Sungkiang, bigod, after a fearful cut-and-thrust in which they lost sixty dead and a hundred wounded – and friend Frederick got a hundred and thirty *thousand* bucks commission from the China merchants.

Jen-kan was disposed to laugh the whole thing off, but I wasn't so sure. It was beyond belief . . . and then again, it wasn't; I'd only to remember that bright eye and reckless grin, and thank God I was well clear of the dangerous young son-of-a-bitch. And take note, he'd done a small but significant thing: he'd knocked the first dent in the invincible Taiping armour, and started something that was to change the face of China. Little mad Fred. But at the time I knew only what Jen-kan told me, heaving with merriment at the thought of how affronted Lee would be to have this Yankee pup nipping his ankle. "Will he be more wary now, when he marches on Shanghai?" he wondered.

I was doing some wondering on my own account, as July wore out, for Lee was due to march in late August, with me two days ahead of him, and I was counting the time with a will. And then, just after the turn of the month, Jen-kan showed what lay behind his genial mask, and frightened the life out of me.

We were boozing in his *yamen* after luncheon, and he was telling me of Ward's latest exploit – a slap at another Taiping outpost, Chingpu, with three hundred men. Unluckily for him the rebels had ten thousand under two good leaders, Chow the Taiping, and Savage, a Royal Navy deserter; they'd torn Ward's attack to bits, killing about a hundred, and the bold Fred had been carried home with five wounds.

"But they say he will come back to Chingpu!" cries Jen-kan. "Poor fellow! Loyal Prince Lee himself has gone down from Soochow to take command; he will crack this Ward under his thumb-nail, and then . . ." he beamed, filling my glass, ". . . he will sweep on to Shanghai."

I sat up at this. "When do I go? Two weeks?"

He studied me for a long moment, with his fat crafty grin, and pulled his old robe round his big shoulders. "Let us talk outside . . . in English," says he, collaring the bottle, and we strolled out into the warm sunshine, Jen-kan blinking contentedly at his miniature garden – you know the kind of thing, from Chinese exhibitions: dwarf trees and flowers set among tiny streams and lakes and waterfalls, with doll's-house pagodas and bridges all to scale, like Lilliput.

"Why do we love things in little?" muses Jen-kan, admiring the line of tiny palms that fringed the garden. "Do they make us feel like giants . . . or gods, perhaps?" He sipped his wine. "Speaking of gods, I have often meant to ask you . . . what did you think of the Heavenly King?"

Now, neither of us had ever mentioned my visit to the Palace, though I was certain he knew about it. And while he was no fanatic, like Lee, I supposed he must be devoted to the Heavenly Loose-screw, so I hesitated how to answer. He settled his broad bottom on a rock under a tree. "I ask, because I am curious to know what you will tell Mr Bruce."

"What d'you think I'll tell him?" says I, wary-like, and he grinned, and then chuckled, and finally laughed so hard he had to set down his glass. He blinked at me, his shoulders shaking.

"Why, that he is a debauched, useless imbecile!" cries he. "What else can you say, except that he is a poor deranged mystic, a hopeless lunatic who makes an obscene parody of Christianity? That is the truth, and that is what you will tell Mr Bruce!"

He took a deep swig, while I stood mum and a mite apprehensive; what he'd said was a capital offence in these parts, and for all I knew, listening might be, too. He shook his head, grinning.

"Oh, but you should have seen him once! In the old days. To know him then, my dear Sir Harry . . . I intend no blasphemy, but it was to understand the force that must have lived in Christ, or Buddha, or Mahomet. And now, poor soul . . . a mad shell, and nothing left within except that strange power that can still inspire devotion in folk like the Loyal Prince Lee." He chuckled. "Even in people like me, sometimes. Enough to make me wish you had not seen him that night. I would have prevented it, but I learned of Lee's intention too late – those were my men who intervened in the garden . . . unsuccessfully. Four of them died." He gave an amused snort that made my skin crawl. "And, do you know – next day Lee and I greeted each other as usual, and said – nothing! We Taiping politicians are very discreet. Let me fill your glass."

I wasn't liking this one bit. He'd never been this forth-coming before, and when great men wax confidential I find myself taking furtive looks over my shoulder. I just had to think of Palmerston.

"I saw Lee's purpose, of course," says the pot-bellied rascal. "He hoped you would fall under our divine ruler's spell, become a fanatical advocate of Anglo-Taiping alliance, and convince Mr Bruce likewise." He shook his bullet head. "Poor Lee, he is such an optimist. With respect, my dear Sir Harry, soldiers should not meddle in affairs of state." I was with him there. "For now I was in a difficulty. Until that night I had accepted, though without enthusiasm, Lee's plan of marching on Shanghai and forcing Britain's hand. But once you had seen the Tien Wang . . . well, I asked myself what must follow when you reported his deplorable condition to Mr Bruce. Alas," he consoled himself with another hefty gulp, "it was all too plain. Whatever force we took to Shanghai, we could never persuade Britain to recognise a regime led by such a creature! Mr Bruce would only have to picture the reaction of Prince Albert and the Church of England. They would fight us, rather. No . . . whatever hope we had of an alliance must perish the moment you set foot in Bruce's office."

If there's one thing that can make me puke with terror, it's having an Oriental despot tell me I'm inconvenient. "You think I'd be giving Bruce news?" I blurted. 'Dammit, the whole world knows your Heavenly King's a raving idiot!"

"No, I think not," says he mildly. "Some may suspect it, but most charitably regard the rumours as Imp propaganda and missionary gossip. They would not *know* the full deplor-able truth . . . until you told them." He looked wistfully at the bottle, now empty. "And then, we agree, Mr Bruce would reject us – and Lee would take Shanghai by storm, with all the horrors of sack and slaughter inevitable in such a victory, and we would be at war with Britain. A war we could not hope to win." He sighed heavily. "It seemed to me that our only hope must be that your report never reached

130

Mr Bruce, in which case, happily ignorant of the Tien Wang's condition, he might well allow Lee to occupy Shanghai peacefully. Ah . . . you are not drinking, Sir Harry?"

My reply to this was an apoplectic croak, and he brightened.

"In that case, may I take your glass? Being fat, I am slothful, and it seems a long way to the house for another bottle. I thank you." He drained my glass and wiped his lips contentedly. "I do like port, I confess."

"But . . . but . . . look here!" I interrupted, babbling. "Don't you see, it won't matter a bit if they know the Heavenly King's cracked! Because I can tell 'em that you're not, and that you're guiding the revolution . . . sir . . . not that mad doxy-galloper! I swear that when Bruce knows you're in charge – why, he'll be far more inclined to accept the Taiping, knowing you have it in hand . . . make a treaty, even –"

"Why, you are jolly kind!" beams the bloated Buddha. "But, alas, it would not be true. Lee is already as powerful as I, and when he succeeds at Shanghai, whether by persuasion or storm, it will be a triumph which cannot fail to enhance him and eclipse me utterly. It was while I was considering your own position that this fact burst on me with blinding force – I could see no issue at Shanghai that would not increase Lee's power and undermine my own. And that was terrible to contemplate . . . no, it is no use, we must have the other bottle!"

And he was off to the house like an obese whippet, kilting up his robe, his fat calves wobbling, while I sat alarmed and bewildered. He came back flourishing a bottle, laughing merrily as he resumed his seat and splashed port into our glasses.

"Your good health, Sir Harry!" chortles he, damn his impudence. "Yes . . . terrible to contemplate. But you mustn't think I'm jealous; if Lee were a realist, I would make way for him, for he is a splendid soldier who might win the war and establish the Heavenly Kingdom. I hoped so, once." He shook his head again. "But of late I have seen how blind is his fanaticism, how implicitly he will obey every insane decree from that lunatic he worships. Between them they

131

would make the Taiping a headless centipede, poisonous, clawing without direction – and there would never be an end to this abominable war of extermination. Oh, that's what it is!" He laughed heartily, chilling my blood. "Do you know why we and the Imps never take prisoners? Because if we did, we could not hold our armies together – if they knew they could be taken prisoner, they would not fight. Consider that hideous fact, Sir Harry, and have some more port." He reached for the bottle, and I realised he was watching me intently, his fat creased face grinning most oddly.

"Between them, Lee and the Tien Wang will destroy the Taiping," says he slowly, "unless I can prevent them. And that I can only do if I retain my power – and diminish that of Loyal Prince Lee. A grievous necessity," sighs the fat hypocrite, beaming happily. "Now, Sir Harry, I wonder if you can foresee – as a strictly neutral observer – how that might be brought about?"

Well, I'd seen where the blubbery villain was headed for some minutes past, and what between flooding relief and fury at the way he'd scared the innards out of me first, I didn't mince words.

"You mean if Lee falls flat on his arse at Shanghai!"

He looked puzzled – doubtless the expression was seldom heard in the Hong Kong mission where he'd worked. "If Lee were to fail at Shanghai," I explained. "If he tried to take the place and couldn't."

He sucked in port noisily. "But is that possible? Obviously, you have a vested interest in saying that it is, but my dear Sir Harry –" he leaned forward, glittering piggily, "I have been entirely frank with you – dangerously frank – and I trust you to be equally candid with me. You know Mr Bruce's mind; you know the position at Shanghai. Could Lee be made to fail?"

Of course he knew the answer; he'd been studying it for weeks. "Well, in the first place," says I, "he'll not scare Bruce into letting him walk in. He'll have to fight – and as I told you at our first meeting, it won't be against a mob of useless Imps who'll fall down if a Taiping farts at them." I waited until his bellow of mirth had subsided. "He'll be meeting British and French regulars for the first time – not many of 'em, but they can be reinforced, given time. We have Sikhs at Chusan, two regiments at Canton –"

"Three," says he. "I have information."

I'll bet he had. "With the fleet lying off Peiho – oh, and this gang of Fred Ward's for what it's worth –"

"Lee will have fifty thousand men, remember! Could Shanghai resist such a force?"

The temptation to say we could lick him from China to Cheltenham was irresistible, so I resisted it. He knew the case better than I did, so there was nothing for it but honesty.

"I don't know. But it could have a damned good try. If Bruce had warning, *now*, by a messenger he trusted . . ." I hung on that for a moment, and he nodded ". . . he'd have two weeks to garrison before Lee arrived. In which case you can wish Lee luck, because by God he'll need it!"

If you've ever seen a fat Chinaman holding four aces, you'll know how he was staring at me as he envisaged the delightful prospect of Lee disgraced, himself supreme – the deliberate sacrifice of hundreds, perhaps thousands, of Taiping lives, and the certain loss of Shanghai to the Taiping cause forever, were mere trifles so long as Jen-kan won his political battle over Lee.[17] Suddenly he gave a little crowing laugh, and filled my glass.

"You confirm my conclusions exactly!" cries he. "Lee will certainly be defeated before Shanghai. Of course, in contriving this I am compromising myself most dangerously, but I know Mr Bruce will be discreet; he and H.M. Government have much to gain from an enlightened control in the Taiping movement. The steamships order, for example, need not be affected by our brief mutual hostilities at Shanghai, which will soon be forgotten. Britain can resume her policy of neutrality, and left to ourselves we shall defeat the Manchoos." He raised his glass to me. "Your own immediate profit should be considerable – you will be the hero who brought the momentous warning that saved Shanghai. I drink to your further advancement, my friend." He smacked his liver lips and leaned back, blinking up at the sunlight filtering through the fronds overhead. "I foresee happy times."

He had it all pat, the fat, grinning, ruthless scoundrel – but, d'you know, I can't say he was a whit worse than any other statesman of my acquaintance, and a sight jollier than most. I asked when I would go.

"Tonight," says he, "it is all arranged, with complete secrecy. I shall easily conceal your absence until the appropriate time, two weeks hence, when I will send word to Lee – who should be at Chingpu by now – that his advance to Shanghai can begin." He giggled and took another mammoth swig of port. "Your escort will take you as far as Chingpu, by the way, where by all accounts your friend Mr Ward will be in the vicinity. But you will keep well clear of Chingpu itself. Lee would not be pleased to see you." He turned to grin at me. "We know what you will tell Mr Bruce of the Heavenly King (regrettable, but there it is), and of the Loyal Prince Lee . . . I wonder what you will say of Hung Jen-kan?"

"That he drinks port at the wrong time of day."

He choked on his glass. "You intend to ruin my reputation, in fact. Ah, well, I am sure Mr Bruce will receive an honest account from you. The fact that it will be totally misleading is by the way." He heaved another of his mountainous sighs.

"You imagine I act out of unscrupulous self-interest; true, all revolutionaries do. They agitate and harangue and justify every villainy in the name of high ideals; they lie, to delude the people, whom they hold in contempt. They seek nothing but their personal ends – my only defence is that my ends are modest ones. I seek power to see the revolution accomplished; after that, I have no wish to rule. I want the biggest library in China, and to visit my cousins in San Francisco, and to read the Lesson, just once, in an English country church." He began to shake with laughter again. "Tell Mr Bruce that. He won't believe a word of it. Oh, and you will not forget to mention the steamships? An order worth a million, remember – whatever happens with Lee." He looked like a contented pig. "As Superintendent of Trade, Mr Bruce will not overlook the importance of the almighty dollar."[18]

❀ I hadn't arrived at Nanking in any great style, but it was Pullman travel compared to the way I went, under hatches on a stinking Yangtse fish-barge, with two of Jen-kan's thugs for company. I daren't show face until we were well away from the city, white *fan-quis* being as common in those parts as niggers in Norway; not that I'd have been hindered, but Jen-kan might have had awkward explanations to make if it got about that Flashy was heading east ahead of time. So we spent a day and night in the poisonous dark and came ashore somewhere on the Kiangyin bend, where two more thugs were waiting with ponies. Farther down, the river was infested by gangs of Imp deserters and bandits (no doubt the Provident Brave Butterflies were spreading their wings, among others), and while the land to the south was swarming with Taiping battalions, Jen-kan had reckoned we'd make better and safer time on horseback, taking a long sweep to come in by Chingpu, where Frederick T. Ward's foreign legion was preparing to have another slap at the Taiping garrison.

I don't remember much about that ride, except that I was damned stiff after months out of the saddle, but I know we raised Chingpu on a misty dawn, looking down from a crest to the town, perhaps a mile away. It was wooded country, with paddy here and there, and many waterways – you could see the little mat sails beetling along among the dykes, ever so pretty in the pearly morning light; it would have been quite an idyllic scene if there hadn't been the deuce of a battle going on round Chingpu's high mud walls.

We'd heard the guns before we came in view, and they were banging away splendidly, wreathing the walls and gate-towers in thick grey smoke, while dead to our front great disorderly lines of men were advancing to the assault. To my astonishment I saw they were Imps, straggling along any old how, but in the van there was a fairly compact company in green caps, and I knew these must be Ward's people. Without a glass I couldn't make them out clearly, but they were holding together well under the fire from the walls, and presently they were charging the main gate, while the Imp supports milled about and let off crackers and waved banners in fine useless style.

Farther back, behind the attackers, were more Imp battalions by a river-bank, with a gunboat blazing away at nothing in particular, and about a mile away on my right was a low hill on which a couple of banners were flying, with a number of mounted men wheeling about and occasionally dashing out to the attacking force. Gallopers; the hill must be the attackers' head-quarters, so it behoved me to make for it. I was just pointing it out to my escort when there was a tremendous pandemonium from the plain before the town, the boom of guns and crackle of musket-fire redoubled, the crimson Taiping banners were waving wildly along the walls, and suddenly in the smoke-clouds before the gate there was a great glare of orange light followed by the thunderous roar of an explosion.

That was Ward's lads mining the main gate, and as the smoke cleared, sure enough, one of the supporting towers was in ruins, and green caps were surging into a breach as wide as a church. At this the Imps, seeing their side winning, set up a huge halloo and went swarming in to join the fun; in a moment the whole space before the breach was choked with men, while the supporting lines, throwing disorder to the winds, crowded in behind, blazing away indiscriminately – and that should have been the end of Chingpu. What the attackers had forgotten, or didn't know, was that they were assaulting a stronghold commanded by Loyal Prince Lee. They were about to find out, and it was a sight to see.

All along the front wall it was like an enormous football scrimmage; there must have been hundreds trying to get to the breach, and more arriving every second. On the side wall nearest to me there wasn't a single attacker, and now a banner waved on the battlements, a side-gate opened, and out came a column of Taiping red-coats, trotting orderly four abreast. They streamed out, hundreds strong, rounding the front angle, and went into the attacking mob like a scarlet thunderbolt. At the same moment, from the other side of the town, a second Taiping column completed the pincer movement, the black silk flags went up, and within five minutes there wasn't a living attacker within quarter of a mile of Chingpu, and the whole Imp rout was streaming back towards the river, utterly broken. I never saw a neater sally in my life; as the Taipings broke off the pursuit and began to strip the dead, I reflected that it was as well Jen-kan wasn't seeing this, or he might have entertained doubts about · Shanghai's ability to hold Lee at bay.

But you don't dally on the touch-line when the game's over; I wheeled my pony and made for the head-quarters hill, keeping well to flank of the fleeing Imps, with my escort thundering along behind. The gallopers and standard-bearers were streaming away over the brow, so I circled the hill and found myself in a little wood beyond which lay a broad sunken road, with what looked like a party of sightseers coming down it. There was a disconsolate chap in a green cap carrying a banner which he was plainly itching to throw away, a few stragglers and mules, two minions carrying a picnic basket, and finally, flanked by a galloper with his arm in a bloody sling, and a noisy cove in a Norfolk jacket and gaiters, came a sedan chair, borne by perspiring coolies and containing Frederick T. Ward.

I almost didn't recognise him at first, for he was swathed in bandages like an Egyptian mummy, with his leg in a splint and a big plaster on his jaw, but it didn't stop him talking, and I'd have recognised that staccato Yankee voice anywhere. The Norfolk jacket had just finished roaring, in a fine Dixie accent, that he didn't know wheah Ned Forrestuh wuz, an' he didn't dam' well cayuh, neethuh, an' if Forrestuh had jest *waited* till the flanks wuz covered they wouldn't ha' bin cotched like a nigguh with his pants down in the melon-patch, it was downright hoomiliatin'.

"Now, you find him damned quick!" snaps Ward. "If he got out – and I hope to God he did – you tell him to get back to Sungkiang with every man he's got! No, the hell with the gunboat, let the Imps worry about it! For all the good it

137

was we'd ha' been better with a canoe! Now, get going –
Sungkiang, remember! Spitz, find the doctor – I want *our*
casualty count – not the Imps! Goddam it, if only I could
walk!"

"An' whayuh the hell do Ah git goin' *to*?" bawled the
Norfolk jacket, raising arms to heaven. " 'Lessn Forrestuh's
daid, he'll be back at the rivuh by naow, an' . . . holy
baldhead, who the hell is *that*?"

I had reined up by the road, and he was gaping at me, so
I gave a cheery wave and sang out: "Just a tourist, old fellow.
Hollo, Fred – been in the wars, I see!"

None too tactful, you may say, but no reason for the
Norfolk jacket to leap three feet and yell: "Cover him, Spitz!
He's a *chang-mao*!"

"Don't be a damned fool, I'm nothing of the sort!" says
I. "Do I look like one?"

"They do!" he roars, pointing, and I realised that Jen-kan's
four thugs were lurking modestly behind me, on the fringe
of the wood, and there was no denying, they had Taiping
haircuts.

"Hold your fire!" I shouted, for Spitz, the wounded galloper, was unlimbering an enormous pistol. "Ward, I'm
Flashman! We're friends! They're not Taipings . . . well,
they are, but they ain't hostile! Call him off, Fred, will
you?"

He was looking at me as though I were a ghost, but he
signed Spitz to put up his piece. "What'n tarnation are you
doing here?"

"Going to Shanghai," says I. "So will you, if you've any
sense."

"He's an Englishman!" cries the Norfolk jacket. "Like
Trent an' Mowbray! Ah kin tell by his voice!"

"I know what he is!" says Ward impatiently, and to me:
"I thought you were at the bottom of the Yangtse! Where
the dooce have you been?"

"That's a long story. First, if you don't mind . . ." And I
turned and waved away my escort, who wheeled and vanished
into the wood on the instant, like sensible lads. Spitz raised
a great outcry, and the Norfolk jacket waved his arms.

"Savage is English, too, an' *he*'s with the Taipings!" he

138

bellowed. "Seed the son-of-a-bitch on the wall this mawnin', bold as brass –"

"I told you to go find Forrester!" barks Ward, and winced. "Damn this leg! Spitz, *will* you get that casualty count!" D'you know, they went like lambs; he was still young Fred Ward, but he'd grown some authority, all right.

"Well, I swan!" He shook his head at me. "You back in British service, or what? I thought you said they busted you over that Pearl River business?"

"No-o, you said that, and I didn't contradict you. I'm still staff colonel."

"Is that a fact?" He was grinning, although the pale young face was pinched with pain. "And those four – were they on the staff, too? Oh, who cares! Come on, Dobbin!" He waved to the coolies, who heaved up the sedan again. "They don't gallop, exactly, and I'd as soon the Long-Hairs didn't catch up with me!"

I told him about Lee's forthcoming advance as we went, not mentioning Jen-kan, and he never took those bright black eyes off me, although he winced and gasped as he was bounced along. When I'd done, he whistled and swore.

"Well, there goes Sungkiang, I guess. In which case, the hell with it, I'm going to France, and have a rest." He squinted at me. "It's *pukka* – that Lee's coming?"

"Yes, and the less you say about it, the better. We don't want him to know he's expected, do we? But, look here – if you can't hold Sungkiang, hadn't you better pull back to Shanghai?"

"I've got a contract to hold the dam' place!" says he. "If I don't, Yang Fang'll want his money back – and he's my father-in-law! Anyway, your man Bruce doesn't want me anywhere near Shanghai – I'm a confounded mercenary nuisance, old boy, dontcherknow?" He laughed bitterly. "The damned dummy! Why, if he'd supported me with arms and men, we'd ha' had a half dozen Taiping places by now, and Lee'd never get within twenty miles o' the coast! But all I get is Imps, and *they* don't fight – you saw that mess just now? And I had to lay there and watch! Say, I sure hope Ned Forrester got out, though!"

I said, if Bruce wasn't helpful, why didn't he try his own

139

American consulate, and he hooted and said they were even more timid than the British or French. "They're all glad enough to hide behind us, though, preserving their darned neutrality – and counting their dividends! Ain't they, though? Oh, I reckon not!" He lay back, gasping and stirring to try to ease his wounds. "God, but I'm tired!"

We were out on the paddy by now, threading along the causeways, and on either side the plain was dotted with groups of fugitives, streaming away from Chingpu – Imps, mostly, but a few in green caps, white men and little dark-skinned chaps who I guessed were Filipinos. They hailed Ward whenever we came within earshot, and he shouted back, although his voice was weak, calling: "All right, boys! Good for you! See you in Sungkiang! Pay-day's coming, you bet! Hurrah!" And they hurrah-ed back, waving their caps, and trudged on through the paddy.

There was no sign of pursuit, and now we called a halt to eat and rest Ward's bearers. The picnic basket proved to contain enough for a banquet, with hams, cold roasts and fowls, fruit, chocolate, and even iced champagne, but Ward contented himself with a loaf of bread which he ate in handfuls, soaking each bite in rum. The rest went in no time, for a party of green-cap stragglers came up, and Ward waved them to pitch in; they were Filipinos under a most ill-assorted pair, a huge broken-nosed American with his shirt open over his hairy barrel chest, who looked and talked like a hobo, and a slim little Royal Navy chap with a wing-collar and a handkerchief in his sleeve; Ward called them Tom and Jerry. And now came Spitz, trotting his near-foundered horse, with the news that Ned Forrester was slightly wounded, but that casualties had been heavy.

"There voss a huntret killed, and ass many wounded," says he, pulling a cold fowl to pieces in his great hands and stuffing it down. Tom swore and Jerry tut-tutted, but Ward just laid down his loaf, closed his eyes, and recited the Lord's Prayer aloud, while we all left off eating and stood about with bowed heads, holding drumsticks and glasses.

"Ay-men," says Ward at last, "so we've got a hundred fit to fight. All right, Jerry – you and Tom make for Shanghai, tell Vincente Macanana I need two, three hundred recruits, and I don't mean Imp deserters. American and British, Russki, French, and all the Filippinos he can raise; kit 'em out at the camp, ten bucks apiece to sign on – no more or they'll take it an' quit right there. Force march to Sungkiang – and see here, Tom, I want 'em there in three days, no later, comprenny?"

"Dunno, old boy," drawls Jerry, shaking his head. "The well's pretty dry; may have to take some odd customers."

"Ticket-o'-leave men," growls Tom. "Bums. Dagoes."

"I don't give a hoot how odd they are so long as they can stand up and shoot! That's all they'll have to do when Lee lays siege to Sungkiang." Ward was looking more chipper now; he laughed at their glum faces and struggled up in his sedan to clap Tom on the back with his good hand. "No room for drills on the parapet, old fellow! Just bang and reload and knock down *chang-maos* like ninepins! Who knows an easier way of making a hundred a week, eh? That's the life in the Green-headed Army!"

"Will t'ree hunnert hold the place, I ask?" grumbles Spitz, and Ward rounded on him, grinning.

"Why, how you talk! Easy as pie! Tumble over their black bannermen and they'll run as fast as . . . as *we* did that first time *we* attacked Sungkiang. 'Member, Jerry? I know you don't, Tom, 'cos you were blind drunk an' snoring in the bottom of a sampan. Yes, you were, too! Oh, you needn't smirk so virtuous, either, Jerry! Who ran the boat aground?" He laughed again, eagerly. "But we came back, didn't we? Threw the Long-Hairs clear out o' the place, didn't we? And we're not giving it up, no, sir! Not while I can lay in a sedan chair an' give orders!"

Just listening to him, shot full of holes and chortling like a schoolboy, I could see Brooke on that rusty little steamer on Skrang river, slapping the table bright-eyed and urging us to sing, because we were only outnumbered a hundred to one by head-hunting pirates, and weren't we going to give 'em what for in the morning? They were a matched pair of madmen, Ward and Brooke, the kind who don't think a cause worth fighting unless it's half lost to start with, pumping their own crazy optimism into their followers by sheer force of will – for now Jerry was smiling and Tom grinning, and

141

even Spitz, the surly Switzer, was looking less sour, while the Filippinos were laughing and chattering as Ward joked and harangued their officers.

I can't stand 'em, myself, these happy heroes; they'll do for us all if we don't watch out. Brooke damned near did for *me*, and F. T. Ward was just the man to have finished the job, as appeared presently when the others had gone off, and I said I must be pushing on to Shanghai myself. He lay quiet a moment, and cleared his throat.

"You wouldn't feel like taking some furlough, would you . . . colonel? I mean . . . oh, fellows like Tom and Jerry are just grand, you know, but . . . well, it'll take more'n pluck to hold Sungkiang, after today, and I could sure use a good man."

"Come, Fred," says I, "you know quite well I'm a Queen's officer, not a wild goose." Being tactful, you see; I'd sooner have gone on a polar expedition with Cetewayo.

"Oh, sure!" cries he airily. "I know that! I didn't mean anything permanent, just . . ." He gave me his cocky urchin grin, so young in that worn, pain-creased face. "Well, you took time off to run opium, didn't you? An' this job pays five hundred bucks a week, *and* commission on every town we take –"

"Like Chingpu, you mean? My, how you tempt a fellow . . ."

"Listen, I'll take Chingpu, don't you fret!" cries he. "Chingpu an' twenty more like it, you'll see! Once I get rested up, an' get a good bunch of fellows together, an' lick 'em into shape –"

"Frederick," says I, because for some reason I'd conceived an affection for the young idiot, "listen to me, will you? I've been twenty years in this game, and I know what I'm saying. Now, within the limits of raving lunacy, you're a good sort, and I don't want to see you come to harm. So my advice to you is . . . retire. The money ain't worth it; nothing's worth it. You're lying there like a bloody colander, and if you don't see sense, why, you'll finish up under the paddy, sure as fate . . ."

"I'll finish up in Pekin!" cries he, and his black eyes were shining fit to sicken you. "Don't you see, this is just a beginning! I'm learning my trade here – sure, I'm making mistakes, and sure, I don't know one little bit about soldiering compared to you! But I will. Yes, sir. I've got the most important thing behind me – a bankroll from the China merchants, and the longer I stay in the field, the better I'll get, and I'm going to build me the Green-headed Army into something that'll sweep the Taipings out of China! And then I'll have won the Emperor's war for him. And then . . ." he laughed and sat back against his cushions, ". . . then, mister, you're going to dine out on how you ran poppy an' fought pirates with Frederick Townsend Ward!"

I watched his sedan jogging away across the plain in the wake of his tatterdemalion regiment, and thought, well, there's another damned fool gone to collect the wages of ambition. I was right – and wrong. He found his bed in the paddy, as I'd foretold, and hardly anyone remembers even his name nowadays, but you may say that without him Chinese Gordon might never have had a look-in. You can read about 'em both in the books, and shudder (I'll tell you my own tale of Gordon another time, if I'm spared); for the moment I'll say only that while Gordon finished the Taiping business, it was young happy-go-lucky Fred who broke the ground for him, and turned that drunken mob of green caps into one of the great free companies: the Ever-Victorious Army. Aye, Ward and Gordon: a good pair to stay away from.[19]

❀ I reached Shanghai at midnight, and the smell of fear was in the air already. Word had run ahead of Ward's debacle at Chingpu, and that it had been caused by none other than the terrible Loyal Prince Lee himself, who could now be expected to sweep on and overwhelm the city. Even the street lanterns seemed to be burning dimmer in apprehension, and I never saw fewer civilians or more troops abroad in the consular district; usually gates were wide, with lights and music from the houses within, and carriages and palkis moving in the streets; tonight the gates were closed, with strong piquets on guard, and occasional files of marines hurrying along, their tramp echoing in the silence.

Bruce had gone to bed, but they rousted him out, and for once his imperturbability deserted him; he stared at me like a stricken seraph, hair all awry where he'd hauled off his nightcap, but once he'd decided I wasn't dead after all he wasted no time, but called for lights to his study, thrust me into a chair, ordered up brandy and sandwiches and told me to talk as I ate.

"You've got two weeks," I told him, and launched into it – the date of Lee's advance, his probable strength, Jen-kan's conspiracy to ensure his failure – at which he exclaimed in disbelief and even Slater, his secretary, stopped taking notes to gape at me – and then such secondary matters as their detention of yours truly, and those impressions I'd formed which seemed important in the present crisis. I talked for an hour, almost without pause, and he hardly said a word till I'd done, when:

"Thank God I sent you to Nanking!" says he. "We've been growing surer by the week that he was coming, but no hint of the date – you're positive we have two weeks?"

"Ten days, if you like, certainly no less. It's my guess

144

he'll put paid to Ward at Sungkiang before he marches on Shanghai."

"It would be a public service if he did!" exclaimed Bruce. "That Yankee upstart is a greater embarrassment than the French priests!"[20]

"He might buy you a few days if he's strong enough," I reminded him. "I'd turn a blind eye to his recruiting, anyway, if I were you."

He sniffed, but said he'd make a note of it, and then told me with some satisfaction how he'd been urging the consuls and the Imps for weeks past to put the city in a state of defence; now that they had definite word, and a date, his hand would be strengthened tremendously, and by the time they had improved the fortifications and called in more troops, Lee could whistle for Shanghai, however many Taipings he had at his back. For which, he said handsomely, they were deeply indebted to me, and Lord Palmerston should know of it.

Well, I always say, credit and cash, you can never have too much of either, but the best news he gave me was that he was sending me north without delay to join Elgin, who had just made his landing at the mouth of the Peiho with Grant's army, and was preparing to advance on Pekin. "There is nothing you can do here, now, my dear Sir Harry, to compare with what you have already done," says he, all smiles, "and it is of the first importance that Lord Elgin himself should have your account of the Taipings without delay. There will be endless chin-chinning with the Emperor's people, you may be sure, before he reaches Pekin, and your intelligence will be of incalculable value."

I heard him with relief, for I'd been fearful that he'd want to keep me by him to advise about Lee's army, and if there was one place I'd no desire to linger just then, it was Shanghai. You see, Bruce, like Jen-kan, might be certain that Lee was going to get a bloody nose, but I wasn't; I'd seen his long-haired bastards making mincemeat of Soochow, and I'd no wish to be among the gallant defenders when their black flags went up before our walls. So I looked knowing and serious, and admitted that I'd be glad to get back to

145

proper campaigning again, and he and Slater exchanged glances of admiration at this soldierly zeal.

They couldn't wait to be rid of me, though; I'd been looking forward to a few days loafing and being lionised, and several restorative romps with my Russian man-eater at the hairdresser's – I hadn't had a woman since my last bout with Szu-Zhan (God, what an age ago that seemed) and I didn't want to forget how it was done. But no; Bruce said I must take the fast steam-sloop for the Peiho that very morning, because Elgin would be in a sweat to have me on hand, and mustn't be kept waiting. (It's astonishing, how even the best men start falling over themselves in a fret when it's a question of contenting their elder brother.)

So now you find Flashy beating nor'-west by south or whatever the proper nautical jargon may be, thundering amain o'er the trackless waste o' waters – which I did by dossing for fourteen hours straight off, and if there was a typhoon it was all one to me. For the first time in months – since I boarded the steamer *Yangtse*, in fact – I was free of all care, content to be tired, with nothing ahead but a safe, leisurely campaign in good company, while behind lay the nightmare, ugly and confused; not near as bad as some I've known, but disturbing enough. Perhaps it was those unreal weeks in Taipingdom that made the memories distasteful; stark danger and horror you can either fight or run from, but madness spreads a blight there's no escaping; it still made me feel vaguely unclean to think of Lee's sharp, crazy eyes, or the blank hypnotic gaze of the arch-lunatic on that incredible night, with the joss-stench like a drug, and those wonderful satin bodies writhing nakedly . . . by Jove, there's a lot to be said for starting a new religion. Or the Bearer of Heavenly Decrees, maddeningly out of reach . . . and far better, the lean face smiling wickedly above the chain collar, and the long bare-breasted shapeliness lounging at the rail. And then the crash of shots, the screaming faces and whirling blades surging out of the mist . . . masked figures and steel claws dragging me through the dark . . . red-coated legions stamping up the dust like Jaggernauts . . . black silk flags and burned corpses heaped . . . a fat, smiling yellow face telling me I knew too much to live . . . a crippled figure swathed in

146

bandages urging on his fools to die for a handful of dollars
. . . that same boy's face distorted with horror as a cageful
of poor wretches was plunged to death in a mere spiteful
gesture. Surely China must have exhausted its horrors by
now?

So I thought, in my drowsy waking, like the optimistic
idiot I was. You'd think I'd have known better, after twenty
years of counting chickens which turned out to be ravening
vultures. For China had done no more than spar gently with
me as yet, and the first gruesome round of the real battle
was only three days away.

That was the time it took from the Yangtse to the mouth
of the Peiho, the great waterway to Pekin, and you must
take a squint at the map if you're to follow what happened
to me next. The mouth of the Peiho was guarded by the
famous Taku Forts, from which we had been bloodily repulsed the previous year, when the Yankees, watching on
the touchline, had thrown their neutrality overboard in the
crisis and weighed in to help pull Cousin John Bull out of
the soup.[21] The Forts were still there, dragon's teeth on
either bank, and since Elgin couldn't tell whether the
Manchoos would let us pass peacefully or blow us to bits,
he and Grant had wisely landed eight miles farther up the
coast, at the Pehtang, from whence they and the Frogs
could march inland and take the Forts from the landward
side, if the Chinks showed any disposition to dispute our
passage.

From the Peiho mouth to the Pehtang the sea was covered
with our squadrons; to the south, guarded by fighting ships,
were the river transports waiting to enter the Peiho when the
Forts had been silenced; for the moment they lay safe out of
range. Farther north was the main fleet, a great forest of
masts and rigging and smoking funnels – troop transports
with their tow vessels, supply ships, fighting sail, steamships,
and gunboats, and even junks and merchantmen and sam-
pans, with the small boats scuttling between 'em like water-
beetles, rowed by coolies or red-faced tars in white canvas
and straw hats. It takes a powerful lot of shipping, more than
two hundred bottoms, to land 15,000 men, horse, foot, guns,
and commissariat, which was what Grant and Montauban

147

had done almost two weeks earlier, and by all accounts it was still bedlam at the Pehtang landing-place.

"Won't have you ashore until tomorrow, colonel, at this rate," says my sloop commander, and being impatient by now to be off his pitching little washtub, I took a look at the long flat coast-line a bare mile away, and made a damned fool suggestion.

We were about half-way between Peiho and Pehtang, in the middle of the fleet, but over on the coast itself there seemed to be one or two flat-bottoms putting in, landing horses on the beach. "Could your launch set me down yonder?" says I, and he scratched his head and said he supposed so, with the result that half an hour later we were pitching through the surf to an improvised landing-stage where a mob of half-naked coolies were manhandling a pontoon from which *syces* were leading horses ashore – big ugly Walers, they were, rearing and neighing like bedamned as they shied at the salt foam. There was a pink-faced youth in a red turban and grey tunic cussing the handlers richly as I splashed ashore.

"Get your fingers in his nose, can't you?" squeaks he. "Oh, my stars! He ain't a sheep, you know!"

I hailed him, and his name was Carnac, I remember, subaltern in Fane's horse, an enterprising lad who, like me, had decided to come in by a side door. The Walers were remounts for his regiment, which he reckoned was somewhere on the causeway between Pehtang and Sinho – a glance at the map will show you how we were placed.

"Fane don't care to be kept waiting," says he, "and we'll need these dam' screws tomorrow, I imagine. So I'm going to take 'em over there while the tide's still out –" he gestured north over the mud-flats which stretched away for miles into the misty distance. "Our people ought to be in Sinho by now. That's over there." And he pointed dead ahead. "About five miles, but there may be Tartars in between, so I'm taking no chances."

"Stout fella," says I. "Got a buckshee Waler for a poor staff colonel, have you? I'm looking for Lord Elgin."

"Dunno where he is – Pehtang, prob'ly," says the lad.

"But Sir Hope Grant's sure to be on the causeway, where we're going."

"He'll do," says I, and when the last of his Walers was ashore, and the *syces* had mounted, we trotted off across the flat. It was muddy tidal sand as far as you could see, with little pools drying in the morning sun, but the mist was burning away, and presently we heard the thump of guns ahead, and Carnac set off at a canter for higher ground to our right. I followed him, scrambling up onto the harder footing of a little plateau dotted with mounds which looked for all the world like big tents – burial places, not unlike Russian *koorgans*. We pushed forward to the farther edge of the plateau, and there we were, in a ringside seat.

Running across our front, about a mile ahead, was the causeway, a high banked road, and along it, advancing steadily to the wail of pipes and rattle of drums, were columns of red-coated infantry, our 1st Division; behind them came the khaki coats of native infantry, and then the blue overcoats and kepis of the Frogs; there must have been two thousand men rolling down to the Manchoo entrenchments where the causeway ended on our left front, with the Armstrong guns crashing away behind them and "Blue Bonnets over the Border" keening in front. Behind the Manchoo entrenchment were masses of Chinese infantry, Bannermen and Tiger soldiers, and on their left a great horde of Tartar cavalry; through Carnac's glass I could make out the red coats and fur hats of the riders, crouched like jockeys on their sheepskins.

Even as we watched, the Tartar cavalry began to move, wheeling away from the causeway and charging en masse away from our advancing columns and out on to their far flank. Carnac stood in his stirrups, his voice cracking with excitement:

"That's the 2nd Division over yonder! Can't see 'em for the haze! By Jove, the Chinks are charging 'em! Would you believe it?"

It was too far to see clearly, but the Tartars were certainly vanishing into the haze, from which came barking salvo after salvo of field pieces, and while our columns on the causeway held back, there was evidently hell breaking loose to their right front. Sure enough, after a moment back came the

149

Tartars, flying in disorder and scattering across the plain, and out of the haze behind them came a thundering line of grey tunics and red puggarees, lances lowered, and behind I saw the red coats of the heavies, the Dragoon Guards. Carnac went wild.

"Look at 'em go! Those are my chaps! Tally-ho, Fane's! Give 'em what for! By crumbs, there's an omen – first action an' we're chasing 'em like hares!"

He was right. The Chinks were all to pieces, with the Indian lancers and Dragoon sabres in among them, and now the columns on the causeway were deploying from the road, quickening their pace as they swept on to the Chink entrenchment. There was the plumed smoke of a volley as they charged, a ragged burst of firing from the Chinks, and then they were into the earthworks, and the Manchoo gunners and infantry were flying in rout, with the Armstrong shells bursting among them. Behind their lines the ground was black with fugitives, streaming back to a village which I supposed was Sinho. Carnac was hallooing like a madman, and even I found myself exclaiming: "Dam' good, Grant! Dam' fine!" for I never saw a smarter right and left in my life, and that was the Battle of Sinho receipted and filed, and the road to the Taku Forts open.

Carnac was in a fever to reach his regiment, and made off for the causeway with his *syces* at the gallop, but I was in no hurry. Sinho was a good three miles away, with swamp and salt-pans and canals in between, and if I knew anything about battle-fields the ground would be littered with bad-tempered enemy wounded just ready to take out their spite on passers-by. I'd give 'em time to crawl away or die; meanwhile I watched the 2nd Division moving in from the plain, and the 1st cheering 'em into the Chinese positions, with great hurrahing and waving of hats. That was where Grant would be, and rather than trot the mile to the causeway which was crowded with our traffic, I presently rode down to the flat and made a bee-line for Sinho across country. I doubted if any sensible Manchoos would be disporting themselves in the vicinity by now; I forgot that every army has its share of idiots.

Down on the salt-flats I no longer had much view; it was

150

nothing but great crusted white beds and little canals, with occasional brackish hollows; ugly country, and after a few minutes there wasn't a soul to be seen anywhere, just the glittering lips of the salt-pans either side, cutting off sight and sound, and only the dry scuff of the Waler's hooves to break the stillness. Suddenly I remembered the Jornada, the Dead Man's Journey under the silent New Mexican moon, and shivered, and I was just about to wheel right and make for the direction of the causeway when I became aware of sounds of true British altercation ahead. I trotted round a salt-bank and beheld an interesting tableau.

Well, there was a Scotsman, an Irishman, and a Chinaman, and they were shouting drunken abuse at each other over a grog-cart which was foundered with a broken wheel. The Paddy, a burly red-head with a sergeant's chevrons, was trying to wrest a bottle from the Scot, a black-avised scoundrel in a red coat who was beating him off and singing an obscene song about a ball at Kirriemuir which was new to me; the Chink was egging 'em on and shrieking with laughter. Various other coolies stood passively in the background.

"Ye nigger-faced Scotch sot!" roars the Murphy. "Will ye come to order, now? I'm warnin' ye, Moyes – I'm warnin' ye! It'll be the triangle and a bloody back for ye if ye don't surrinder that bottle, what's left of it, ye guzzlin' pig, ye! Give over!"

The Scot left off singing long enough to knock him down, and lurched against the cart. "See you, Nolan," cries he. "See your grandmither? She wiz a hoor! Nor she couldnae read nor write! So she had your mither, by a Jesuit! Aye, an' your mither had you, by a b'ilerman! Christ, Nolan, Ah'm ashamed o' ye! Ye want a drink?"

The Irishman came up roaring, and flew at him, and since brawling rankers ain't my touch I was about to ride on, when there was a pounding of hooves behind me, a chorus of yells, and over the lip came a section of Tartar cavalry, bent on villainy. After which much happened in a very short space.

I was off the Waler and shooting under its neck with my Colt in quick time, and down goes the lead Tartar. His mates hauled up, unslinging their bows, and I barely had time to

151

leap aside before my Waler was down and thrashing, feathered with shafts. I turned, ran, and fell, rolling over and blowing shots at the red coats which seemed to be swarming everywhere; out of the tail of my eye I saw the Irishman grabbing a Tartar's leg and heaving him from the saddle; the Scotchman, whom I'd have thought too screwed for anything, was on top of the grog cart, crashing his bottle on the head of another Tartar and then diving on to him, stabbing with the shards. I took an almighty crack on the head, which didn't stun me, but caused me to lose the use of my limbs entirely; then I was being hauled up between two red coats, with evil yellow faces yelling at me from under conical fur hats, and the stink was fit to knock you down – the fact is, they *never* wash; even the Chinese complain. The scene was swimming round me; I remember seeing the Irishman being frog-marched and bound, and the Scot lying on the ground, apparently dead, and that's all.

Now, I say I don't believe I lost consciousness, but I must have done, for piecing events together later, there's a day missing. So they tell me, anyway, but it don't matter. I know what I remember – and can never forget.

There was terrible pain in my wrists and ankles: when the Chinese tie a man up, they do it as tight as possible, so that his hands are quickly useless, and in time will mortify. There was darkness, too, and an agonising jolting: plainly I was carried on one of their ponies. But my first clear recollection is of a foul cell, a foot deep in mud, and no feeling in my hands or feet, which were still bound. I couldn't speak for raging thirst that had dried my tongue and lips bone hard; all I could do was lie in pain, with my senses dulled almost to idiocy – I could hear, though, and I remember that coarse Scotch voice yelling obscenities, and the Irish voice hoarse and begging him to lay off, and the wailing of coolies somewhere near me in the dark.

And then there was blinding light in the cell, and Tartar swine yelling and dragging us to a low doorway, kicking and beating us as we went. I remember recalling that the Manchoos treated all prisoners alike – as vermin – so being an officer meant nothing, not that I could have proclaimed myself, with my tongue like a board. I half-fell out into the light, and was hauled to my feet, and after a moment my vision cleared, and the first thing I saw was a face.

No doubt I'm biased, but it was the most cruel, evil human visage I ever set eyes on, and I've seen some beauties. This one was as flat and yellow as a guinea, grinning in sheer pleasure at our pain, turning to laugh bestially to someone nearby; it had a drooping moustache and a little chin-beard, and was crowned with a polished steel helmet. The figure that went with the face was all in steel and leather armour, even to mailed gauntlets, with a splendid robe of red silk round the shoulders. He was seated on a gilded chair of state, with a great sword across his knees, and beside him stood a nondescript Chink official and a burly Tartar, bare to the waist, with an axe on his shoulder.

We were in a courtyard with high walls, lined by fur-capped Tartars; to my right were half-a-dozen cringing coolies, and to my left, barely recognisable for the mud that plastered them, stood the Paddy and the Scot from the grog-cart; the Irishman had his eyes closed, muttering Hail-Mary; the Scot was staring ahead. His tunic was half-torn off, but I noted dully that it bore the ochre facing of the Buffs, and that he had old cat-scars on his shoulder. My eyes went back to the huge Tartar with the axe, and with a thrill of sheer horror I knew that we were going to die.

Suddenly the brute in the chair spoke, or rather shrieked in Chinese, flinging out a pointing hand of which two fingers were sheathed in nail-cases.

"Filth! Lice! White offal! You dare to show your dog-faces in the Celestial Kingdom, and defile the sacred soil! You dare to defy the Complete Abundance! But the day of your humiliation is coming! Like curs, you have fed your pride for twenty years! Now, like curs, you will hang your heads, lay back your ears, wag your tails, and beg for mercy!" There was foam at his thin lips, and he jerked and glared like a maniac. "Kneel! Kneel down, vermin! Kow-tow! Kow-tow!"

There were squeals and whimpers on my right; the coolies were down and knocking head for dear life. The two Britons on my left, not understanding a word, didn't move, and as the mailed tyrant screamed with rage the little official hurried forward, snarling in a fearful parody of English:

153

"Down! Down to legs! Down to Prince Sang! Makes kill! See! Makes kill!"

He was gesticulating at the big Tartar, who stumped forward grinning, flourishing that awful axe above his head with both hands. There was no doubt what was demanded – and the alternative. It was enough for me: I was down and butting my way to the Antipodes before the little bastard had done speaking. I still thought we were doomed, but if a timely grovel would help, he could have it from me and welcome; you don't catch Flashy standing proud and unflinching at the gates of doom. There was one who did, though.

"Down! Down to Prince Sang! Not – makes kill! Not kow-tow, makes kill! Kow-tow! Kow-tow!" The official was screaming again, and with my head on the earth I stole a sideways glance. This is what I saw.

The Paddy was a brave man – he absolutely hesitated. His face was crimson, and he glared and gulped horribly, and then he fell to his knees and put his face in the dust like the rest of us. Beyond him the Sawney was standing, frowning at the Prince as though he couldn't credit what he'd heard; his mouth was hanging slack, and I wondered was he still drunk. But he wasn't.

"Ye *what*?" says he, in that rasping gutter voice, and as the Prince glared and the little official jabbered, I heard the Irishman, hoarse and urgent:

"Fer God's sake, Moyes, get down! Ye bloody idiot, he'll kill ye, else! Get down, man!"

Moyes turned his head, and his eyes were wide in disbelief. By God, so were my ears. For clear as a bell, says he:

"Tae a —in' Chink? Away, you!"

And he stood straight as he could, stared at Prince Sang, and stuck out his dirty, unshaven chin.

For a full ten seconds there wasn't a sound, and then Sang screamed like an animal, and leaped from his chair. The Tartar, square in front of Moyes, brought the glittering axe-blade round slowly, within inches of the Scot's face, and then whirled it up, poised to strike. The official repeated the order to kow-tow – and Moyes lifted his chin just a trifle, looked straight at Sang, and spat gently out of the corner of his mouth.

154

Sang quivered as though he'd been struck, and for a moment I thought he'd spring at the bound man. But all he did was glare and hiss an order to the Tartar, who raised the axe still higher, his huge shoulders bunched to strike. The Irishman's voice sounded in a pleading croak:

"Jaysus, man – will ye do as he bids ye, for the love o' Mary? Ye'll be kilt, ye fool! He'll murther ye!"

"That'll mak' him a man afore his mither," says Moyes quietly, and for flat, careless contempt I never heard its equal. He stood like a rock – and suddenly the axe flashed down, with a hideous thud, his body was sent hurtling back, and I was face down in the dirt, gasping bile and sobbing with horror.

That was how it happened – the stories that he laughed in defiance, or made a speech about not bowing his head to any heathen, or recited a prayer, or even the tale that he died drunk – they're false. I'd say he was taken flat aback at the mere notion of kow-towing, and when it sank in, he wasn't having it, not if it cost him his life. You may ask, was he a hero or just a fool, and I'll not answer – for I know this much, that each man has his price, and his was higher than yours or mine. That's all. I know one other thing – whenever I hear someone say "Proud as Lucifer", I think, no, proud as Private Moyes.[22]

But I'd no time for philosophy just then; I was numb with shock and a blinding pain in my wounded head as they dragged us back to our cell, still in mortal fear of our lives; someone, I believe it was a coolie, loosed my bonds and poured water over my face and down my throat, and I remember the excruciating pain as the blood flowed back to my hands and feet. Gradually it eased, and I must have slept in that bed of stinking mud, for suddenly I was awake, and it was freezing cold, and though my skull was still aching dully, I was clear-headed – and I was alone in the cell and the door was open.

By the cold, and the dim light, it could only be dawn, and there was a cannonading shaking the ground, from not far away. It stopped of a sudden, with much Chinese yelling, and then came the crash of exploding Armstrongs, followed by a distant rattle of musketry, growing closer, and culminat-

155

ing in a babble of voices cheering. More shots, and steps pounding outside, and a voice bellowing excitedly: *"En avant! En avant! Chat huant! Chat huant!"*, and as I scrambled up, soaked in mud, I was thinking: "Frogs, and Bretons, at that!"[23] and I stumbled from the cell into the arms of a big cove in a blue overcoat and kepi, who gave back roaring in disgust from this muddy spectre pawing at him.

This was how it was. I'd been taken prisoner by the Tartars on the afternoon of August 12, and carried by them to the village of Tang-ku, the last Chink outpost before Taku Forts. I'd been groggy with the clout on my head until next day, when we'd been dragged out to the yard where Moyes was murdered. I must have lain in the cell through the next night, and when our people attacked Tang-ku at dawn on the 14th, and the Chinese fired a few salvoes and abandoned the place, leaving us unheeded – why, there I was. Where the Irishman and the coolies had gone, I'd no notion, but I gave it some thought while a Frog rifleman helped me back to a field dressing-station – and decided to be French for the moment. I mort-de-ma-vied and sacred-blued like anything while an orderly flung water over me to disperse my filth and then clapped a cold compress on my battered scalp. I gave him a torrent of garlic gratitude and withdrew from the bedlam of the station, muttering like an Apache, and considering, now that the peril was past, how to preserve my precious credit.

You see, I'd grovelled, and been seen to grovel, to that infernal Chink warlord – but only by a Paddy sergeant who didn't know me from Adam; besides, I'd been in khaki mufti and so plastered with dung as to be unrecognisable. I doubted if the Mick had even seen me at the grog-cart, it had all happened so quickly – so now, if I minded my step for a while, and covered my tracks, there was no earthly reason why the inconvenient Fenian (wherever he was) or anyone else, should ever identify the spruce and heroic Flashy, who would shortly appear at head-quarters, with the craven scarecrow who'd been first to knock head before the heathen's feet. Ve-ry good; all we needed was a razor and somebody's clean shirt and trousers . . .

It's a crying shame, as I keep telling Royal Commissions,

156

that among all the military manuals there ain't a line about foraging and decorating, those essential arts whereby the soldier keeps body and soul together in adversity. Offered to write 'em one, but they wouldn't have it, more fool them, for I've lifted everything from chickens to Crown Jewels, and could have set generations of young fellows right, if they'd let me. It was child's play to kit myself out after Tang-ku; the two miles back to Sinho was a carnival of support troops and baggage following the advance, setting up tents and quarters, and a great confusion through which I ambled, airing my French when I had to, and being taken, no doubt, for a rather unkempt commissariat-wallah, or a correspondent, or a Nonconformist missionary. Within ten minutes I'd replaced my soiled garments with a fine tussore coat, coolie pants, solar helmet, and umbrella, with a handsome morocco toilet case in my back pocket – and if you think that outlandish, let me tell you that armies were a deal more informally attired in my day. Campbell at Lucknow looked like a bus conductor, and old Raglan in the Crimea appeared to have robbed a jumble sale.

So when I'd shaved in a quiet corner, got rid of my bandages, and covered my cracked sconce with the topi, I was in pretty good fig, though feeling like a stretcher case. I hopped aboard an empty Frog ammunition cart going back to Sinho, spied Grant's marker by a covered wagon, and strolled up to report, swinging my gamp. Two staff infants were within, Addiscombe all over 'em.

"Hollo, my sons!" cries I cheerily, with my head splitting. "I'm Flashman. Not a bit of it, sit down, sit down! Don't tell me you haven't learned the great headquarters rule yet!"

They looked at each other, blushing and respectful in the presence of the celebrated beau sabreur. "No, sir," says one, nervously. "What's that?"

"Hark'ee, my boy. If bread is the staff of life, what is the life of the staff?"

"Dunno, sir," says he, grinning.

"One long loaf," says I, winking. "So take your ease, and tell me where's Sir Hope Grant?"

They said he was with the 60th, and when I inquired for

157

Elgin, they looked astonished and told me he was back at Pehtang.

"You mean I've trekked all across those confounded mud-flats for nothing? Now, that's too bad! Ah, well, Pehtang it must be. My compliments to Sir Hope, and tell Wolseley that if I hear he's been fleecing you young chaps at piquet, I'll call him out. So long, my sons!"

Alibi nicely established, you see, with two gratified young gallopers reporting that Flashy had just tooled in from the coast (which was true, give or take a couple of days). I could now depart for Pehtang in the certainty that no one would ever imagine I'd been near Tang-ku, and the scene of my shame. It's just a question of taking thought and pains, and well worth it.

I was feeling decidedly flimsy by now, and wondering if I'd last as far as Pehtang, but by good luck the first man I ran into outside Grant's wagon was Nuxban Khan, who'd been second to my blood-brother, Ilderim Khan, in the irregular horse at Jhansi. He hailed me with a great whoop and roarings in Pushtu, a huge Afghan thug in a sashed coat and enormous top-boots, grinning all over his dreadful face as he demanded how I did, and recalling those happy days when the Thugs all but had me outside the Rani's pavilion until he and Ilderim and the rest of the Khyber Co-operative Society arrived to carve them up so artistically. He was a great man now, *rissaldar* in Fane's Horse, and when he heard where I was bound nothing would do but I must travel in style in the regimental gig.

"Shall Bloody Lance walk, or ride like a common *sowar*? No, by God! Thou'lt ride like a rajah, old friend – ah, the Colonel husoor's pardon! – for the honour of Ilderim's band! Aye, Ilderim! He ate his last salt at Cawnpore, peace be with him!" Suddenly there were tears running down his evil face. "Bismillah! Where are such friends as Ilderim today? Or such foes? Have ye seen these Tartars, Bloody Lance? Mice! Aye, but we'll go mouse-hunting anon, thou and I!" Then he was shouting. "Hey, Probyn Sahib! Probyn Sahib! See who is here!"

And now he was making me known to Probyn, whom I'd never met – tall, handsome, soft-spoken Probyn, whom some

158

called the best irregular cavalryman since Skinner (though I'd have rated Grant above both). He was only a subaltern in his regular regiment, yet here he was, with an independent command of his own, and a V.C. to boot. He in turn presented a few of his officers, Afghans to a man, and as ugly a crowd as ever crossed the border, and it made me feel downright odd, when he indicated me as "Flashman bahadur", to see how they straightened and beamed and clicked their heels.

D'you know, it was like coming home? Suddenly, among those wicked friendly faces, with Nuxban exclaiming and Probyn smiling and eyeing me respectfully, the terror of the past two days melted away, and even my head didn't ache so fierce. I realised what it was – for the first time, in China, I wasn't alone: I had the best army on earth with me, the bravest of the brave, terrible men who hailed me as a comrade, and an admired comrade, at that – unless your belly's as yellow as mine, you can't imagine what it means. I felt downright proud, and safe at last.

Probyn rode along with me when I rolled off in Nuxban's gig, and for the first time I had a proper look at the great British and French army camped outside Sinho. On either side of the causeway road stretched the long lines of tents, white and khaki and green, with the guidons fluttering and the troops at exercise or loafing: here was a company of Frogs with their overcoats and great packs counter-marching on the right of the road to "Marche Lorraine", in competition with a Punjabi battalion, very trim in beards and tight puggarees, drilling to "John Peel" on the left; there was a Spahi squadron practising wheels at the gallop, the long cloaks flying, and a line of Probyn's riders, Sikhs and Afghans in shirt-sleeves, taking turns to ride full tilt past an officer who was tossing oranges in the air – they were taking 'em with their sabres on the fly, roars of applause greeting each successful cut.

"Fane's boys will be doing it with grapes tomorrow, I expect," says Probyn.

I said it was a pity the Chinese Emperor couldn't see 'em, and be brought to his senses – the neat artillery parks and rocket batteries, the endless lines of supply carts and ord-

159

nance wagons, manned by the milling Coolie Corps, whiskered Madrassis wrestling in their loin-cloths, brawny Gunners playing cricket on a mat wicket, bearded Sikhs grinding their lance-points on the emery wheel, green-jacketed 60th riflemen close-order-drilling like clockwork, a squadron of Dragoon Guards trotting by, each pith helmet and sloped sabre at an identical angle, Royals in their shirt-sleeves mingling with the Tirailleurs to swap baccy and gossip (it's damned sinister, if you ask me, how the Jocks and Frogs always drift together), and something that would have made his Celestial Majesty's eyes start from his princely head – two *sowars* of Fane's in full fig being *carried* carefully to their horses by their mates for guard-mounting, so that no speck of dust should blemish the perfection of tunic and long boots, or the polish of lance, sword, pistols, and carbine. Probyn eyed them jaundiced-like, stroking his fair moustache.

"If they take the stick[24] again, Fane'll be insufferable," says he. "What, you'd like the Manchoo Emperor to see all this? Don't fret, old fellah – he will."

He left me at the causeway, and I drove on alone to Pehtang, a moth-eaten village on the river boasting one decent house, where Elgin and his staff were quartered. I tiffined first with Temple of the military train, who deafened me with complaints about the condition of our transport – poor forage for the beasts, useless coolies, officers overworked ("for a miserly nine and sixpence a day buckshee, let me tell you!"), the native ponies were hopeless, the notion of issuing a three-day cooked ration in *this* climate was lunacy, and it was a rotten, piddling war, anyway, which no one at home would mind a bit. It sounded like every military train I'd seen.

"Frogs just a damned nuisance, of course – no proper provision, an' three days late," says he with satisfaction. "How the blazes Bonaparte ever got 'em on parade beats me. We should go without 'em."

Everyone says that about the French, and it's gospel true – until it's Rosalie's breakfast time*, and then Froggy'll be first into the breach ahead of us, just out of spite.

* Time for action. Rosalie was the long French sword-bayonet.

160

Elgin was in the backyard of his house, stamping about in his shirt-sleeves, snapping dictation at Loch, his secretary, while my Canton inquisitor, Parkes, sat by. I heard Elgin's sharp, busy voice before I saw him; as I halted in the gateway he turned, glaring like a belligerent Pickwick, and hailed me in mid-sentence with a bark and a wave.

". . . and I have the honour to refer your excellency to the Superintendent's letter of whenever-it-was . . . Ha, Flashman! At last! . . . and to repeat the assertion . . . wait, Loch, make that warning . . . aye, the warning conveyed in my notes of so-and-so and so-and-so . . . that unless we have your assurance . . . solemn assurance . . . that our ultimatum will be complied with directly . . ."

Still dictating, he rummaged in a letter-case and shoved a packet at me; to my astonishment it was addressed in my wife's simpleton scrawl, and I'd have pocketed it, but Elgin waved me peremptorily to read it, so I did, while he went on dictating full spate.

"Oh, my Darlingest Dear One, how I *long* to *see* you!" it began, and plunged straight into an account of how Mrs Potter was *positive* that the laundry were pinching our Best Linen sheets and sending back rubbish, so she had approved Mrs Potter's purchase of one of Williamson's new patent washing-machines and did I think it a *Great Extravagance*? "I am sure it must prove *Useful*, and a *Great Saving*. Shirts require no hand-rubbing! Qualified Engineers are prompt to carry out repairs, tho' such are seldom necessary Mrs Potter says." She (Elspeth, not Mrs Potter) loved me Excessively and had noticed in the press an Item which she was sure I must find *droll* – a Bishop's daughter had married the Rev. Edward Cheese! *Such* a comical name! She had been to Hanover Square to hear Mr Ryder read "MacBeth" – most *moving* altho' Shakespeare's notions of Scottish speech were *outlandish* and *silly*, and she and Jane Speedicut had been twice to "The Pilgrim of Love" at the Haymarket, and Jane had wept in a most *Affected* way "just to attract Attention, which she needn't have bothered in that unfortunate lilac gown, *so* out of style!!" She missed me, and *please*, I must not mind about the washing-machine for if she hadn't Mrs P. might have Given Notice! Little Havvy hoped his Papa would kill a Chinaman, and enclosed a picture of Jesus which he had drawn at school. "Oh, come to us soon, soon, dear Hero, to the fond arms of your Loving, *Adoring* Elspeth. x x x x x!!!"

I ain't given to sentimental tears, but it was a close thing, standing in that hot, dusty yard with the smell of China in my nostrils, holding that letter which I could picture her writing, sighing and frowning and nibbling her pen, rumpling her golden curls for inspiration, burrowing in her dictionary to see how many s's in "necessary", smiling fondly as she kissed young Havvy's execrable drawing – eleven years old the little brute was, and apparently thought Christ had a green face and feathers in his hair. If she'd written pages of Undying Devotion and slop, as she had in our young days, I'd have yawned at it – but all the nonsense about washing-machines and "MacBeth" and Jane's dress and the man Cheese was so . . . so *like* Elspeth, if you know what I mean, and I felt such a longing for her, just to sit by her, and have her hand in mind, and look into those beautiful wide blue eyes, and tear off her corset, and –

"Flashman!" Elgin was grasping my hand, demanding my news. "Ha! I'm glad to see you! You were despaired of at Shanghai!" The sharp eyes twinkled for an instant. "So you'll write directly to reassure that bonny little wife whose letter I brought, hey? She's in blooming health. Well, sit down, sit down! Tell me of Nanking."

So I did, and he listened with his bare forearms set on the table, John Bull to the life; he'd be fifty then, the Big Barbarian, as the Chinese called him, bald as an egg save for a few little white wisps, with his bulldog lip and sudden barks of anger or laughter. A peppery old buffer, and a deal kinder than he looked – how many ambassadors would call on a colonel's wife to carry a letter to her man? – and the shrewdest diplomatic of his day, hard as a hammer and subtle as a Spaniard. Best of all, he had common sense.

He'd made a name in the West Indies and Canada, nego-tiated the China treaty which we were now going to enforce, and had saved India, no question, by diverting troops from China at the outbreak of the Mutiny, without waiting orders from home. As to his diplomatic style – when the Yankees still had their eye on Canada, and looked like trying annexation, Elgin went through Washington's drawing-rooms like a devouring flame, wining and dining every Southern Democrat he could find, dazzling 'em with his blue blood, telling 'em racy stories, carrying on like Cheeryble – and hinting, ever so delicate, that if Canada joined the Great Republic, it would give the Northern Yankees a fine majority in Congress, with all those long-nosed Scotch Calvinists (to say nothing of French Papists) becoming American voters overnight. *That* set the fire-bells ringing from Charleston to the Gulf, and with the South suddenly dead set against annexation – why Canada never did join the U.S.A., did she? Wily birds, these earls – this one's father had pinched all the best marbles in Greece, so you could see they were a family to be watched.[25]

"An unsavoury crew of fanatics," was his comment when I'd told him of the Taipings. "Well, thanks to you, we should be able to keep them from Shanghai, and once the treaty's signed, their bolt's shot. The Imperial Chinese Government can set about 'em in earnest – with our tacit support, but not our participation. Eh, Parkes?"

"Yes . . . the trouble is, my lord," says Parkes, "that those two terms have a deplorable habit of becoming synonymous."

"Synonymous be damned!" snaps Elgin. "H.M.G. will not be drawn into war against the Taipings. We'd find ourselves with a new empire in China before we knew it." He heaved up from the table and poured coffee from a spirit kettle. "And I have no intention, Parkes, of presiding over any extension of the area in which we exhibit the hollowness of our Christianity and our civilisation. Coffee, Flashman? Yes, you can light one of your damned cheroots if you want to – but blow the smoke the other way. Poisoning mankind!"

There you have three of Elgin's fads all together – he hated tobacco, was soft on Asiatics, and didn't care for empire-building. I recall him on this very campaign saying he'd do anything "to prevent England calling down God's curse on herself for brutalities committed on yet another feeble Oriental race." Yet he did more to fix and maintain the course of British empire than any man of his day, and is remembered for the supreme atrocity. Ironic, ain't it?

The letter he'd been dictating had been yet another demand to the local Manchoo governor for free passage to Pekin, which the Chinks had previously agreed to – and were now hindering for all they were worth, as at Sinho and Tang-ku.

"Perhaps when we've stormed the forts they may realise the folly of resistance," says Loch. He was a tall, grave young file with a great beard, who looked a muff until you learned he'd been a Navy middy at 13, aide to Gough at 17, adjutant of Skinner's Horse at 23, and come through Sutlej and Crimea. Parkes laughed.

"Why should they? The Emperor's not there; he won't suffer. Nor his ministers, Prince Sang and the like, who feed him vain lies about sweeping us into the sea. The Emperor believes them, the decree goes forth, the local commanders put up a futile fight, and send wild accounts to Pekin of how they've licked us. So the fool's encouraged in his folly, and all his concubines clap their little hands and tell him he's lord of creation."

"He's bound to learn the truth eventually, though."

"In the Imperial Palace? My dear Loch, it's another world! Suppose they *do* learn they've lost Sinho, for example – it won't have happened before their eyes, at Pekin, so . . . it simply didn't happen, you see? That's Chinese Imperial logic."

"Who's Prince Sang?" I asked, remembering the swine who'd had Moyes butchered – and to whom I'd kow-towed.

"A brute and a firebrand," grunts Elgin. "Prince Sang-kol-in-sen – our fellows call him Sam Collinson. Mongol general commanding the Emperor's forces; he's in the Taku Forts this minute, which is why we'll certainly have to fight for them." 'Nuff said; I'd met Prince Sang.

I asked when we'd advance on the forts, and he glowered and said, in a week, twiddling his scanty wing of hair, a sure sign of irritation.

"We're too damned cumbersome by half!" says he. "I told Palmerston five thousand men would do; but no, Parliament thinks we're still fighting the damned Bengal sepoys, so we must have three times that number." He champed and

164

snorted, tugging away. "A confounded waste of men, material, and time! Wait till the Commons get the bill, though! And to be sure, the fools of public will ask what it was for – they'll expect victories, a dozen V.C.s, and enough blood and massacre to make their flesh creep. Well, they'll not get 'em if I can help it! This is not a war, but an embassy. And this is not an expeditionary force, it's an escort!"

He'd gone quite pink, and by the way Parkes was pulling his nose and Loch studying the distance, I could guess it was a well-played air. After a moment he left off trying to pull his hair loose.

"Our assault on Taku will take a week to prepare because the field command changes daily, to keep the French happy – Grant handed over to Montauban *during* our attack on Sinho, if you please! Oh, 'twas safe enough, and Montauban's a sensible man – but it's not a system that makes for expedition. We'd have been better with a small, mobile force – and no French.[26] Ah, well!" He gave his hair a final wrench and suddenly grinned. "We shall have to see. Eh, Loch? As our old nurses would have said, 'a sair fecht'. For your benefit, Parkes, that means a long, weary struggle."

How long, I asked Parkes when he showed me to my billet, and he pursed his lips officially.

"To Pekin? Oh, a month, perhaps . . . six weeks?"

"God save us – you ain't serious?"

"I try to be. Elgin's perfectly correct – we're too many, and Sir Hope, with his many fine qualities is . . . methodical. What with the French, and the Manchoos lying and procrastinating at every step . . . well, as his lordship's interpreter, I expect to be chin-chinning to Chinamen quite excessively." He paused in my doorway and gave a resigned sigh. "Ah, well . . . at least it should be a quiet little war. We dine at six, by the way; a coat is sufficient."

✿ The great Taku Forts went down on the 21st, as advertised, to the astonishment of the Manchoos, who thought them impregnable, and the chagrin of the Frogs, who had violently opposed Grant's plan of attack. They wanted to assail the forts on both sides of the river; Grant said no, settle the Great North Fort and the job's done. Montauban squawked and hooted, saying it was an affront to military science, but Grant just shook his head: "North fort goes, rest'll submit. You'll see. Bonjour," and carried on, humming bull-fiddle tunes. His force might be unwieldy, as Elgin said, but it was damned expert: he built two miles of road to the approaches, had volunteers swimming the river by night to mine the defences, hammered the place with siege guns and a naval bombardment, and sent in the infantry with pontoons and ladders to carry the walls – and sure enough, the infuriated Crapauds made sure they got in first.

Your correspondent bore no part beyond loafing up, when the Chinese guns had been safely silenced, to offer cheer and comfort to Major Temple before the final assault. A week ago he'd been damning his coolies for useless, but now he was in a desperate fret for their welfare – they were to carry in the scaling ladders in the teeth of cannon, jingal-fire, spears, stinkpots and whatever else the Manchoos were hurling from the walls, and Temple, the ass, was determined to go in with them. I found him croaking under his brolly, waiting for the word, but for once his complaint wasn't a military one.

"These bloody magistrates!" cries he. "Have you seen the *China Mail*? Heenan's been held to bail at Derby, an' he an' Sayers are to be charged with assault! Damned nonsense! Why can't they leave sport alone?[27] Ahah!" he roars, waving

166

to the Frog colonel. "Ready, are we? Sortons, is that it? Come on, you chaps! China forever!" And he was away, bounding over the ditches, with his yellow mob at his heels and the Frog infantry in full cry, bursting with la gloire. They had warm work crossing the moats and canals, but they and our own 44th and 67th carried the walls with the bayonet – and as Grant had said, out came the white silk flags on the other forts. Four hundred Manchoos were killed out of five hundred; we lost about 30, and ten times as many wounded. The coolies behaved famously, Temple said.

Parkes and Loch and I were in the party sent across the river to arrange terms with Hang-Fu, the local mandarin, a leery ancient with the opium shakes who received us in a garden, sitting on a chair of state with a mighty block of ice underneath to keep him cool, and his minions carrying his spectacles and chopsticks and silver watch in embroidered cases. He served us champagne, but when Parkes demanded a signed surrender the old fox said he daren't, not being military, and Prince Sang had already left up-river.

Parkes then came all over diplomatic, promising to blow the forts to kingdom come, at which Hang-Fu said, well, the Emperor would be graciously pleased to give us temporary occupation of them (which we already had) and we could take our gunboats up to Tientsin. Parkes almost had to take him by the throat to get it in writing, and then we ploughed back to the boat in the dark, past the huge gloomy fort-buildings, with slow-fuse mines which the Chinks had thoughtfully left behind exploding here and there. (Another trick was to bury cocked gun-locks with bags of powder, for the unwary to tread on; subtle, eh? – and yet some of their fort guns were wooden dummies.) I was never so glad to get back to a boat in my life.

So now the way was clear, and with the gunboats leading the way up the twisty moonlit river, it began: the famous march on Pekin, the last great stronghold on earth that had never seen a white soldier, the Forbidden City of the oldest of civilisations, the capital of the world, to the Chinese, having dominion over all mankind. And now the foreign devils were coming, the whining pipes echoing out across the sodden plain, the jaunty little *poilus* with their kepis tilted, stepping it out, the jingling troopers of Fane's and Probyn's with the sun a-twinkle on their lance-heads, the Buffs swinging by to the odd little march that Handel wrote for them (so Grant told me)[28], the artillery limbers churning up the mud, the Hampshire yokels and Lothian ploughboys, the Sikhs and Mahrattas and Punjabis, McCleverty bare to the waist in the prow of his gunboat, Wolseley halting his pony to sketch a group of coolies, Napier riding silent, shading his eyes ahead, Elgin sitting under the awning of *Coromandel* fanning himself with his hat and reading *The Origin of Species*, Montauban careering up and down the columns with great dash, chattering to his staff, Grant standing by the roadside, tugging his grizzled whiskers and touching his cap to the troops who cheered him as they marched by. Fifteen thousand horse, foot and guns rolling up the Peiho, not to fight or to hold or to conquer, but just so that the Big Barbarian could stand before the Son of Heaven and watch him put his mark on paper. "And when he does," says Elgin, "the ends of the earth will have met at last, and there will be no more savage kings for our people to subdue. We've come a long way from our northern forests; I wonder if we were wise."

The Chinese evidently thought not, for having given us fawning assurance of free passage and no resistance, they hampered us every yard to Tientsin. Transport and beasts had vanished from the country, the local officials used every excuse to delay us, and to make things worse the weather was at extremes of broiling heat and choking dust or deluges of rain and axle-deep mud[29]. Fortunately the Manchoos hadn't had the wit to break bridges or block channels, and the peasantry, with a fine disregard for Imperial policy, were perfectly ready to repair our road and sell us beef and mutton, fruit, vegetables and ice at twenty times their proper price. Snug on *Coromandel*, I could endure our leisurely progress, but Parkes was plumb in the path of all the Manchoos' growing insolence and deceit, and I could see his official smile getting tighter by the hour.

"At this rate we may reach Pekin by Christmas. The more we submit to their lies and hindrance, the less they respect us." He was at the rail, glaring coldly at the glittering salt-

168

heaps that lined the banks below Tientsin. "In '58, after we shelled Canton, the river banks were black with Chinese – kow-towing. You will observe, Sir Harry, that they do not kow-tow today. Much as I admire our chief, I cannot share his recently-expressed satisfaction that in these enlightened times we no longer require every Chinaman to take off his hat to us."

But even Elgin's patience was beginning to wear thin. Somehow he preserved a placid politeness through every meeting with Manchoo officials who barely concealed their satisfaction in wasting time and frustrating our progress, but afterwards he'd be in a fever to get on, snapping at us, tugging his fringe, urging Grant and Montauban with an energy that stopped just short of rudeness; Montauban would bridle and Grant would nod, and then we staff-men would get pepper again. He was bedevilled, trying to keep the Chinks sweet and the advance moving, fearful of provoking downright hostility, but knowing that every hour lost was time for the war party in Pekin to get their nerve back after Taku; we knew Sang-kol-in-sen was back in the capital, urging resistance, and Elgin in his impatience was being tempted by a new Manchoo ploy – speedy passage to Pekin in return for a promise of active British help against the Taipings, which he daren't concede or bluntly refuse.[30]

It took us ten crawling days to cover sixty miles to Tientsin, a stink-hole of salt-heaps and pi-dogs – and smiling Manchoo mandarins sent by Pekin to "negotiate" our further progress. They talked for a full week, while Parkes risked apoplexy – and Elgin nodded gravely, with his lip stuck out. Finally, after interminable discussion, they agreed that we might advance to Tang-chao, eleven miles from Pekin – provided we didn't take artillery or too many gunboats to alarm the people – and from there Elgin and Baron Gros might go into Pekin with a thousand cavalry for escort, and sign the damned treaty. It seemed too good to be true – although Grant looked grim at the smallness of the escort – but Elgin accepted, hiding his satisfaction. And then the mandarins, smiling more politely than ever, said of course they couldn't confirm these arrangements, but doubtless Pekin would do so if we were patient a little longer . . .

169

If Bismarck or D'Israeli or Metternich had had to sit through those interminable hours, listening to those bland, lying old dotards, and then received that slap in the face, I swear they'd have started to scream and smash the furniture. Elgin didn't even blink. He listened to Parkes's near-choked translation of that astounding insolence, thanked the mandarins for their courtesy, stood up, bowed – and told Parkes, almost offhand, to pass 'em the word that they now owed Britain four million quid for delays and damage to our expedition. Oh, aye, and the treaty would now contain a clause opening Tientsin to European trade.

Back on *Coromandel* he was grimly satisfied. "Their bad faith affords the perfect excuse for proceeding to Pekin forthwith. Sir Hope, the army will no longer halt when discussions take place; if they want to talk we'll do it on the march. And if they don't like it, and want a fight, they can have it."

Suddenly everyone was grinning; even Parkes was delighted, although he confided to me later that Elgin should have taken a high hand sooner. Elgin himself looked ten years younger, now that he'd cast the die, but I thought exuberance had got the better of him when he strode into the saloon later, threw *The Origin of Species* on the table, and announced:

"It's very original, no doubt, but not for a hot evening. What I need is some trollop."

I couldn't believe my ears, and him a church-goer, too. "Well, my lord, I dunno," says I. "Tientsin ain't much of a place, but I'll see what I can drum up –"

"Michel's been reading *Dr Thorne* since Taku," cries he. "He must have finished it by now, surely! Ask him, Flashman, will you?" So I did, and had my ignorance enlightened.[31]

It was bundle and go now. We left 2nd Division at Tientsin, shed all surplus gear, and cracked away at twice our previous pace, while the Manchoos plagued Elgin with appeals to stop the advance – they would appoint new commissioners, they had further proposals, there must be a pause for discussion – and Elgin replied agreeably that he'd talk to 'em at Tang-chao, as agreed. The Manchoos were frantic, and now we

170

saw something new – great numbers of refugees, ordinary folk, streaming *towards* us from Pekin, in evident fear of what would happen when we arrived. They flooded past us, men, women, and children, with their possessions piled on rickety carts – I remember one enormous Mongol wheeling four women in a barrow. But no sign of armed opposition, and when our local guides and drivers decamped one night, spirits were so high that no one minded, and Admiral Hope and Bowlby, the *Times* correspondent, took over as mule-skinners, whooping and hawing like Deadwood Dick. We swung on up-river, the gunboats keeping pace and the Frog band thumping "Madelon", for now Pekin was barely thirty miles ahead, and we were going to see the elephant at last, seven thousand cavalry and infantry ready for anything, not that it mattered for the Manchoo protests had subsided to whines of resignation, and we were coming home on a tight rein, hurrah, boys, hurrah!

And the dragon . . . waited.

*   *   *

It happened the day after we held divine service in a big temple, and afterwards there was much fun while we looked over a book of pictures which Beato, who'd been photographing the march, presented to Elgin. Word came that new Manchoo commissioners, including the famous Prince I, were waiting just up ahead, at Tang-chao, and they hoped the army would camp on the near side of the town while we negotiated the details of Elgin's entry to Pekin.

"Go and see him," says Elgin to Parkes, so on the Monday, in the cool of a beautiful dawn, about thirty of us set out to ride ahead. There was Parkes, Loch, De Normann from Bruce's office, Bowlby of *The Times*, and myself, with six Dragoon Guards and twenty of Fane's *sowars* under young Anderson, as escort. Walker, the Q.M.G., and Thompson of the commissariat rode along to inspect the camp site.

We trotted up the dusty road, myself in the lead as senior officer, with Parkes (who rode like an ill-tied sack of logs,

171

by the way). To our right was the river, half a mile off, and on our left empty plain and millet fields to the horizon. Beyond a little village we were met by a mandarin with a small troop of Tartar cavalry, who said he would show us our camp-site; it proved to be to the right of the road, where the river took a great loop, near a village called Five-li Point. Walker and I thought it would do, although he'd have preferred to be closer to the river, for water; the mandarin assured us that water would be brought to us, and as we rode on he chatted amiably to Parkes and me, telling us he'd been in command of the garrison we'd defeated at Sinho.

"As you can see." He touched the button on his hat; it was white, not red. "I was also degraded by losing my peacock feather," he added, grinning like a corpse, and Parkes and I made sounds of commiseration. "Oh, it is no matter!" cries he. "Lost honours can be regained. As Confucius says: Be patient, and at last the mulberry leaf will become a silk robe."

I remember the proverb, because it was just then that I chanced to look round. The six Dragoons had been riding immediately behind Parkes and me since we set out, in double file, but I'd paid 'em no special heed, and it was only as I glanced idly back that I saw one of them was watching me – staring at me, dammit, with the oddest fixed grin. He was a typical burly Heavy with a face as red as his coat under the pith helmet, and I was just about to ask what the devil he meant by it when his grin broadened – and in that moment I knew him, and knew that he knew me. It was the Irishman who'd been beside me when Moyes was killed.

I must have gaped like an idiot . . . and then I was facing front again, chilled with horror. This was the man who'd seen me grovelling to Sam Collinson, my abject companion in shame – and here he was, riding at my shoulder like bloody Nemesis, no doubt on the point of denouncing me to the world as a poltroon – it's a great thing to have a conscience as guilty as mine, I can tell you; it always makes you fear far more than the worst. My God! And yet – it couldn't be! the Irishman had been a sergeant of the 44th; this was a trooper of Dragoon Guards. I must be mistaken; he hadn't been

172

staring at me at all – he must have been grinning at some
joke of his mate's, when I'd caught his eye, and my terrified
imagination was doing the rest –

"Where the hell d'you think you're goin', Nolan?" It was
the Dragoon corporal, just behind. "Keep in file!"

Nolan! That had been the name Moyes had spoken – oh,
God, it was him, right enough.

I daren't look round; I'd give myself away for certain. I
must just ride on, chatting to Parkes as though nothing had
happened, and God knows what I said, or how much farther
we rode, for I was aware of nothing except that my cowardly
sins had found me out at last. You may think I was in a great
stew over nothing – what had the great Flashy to fear from
the memory of a mere lout of a trooper, after all? A hell of
a deal, says I, as you'll see.

But if I was in a state of nervous funk for the rest of
the day, I remember the business we did well enough. At
Tang-chao, we met the great Prince I, the Emperor's cousin,
a tall, skinny crow of a Manchoo in gorgeous green robes,
with *all* his nails cased; he looked at us as if we were dirt,
and when Parkes said we hoped the arrangements agreed for
Elgin's entry to Pekin were still satisfactory to their side, he
hissed like an angry cat.

"Nothing can be discussed until the barbarian leader has
withdrawn his presumptuous request for an audience with the
Son of Heaven, and begged our pardon! He does not come
to Pekin!"

Parkes, to my surprise, just smiled at him as though he
were a child and said they must really talk about something
important. Elgin was going to Pekin, and the Emperor would
receive him. Now, then . . .

At this Prince I went wild, spitting curses, calling Parkes
a foreign cur and reptile and I don't know what, and Parkes
just smiled away and said Elgin would be there, and that was
that. And in this way the time passed until (it's a fact) six
o'clock, when Prince I had cursed himself hoarse. Then
Parkes got up, repeated for the four hundredth time that
Elgin was going to Pekin – and suddenly Prince I said, very
well, with a thousand cavalry, as agreed. Then in double
time he and Parkes settled the wording of a proclamation

173

informing the public that peace and harmony were the order of the day, and we retired to the quarters that had been prepared for us, and had dinner.

"Who said the Chinese were negotiators!" scoffs Parkes. "The man's a fool and a fraud."

"He caved in very suddenly," says Loch. "D'you trust him?"

"No, but I don't need to. Their goose is cooked, Loch, and they know it, and because they can't abide it, they squeal like children in a tantrum. And if he goes back on his word tomorrow, it doesn't matter – because the Big Barbarian is going to Pekin, anyway."

It was arranged that in the morning, while De Normann and Bowlby (who wanted some copy for his rag) would stay in Tang-chao with Anderson and the *sowars*, the rest of us would return to the army, Parkes and Loch to report to Elgin, Walker and I to guide them to the camp site. The others turned in early, except for Parkes, who had invited one of the lesser mandarins over for a chat, so I retired to the verandah to rehearse my anxieties for the umpteenth time, able to sweat and curse in private at last.

Nolan knew me. What would he say – what *could* he say? Suppose he told the shameful truth, would anyone believe him? Never. But why should he say anything – dammit, he'd grovelled, too . . . I went all through my horrid fears again and again, pacing in the dark little garden away from the house, chewing my cheroot fiercely. What *would* he say –

"A foine evenin', colonel," was what, in fact, he said, and I spun round with an oath. There he was, by the low wall at the garden foot – standing respectfully to attention, rot him, the trooper out for an evening stroll, greeting his superior with all decorum. I choked back a raging question, and forced myself to say nonchalantly:

"Why, I didn't see you there, my man. Yes, a fine evening."

I hoped to God it was too shadowy for him to see me trembling. I lit another cheroot, and he moved forward a step.

"Beg pardon, sorr . . . don't ye remember me?"

I had myself in hand now. "What? You're one of the dragoons, aren't you?"

"Yes, sorr. I mean afore that, sorr." He had one of those soft, whiny, nut-at-ahl Irish brogues which I find especially detestable. "Whin I wuz in the 44th – afore dey posted me to the Heavies. Shure, an' it's just a month since – I think ye mind foine."

"Sorry, my boy," says I pleasantly, my heart hammering. "I don't know much of the 44th, and I certainly don't know you." I gave him a nod. "Good-night."

I was turning away when his voice stopped me, suddenly soft and hard together. "Oh, but ye do, sorr. An' I know you. An' we both know where it wuz. At Tang-ku, when Moyes got kilt."

What should an innocent man say to that? I'll tell you: he turns sharp, frowning, bewildered. "When *who* was killed? What the devil are you talking about? Are you drunk, man?"

"No, sorr, I'm not drunk! Nor I wuzn't drunk then! You wuz in the yard at Tang-ku whin they made us bow down to yon Chink bastard –"

"Silence! You're drunker than David's sow! You're raving! Now, look here, my lad – you cut along to your billet and I'll say no more –"

"Oh, but ye will! Ye will dat!" He was shaking with excitement. "But first ye'll listen! For I know, ye see, an' I can say plenty more –"

"How dare you!" I forced myself to bark. "You insolent rascal! I don't know what you're talking about, or what your game is, but another word from you and I'll get you a bloody back for your damned insolence, d'ye hear?" I towered, outraged, glaring like a colonel. "I'm a patient man, Nolan, but . . ."

It was out before I knew it, and he saw the blunder as soon as I did. The eyes bulged with triumph in his crimson face.

"Whut's dat? Nolan, d'ye say? An' if ye don't know me, how the hell d'ye know me name, den?"

In fact, I'd heard his corporal use it that day, but in my panic I remembered only Moyes at the grog-cart. I was speechless, and he rattled on excitedly:

"It wuz you! By the Virgin, it *wuz* you in that yard, crawlin' wid the rest on us, me an' the coolies – iveryone but Moyes! I didn't know yez from Rafferty's pig – till I seed ye in the lines, two days since, an' rec'nised ye! I did that! An' I asked the boys: 'Who's dat?' They sez: 'Shure, an' dat's Flash Harry, the famous Afghan hero, him that wan the Cross at Lucknow, an' kilt all the Ruskis, an' that. Shure, 'tis the bravest man in th'Army, so it is.' Dat's whut they said." He paused, getting his breath back in his excitement, and for the life of me I could only mouth at him. He stepped closer, breathing whisky at me. "An' I sez nuthin', but I thinks, is that a fact, now? 'Cos I seen him when he wuzn't bein' so bloody heroical, lickin' a Chinese nigger's boots an' whinin' fer his life!"

If I'd been heeled, I'd have shot him then and there, and damn the consequences. For there was no doubt he had me, or where he was going. He nodded, bright-eyed, and licked his coarse lips.

"Aye, so I got to studyin'. An' whut d'ye think? Sez I to meself, 'Shure, whut a hell of a pity it'd be, if this wuz to get about, like.' In the Army, ye know? I mean – even if iveryone said, och, it's just Paddy Nolan lyin' again – d'ye not think there's some might believe the shave*, eh? There'd be questions, mebbe; there might even be wan hell of a scandal." He shook his head, leering. "Talk, colonel. Ugly talk. Ye know what I mean? Bad for the credit o' th'Army. Aye, a bloody back's a sore thing, so it is – but it heals faster'n a blown reppitation." He paused a moment. "I'd think, meself, it'd be worth keepin' quiet. Wouldn't you, colonel?"

I could bluster still – or not. Better not; it would be a waste of time. This was a cunning swine; if he spread his story as well as he'd summed it up, I was done for, disgraced, ruined. I knew my Army, you see, and the jealousies and hatreds under the hearty grins. Oh, I didn't lack for enemies who'd delight in sniffing it all out, prying till they found Carnac, compared dates, put two and two together – where had I been on August 13, eh? Even if I could bluff it away, the mud would stick. And this sly peasant could see clear through; he

* Rumour.

176

knew he didn't have to prove a thing, that being guilty I'd be ready to fork out to prevent any breath of rumour –

"Sir Harry! Are you there?" It was Parkes's voice, calling sharply from the verandah twenty yards away; his figure was silhouetted against the glow from the house. "Sir Harry?"

Nolan took a swift step back into the shadows. " 'Tis another word we'll be havin' tomorrow, colonel – eh?" he whispered. "Until den." I heard his soft chuckle as I turned to the house, still stricken dumb, with Parkes crying: "Ah, there you are! Care for a nightcap?"

How much sleep I got you may imagine. I couldn't defy the brute – the question was whether it was safer to pay squeeze and risk his blabbing another day, or kill him and try to make it look accidental. That was how desperate I was, and it was still unresolved when we saddled up at dawn to ride back to the army. As the party fell in under the trees, a sudden reckless devil took hold of me, and I told the dragoon corporal I'd inspect the escort; Parkes cocked an amused eyebrow at this military zeal, while the corporal bawled his troopers into mounted line. I rode slowly along, surveying each man carefully while they sweated in the sun; I checked one for a loose girth, asked the youngest how long he'd been in China, and came to Nolan on the end, staring red-faced to his front. A fly settled on his cheek, and his lip twitched.

"Let it be, my boy," says I, jocular-like. "If a fly can sit still, so can you. Name and service?"

"Nolan, sorr. Twelve years." His brow was running wet, but he sat like a statue, wondering what the hell I was about.

"Trahnsferred las' month, sir, when 44th went dahn to Shang'ai," says the corporal. "Cavalry trained, tho'; in the Skins, I b'lieve."

"Why'd you transfer, Nolan?" I asked idly, and he couldn't keep his voice steady.

"If ye please, sorr . . . I . . . I tuk a fancy to see Pee-kin, sorr."

"Looking for excitement, eh?" I smiled. "Capital! Very good, corporal – form up."

If you ask what I was up to . . . why, I was taking a closer look by daylight – and unsettling the bastard; it never hurts.

177

But it was a wasted effort, for in the next hour everything changed, and even disgrace and reputation ceased to matter . . . almost.

The road had been empty coming up, but from the moment we left Tang-chao we were aware of a steady movement of Imperial troops – a few odd platoons and half-sections at first, and then larger numbers, not only on the road but in the paddy and millet-fields either side. What seemed most odd, they were moving in the same direction as ourselves – towards our army. I didn't like the look of 'em above half, but there was nothing to do but forge ahead. We rode at a steady canter for about an hour, past increasing numbers, and when we came to Chang-kia-wan, about half-way home, the town was thick with them, and there was no doubt of it: we were in the middle of a thumping big Imperial army. Parkes wanted to stop to make inquiries, the ass, but as senior officer I wouldn't allow it, and we cantered out of the place – and had to skirt the road to pass a full regiment of Bannermen, great ugly devils in bamboo armour who scowled and shouted abuse at us as we thundered by.

"What can this mean?" cries Parkes, as we drew clear. "They cannot intend to put themselves in Sir Hope's way, surely?"

"They ain't going to a field day!" says I. "Colonel Walker, how many d'you reckon we've come through?"

"Ten thousand, easily," says he. "But God knows how many there are in the millet-fields – those stalks are fifteen feet high."

"Take the rear, and keep 'em closed up!" says I. "Forward!"

"My dear Sir Harry!" cries Parkes. "Surely we should stop and consider what is to be done!"

"What's to be done is get to the Army. Close up, there!"

"But, my dear sir! They cannot mean any treachery, I –"

"Mr Parkes," says I, "when you've ridden through as many armies as I have, you learn how to smell mischief – and it's breast-high here, I can tell you."

"But we must not exhibit any signs of distrust!"

"Right you are," says I. "Anyone who pukes or soils himself will answer to me!" Which had the troopers haw-

178

hawing, while Parkes looked furious. "Really, sir – if they intended any harm, would they advance in full view? Why, the country to our right is quite clear!"

So it was, and the millet was so high to the left that for a moment we seemed all alone. I glanced right – and Walker was doing the same thing. Our eyes met, and I grabbed Parkes's bridle as we rode, heading him out to the right, while he demanded to know what I was about.

"You'll see," I told him. What Walker and I had noticed was a big nullah away on the right, and now we went for it full lick, turning down its lip as we reached it, and Parkes gave a great cry of astonishment, and would have reined in, but I kept him going.

"In full view, eh?" says I. "That settles it!"

There were three thousand Tartar horsemen in that nullah if there was one, dismounted, with drawn sabres, and they gave a great roar at the sight of us. But now I had us heading left again, towards the road and the little village beyond which lay the camp-site to which our army would presently be advancing. As we thundered past it a little group of horsemen broke cover, led by a mandarin who yelled at us to keep away. Beyond him I could see the guns in the trees.

"Masked battery!" cries Walker. "Jesus – look at that!"

As we came through the fringe of trees to the camp-site, the whole eastern horizon seemed to be moving. Immediately to our left, a long bund stretched away, and it was lined with heavy guns, covering the camp-site; in the millet behind the bund the country was alive with Tiger soldiers, the black and yellow stripes clear to be seen, but on the eastern flank of the plain was the sight that had brought Walker up in his stirrups – long lines of Tartar cavalry, advancing at the walk, thousands upons thousands of them. We raced out into the unoccupied camp-site, and suddenly Parkes reined in, white-faced.

"Sir Harry! Stop, if you please!" I reined up, and the whole troop followed. "Sir Harry, I am returning to Tang-chao! I must inform Prince I of this . . . this extraordinary proceeding!"

I couldn't believe it – and then I realised his pallor wasn't fear, but anger. He was in a positive fury, so help me.

179

"Good God!" I cried. "D'you think he doesn't *know*?"

"It is impossible that he should! Mr Loch, will you return to Lord Elgin at once, and inform him of what is happening? Sir Harry, I must ask for a small escort, if you please. One trooper will be sufficient."

I'm a true-blue craven, as you know, but I'm also too old a soldier to waste time raving. "You'll never come out alive," says I.

"No, you are mistaken. I shall be perfectly safe. My person is inviolate."

D'ye know, it was on the tip of my tongue to holler "It may be in bloody lilac stripes for all the good it'll do you!" but I kept a grip, thinking in the saddle. It must be a good ten miles to the army, with God knew how many Chinese along the road; if there was trouble it would be here, and the risk of cutting and running was appalling. The prospect of returning to Tang-chao was even worse – except for one thing. Parkes was right: *he* was inviolate. Whoever the Chinks cut up, it wouldn't be Her Majesty's biggest diplomatic gun bar Elgin himself; they wouldn't dare that. It came home to me with blinding clarity that the one safe place in the whole ugly mess was alongside H. Parkes, Esq.

"Very good, Mr Parkes," says I. "I'll ride with you. Corporal, detail two dragoons as escort. Mr Loch, take one trooper, ride to the army, inform Sir Hope and Lord Elgin. Colonel Walker, remain here with the rest of the party to observe; retire at discretion. Corporal," I drew him aside; he was a rangy lantern-jawed roughneck with a tight chin-strap. "If it gets ugly, scatter and ride through, d'ye hear? Get to Grant – whatever anyone else says, tell him – Flashy says 'Close up.' Mind that. I'm counting on you . . . Mr Loch, what the dooce are you waiting for? Be off – at a steady canter! Don't run! Mr Parkes, I suggest we lose no time!"

Doing my duty by the army, you see, before bolting to what I hoped to God was safety. I glanced round: Tartar cavalry two miles to the left, closing slowly; masked batteries on the bund – and now the concealed Tartars emerging from the nullah to the right, streaming down in a great mass. The camp-site was a death-trap . . . but Grant would steer clear

180

of it. I slapped Parkes's screw, and we raced away, the two dragoons at our heels, back through the trees and on to the Tang-chao road.

Before we'd gone a mile I was breathing easy; whether all the troops we'd seen coming down had now reached the camp-site, I don't know, but the way was clear, and when we met Chinese they didn't attempt to stay us. We were in Tang-chao under the hour, and while Parkes hurried off to find Prince I, I set the dragoons searching for Anderson and the others. It was only then that I realised one of my dragoons was Nolan. Hollo, thinks I, we may find advantage in this yet.

Tang-chao ain't a big place, and I found two Sikh troopers near the bazaar. Bowlby Sahib was buying silk, says they, grinning, and sure enough he was festooned in the stuff, with his money on the table while the vendor shook his sticks to determine the price, with Anderson and De Normann chaffing and half a dozen *sowars* chortling round the stall.

"I can't gamble with *Times* money!" Bowlby was laughing, pink in the face. "Delane will go through my accounts himself, I tell you! I say, Anderson, tell him to name a price and I'll cough it up, hang it!"

I tapped Anderson's arm. "Everyone to the square, quietly, in two's and three's. No fuss. We're riding in ten minutes."

Good boy, Anderson; he nodded, called a joke to De Normann, passed word to his *jemadar*, and the Sikhs began to drift off, slow and easy. I left him to bring Bowlby, and went to find another horse from our two remounts; I ride thirteen stone, and if there was one thing I wanted it was a fresh beast.

Anderson had his troop ready in the square by the temple – loafing so as not to attract notice, I was glad to see – and there was nothing to do but wait for Parkes and tell De Normann and Bowlby what had happened. It was roasting hot now, in the dusty square; the beasts stamped and jingled, and the *sowars* yawned and spat, while Anderson strolled, hands in pockets, whistling; my nerves were stretching. I can tell you, when there was a clatter of hooves, and who should it be but Loch, with two *sowars* carrying white flags on their lance-points, and young Brabazon, a staff-walloper.

Yes, Loch had seen Grant, and after reporting had felt bound to return for Parkes and me; he said it almost apologetically, blinking and stroking his beard, while I marvelled at human folly. The Imps were in greater force than ever at the camp-site, and in Loch's opinion, presenting a most threatening appearance, but while Montauban had been all for a frontal attack, Grant was sitting tight, to give us time to get clear. That cheered me up, for if he didn't advance the Imps would have nothing to shoot at, and all might blow over; but it was still gruelling work waiting for Parkes; I beguiled the time trying to think of fatal errands on which I might despatch Trooper Nolan, who was sitting aside, puffing his pipe, his bright little eyes sliding every so often in my direction.

Suddenly here was Parkes, riding alone, pausing to scribble furiously in his note-book, and in a fine taking. "I am out of all patience with I!" snaps he. "He is a lying scoundrel! Sam Collinson has been at work, stirring up resistance, and what d'you think I had the effrontery to say? That it is all our fault for insisting on Lord Elgin's entering Pekin!"

"You said that?" says Loch, puzzled.

"What? Of course not! I said it!" cries Parkes, and as God's my witness, they began to discuss the personal pronoun. One thing rapidly became clear: the Chinks had repudiated the agreement made only yesterday, and were now vowing that unless Elgin withdrew his demand, they were ready to fight. "There can be no peace!" Prince I had shouted at Parkes. "It must be war!"

I gave the word to Anderson, and we were off at the canter, stretching to a gallop as we left the town. With luck, we might pass through before the explosion came, but barely a mile out on the road Parkes's horse fell, and although he remounted, I could see that his beast, and De Normann's, would never stay the course. I slowed to a trot, wondering what the devil to do; if it came to the pinch, they could damned well take their chance, but for the moment we must hold together and hope. By God, it was a long ride, with my ears straining for the first crack of gunfire ahead; if only Grant held off a little longer . . .

182

We passed through Chang-kia-wan again, in a solid phalanx with the Sikh *sowars* around us, thrusting by main force through streets choked with jingal-men and Tiger soldiers who sneered and spat but kept their distance from those razor-sharp lance-heads. Then we were out and trotting down the long slope towards the distant camp-site; the plain either side was black with Imps, foot and horse; the huge coloured banners were streaming in the breeze, paper standards were flapping and filling, their horns were blaring and cymbals clashing, every group we passed turned to scream execrations at us; suddenly before us was a troop of Manchoo artillery, absolutely slewing round their great dragon-headed brass pieces to threaten us. I looked back – De Normann and Bowlby had fallen behind on their foundering hacks, and Parkes seized my elbow. "Sir Harry! Sir Harry, we must decide what is best to be done!"

They're smart in the diplomatic, you know, and in a moment the others had caught fire from his inspiration. Loch said that in such moments decisions should be arrived at quickly, De Normann urged the necessity of calm, and Brabazon cried out that since Parkes was the chief negotiator, he must say how we should proceed.

"Shut your bloody trap!" I roared. "Anderson – wheel right!" If there was a way through – for anyone lucky enough to have a fresh horse, anyway – it was beyond the big nullah, where we might skirt round to the army. We swung off the road, and in that moment there was a thunderous roar of cannon from far ahead, and I knew the masked batteries were in action; a breathless pause, and then as Armstrong shells began to burst among the Imps, pandemonium broke loose. I yelled to Anderson to hold them together as we surged forward through the milling infantry, and here was Bowlby clattering up, brandishing his pistol.

"Now we'll see how these yellow fellows can fight!" cries he. I roared to him to holster his piece, heard Parkes yelling in front of me, and saw that he and Loch had reined up by a little silk pavilion where a mandarin was sitting a Tartar pony, with officers at his back; it was our acquaintance of yesterday, who had lost his spurs at Sinho. As I rode up to them, Parkes was shouting something about safe-conduct, but now there was a crowd of angry Imps in the way; they'd spotted us as enemy, clever lads, and were crowding in, waving fists and spears; suddenly there seemed to be contorted yellow faces all round us, screaming hate. Above the din I heard the mandarin cry out something about a prince; then Parkes was calling across the crowd to me. "Wait for us, Sir Harry! Prince . . ." And then he and Loch and one of the *sowars* were galloping off with the mandarin.

"Come back!" I roared. "Parkes, you idiot!", for it was plain that our one hope was the mandarin, and we should all stay with him. Roaring to Anderson to hold on, I drove through the press in pursuit; by the time I'd cleared that howling mob my quarry was wheeling into a gully a furlong ahead, and I cursed and thundered after them. I plunged into the gully, and there they were, not twenty paces off, reined up before a group of magnificently-armoured Manchoo horsemen, banners planted in the turf beside them, and Parkes was pointing to the white rag on the *sowar*'s lance-point. I pulled up, and the leader of the Manchoos was standing in his stirrups, screaming with laughter, which seemed damned odd till I saw who it was: Prince Sang-kol-insen. In fine voice he was.

"You ask safe-conduct! Foreign filth! Crawling savages! You who would shame the Son of Heaven, and who come now treacherously to attack us! Barbarian lice! Offal! And now you come whining –"

The rest was lost in howls of hatred as his followers closed in; I saw Parkes struggling with a mounted rider, and thought "McNaghten!"[32] Loch was knocked flying from the saddle, and the Sikh was thrashing with his lance as they bore him down. I didn't linger; I was round and out of that gully like a guilty squirrel – and slap in front of me was a boiling crowd of Imp braves, with Anderson's party struggling desperately in the middle. A musket barked, and I saw a Sikh reel in the saddle; then the sabres were out, Sikhs and dragoons laying about them, with Anderson yelling to close up; a ragged volley of musketry, a Sikh going down, the answering crash of revolver fire, Bowlby blazing away wild-eyed until he was dragged from the saddle, Nolan bleeding from a sword-cut on the brow as he drove through the press – I heard him shriek as he pitched forward over his horse's head into the crush. It didn't matter now; I stared appalled at that hideous mêlée, and turned to flee.

But they were streaming out of the gully, too, Tiger soldiers with drawn swords, and at their head the white-button mandarin and half a dozen mounted monsters in black bamboo armour and helmets, brandishing pennoned spears and screaming blue murder. I put my beast to the bank; he scrambled up, reared, and fell back, and I rolled clear just in time. There was a side-gully and I raced up it, howling as I went, and came down headlong over a pile of stones; I scrambled afoot, mouthing vainly for help, there wasn't a friendly soul in sight, Loch and Parkes might be dead by now, hacked to pieces – well, by God, thinks I, if it must be, I'll make a better end than that. I swung to face them, whipping out my sabre and dropping a hand to my pistol-butt as that devil's horde bore down on me.

Even for old Flashy, you see, there comes the moment when you realise that, after a lifetime of running, you can't run any longer, and there's only one thing for it. I gritted my teeth and ran at them, spun the weapons in my hands, and bawled in my best Chinese:

"Quarter! I surrender! I'm a British staff colonel and you touch me at your peril! My sword, your excellency!"[33]

✿ For a well-decorated hero I've done a deal of surrendering in my time – which is doubtless why I remain a well-decorated hero. Piper's Fort, Balaclava, Cawnpore, Appomattox – I suppose I can't count Little Big Horn, because the uncivilised rascals wouldn't accept it, try as I might – and various minor capitulations. And if there's one thing I've learned, which young military men should bear in mind, it's that the foeman is generally as glad to accept your surrender as you are to give it. Mind you, he may turn spiteful later, when he's got you snug and helpless (I often do), but that's a risk you must run, you know. Most of my captors have been decent enough.

The Chinese were not. You'd have thought, the trouble I saved 'em, they might have shown me some consideration, but they didn't. For two days I was confined in a stinking wooden cage no bigger than a trunk, unable to stand or lie, but only to crouch painfully while I was exhibited in the temple square at Tang-chao to a jeering mob who spat and poked and shovelled ordure through the bars. I was given no food or drink beyond a filthy rag soaked in water, without which I'd have died – but I was in paradise compared with Parkes and Loch, who had survived only to be dragged to the Board of Punishments in Pekin.

The worst of it was not knowing. What would they do to me? Where were the others? What had happened at Five-li Point? The Manchoo thugs who guarded my cage, and egged on the mob to torment me, gloated about the terrible slaughter they'd inflicted on our army – which I knew was lies, for they couldn't have licked Grant, and why wasn't Tang-chao choked with prisoners like myself? But I didn't know that in fact Grant had thrashed their ambush out of sight, with our cavalry driving *twenty thousand* Tartar horsemen pell-mell, and even riding round the walls of Tang-chao before withdrawing to Grant's new position at Chang-kia-wan. Nor could I guess that Elgin was furiously demanding our release – or that the Manchoos were refusing even to talk.

It beats belief, but those lordly idiots at the Imperial Court still wouldn't accept the evidence of their senses. No, their army hadn't been driven like sheep; no, it was impossible that the insolent barbarians could approach Pekin; no, it wasn't happening at all. So they were telling each other, with Sang-kol-in-sen and Prince I spitting venom into the ear of their imbecilic Emperor, convincing the poor dupe that the sound of our guns twenty miles away was merely our last despairing gasp, and that presently we should be laid in the dust at his feet. They were ready to try to prove it, too, as you shall see.

I knew only from my guards that Pekin had proclaimed that we prisoners would be executed the moment our army advanced; I hadn't heard, thank God, that Elgin's reply was a flat defiance: he was coming to Pekin, and if a hair of our heads was hurt, God help the Emperor. Looking back now in safety, I can say he was right; if he'd weakened, those Manchoo idiots would have thought they'd won, and murdered us in sheer gloating exuberance, for that's their style. But as long as he was coming on, with blood in his eye, they held their hands out of secret fear. And he was coming, the Big Barbarian, at the double and tugging his hair; even while I crouched in that hellish cage, and while they were dying by inches in the Board of Punishments, Grant was throwing aside his map and thrusting his *sgian dhu* into his boot, and Montauban was haranguing his *poilus* as they stuffed their cartridge-pouches. It was different, then; touch a Briton, and the lion roared once – and sprang.

They came like a whirlwind on the third day of our captivity, with a thunderous prelude of artillery that had me craning vainly at the thick wooden bars; the townsfolk scattered in panic to get out of the way as Chinese troops came pouring through the square, horse, foot and guns streaming through to the Pekin road. I was croaking with hope, expecting any moment to see the beards and puggarees and lance-heads galloping into view, when I was dragged from my cage and hauled before an armoured horseman. My cramped limbs wouldn't answer at first, but when they lashed my wrists by a long rein to his crupper, and the swine set off up the street – well, it's astonishing how you can hobble when you have to. I knew if I fell I'd be dragged and flayed to pieces, so I ran stumbling with my arms being half-torn from their sockets. Fortunately the road was so crowded with troops that he couldn't go above a trot; we must have been about a mile beyond the town, and more artillery was booming close at hand, when we came in view of an enormous bridge built of great marble blocks; it must have been thirty yards wide by three hundred long, spanning the muddy yellow Peiho. This was the bridge of Pah-li-chao, and here I saw an amazing sight.

On the approaches to the bridge, and for miles to my left, was drawn up the Chinese Imperial Army. I've heard there were thirty thousand; I'd say double that number, but no matter. They stood in perfect parade order, regiment on regiment stretching away as far as I could see: Tartar cavalry in their coloured coats and conical fur hats, lances at rest; rank after rank of massive Bannermen in clumsy armour and barred helms; Tiger soldiers like yellow Harlequins, chanting their war-song; robed jingal-men, two to a piece, their fuses smouldering; half-naked Mongol infantry like stone Buddhas with drawn swords; armoured horsemen with long spears and antique firearms, their wide plated coat-skirts giving them the appearance of gigantic beetles; pig-tailed musketeers in pyjama dresses of black silk and yellow pill-box hats; batteries of their ridiculous artillery, long-barrelled ancient cannon with muzzles carved in fantastic dragon mouths, the stone shot piled beside them, crashing out ragged salvoes that shook the ground – and over all fluttered banners of every hue and design, shimmering in the sunrise, great paper tigers and hideously-featured effigies to frighten the enemy. Above the explosion of the guns rose the hellish din of gongs and cymbals and fifes and rattles and fireworks – China hurling defiance at the barbarians. The noise swelled to a deafening crescendo as the guns fell silent; then it too died to a conclusion, and through the ranks of the tremendous host swept a roar of human sound, pealing out into a final great shout – and then silence.

Silence . . . a dead, eery quiet over the flat fields before the army, stretching off into the eastern haze. Nothing to be heard but the soft flap of a silk banner, the clink of a stirrup-iron, the gentle swirl of a tiny dust-devil on the marble flags of the bridge, until out of the hazy distance came the far-off voice of a bugle, followed by the faintest of whispers down the wind, a piper playing "Highland Laddie", and the great Imperial army bristled down its length like an angry cat and the horns and cymbals blared again in deafening reply.

My horseman gave an angry shout and spurred up the bridge so suddenly that I was thrown off my feet and dragged across the flags until I managed to stumble up after him. He cast me loose before a knot of mounted officers on the summit; their leader was an ugly, pock-marked mandarin in black plate armour and a pagoda helmet, who flourished a fighting-iron at me.

"Throw this pig in with the rest of the herd!" he bawls, and I saw that behind him, on the parapet, was another of their infernal cages; an iron one this time, as long as an omnibus, containing half a dozen ragged wretches. I was seized and thrust up on to the parapet and through the low iron door; a cry of astonishment met me, and then Brabazon was gripping my hand – a ragged, hollow-eyed Brabazon with his arm in a tattered sling; he was as filthy as I.

"Colonel Flashman! You're alive! Oh, thank God! Thank God you're safe, sir!"

"You call this safe, do you?" says I. He stared, and cackled.

"Eh? Oh, my word – not too safe, perhaps! No . . . oh, but it's famous to see you, sir! You see, we feared we were the only . . ." He gestured at his companions – a couple of Sikhs, trying to sit up to attention, a dragoon half-slumped down against the bars, a frail little stick of a man with long silver hair, in a priest's robe. "But Mr Parkes, sir? Mr Loch? What of them?"

I said I believed they were dead. He groaned, and then cried: "Well, at least you're alive, sir!", and the dragoon chuckled, raising his head.

"Shure, an' why wouldn't he be? Ye don't kill Flash Harry that easy – do ye, colonel?" says Trooper Nolan.

He had a bloody bandage round his brow, and there was dried blood on his cheek, but he was wearing the same slack, calculating grin as he stared at me across the cage. Brabazon gobbled indignantly.

"It's not for you to say so, my man! How dare you address an officer in that familiar style?" He grimaced admiringly at me. "Mind you, it's true what he says, sir! They can't keep you down, can they? I'm sure he meant no harm, sir!"

"None taken, my boy," says I, and sank down in the straw opposite Nolan. I'd forgotten all about the blackmailing brute – and now my fears came rushing back at the sight of that knowing peasant grin. You may think I should have had more immediate cares, but the very sight of these five other prisoners had sent my spirits soaring. Plainly they were regarding us as hostages, and would keep us alive to the bitter end – and when we were free again, there would still be Nolan. I could see he was already contemplating that happy prospect, for when a renewed cannonade by the Chink guns took Brabazon to the bars for a look-see, he leaned forward towards me and says quietly:

"Shure, an' mebbe we'll be havin' our little talk after all, colonel."

"Any talking we do can wait until we're out of this," says I, equally quiet. "Until then, hold your tongue."

His grin faded to an ugly look. "We'll see about dat," he whispered. "Whether I hold it or not . . . depends, does it not, sorr?"

He sat back against the bars, glowering truculently, and just then there was a sudden uproar on the bridge, and Brabazon was shouting to me to come and look. Smoke was swirling over the bridge from the nearest battery, but when it cleared I saw that the mandarin and his staff were at the parapet just beneath us, pointing and yelling excitely, and there, far out on the plain, where visibility ended in a bright haze flecked gold by the morning sun, little figures were moving – hundreds of them, advancing out of the mist towards the Imperial army. They couldn't be more than a mile away, French infantry in open order, rifles at the trail;

190

their trumpets were sounding through the thunder of the Chinese guns, and as the stone shot kicked up fountains of dust among them they held on steadily, moving directly towards us, the Tricolour standards waving before them.

"Oh, vive la France!" mutters Brabazon. "Strange little buggers. See 'em strut, though! Stick it, you Frogs!"

The Chinese horns and gongs were going full blast now, and there was more hullaballoo and racing about on the bridge as lines of British and Indian infantry came into view on the French left flank; in between there was a little line of dust, thrown up by hooves, and above it the twinkling lance-points and the thin slivers of the sabres: Fane's Horse and the Dragoon Guards, knee to knee. Down beyond the parapet the Chinese gunners were labouring like billy-be-damned; their shot was churning the ground all along the allied line, but still it came on, unhurried and unbroken, and the Chinks were yelling exultantly in their ranks, their banners waving in triumph, for out on the plain could be seen how small was our army, advancing on that mighty mass of Imperials, who outflanked it half a mile on either side. Brabazon was muttering excitedly, speaking my own thought:

"Oh, run away, you silly Chinamen! You ain't got a hope!"

There was a great stir to the Imperial right, and we saw the Tartar horse were advancing, a great mass swinging out to turn the British flank; the Armstrong shells were bursting above them, little flashes of flame and smoke, but they held together well, weathering it as their stride lengthened to a canter, and Brabazon was beating his fist on the bars.

"My God, do they think Grant's asleep? He's been up for hours, you foolish fellows – look! Look there!"

For suddenly a trumpet was shrilling from the allied line, and like a gate swinging on its hinge our cavalry came drumming out of the centre, sweeping round in a deadly arc, the lances going down and the sabres twinkling as they were advanced; like a great fist they tore into the Tartar flank, scattering them, riding them down; as the enemy cavalry wavered and gave back, with Fane's and the Dragoons tearing into their heart, there was another blast of trumpets, and Probyn's riders came charging in to complete the rout.

Brabazon was bellowing like a madman, and the two Sikhs were dancing at the bars: *"Yah sowar! Sat-sree-akal! Shab-ash!"*

Suddenly one of the Sikhs yelled and fell back, blood welling from a gash in his thigh. Nolan caught him, swearing in amazement, and then we saw the Bannerman on the bridge beneath us, screaming curses and brandishing a bloody spear. The mandarin's staff were shaking their fists at the cage, until the crash of an Armstrong shell on the bridge end sent them headlong for cover; another burst on the far parapet, splinters whining everywhere; the Armstrongs had ranged on the Chinese guns' positions, and through the thunder of the Imperial salvoes we could hear the thumping strains of the "Marseillaise"; there were the dear little Crapauds storming into the Chinese forward positions, with the Armstrong bursts creeping ahead of them; behind the Chink front line it was like an antheap kicked over, and then another shell burst plumb on the summit of the bridge and we were dashed to the floor of the cage.

When I raised my head Brabazon was back at the bars, staring down in disgust at a bloody palpitating mass on the flags which had been a Bannerman, or possibly two. The ugly mandarin was standing beside it, staring at a bloody gash on his hand, and Brabazon, the eternal oaf, had to sing out:

"Take that, you villain! That'll teach you to attack a prisoner!"

The mandarin looked up. He couldn't understand the words, but he didn't need to. I never saw such livid hate in a human face, and I thought we were goners there and then. Then he strode to the cage, gibbering with fury.

"Fan-qui scum! You see this?" He flourished his bloody hand. "For every wound I take, one of you dies! I'll send his head back to your gunners, you spawn of the White Whore!" He turned to scream orders to his men, and I thought, oh Jesus, here goes one of us, but it was evidently a promise for the future, for all their response was to line the parapet and blaze away with their jingals at the Frogs, who were still engaged in the forward entrenchments three hundred yards away.

"What did he say?" Brabazon was demanding. "Sir – what was he shouting at us?"

None of them understood Chinese, of course. The unwounded Sikh and the little priest were bandaging the wounded man's leg; Nolan was a yard off, slightly behind me; Brabazon at my side, questioning. And in that moment I had what I still maintain was one of the most brilliant inspirations of my life – and I've had one or two.

Hoaxing Bismarck into a prize-fight, convincing Jefferson Davis that I'd come to fix the lightning-rod, hitting Rudi Starnberg with a bottle of Cherry Heering, hurling Valentina out of the sledge into a snow-drift – all are fragrant leaves to press in the book of memory. But I'm inclined to think Pah-li-chao was my finest hour.

"What did he say, sir?" cried Brabazon again. I shook my head, shrugging, and spoke just loud enough for Nolan to overhear.

"Well, someone's in luck. He's going to send one of us under a white flag to the Frogs. Try to make terms, I suppose. Well, he can see it's all up."

"Good heavens!" cries Brabazon. "Then we're saved!"

"I doubt that," says I. "Oh, the chap who goes will be all right. But the Frogs won't parley – I wouldn't, if I commanded 'em. What, trust these yellow scoundrels? When the game's all but won? No, the French ain't such fools. They'll refuse . . . and we know what our captors will do then . . ." I looked him in the eye. "Don't we?"

Now, if we'd been a directors' meeting, no doubt there'd have been questions, and eleventeen holes shot in my specious statement – but prisoners in a cage surrounded by blood-thirsty Chinks don't reason straight (well, *I* do, but most don't). Anyway, I was the bloody colonel, so he swallowed it whole.

"My God!" says he, and went grey. "But if the French commander knows that five lives are –"

"He'll do his duty, my boy. As you or I would."

His head came up. "Yes, sir . . . of course. Who shall go, sir? It ought to be . . . you."

I gave him my wryest Flashy grin and clapped him on the shoulder. "Thanks, my son. But it won't do. No . . . I think

193

we'll leave it to chance, what? Let the Chinks pick the lucky one."

He nodded – and behind me I could almost hear Nolan's ears waving as he took it all in. Brabazon stepped resolutely away from the cage door. I stayed at the bars, studying the mandarin's health.

There had been a brief lull in the Armstrong barrage, but now they began again; the Frogs were trying to carry the second line of works, and making heavy weather of it. The jingal-men were firing volleys from the bridge, the ugly mandarin rushing about in the smoke, exhorting 'em to aim low for the honour of old Pekin High School, no doubt. He even jumped on the parapet, waving his sword; you won't last long, you silly sod, thinks I – sure enough, came a blinding flash that rocked the cage, and when the smoke had cleared, there were half a dozen Manchoos splattered on the marble, and the mandarin leaning on the parapet, clutching his leg and bawling for the ambulance.

My one fear was that he'd have Brabazon marked down as his victim, but he hadn't. He was a man of his word, though; he screamed an order, there was a rush of armoured feet, the cage door was flung open, a Manchoo officer poked his head in, shrieking – and Trooper Nolan, glaring desperately about him, had made good and sure he was closest to the door. The Manchoo officer shouted again, gesturing; Nolan, wearing what I can best describe as a grin of gloating guilt, took a step towards him; Brabazon was standing back, ramrod-straight, while I did my damnedest not to catch the chairman's eye.

"Take him!" yells the officer, and two of his minions plunged in and flung Nolan from the cage. The door slammed shut, I sighed and loafed across to it, looking down through the bars at him as he stood gripped by two Bannermen.

"Be sure and tell 'em about Tang-ku Fort," says I softly, and he goggled in bewilderment. Then, as they ran him to the parapet, he must have realised what was happening, for he began to struggle and yell, and I staggered back from the door, crying to Brabazon in stricken accents:

"My God! What are they doing? Why, that lying hound of a mandarin – ah, no, it cannot be!"

They had forced Nolan to his knees before the wounded mandarin, who left off bellowing long enough to spit in his face; then they hauled him up on to the parapet, and while two gripped his arms and bent him double, a third seized his hair and dragged his head forward. The officer drew his sword, shook back his sleeve, and braced himself.

"Mother o' mercy! Oh, Christ, don't –!"

The scream ended abruptly – cut off, as you might say, and I sank my face into my hands with a hollow groan, reflecting that who steals my purse may get away with it, but he who filches from me my good name will surely find his tits in the wringer.

"The filthy butchers!" roars Brabazon. "Oh, the poor fellow! But why, in heaven's name, when they'd said –"

"Because that's the kind of swine John Chinaman is!" I growled. "They lie for the pleasure of it, Brabazon!"

He gritted his teeth and drew a shuddering breath. "And my last words to him were a rebuke! Did you . . . did you know him well, sir?"

"Well enough," I said. "A rough diamond, but . . . Here, how are the Frogs getting along?"

In fact, they were making capital progress, bayonetting away with élan in the second entrenchment, and while the Chinese positions to the right were hidden by smoke, from the sounds of things the British attack was going well. The Imps seemed to be giving back all along the line; hundreds of them were streaming over the bridge, with officers trying to rally them, riding about and howling, but there was only one way the battle could go – the question was, would they slaughter us before we could be rescued? Torn between terror and hope, I reckoned it was odds on our preservation, unless that reckless fool of a mandarin stopped another splinter – in which case we'd better chivvy up the priest, he being well stricken in years and presumably in a state of grace. I looked anxiously for the mandarin, and saw he was being held up by two of his pals while directing operations; but the Armstrongs seemed to have given over for the moment, and clattering up the bridge came a cavalcade of gorgeously-armoured nobles, accompanied by standard-bearers; my heart rose in my throat as I saw that their leader was Sang-kol-in-sen.

He was reining up, addressing the mandarin, and now the whole gang turned towards the cage, the mandarin pointing and yelling orders. My knees gave under me – hell, were they going to serve us as they'd served Nolan? The Bannermen swarmed in and three of us were hauled out – they left the Sikhs, and in a moment I understood why. For they flung us down on the flags before Sang's horse, and that ghoulish face was turned on us, pale eyes glaring under the wizard's helmet, as he demanded to know if any of us spoke Chinese.

Now, he wasn't asking *that* for the purpose of execution, so I hauled myself upright and said I did. He considered me, frowning malevolently, and then snarled:

"Your name, reptile?"

"Flashman, colonel on the staff of Lord Elgin. I demand the immediate release of myself and my four companions, as well as –"

"Silence, foulness!" he screamed, on such a note that his pony reared, and he hammered its head with his mailed glove to quiet it. "Snake! Pig!" He leaned down from the saddle, mouthing like a madman, and struck me across the face. "Open your mouth again and it will be sewn up! Bring him!" He wheeled his mount and clattered away, and I was seized, my wrists bound, and I was flung bodily on to a cart. As it rolled away I had one glimpse of Brabazon looking after me, and the little priest, head bowed, telling his beads. I never saw them again. No one did.[34]

*   *   *

This may seem an odd time to mention it, but my entry to Pekin recalls a conversation which I had a couple of years ago with the eminent wiseacre and playwright, George B. Shaw (as I call him, to his intense annoyance, though it don't rile him as much as "Bloomsbury Bernie"). I was advising him on pistol-play for a frightful pantomime he was writing about a lynching in a Kansas cow-town[35]; discussing hangings set him off on the subject of pain in general, and he advanced the fatuous opinion that mental anguish was worse than

196

physical. When I could get a word in, I asked him if spiritual torment had ever made him vomit; he allowed it hadn't, so I told him what my Apache wife had done to Ilario the scalp-hunter, and had the satisfaction of watching our leading dramatist bolting for the lavatory with his handkerchief to his mouth. (Of course, I didn't get the better of him; as he said later, it was the *thought* that had made him spew, not pain itself. The hell with him.)

I reflect on this only because the most prolonged pain I ever endured – and I've been shot, stabbed, hung by the heels, flogged, half-drowned, and even stretched on the rack – was on the road into Pekin. All they did was tie my hands and feet – and pour water on my bonds; then they hauled my wrists up behind me and tied 'em to a spar above the cart, and set off at a slow trot. The blazing sun and the bouncing cart did the rest; I'll not describe it, because I can't, save to say that the fiery agony in wrists and ankles spreads through every nerve of your body until you're a living mass of pain, which will eventually drive you mad. Luckily, Pekin is only eleven miles from Tang-chao.

I don't remember much except the pain – long rows of suburbs, yellow faces jeering and spitting into the cart, a towering redoubt of purple stone topped by crenellated turrets (the Anting Gate), foul narrow streets, a blue-covered carriage with the driver sitting on the shaft – he called to his passengers to look, and I was aware of two cold, lovely female faces regarding me without expression as I half-hung, whimpering, in my bonds. They weren't shocked, or pitying, or amused, or even curious; merely indifferent, and in my agony I felt such a blazing rage of hatred that I was almost exalted by it – and now I can say, arrant coward that I am, that at least I understand how martyrs bear their tortures: they may have faith, and hope, and all the rest of it, but greater than these is blind, unquenchable red anger. It sustained me, I know – the will to endure and survive and make those ice-faced bitches howl for mercy.

It must have cleared my mind, for I remember distinctly coloured pagoda roofs bigger than I'd ever seen, and a teahouse with dragons' heads above its eaves, and the great scarlet Gate of Valour into the Imperial City – for Pekin, you

197

must know, is many cities within each other, and innermost of all is the Forbidden City, the Paradise, the Great Within, girded by gleaming yellow walls and entered by the Gate of Supreme Harmony.

There are palaces for seven hundred princes within the Imperial City, but they pale before the Great Within. It is simply not of this world. Like the Summer Palace, outside Pekin, it's entirely cut off from reality, a dreamland, if you like, where the Emperor and his creatures live out a great play in their stately halls and gorgeous gardens, and all that matters is formality and finger-nails and fornication. Nothing is seen or heard of the rest of mankind, except what his ministers think fit. There he dwells, remote as a god, sublime not in omniscience but in ignorance, lost to the world. He might as well be in the Athenaeum.

I saw most of it, later – the Palace of Earthly Repose, for the Emperor's consort; the Temple of Imperial Ancestors, for sacrifices; the Gate of Extensive Peace, a hundred and ten feet high, for kow-towing; the Hall of Intense Mental Exercise, for studying Confucius; the Temple of the Civic Deity – don't know what that's for, paying rates, I dare say – and the library, the portrait hall, and even the office of the local rag, the *Imperial Gazette*, which circulates every day to all the nobles and officials in China. That's the unreality of the country – they nail thieves' hands together, and have a daily paper.

For the moment all I saw was the great gilt copper tower in which incense is kept perpetually burning, filling the city with its sweet, musky odour; and beyond it the holy of holies, the Palace of Heavenly Tranquillity (which it ain't). I was dragged in through a round doorway, and flung into a great room utterly bare of furniture, where I lay for several hours on a cold marble floor, too sick and sore and parched even to move, or to do anything except groan. I must have slept, for suddenly I was aware of tramping feet, and a door crashing open, and the glare of torches, and the revolting face of Sang-kol-in-sen glaring down at me.

He was still in full martial fig, brazen breastplate, mailed gloves, spurred greaves, and all, but with a fur-lined robe of green silk over his shoulders. He was bare-headed, so I had the benefit of his bald Mongol skull as well as the obscene little beard on the brutal moon-features. He fetched me a shattering kick and shouted:

"Get on your knees, louse!"

I tried to obey, but my limbs were so painful that I pitched over, and received several more kicks before I managed to kneel, croaking for a drink of water. "Silence!" he bawled, and cuffed me left and right, cracking the skin with his brass fingers. I crouched, sobbing, and he laughed at me spitefully. "A soldier, you!" He kicked me again. He didn't seem to remember me from Tang-ku Fort, not that that was any comfort.

There were two Manchoo Bannermen flanking the door, and now came two others, bearing an open sedan in which sat Prince I, the skull-faced monster who had raved and shrieked at Parkes at Tang-chao. He looked even more of a spectre in the glare of torchlight, sitting lean and motionless in his shimmering yellow robe, hands on knees – the silver cases on his nails came half-way down his shins. Only his eyes moved, gleaming balefully on me. To complete the comedy trio there was a burly, thick-lipped Manchoo in dragon robes, his fingers heavy with rings, a ruby button in his hat. This, I was to learn, was Sushun, the Assistant Grand Secretary of the Imperial Government, a vulture for corruption and the Emperor's tutor in vice and debauchery, on which, to judge by his pupil's condition, he must have been the greatest authority since Caligula. To me, for the moment, he was only another very nasty-looking Manchoo.

"Is this the creature?" growls Sang, and Prince I nodded imperceptibly, and piped in his thin voice: "He was with Pa-hsia-li when that lying dog deceived us at Tang-chao."

"Then he may go the way of Pa-hsia-li," snarls Sang. "It is enough for the moment that he is what the barbarian scum call an officer. An officer!" He stooped to scream in my face: "Who is your commander, pig-dung?"

"General Sir Hope –" I was beginning, and he knocked me flying with his boot.

"You lie! You have no generals! Who commands your ships?"

"Admiral Ho –"

199

He screamed and stamped on my arm, agonisingly. "Another lie! You have no admirals! You are barbarian swine – you have no nobles, no officers, no generals or colonels or admirals! You have animals who grunt louder than the rest, you offal! That is all!" He was bent over me, raving, spraying me with his spittle, glaring like a maniac. Then he straightened up, snarling, and snapped an order to the Bannermen.

I was huddled, babbling to be let alone, terrified as much by the brute's frenzied ranting as by what he might do to me. And what happened now reduced me to the final depth of fear.

The Bannermen were carrying in a stool, on which was seated a naked Chinese, a white, shuddering figure who seemed to have no arms – until I realised that they were clamped tight against his body by a horrible coat of meshed wire, bound so tight that his flesh protruded through the spaces in obscene lumps about the size of finger-tips. It covered him from neck to knee, and I've seen nothing more disgusting than that trembling, rippled skin in its hideous wire casing.

They plumped the stool down in front of me, the poor wretch slobbering with terror.

"The wire jacket," says Sang, grinning. "Even a benighted worm of a *fan-qui* must have heard of it." Without taking his eyes from me he beckoned, and one of the Bannermen came forward, carrying an open razor. He laid the shining blade on the victim's shoulder, and the fellow jerked and squealed at the touch of the steel. Sang watched me, and then nodded, the Bannerman flicked his wrist, the trembling mouth before me gaped in a dreadful scream, and one of the flesh-lumps had vanished, replaced by a tiny disc of blood which coursed down the naked arm.

Sang bellowed with laughter, absolutely slapping his sides, and the burly Sushun came forward, chuckling, to peer at the wound. I turned my head aside, gagging, and received a stinging slap across the face.

"Watch, coward!" roars Sang, and slapped me again. "Now," says he, "a wearer of the wire jacket has been known to receive as many as ten thousand cuts . . . and still live.

200

Indeed, he may live for months, if the executioner is patient, and eventually he will have no skin at all." He laughed again, enjoying my terror. "But if a quicker despatch is desired . . ." He nodded again, and the Bannerman's razor streaked down the full length of the victim's arm.

I didn't faint. I could wish I had, for I'd have been spared the tortured screaming, and the diabolical laughter, if not the bloody pool which remained on the marble after they'd carried that babbling wretch out of the room. I wonder I didn't go crazy; I fairly grovelled to these fiends, begging them to let me be, not to cut me, anything so they spared me that unthinkable cruelty. Oh, I've faced some horrors in my time – Narreeman and her knife, Mimbreno squaws out for an evening's amusement, Malagassy inquisitors, and Ignatieff with his knout, but nothing more ghastly than the gloating enjoyment of those two devils, Sang and Sushun. Prince I sat in the background, immobile, his face expressionless.

"You have seen, dog-dirt," snarls Sang. "Now hear. You will wear the wire jacket, I swear, and when your foul carcase has been flayed, an inch at a time, it will be thrown to the maggots – and still you will be living. Unless you obey to the uttermost the orders we give you. Do you hear me, kite?"

I'd do anything, I whined, anything he asked, and he seemed satisfied and kicked me again for luck. He thrust his face into mine, dropping his voice to a mere rasp:

"You are to be honoured beyond your bestial imagining. You are going into the Divine Presence, and you will go like the crawling animal you are, on your knees, and you will speak. This is what you will say." He gestured to Sushun, and the burly brute swaggered forward, towering over me, and shouted:

"I am a Banner chief in the Red-haired Army, a trusted creature of the Big Barbarian. See, I lay at your Divine Feet the unworthy sword which, misbegotten foreign slave that I am, I dared to raise in revolt against the authority of the Complete Abundance. I was misled by evil counsellors, my master the Big Barbarian and the arch-liar Pa-hsia-li, who tempted me from my allegiance to the glorious Kwa-Kuin, the Tien-tze, the Son of Heaven. I marched in their army,

201

which prevailed by lies and treachery against the trusting and unwary generals of the Divine Emperor. At Sinho, for example, we succeeded only by despicable fraud, for our leaders bade us perform the kow-tow before the Imperial soldiers,[36] and when they approached in good faith we fired on them treacherously and so overcame them for the moment. Thus we continued, in stealth and trickery, lying shamelessly to the Imperial ambassadors when they besought us gently to repent our rebellion and return to our duty to you, the Son of Heaven who rules All Under the Skies. Pa-hsia-li lied, the Big Barbarian lied, we all lied, but now we see our error; we tremble under the just wrath of your servant, Prince Sang, who has chastised us; dismay and fear spread through our ranks, our soldiers run crying away, our evil leaders cannot control them. The Big Barbarian bites his nails and weeps in his tent; all our soldiers and sailors weep. We beg your Divine Forgiveness, kneeling, and acknowledge your supremacy, oh Son of Heaven. Be merciful, accept our homage, for we were misled by evil people."

Well, I've talked greater rubbish in my time; he could have it signed and witnessed if he wanted. But even in my abject terror, kneeling almost in the blood of the wire jacket victim, with those madmen screaming at me, I couldn't help wondering what mortal use they thought it would be. Within a week their precious Son of Heaven was going to be brought face to face with the Big Barbarian, who'd make him eat crow and like it; the despised Red-headed soldiers would march the sacred streets of the Forbidden City, and get drunk, and piss against his temple walls, and accost his women, and kick his mandarins' backsides if they didn't stir themselves. And since nothing in Heaven or earth could prevent that – and Sang and Sushun and Prince I _knew_ it – what was the point of stuffing the Emperor's ears with nonsense at the eleventh hour, when he'd learn the dreadful truth at the twelfth?

I still didn't understand, you see, the blind arrogant stupidity of the Manchoo mind – that even if Elgin stood in the Emperor's presence, his ministers would still pretend he wasn't there at all; that they'd be whispering him just to wait, this foreign pig would be brought to book presently, and his army thrashed; that none of it was happening, because it

202

couldn't happen, Q.E.D. And in the meantime, here was a high-ranking British Officer to tell him the same tale, what more proof could His Majesty want?

They had me rehearsing it now, and you may be sure I howled it with a will, even throwing in corroborative detail of my own about how my family (including little golden-headed Amelia, of blessed memory) were held hostage by Elgin's villains, to coerce me into rebellion against my better judgment. D'you know, they were delighted – I ain't sure they didn't believe it. Sang bellowed and kicked me with enthusiasm, and Prince I said coldly they had chosen well. Sushun spat on me to show his approval. Then:

"Strip the swine!" cried Sang, and the Bannermen cut my cords, tore off my clothes, gave me a rag of loin-cloth such as coolies wear, and replaced my bonds with ponderous steel fetters whose links must have been two inches thick. I now looked abject enough to satisfy them, but they kept my lancer tunic, belt, boots and spurs, to show their lord and master, and produced a ridiculous Oriental sword which would be laid at his Divine Feet during my speech to the throne. Then they left me for about an hour, half-dead with pain and fear and icy cold, mumbling over the farrago of drivel that I knew I would be repeating for my very life. But after that . . .

Suddenly it was on-stage with a vengeance, with the Bannermen hauling me out and along passages and up stairways, beating me with their spear-shafts while I laboured with the dead-weight of my chains. We passed through chambers where Chinese officials stared curiously, and uniformed Bannermen guarded the round crimson doorways; I remember a carpeted gallery crammed with porcelain statues of grotesque figures with enormous teeth and staring eyes; then they were driving me out across a polished marble floor like a frozen lake, reflecting a great hall as long and high as a church, with a bass gong booming hollowly in its emptiness. Huge vases, three times the height of a man, stood on either side of that cavernous apartment, which was lit by great lanterns with candles of perfumed wax; three-quarters of its length was only dimly-lighted, but at the far end, above three tiers of broad marble steps, was a dais on which was seated a golden

203

figure, shining in the flames of the great candlebranches flanking his throne, a massive ebony contraption inlaid all over with mother-of-pearl. Robed figures, about a dozen of them, stood on the steps, to either side; there was Sang, and Prince I, and Sushun, but I had little chance to take 'em in, for my Bannermen flung me headlong, and I had to crawl the whole damned way, dragging those beastly irons, and staring at the reflection of the naked, bearded wretch in the glassy floor beneath me. Hollo, Flashy, old son, I thought, bellows to mend again, my boy, but you keep going and speak civil to the gentleman and you'll get a sugar-plum at tea.

The gong had stopped, and the only sounds in that joss-laden silence were clanks and laboured breathing; I reached the steps, and under the Bannermen's proddings dragged my way upwards, kow-towing all the way; thirty-three of them were there, and then I stopped, sprawled stark, with a pair of yellow velvet boots just ahead, and the hem of a robe that seemed to be made of solid gold inlaid with emeralds.

"He doesn't look like a soldier," said a drowsy voice. "Where is his armour? Why is he not wearing it?"

"Your slave, kneeling, begs Your Imperial Majesty to look on these rags of garments which the Red-headed savages wear." This was Sang, and it was the first time I'd heard him speak at anything but the top of his voice. "They have no armour."

"No armour?" says the other. "They must be very brave."

That's foxed you, you bastard, thinks I, but after a minute Sushun explained that we were so bloody backward we hadn't thought of armour yet, and Sang cried aye, that was it.

"No armour," says the drowsy voice, "yet they have great guns. That is not consistent. You – how is it that you have guns, but no armour?"

"Address the Son of Heaven, pig!" yells Sang, and the Bannermen bashed me with their spear-shafts. I scrambled to my knees, looked up – and blinked. For if the fellow on the throne wasn't Basset, my orderly from the 11th Hussars, he was dooced like him, except that he was Chinese, you understand. It was just one of those odd resemblances – the same puffy, pasty, weak young face and little mouth, with a pathetic scrap of hair on the upper lip; but where Basset's eyes had been weasel-sharp, this fellow's were watery and dull. He looked as though he'd spent the last ten years in a brothel – which wasn't far wrong.[37] All this I took in at a glance, and then hastened to answer his question.

"Our guns, majesty," says I, "were stolen from your imperial army." At least that ought to please Sang, but with a face like his you couldn't be sure.

"And your ships?" says the drowsy voice. "Your iron ships. How do you make such things?"

By George, this wasn't going according to Sushun's scenario at all. Here was I, all ready with a prepared statement, and this inquisitive oaf of an Emperor asking questions which I daren't answer truthfully, or Sang would have my innards all over the yard.

"I know of no iron ships, majesty," says I earnestly. "I think they are a lie. I have never seen them."

"I have seen pictures," says he sulkily, and thought for a moment, an unhappy frown on his soft yellow face. "You must have come to the Middle Kingdom in a ship – was it not of iron?" He looked ready to cry.

"It was a very old wooden ship, majesty," says I. "Full of rats and leaked like a sieve. I didn't want to come," I cried on a sudden inspiration, "but I was seduced from my allegiance to your Divine Person by evil people like Pa-hsia-li and the Big Barbarian, you see, and they made me a Banner chief in the Red-headed Army and a trusted creature of the Big Barbarian himself, and . . ."

It was the only way I could get into Sushun's speech and forestall further embarrassment; I poured it out, keeping my eyes lowered and knocking head obsequiously at intervals, and putting a heart-rending pathos into my final appeal for his Divine Forgiveness. If he'd then said, what about all these railways and telegraphs and the Crystal Palace, hey, I'd have been stumped, but he didn't. Silence reigned, and when I stole a glance up at the Imperial Throne, damned if he hadn't gone to sleep! Bored stiff, no doubt, but highly disconcerting when you've been pleading for your life, and

Sang and Sushun glaring like Baptists at a Mass. None of 'em seemed to know what to do; the Son of Heaven smacked his lips, broke wind gently, and began to snore. There were whispered consultations, and finally one of them went off and returned with a stout little pug in a plain robe, who approached the throne, knocked head, and began to tickle the royal ankle.

The Emperor grunted, woke, stared around, and asked sleepily which tortoiseshell was turned over tonight.

"The Fragrant Almond Leopardess, oh Kwa-Kuin Ruling the World," squeaks the stout party, and the Emperor pulled a face.

"No!" says he petulantly. "She is large and clumsy and without culture. She sings like a crow." He sniggered, and Sang and the others, who'd been mirroring his disapproval, chuckled heartily. "Let it be the Orchid," says the Emperor, sighing happily, and everyone beamed; I may even have nodded approbation myself, for he looked at me again, and frowned.

"I saw a picture of an iron ship with three great chimneys," says he sadly, and then he got up unsteadily, and everyone dropped to their knees, crying: "There cannot be two suns in the heaven!" and knocked head vigorously. I watched him shuffle off, attended by the stout fellow; he walked like an old, sick man, for all he couldn't have been thirty. The Solitary Prince, Son of Heaven, the most absolute monarch on earth, yearning for a trip on a steamship.

The fact remained that he hadn't told 'em to give Flashy a pound from the till and a ticket to Tooting; I doubted if Sang would either, for while I'd done my damnedest to carry out his orders, I knew I hadn't made much of a hit, and if he was displeased . . . my fears were realised as I was abruptly jerked to my feet, and that hateful voice was snarling at the Bannermen:

"Put him below! Tomorrow he can join the other barbarian curs in the Board of Punishments."

My blood froze at the words, and as they seized my fetters I was foolish enough to protest. "But you swore to let me off! I said what you wanted, didn't I? You said you'd spare me, you lying beast!"

206

He was on me like a tiger, striking viciously at my face while I cowered and yammered. "I said I would spare you the wire jacket!" he shouted, and fetched me a final clip that knocked me down. "So, I will spare you . . . the wire jacket! You may yet come to beg for it as a blessed release! Away with him!"

They hauled me off, and since I was in such fear that I woke the echoes with my roaring, they gagged me brutally before rushing me down a spiral stairway. It wasn't the way we'd come, and I was expecting stone cells and dripping walls, but evidently they didn't have such amenities in the Emperor's private apartments, for the room they thrust me into seemed to be a furniture store, dry and musty, but clean enough, with chairs and tables piled against the walls. The swine made me as comfortable as possible, though, throwing me back down on a narrow wooden bench and shackling my wrists so tightly beneath it that I couldn't budge an inch and must lie there supine with my legs trailing on the floor either side. Then they left me, a prey to the most horrid imaginings, and unable even to whine and curse by reason of my gag.

The Board of Punishments . . . I'd heard of it, and horrid rumours of what happened there – if I'd known what Parkes and Loch and the others were already suffering, I'd have gone off my head. Mercifully, I didn't know, and strove to drive the awful fears out of my mind, telling myself that the army was only a few miles away, that even mad monsters like Sang must realise the vengeance that Elgin would take if we were ill-treated, and hold his hand . . . and then I remembered Moyes and Nolan, and the vicious, mindless spite with which they'd been murdered, and I knew that my only hope was that rescue would get here in time. They were so close! Grant and the Frogs and Probyn and Nuxban Khan and Wolseley and Temple, those splendid Sikhs and Afghans and Royals; I could weep to think of them in their safe, strong, familiar world, loafing under the canvas, sitting about on Payne & Co's boxes, reading the *Daily Press*, chewing the rag about . . . what had it been, that evening a century ago, before we rode to Tang-chao . . . oh, aye, the military steeplechase at Northampton, won by a Dragoon over twenty fences and three ploughs, and spectators riding alongside had spoiled sport . . . "Goin' to ride next year, Flash?" "Garn, he's top-heavy!" "They say the Navy are enterin' in '61 – sailors on horseback, haw-haw!" That's how they'd be gassing and boozing and idling away precious time, the selfish bastards, while I was bound shivering and naked and near-demented with fear of what lay ahead . . .

I must have dozed, for I came awake freezing cold, racked by pain where the sharp edges of the bench were cutting into the back of my shoulders and thighs. It was still night, for the window was dark, but through the lattice door light was streaming, light that moved – someone was quietly descending the stairway to my prison. There was a murmur of Chinese voices just outside: one a falsetto squeak that I seemed to have heard before, and the other . . . even to my battered senses it was one of the loveliest human sounds I'd ever listened to, soft and tinkling as a silver bell, the kind of voice a happy angel might have had – a slightly excited, tipsy angel.

"Is this the room, Little An?" it was whispering. "You're sure? Well, take me in, then! Hurry, I want to see!"

"But, Orchid Lady, it is madness!" whimpers Squeaker. "If we were seen! Please, let us go back – I'm frightened!"

"Stop trembling or you'll drop me! Oh, come on, fat, foolish, frightened Little An – be a man!"

"How can I? I'm a eunuch! And it's cruel and mean and unworthy to taunt me – aiee! Oh! You pinched me! Oh, vicious, when you know I bruise at the least nip –"

"Yes, so think how you'll bruise when the Mongols take their flails to you, little jelly . . ."

"You wouldn't!"

"I would. I will, unless you take me in and let me see – now."

"Oh, this is wilful! It's wicked! And dangerous! Please, dear Imperial Concubine Yi, why can't we just go upstairs and –"

"Because I've never seen a barbarian. And I'm going to, dear Little An." The lovely voice chuckled, and began to sing softly: "Oh, I'm going to see a barbarian, I'm going to see a barbarian . . ."

"Oh, please, please, Orchid Lady, quietly! Oh, very well —"

The door opened, and light flooded into the room.

❀ Dazzled, all I could make out at first was a short, stout figure carrying someone – a child, by the look of it. Then the lantern was placed on a cupboard, so that it shone down on me, and as they advanced into the room I saw that the bearer was the portly cove who'd scratched the Emperor's foot in the Hall of Audience; his burden was wrapped in a scarlet silk cloak with a hood keeping the face in shadow.

"Well!" hisses the eunuch. "There it is – I hope you're satisfied! Risking our lives just to gape at that monster – to say nothing of the scandal if it were known that the Empress of the Western Palace was sneaking about –"

"Oh, shut up, pudding," says she in that silvery chuckle. "And put me down."

"No! We're going – we must, before –"

"Put me down! And close the door."

He gave a hysterical whimper and obeyed, and she circled the bench none too steadily, giggling and clutching the cloak tightly under her chin. She craned foward to look at me, and the light fell on the most beautiful face I've ever seen in my life.

I've said that of three women, and still do – Elspeth, Lola Montez . . . and Yehonala Tzu-hsi, the Orchid, the incomparable Yi Concubine. And it's true of each in her own way: fair Elspeth, dark Lola . . . and Yehonala was the Orient, in all its pearly delicacy of flower-like skin, lustrous black eyes, slender little nose, cherry mouth with the full lower lip, tiny even teeth, all in a perfect oval face; add that her hair was blue-black, coiled in the Manchoo style – and you ain't much wiser, for there are no words to describe that pure loveliness. Who could have guessed that it masked a nature compounded of all the seven deadly sins except envy

210

and sloth? But even when you knew it, it didn't matter one damned bit, with that breath-taking beauty. She said it herself: "I can make people hate me – or love me with blind worship. I have that power."

All I knew then, as she surveyed me, swaying and tittering excitedly, was that I'd never seen the like, and I can pay the little heart-stopper no higher tribute than to say that my first wish was that I had my uniform and a shave – being flat on your back, gagged and bound in a filthy loin-cloth, cramps the style no end. My second thought was that whoever had painted her mouth purple and her eyelids silver, with devil's streaks slanting up the brows, had done her no service – and then I noticed that the black pupils were shrunk to pin-points, and the perfect lips were loosely open. She was rollicking drunk on opium. Her first words confirmed it, I'd say.

"Ughh! He's . . . disgusting. Not human! Look at the hair on his chest – like an ape!" She shivered deliciously. "Are they *all* like this?"

"What did you expect?" pipes An fearfully. "I told you, but you wouldn't listen! Yes, they're all like that – some are even worse. Revolting. Now, please, come away –"

"They can't be uglier than this! See his dreadful great nose – like a vulture's beak! And his ears! And his hair!" She gurgled hysterically, and the lovely face came closer, wrinkling delicately. "He smells, too – ugh!"

"They all smell! Like sour pork! Oh, Orchid Lady, why do you wait, staring at the beastly thing! He's a barbarian! Very well, you've seen him! And unless we make haste –"

"Be quiet! I want to look at him . . . he's grotesque! Those huge shoulders . . . and his skin!" She put out a slim white hand, whose silver nails were two-inch talons, and brushed my chest with her finger-tips. "It's like ox-hide – feel!" She squeaked with delight.

"I'll do no such thing! And neither will you – stop it, I say! Eegh! To touch that foulness – how can you bear it? Oh, Orchid, mistress, I beg you, come before anyone finds us!"

"But his arms and legs, An – they're enormous! Like an elephant. He must," says she, all tipsy solemnity, "be terribly strong . . . strong as a bull, wouldn't you think?"

211

"Yes, as a bull – and quite as interesting! Imperial Concubine Yi, this is not fitting! Please, I implore you – let us go quickly!"

"In a moment, stupid! I'm still looking at him . . ." She took an unsteady pace back, head on one side. "He's an absolute monster . . ." She giggled again, her knuckles to her lips. "I wonder . . ."

"What! What do you wonder? Eh? Aha! I know what you wonder! Oh, vile! Shameless! Come away this instant! No, no –"

"I just want to *look*, fool! You wouldn't care if it was a horse, or . . . or a monkey, would you? Well, he's just a barbarian . . ." And before he could stop her she had swayed forward, laughing, and yanked at my loin-cloth; there was a rending sound, Little An screamed, averted his eyes, tried to drag her away, succeeded in pulling the cloak from her shoulders – and while her ladyship, oblivious, blinked in drunken contemplation, I returned the scrutiny with interest; in fact, I near swallowed my gag.

I should explain that she had looked in while returning from duty in the Emperor's bed, and consequently was still in uniform. Or rather, out of it – and his majesty's tastes were curious. She was dressed in enormous wings of peacock feathers, attached from shoulder to wrist, and high-soled Manchoo slippers from which silver cross-garters wound up to above her knees. The effect was striking; she was one of your slim, perfectly-shaped, high-breasted figures, with skin like alabaster – as I said, I never saw the like. She would have made a stone idol squeal.

"Put it back! Stop it! Don't look!" Little An was in a frenzy, dropping to his knees beside her, pawing distraught. "For pity's sake, Orchid Lady! Please, come away quickly, before . . . oh, Gods! What are you doing?"

It was a question which, had I not been gagged, I might well have echoed – rhetorically, since there was no doubt what she was doing, the wicked, insolent little flirt. She had detached a plume from her peacock wing and was tickling lasciviously, humming what I took to be an old Chinese lullaby and going into delighted peals at the visible result of her handiwork.

212

"Oh, buffalo!" she exclaimed, clapping her hands, while Little An stared in horror and absolutely beat his forehead with his fists, and the hapless victim struggled helplessly, distracted and outraged – for I have my dignity, dammit, and I bar being unbreeched and assailed by opium-sodden houris, however bewitching, without even a by-your-leave.

"Oh, horrible! Impossible!" Little An fairly gibbered. "Oh, lady – dear Orchid, please come away! See, I lie at your feet, I beg, I beseech – stop, stop! If someone should find us –"

"That would be unlucky – for them." She stopped tickling, and laid hold. "Oh-h! Little An," says she breathlessly, "go outside . . . and guard the door."

He gave a frenzied neigh. "What will you do?" he squealed, which was as foolish a question as ever I heard, considering my condition and her behaviour. "No! I forbid it! You cannot! It is sacrilege, blasphemy – awful! It is improper –"

"Do you want to be alive tomorrow, Little An?" The voice was as musically soft as ever, but there was a note in it to bristle your hair. "Go out, keep watch . . . and wait till I call. Now."

He gave a last despairing wail and fled, and she teased fondly for a moment, breathing hard, and then leaned over to look into my face, possibly to make sure I wasn't going to sleep. Dear God, but she was lovely; the purple mouth was wide, panting violet-scented breaths, the black eyes were glittering as she laughed and called softly:

"Oh, An – he is *so* ugly! I can't bear to look at him!"

"Then don't!" His piping came faintly through the door. "Don't look! Don't do anything! Don't touch it – him! Remember who you are, you bad, lascivious wretch – you're the Imperial Concubine Yi, beloved of the Complete Abundance, mother of his only child, Moon to the Heavenly Sun! Here – are you listening?"

"What did you say about complete abundance?" chuckled the drunken hussy, and dropped her silk cloak over my face, to cut off her view, no doubt, damn her impudence. Her hands gripped my chest as she swung nimbly astride, her knees either side of my hips; for a moment she was upright,

213

playing and fondling while I lay fit to burst, and then with a long shuddering sigh she sank slowly down, impaling herself, gliding up and down with maddening deliberation, and what could I do but close my eyes and think of England?

* * *

An said afterwards that it was incredible, and but for the gag I'd have cried "Hear, hear!", supposing I'd had breath to do it. But while I wouldn't have missed it for the world, it was deuced unnerving – being ravished is all very well, especially by the most accomplished wanton in China, if not all Asia, but when you're utterly helpless, and she has finally worked her wicked will and lain sated and moaning drunkenly on your manly chest, only to draw away suddenly with a cry of "Ugh, how he stinks!", and then plucks away the cloak for another look and shudder at you . . . well, you're bound to wonder about the future, if you follow me.

Little An had it all settled, rot him. When she called, he waddled in, sulking furiously, and said that if she'd *quite* finished behaving like a rutting sow he would carry her to bed, and then slit the barbarian's tongue so that the disgusting brute couldn't blab when they took him to the Board of Punishments. I listened in cold horror, but she reclined gracefully in a chair and says yawning:

"Blood-thirsty little pig, you'll leave his tongue alone – and the rest of him . . ." She stretched luxuriously. "Oh, An! Do you know what it's like when your whole body melts in such ecstasy that you feel you'll die of bliss? No, of course you don't. But I do . . . now. I thought Jung was wonderful, but . . . oh, Jung was just a boy! This was like . . . who was that ancient god who used to rape everyone? It doesn't matter." She waved a languid wing in my direction. "Carry me upstairs . . . and have him taken to the Wang-shaw-ewen. Put him in –"

"Are you mad? Has lechery disordered your wits? What the devil is he to do in the Wang-shaw-ewen?"

"Die a happy barbarian," purrs madam. "Eventually. Unless I tire of him first . . . which is unimaginable." She sighed happily. "Of course, all that horrid hair must be

214

shaved from his body, and he must be bathed in musk for that awful odour, and dressed decently –"

"You *are* mad! Take that . . . that *thing* to your own pavilion!" He gargled and waved his arms. "And when the Emperor hears of it, or Prince Kung – or your enemies, Sang and Sushun and the Tsai Yuan –"

"Oh, don't be silly! Who would be so brave – or foolish – as to tell on the Concubine Yi? Even you aren't so stupid . . . are you, Little An?" Just for a second the silvery voice hardened on that chilly note, and then she had risen, staggered, giggled, and broken into a little-girl sing-song: "I'm hungry, An! Yes, I am, An! And I want some pickles, An, and roast pork, and cherries, and lots of crackling, and sugared lotus seeds, and a cup of honeysuckle tea . . . and then sleep, sleep, sleep . . ." She leaned against him, murmuring.

"But . . . but . . . oh, it's the infernal black smoke! It makes you mad, and irresponsible . . . and . . . and naughty! You don't know what you're saying or doing! Please, dear Orchid Lady, little Empress, listen to reason! You've enjoyed the beastly fellow – ugh! – isn't it enough? You say no one would tell – but how if the Emperor came to your pavilion and found that . . . that creature –"

"The Emperor," says she drowsily, "will never get out of his bed again. Why should he, when I'm always in it? But if he did, and caught me with twenty barbarians . . . d'you know what? He'd forgive me." She brushed a wing playfully across his face. "If you were a man, Little An, you'd know why. My barbarian knows why!" She pushed away from him, laughing, and skipped unsteadily to my bench, beating her wings. "Oh, yes, he knows why! Don't you, my ugly, hairy barbarian – so ugly, except for the happy part . . . See? Oh, An, I'm so happy!"

"Stop it! Stop it at once, I say!" He pulled her away; he was nearly in tears. "I won't have it, d'you hear! It's not decent – you, a great Manchoo lady – how can you think of that animal –"

"Oh, leave me alone – look, you've torn my wing!" The lovely mouth pouted as she smoothed her feathers. "You'll make me angry in a minute, Little An – I should have you beaten for that – yes, I will, you blubbery little ape –"

"Have me beaten, then!" he squealed, in sudden passion. "Beat me for a torn wing – and what of your torn honour? You, Yehonala, daughter of a knight of the Banner Corps, mother of Tungchi, the seed of Heaven, to forget your loyalty to the Emperor! You indulge your wicked lust with this peasant savage – you, whose life's duty is the solace and comfort of the Solitary Prince! Shame on you! I'll have no part in it, and you can beat or kill me if you like!" He finished on a fine fearful flourish. "It's not good enough!"

I've taken part in some damned odd scenes in my time, but I imagine a visitor to that room just then would have agreed that the present spectacle was unique. There we were among the furniture and dust-sheets: on my left, in brown robe and pill-box hat, twenty diminutive stone of blubber shrilling like a steam whistle; on my right, topping him by a head in her pearl-fringed block shoes, that incredible ivory beauty, her nudity only enhanced by the ridiculous trailing peacock wings and silver garters; they faced each other across the supine form of the pride of the 17th Lancers, trussed, gagged, and stark as a picked bone, but following the debate with rapt attention. My admiration, if not my sympathy, was all with Little An, as I looked at that lovely, silver-painted mask of a face beneath the coiled raven hair: suddenly it was wiped clean of drugged laughter, and the cold implacability that looked out of it was frightening. I even left off staring at those excellent jutting tits, which goes to show. I'd not have faced her for a fortune, but when she spoke it was in the same soft, bell-like tone.

"Eunuch An-te-hai," says she, and negligently indicated her feet – and the poor little tub came waddling and sank down like a burst bladder. She touched his cheek gently with a silver talon, and he turned up his trembling pug face.

"Poor Little An, you know I always get my way, don't you?" It was like a caress. "And you always obey, because I am your little orchid whom you have loved since I came here long ago, a frightened little girl to whom you were kind. Remember the watermelon seeds and walnuts, and how you consoled me when my heart was breaking for the boy I loved, and how you shielded me from the anger of the Dowager when I broke her best gold cup and you took the blame, and how you whispered comfort when first you wrapped me in the scarlet cloak and took me to the Emperor's bed, trembling and in tears? 'Be brave, little empress – you will be a real empress some day'. Have you forgotten, Little An? I never shall."

He was leaking like the Drinking Fountain Movement by now, and no wonder. I was starting to feel horny for her again myself.

"Now, because I love you, too, and need you, Little An, I shall be honest with you – as I always am." The silvery voice was sober as a judge's now. "I want this barbarian, for what you call my wicked lust . . . no, no, it's true. And why not, if it pleases me? You talk of honour, loyalty to the Emperor – what loyalty do I owe to that debauched pervert? You know I'm not a woman to him, but a pretty painted toy trained to pander to his filthy vices – what honour is there in that? You know, and pity me – and used to arrange those secret trysts with Jung, the man I loved. Where was my honour then?"

"Jung Lu was a noble, a Manchoo, a Banner Chief who would have married you if he could," he whimpered, pawing her feet. "Oh, please, Orchid, I seek only your good – this thing is a barbarian brute –"

"But if I want him, Little An, mayn't I have him . . . please? He is just a little pleasure . . . a watermelon seed. And he may have another use; you should know of it . . . and of other things, which it will soon be time to tell you." She paused, head lifting. "Yes . . . why not now? This is a good secret place, away from big ears. Go – see that all is safe."

He hopped up, all alarm, popped his head out, and came back nodding nervously. She sat down, motioning him to kneel close, and stroked his fat cheek playfully. "Don't be frightened, small jelly. Just listen." She began to talk, quite unaware that the big ears of the barbarian melonseed were understanding every word.

"Soon, Little An, two great things will happen: the barbarians will take Pekin, and the Emperor will die. No, listen,

217

you fat fool, and keep your babbling to yourself. First, the Emperor. Only I and one discreet physician know it, but in a few weeks he will be dead, partly of his infirmities, but mostly of over-indulgence in the charms of the Yi Concubine. Well, it's a pleasant death, and I give him every assistance. I believe," says this Manchoo Messalina, with a reflective chuckle, "that I could have carried him off tonight, by combining the Exquisite Torment of the Seven Velvet Mirrors with the Prolonged Ecstasy of the Reluctant Shrimp, which as you know involves partial immersion in ice-cold water. But it will be soon, anyway – and who will rule China then, Little An?" She played with her feathers, smiling at his evident terror. "Will it be that amiable weakling, Prince Kung, the Emperor's brother? Or his cousin, the hungry skeleton Prince I? Or that murderous madman, Prince Sang? Or Tungchi, the Emperor's only son – *my* son? Any one of these, or as many others, might become Emperor, Little An – but who will rule China?"

Well, he could guess, all right, and I could have a suspicion myself; I knew nothing of their palace politics, or the immense power of Imperial concubines, but I know women. This one had the spirit, no error, and probably the brains and determination – above all, she had that matchless beauty which could get her whatever she wanted.

"What . . . too frightened even to guess, Little An? Never mind; leave the dying Son of Heaven, and consider the barbarians. Sang, the idiot, still hopes to defeat them – which is why he and his fellow-jackals have been urging the Emperor to go north to Jehol, on an ostensible hunting trip for his health!" She laughed without mirth. "In fact, Sang knows such a departure would be seen as a cowardly flight, and the Emperor would be disgraced – and Sang, having beaten the barbarians in his absence, would step into his shoes as the darling of army and people. Poor Sang! If only he knew it, the throne will soon be vacant, and his intrigues all for nothing. In any event, he will not beat the barbarians; they will be here within two weeks."

"But that is impossible!" Little An started up in horror. "And that you should say so! You, Orchid Lady, who have urged the Emperor to fight to the end – who made him send

218

the silk cord to defeated generals – who made him set the price on barbarian heads!"

"To be sure – a thousand taels for the Big Barbarian's head, isn't it?" She sounded amused. "A hundred for every white head, fifty for their black soldiers? Five hundred for Banner Chiefs like that repulsive thing there!" She waved a wing at me, the awful bitch. "Really, I must make him wear a mask in bed. But of course I urge resistance – you think I like these barbarian swine? Yehonala is the resolute champion of China, and the people know it, and will remember the Banner Knight's daughter – especially when the Emperor is dead. Until he is, I make him fight – who do you think has kept him from fleeing to Jehol, stupid? It is quite wonderful how even such a flabby wreck as the Son of Heaven can be roused to martial ardour . . . in bed."

"But if the barbarians triumph, all is lost –"

"No, little fool, all is gained! The barbarians will come – and go, with their piece of paper. China remains. With a new Emperor – but of course, he must be an Emperor acceptable to the barbarians; they will see to that before they go. And they will countenance no bitter enemies like Sang or Prince I or Sushun –"

"But, forgive me, Orchid Lady – you are their bitterest foe of all!"

"But they don't know that, do they? They think Sang and the ministers control the Emperor – they can't conceive the power that rests in the little lotus hand." She raised one slim silver-taloned pinkie, and laughed. "What, a mere girl, who looks like me? Can you hear the Big Barbarian crying 'Enemy!' when I smile and bid my ladies serve him rose-petal tea and honey cakes in the Birthday Garden? Why, I'm just the dead Emperor's whore – and the mother of his heir. No, to ensure a clear field for my Imperial candidate – whoever he may be – it is necessary only to ensure the complete discredit in barbarian eyes of such rivals as Sang and his reptiles. As the known leaders of resistance, they are ill-regarded already, but I shall contrive their utter disgrace – perhaps even get them hanged, who knows?"

D'you know who she reminded me of? Otto Bismarck. Not to look at, you understand, but in the smooth, sure way she summed it up and lined it out, and had you agog for her to drop the next piece into place – and a bare half-hour since she'd been rogering her soul out, whooping drunk on lust and poppy. And, like dear Otto, she was holding my interest despite my other pressing concerns; come on, come on, I was thinking, let's hear how you're going to get Sang to Tyburn, because I want to be there to swing on the bastard's ankles. Little An, too, was clamouring for information, albeit apprehensively. So she told him – and I wished she hadn't.

"It is simple. Before he dies, the Emperor will issue a final vermilion decree, ordering the execution of all barbarian captives now in the Board of Punishments. For this, the Emperor's advisers, Sang and the rest, will be held responsible, and when the bodies are handed back, and it is seen that they have died by the usual procedures – binding, flogging, bursting, maggots – the barbarians will be in a rage for retribution. Sang will have to make apologies and excuses – that it was the work of brutal underlings, most unfortunate, much to be regretted, and so forth. The barbarians, growling, will accept the apology – and a cash compensation – as they have done in the past. They will bear no love for Sang and his friends, but they will let the matter end there. Unless," she laughed, and it would have frozen your marrow, "there is, among the bodies, one that has died by the wire jacket, or something equally elaborate. For that cannot be excused as the casual brutality of some underling; it will be seen as a calculated, insulting atrocity. Barbarians are very sensitive about such things; they will certainly take vengeance – and I wonder if Sang will escape with his life?"

My soul shrank as I listened; only a Chinese female could plot with such cruel, diabolic cunning. Our prisoners were doomed, then, one of them by the most ghastly torture – just so that this wicked, lovely harpy could bring down her rivals and capture Imperial power. And there was nothing to be done – I didn't even know how many of our fellows had been taken, or who. And it would be done without warning, or hope of rescue . . . that little toad An was at the knots and splices of it already, once he'd babbled out his admiration.

"Oh, Orchid Lady, forgive your kneeling slave!" cries he, and he was weeping buckets, so help me. "Your eyes are on

220

the stars, and mine on the dirt! When shall it be done? And which of them shall it be? For it will be to arrange – the victim must be brought from the Board secretly, lest Sang's people should hear. Afterwards, when the bodies are sent to the barbarian camp, it will be easy to increase their number by that one."

"In a week, perhaps. When the barbarians prepare their final attack on the city. And who will wear the jacket?" She shrugged. "One of their leading people – Pa-hsia-li, perhaps." So they'd got Parkes; I could hear that lazy drawl, see the superior smile, and . . . the wire jacket. "It does not matter. You will see it done. Now," she stood up, stretching, "you will take me up. Oh, but I'm tired, Little An! And hungry! Why did you let me talk so long, you stupid little man!" And she pretended to box his ears, laughing, while he squeaked and feigned anguish.

That was what made my flesh crawl – the sudden capricious change from hellish scheming to playful mischief, from the cold, unspeakably cruel calculation that meant dreadful death for men she'd never seen, to happy high spirits demanding crackling with cherries, and a tea-leaf pillow because her eyes were tired. It's a rare thing, that gift of human translation, although I'd seen it before – always in people who held immense power. I mentioned Bismarck just now; he had it. So did Lakshmibai of Jhansi – and in a way, James Brooke of Borneo, although with him it had to be a conscious act of will. For the others, it was a necessary part of their nature, to be able to turn, in perfect oblivion, from determining the destiny of a nation, or a matter of life and death, to choosing a new hat or listening to music – and then back again, with the mind wiped clean.

Here, in an hour or so, this bonny girl of twenty-five had been subjected to heaven-knew-what debauches with a dying monarch, drugged herself with opium, run the risk of death for the mere whim of seeing some new thing (a barbarian), ravished a helpless captive for the sheer sport of it, rehearsed her plans for securing supreme political power, again at the risk of death, and was now yawning contentedly at the thought of a snack and a good sleep. God knew what her diary held for tomorrow; my point is, it wasn't quite the home life of our own dear Queen, and it takes a nature beyond our understanding to manage it.

Now, as she yawned and hummed and resumed her cloak and hood, she spared a thought for me again, tickling mischievously and skipping away laughing as Little An scuttled in to fend her off. I was to be taken secretly, she reminded him, to the Wang-shaw-ewen, which sounded like some sort of garden (I wondered what Sang would think when his soldiers reported that the wandering boy had vanished into thin air). The little eunuch made a doubtful lip.

"A pity we must be at the trouble of removing a captive from the Board of Punishments," grumbles he, "when we have one to hand." At which she cuffed him soundly, and serve him right.

"Fat savage, would you harm my barbarian? You'll treat him with care and respect, d'you hear, or I'll have you fed to the tiny devil fish, one greasy inch at a time!" She considered me with her secret smile. "Besides, I told you I may have another use for him. Just suppose . . . when the other prisoners have been killed, the barbarians discover that one has been saved, and kindly treated, by the Yi Concubine. Won't they be pleased with her – and with her party at court." She patted his head lightly. "Well, it is a possibility."

"Better he should wear the wire jacket!" pipes he viciously. "He deserves it – after tonight he isn't fit to live! How could you?" He shuddered in revulsion. "Ugh! Disgusting!"

"Why, I believe you're jealous, Little An," she mocked him, as he lifted her in his arms. "Oh, stop sulking! Just because you're weaponless, selfish little hound, am I to have no fun? Oh, no, I'm sorry – that was a mean thing to say! Forgive me, Little An . . ." As he bore her from the room she was apologising to the beastly little bladder, and her last words drifted to my ears, filling me with a new and dreadful fear. "Look, if he does not please me, or I tire of him quickly, perhaps . . ."

The beautiful voice faded up the stairs, and I was left a prey, as they say, to conflicting emotions.

*   *   *

It's a strange thing, but I remember distinctly I wasn't tired when they whisked me out of that lumber room just as dawn was breaking. Twenty-four hours earlier I'd been waking in my cage at Tang-chao. Since then I'd witnessed the battle of Pah-li-chao, arranged the demise of Trooper Nolan, been ill-used and terrified by Sang's thugs, crawled to the Emperor of China, and conferred, so to speak, with his principal concubine. A busy day, you'll allow, but while I'd a right to be played out, body and soul, I wasn't, because I didn't dare to be; I must keep my wits about me. For one stark thought was hammering in my brain above all others when the sha-dowy figures flitted into my room, to unchain and carry me swiftly out, wrapped in a carpet like Cleopatra as ever was – whatever happened now, I must not, for my very life's sake, utter so much as a syllable in Chinese.

It was the grace of God that Little An hadn't been present when I babbled before the Emperor; true, he'd later suggested slitting my tongue, but that presumably had just been native caution – he plainly didn't even suspect that I understood the lingo, or he'd never have permitted Yehonala to pour out her girlish dreams in my hearing. To both of them, I was a mere lump of uncomprehending barbarian beef, and if ever they realised that I'd taken in every word . . . quite. Thank heaven I'd been gagged throughout our meeting, or I might well have spoken at some point . . . "You permit yourself strange liberties, madam," for example.

Well, they *didn't* know, and provided I kept my trap shut, they never would. Only the Emperor and his nobles were aware of my linguistic skill, and I wasn't liable to be meeting them again. In the meantime, I faced the prospect of becom-ing stallion-*en-titre* to that gorgeous little tyrant, which was capital . . . and the possibility, if she tired of me, or it suited her murderous plan, that I'd be the one given the wire jacket when they started butchering prisoners. That wouldn't be for a week; I had that much law in which to escape and take word to Grant that he'd better look sharp if he was to rescue them. Then again . . . escaping would be damned risky; my safest course might well be to lie snug, bulling Yehonala's pretty little rump off, and pray that she'd exempt me from

223

the slaughter, which she seemed inclined to do. Which meant letting the other prisoners go hang; aye, well, it's a cruel world. It was all very difficult, and I must just wait and see what seemed best – best for Flashy, you understand, and good luck to everyone else.

These were my thoughts as I was borne off, and one thing quickly became plain: in the event that escape did eventually seem advisable (and sorry, Parkes, but on the whole I'd rather not) at least it wouldn't have to be from the Forbidden City, which would have been next to impossible. For after my swathed carcase had been carried some way, it was slung aboard a cart, and driven for about two miles through city streets, to judge from the noises. Then the rumble of other traffic and the din of the waking city ceased, our speed picked up, there were several cock-crows, and I guessed we were in open country. After about half an hour the cart slowed to a walk, my carpet was stripped away, I was hauled into a sitting position, and looked about me.

My escort were four men dressed like Little An, which meant they were eunuchs – nominally, at least, for while three were squeaking butterballs, the fourth was lean and whiskered and spoke in a bass croak. There's one who's all present and correct, thinks I, and he probably was. These eunuchs, you see, are an extraordinary gang; in most eastern countries, they're prisoners or slaves who've been emasculated and given charge of the royal womenfolk. But not in China, where they're absolutely *volunteers*, I swear it. It's a most prestigious career, you see, offering huge opportunities of power and profit, and there are young chaps positively clamouring to be de-tinkled so that they can qualify for the job. Not a line of work that would appeal to me, but then I'm not Chinese. However, royal concubines being what they are (and you may have gathered that Yehonala, for one, was not averse to male society) it was sometimes arranged that a candidate escaped the scissors and took up his duties in full working order. I suspect that my chap in the cart was one such, and a capital time he must have had of it, since concubines outnumbered the Emperor by about three hundred to one, and his majesty was so besotted with Yehonala that the others had to look elsewhere for diversion. But

224

fully-armed or not, the eunuchs were the most influential clique at court, as spies, agents, and policy-makers; saving the Emperor, the most powerful man in China was undoubtedly Little An, the Chief Eunuch – and he was right under Yehonala's dainty little thumb.

But I'll digress no longer, for now I have to tell you of one of the most wonderful things I've ever seen, a marvel to compare with any on earth – and no one will ever see it again. There are many beautiful things in the world, mostly works of Nature – a Colorado sunset, dawn over the South China Sea, Elspeth, primroses, cold moonlight on the Sahara, an English woodland after rain. Man cannot make anything to equal these, but just once, in this critic's opinion, he came so close that I'd hate to live on the difference. And it was done by shaping Nature, delicately and with infinite patience, as probably only Chinese artists and craftsmen could have done it. This was what I was privileged to see that September morning.

As I remember, we were leaving a little village, on a narrow road between high stone walls, which took us over a stone bridge and a causeway through a lake to a great carved entrance gate. Beyond that was a courtyard, and a massive building, blazing with gold in the rising sun; we drove past it and a scattering of lesser pavilions, and then it burst on the view in all its perfect, silent splendour, and I gasped aloud in wonder, while the eunuchs squeaked and laughed and nudged each other to see the barbarian stricken dumb as he gazed for the first time on the Summer Palace.

As you may have heard, it was not a palace at all, but a garden eight miles long – but it wasn't a garden, either. It was fairyland, and how d'you describe that? I can only tell you that in that vast parkland, stretching away to distant, hazy hills, there was every beauty of nature and human architecture, blended together in a harmony of shape and colour so perfect that it stopped the breath in your throat, and you could only sit and wonder. I can talk of groves of trees, of velvet lawns, of labyrinths of lakes with pavilioned islands, of temples and summer houses and palaces, of gleaming roofs of imperial yellow porcelain seen through leaves of

225

darkest green, of slow streams meandering through woods, of waterfalls cascading silently down mossy rocks, of fields of flowers, of pebbled paths winding past marble basins where fountains played like silver needles in the sunlight, of deer cropping daintily beneath spreading branches, of willow-pattern bridges, of dark grottoes where pale gold statues shone faintly in the shadows, of lotus pools where swans slept – I can write these things down, and say that they were spread out like a great magic carpet in glorious panorama as far as the eye could see, and what does it convey? Very little; it may even sound vulgar and overdone. But you see, I can't describe how one delicate shade of colour blends into another, and both into a third which is not a colour at all, but a radiance; I can't show you how the curve of a temple roof harmonises with the branches that frame it, or with the landscape about it; I can't make you see the grace of a slender path winding serpentine among the islands of a lake that is itself a soft mirror bordered by ever-changing reflections; I can't say why the ripple of water beneath the prow of a slow-gliding pleasure barge seems to have been designed to complement the shape of barge and lake and lily-pad, and to have been rippling since Time began. I can only say that all these things blended into one great unified perfection that was beyond belief, and damned expensive, too.

It had taken centuries to make, and if all the great artists of the Classical Age and the Renaissance had seen it, they'd have agreed that the fellows who designed it (for design, of course, was its secret and its glory) knew their business. Being a Philistine, I will add only: never talk to me about Art or Beauty or Good Taste or Style, because I've seen the bloody elephant.

I say it was a vast garden, but in fact it was many. The main one was the Ewen-ming-ewen, the Enclosed and Beautiful Garden, a great walled park with palaces which were museums of all Chinese art and civilisation, accumulated through the ages; then there was the Ching-ming-ewen, the Golden and Brilliant Garden, with its hills crowned by a six-storey jade tower and a magnificently ruined lamasery, and the Fragrant Hills, the Jade Fountain Park, the Imperial

226

Hunting Park, the Garden of Clear Rippling Water, and the one to which I was taken, the Wang-shaw-ewen, or Birthday Garden, which was reckoned the most perfect of all, with its views of the whole shooting-match, and beyond that distant Pekin, and the surrounding hills.[38]

This miracle was all for the personal delight of the Emperor and his court; no other visitors ever saw it, which was perhaps as well, since I should think it was by far the richest treasure house there has ever been in the world. To give you a notion, Yehonala's favourite pavilion was a modest cabin covering about an acre, roofed with gold leaf and apparently constructed of marble, jade, and ivory throughout; its scores of rooms were stuffed with priceless fabrics, carpets, and furs, statuary of every precious metal and porcelain, clocks, jewellery, paintings – I remember going along a verandah, looking out at the glorious scenery, and suddenly realising that I was no longer out of doors, but was staring at a wall so cunningly decorated that it appeared to be a continuation of the world outside; I had walked a good ten paces before I discovered that I was no longer seeing reality, but artifice, and when I went back and stood at gaze, I could hardly tell where one ended and t'other began. It was almost sickening to think of the genius and labour that had gone to the making of such a vain thing – yet it was lovely, and as to the movable loot . . . well, an entire wing was devoted to thousands of magnificent silk dresses, scarves, and shawls; you absolutely waded through them; another wing was given over to jewelled ornaments so brilliant and numerous that the eye could not bear to look at them for long; one vast room was filled with the most intricate mechanical toys crusted with gems, jade jack-in-the-boxes, walking dolls, blasted diamond frogs and beetles hopping and scuttling all over the shop, and you'd no sooner escaped them than you were in a room walled in solid silver and carpeted in ermine and sable, with gold racks covered in – ladies' shoes.[39]

That was Yehonala's house – and there were hundreds like it, palaces, temples, museums, art galleries, libraries, summer houses, and pavilions, all crammed with treasures so opulent that . . . why, if those Russian Easter eggs that are so admired had found their way into the Summer Palace,

227

I swear they'd have boiled 'em. God knows what it was all worth – or what it was all for. Greed? Vanity? An attempt to create a luxurious paradise on earth, so that the earth could be forgotten? If the last, then it succeeded, for you forgot the world in an instant. It should have seemed just a great, overstuffed bazaar – but it didn't, probably because of this last detail which I shall tell you, and then I'm done with description: every one of the millions of precious things in the Summer Palace, from the forty-foot jade vases in the Hall of Audience, so fragile that you could read print through them, to the tiny gold thimble on a corner shelf in the room of Yehonala's chief seamstress, was labelled with its description, origin, *and the exact position which it must occupy in the room*. Think of that the next time you drop a book on the table.

Possibly because of recent events, and my new surroundings, my memories of the first two days in that house are all at random. I saw no one but the eunuchs, whose first task was to groom the barbarian and make him fit for human consumption; Little An was early on the scene, scowling sullenly and instructing the lads to see me shaved, scrubbed, and suitably attired – I had to be careful not to understand the shrill directions screamed at me, and to appear to cotton on slowly. I insisted on bathing and shaving myself, and recall sitting in a splendid marble bathing pool, using a jewelled razor on my chest, arms, and legs, and damning (in English) the eyes of the bollockless brigade as they twittered round the brink pouring in the salts and oils to make me smell Chinese. I had a splendid shouting-match with An on the subject of my moustache and whiskers, which he indicated must come off, and which I by Saxon oath and gesture showed I was ready to defend to the last. Finally I removed them – the first time I'd been clean-shaven since I rode as a bronco Apache in Mangus Colorado's spring war party back in '50 – but dug in my heels about my top-hair; I'd been bald, when I was Crown Prince of Strackenz, and looked hellish. (Gad, I've suffered in my time.)

Another memory is of sleeping in silk sheets on a bed so soft I had to climb out and camp on the floor. I suppose I ate, and loafed, but it's fairly hazy until the second night, when they took me in a closed sedan chair to the Imperial apartments in the Ewen-ming-ewen.

This was a piece of pure effrontery on Yehonala's part, and showed not only her supreme confidence in her power, but the extent of that power, and the fear she inspired among the minions of the Imperial court. The Emperor was down in the Forbidden City still, with all his retinue of nobles and attendants, while the Concubine Yi lorded it in the Summer Palace alone – but instead of conducting her illicit amours secretly in her own pavilion, damn if she didn't appropriate his majesty's private apartments, serenely sure that not one of the eunuchs or guards or palace servants would dare to betray her. Little An's spy system was so perfect that I doubt if an informer could have got near the Emperor or any of her enemies, but probably her best security was that almost the whole court worshipped the ground she trod on. "I have that power," remember.

I had no inkling of this when they decanted me at the third of the great halls that made up the Emperor's residence, and led me through a circular side-door to a small dressing-room hung with quilted dragon robes in every conceivable colour – it was just like her, you know, to fig me out in her old man's best gear, although I had no suspicion of what was afoot until Little An began puffing musk at me from a giant squirt, and his assistant applied lacquer to my hair to make it lie down. When they tied a flimsy gauze mask over my face, I thought aha!, and then they bundled me into a corridor and along to a great gilt door where a table stood bearing scores of tortoiseshell plaques, each with a different design worked in precious stones. These were the concubines' tablets, with which his majesty indicated his choice for the night; it was then Little An's task to rout out the appropriate houri, wrap her in the silk cloak, carry her to the gilt door, and shoot her in, no doubt with a cry of "Shop!"

He didn't attempt to carry me, just waved me in and closed the door after me. And through the thin mask I saw enough to confirm my growing suspicions.

Directly ahead of me there was a sort of sloping ramp which led up to an alcove entirely filled by a bed large enough to accommodate the King's Own Yorkshire Light Infantry

229

and a couple of signallers; it was sheeted in purple silk with gold lamé pillows in case anyone wanted to sleep. To the left of the ramp were low ebony tables covered with the kind of bric-a-bric that Susie Willinck had insisted on taking to California, only more expensive: silver opium pipes and skewers, delicate golden chains and fetters, cords of silk and velvet and plaited leather, a tiny cat-o'-nine-tails with minute gems glinting in its lashes, and a scattering of exquisitely-tinted pictures which they wouldn't have shown at the Royal Academy in a hurry. Hang it, this ain't the billiard room, thinks I, and glanced to my right – and forgot everything else.

Yehonala was sitting on a low stool, dabbing her lower lip with a little brush before a dressing-table mirror. She was wearing a robe of some gauzy, shimmering material that changed colour with every movement – a wasted effect, since it was entirely transparent. But it wasn't only the sudden vision of that flawless ivory body that set me gulping and gloating as I surveyed the slender foot and ankle, the slim tapering legs, the smooth curve of belly and rump, the tiny waist, and the splendid conical breasts standing clear of the robe – well, you can see it wasn't . . . it was that perfect face in the mirror, so arrestingly lovely that you couldn't believe it was flesh and blood, and not a picture of some impossible ideal. She glanced at my reflection in the mirror, cool up-and-down.

"You look much better in a mask," says she idly, as she might have addressed her pet Pekingese, pouting her lip to examine it in the glass. "Go to the bed, then, and wait." I didn't move, and remembering that I was an uncomprehending barbarian she pointed with a silver finger-nail, flicking her hand impatiently. "To the bed – there! Go on!"

If there's one thing that can make me randier than a badger it's an imperious little dolly-mop giving me orders with her tits out of her dress. "Don't you believe it, my lass!" growls I in English, and she stopped, brush poised, eyes wide in astonishment – I reckon it was a shock to her to hear the noise the animal made. She gasped as I pulled off my mask, and for an instant there was fear in the dark eyes, so I smiled politely, made her my best bow, and came up behind her

230

stool. Her face set in anger, but before she could speak I had applied the fond caress that I use to coax Elspeth when she's sulking – one hand beneath the chin to pull her head back while you chew her mouth open, the other kneading her bouncers with passionate ardour. They can't stir, you see, and after a moment they don't want to. Sure enough, she stiffened and tried to struggle, writhing on the stool with smothered noises . . . and then she began to tremble, her mouth opened under mine, and as I worked away feverishly at her poonts her hands reached up to clasp behind my head. I disengaged instantly, dropped to one knee by her stool, smiled tenderly into the beautiful bewildered face, squeezed her belly fondly, stole a quick kiss on each tit, and swept her up in my arms as I rose.

"Wait . . . put me down . . . no, let me go . . . wait . . ." But having no Chinese I strode masterfully up the ramp, whistling "Lilliburlero" to soothe her, dropped her head and shoulders on the edge of the bed while holding the rest of her clear with a hand under either buttock, leaned forward in the approved firing position, and piled in, roaring like a Gorgon. I believe she was quite taken aback, for she gave one uncertain wail, gesturing feebly with those dear little white hands, but I'd arranged her artfully in a helpless position, hanging suspended while wicked Harry bulled away mercilessly with his feet on the ground, and what was the poor child to do? I was fairly certain, from the look of the Emperor's bedside tackle, and what I'd heard her tell Little An about Reluctant Shrimps or Galloping Lobsters or whatever it was, that she had never been romped in normal, true British style in her life, but you could see her taking to it, and by the time my knees began to creak – for I spun the business out to the ecstatic uttermost for her benefit – she was in a condition of swoon, as I once heard a French naval officer put it. I was quite breathless myself, and blissfully content, but I knew that wouldn't be the end of it.

She fulfilled, you see, four of the five conditions necessary for what may be called the Australian Ideal – she was an immensely rich, stunningly beautiful, highly-skilled professional amorist with the sexual appetite of a pagan priestess; she did not own a public house. And having spent ten years entertaining a depraved idiot of unspeakable tastes, she was now determined to make the most of Flashy while he lasted, which was until about noon next day, so far as I could judge, and if Little An had offered to carry me away I'd have held out my arms, whimpering weakly. Mind you, it was partly my own fault for being such a susceptible romantic. For it wasn't only her beauty, or passion, or matchless skill in the noble art that were nearly the death of me; it was her pure irresistible charm. When I was ruined beyond redemption, face down and fagged out, thinking, aye well, it's been not a bad life, and who'd ha' thought it would end on the Emperor of China's mattress, in the Chamber of Divine Repose (ha!) on the morning of September 25, 1860? . . . then that perfumed musical whisper would be in my ear, and I'd turn feebly to meet that angelic face with its little smile that pierced me through, and such a wave of sentimental affection would come over me, and a great longing to lock her in my heart forever, and . . . well, somehow, before I knew it, it was boots and saddles again.

❀ In a *Gazette* article entitled "The Fate of the Peiping Captives in the Late War", you may read how Col. Sir H. Flashman "endured a captivity little better than slavery at the hands of his tormentors", who treated him "in the most degrading and insulting manner", and subjected him "to such usage as can seldom have been met with by a British officer in the hands of a savage foreign Power". It's gospel true, and omits only that if the Army had known the circumstances they'd have been lining up to change places with me.

I was fourteen memorable days (and nights) in the Summer Palace of Pekin, held thrall by the notorious Yi Concubine, and since they followed the pattern of the first, you may think I was on velvet, which I was . . . and silk, satin, gauze, fur, grass, marble (which is perishing cold), yellow jade (even colder), Oriental carpet, leather upholstery, a Black Watch tartan rug (wherever that came from), and the deck of a pleasure barge on the Jade Fountain Lake, which was her most extraordinary choice of all, I think. We'd been cruising about, watching a battle between little model gunboats blazing away at each other with tiny brass cannon, when my lady becomes bored, and consequently amorous, and decided she didn't care to wait till we reached shore – so she made every other soul on board (half a dozen female attendants, two eunuchs, and the entire crew) *jump overboard* and flounder ashore in ten feet of water, so that I could rattle her undisturbed. Two of the girls were almost drowned.

From this you might suppose that my sojourn was a continuous orgy; not at all. Most of the time I was confined to Yehonala's pavilion, with a couple of the burliest eunuchs on guard, for she was by no means preoccupied with me in

233

those critical times when she was juggling to catch a crown; sometimes I didn't see her for two days on end – early in my captivity, for instance, she went with the Emperor to Jehol, forty miles away, where she tucked him up to die out of harm's way before returning to Pekin for the showdown with Sang and the barbarians. She was plotting and politicking for dear life then, and I was her Wednesday afternoon football match and brandy-and-cigar in the evening, so to speak – and her week-end picnic. A humiliating position which I was mortal glad of after what I'd been through, and I just prayed she wouldn't lose interest in her new toy before Elgin closed his grip on Pekin. For, incredibly, our army was holding off at the last, fearful that a hostile advance might spell the end of us hostages, yet fearing, too, that delay might be equally fatal.

You may wonder how I knew of this; it arose from Yehonala's remarkable attitude towards me. I said before that she spoke to me as though I were a pet poodle – and that was precisely how she treated me. Not wholly surprising, perhaps; with all the arrogance and ignorance of the well-born Manchoo, she thought of foreigners (and I was the first she'd ever seen, remember) as rather less than human, and exercised no more reticence before me than you do before Poll or your tabby. And since, quite apart from coupling, it was her whim to keep me on hand in her leisure hours, when she walked or sat in the gardens, or boated, or played games with her ladies, I learned a deal by sitting quiet with my ears open. I suspect she paraded me chiefly to tease Little An, who was her constant attendant and couldn't abide the sight of me; they'd talk shop by the lily-pond while Fido sunned himself on the grass, the target of apples playfully tossed by her ladies, and took it all in – how Parkes and Loch had been segregated from the other prisoners, and would make ideal candidates for the wire jacket when the time came; yes, the Emperor's signature was already on the vermilion death warrant, which would be forwarded from Jehol to Pekin whenever she wished; the word from the barbarian camp was that they'd rather negotiate than fight, so she had time in hand if she wished; Prince Kung, the Emperor's brother, could be relied on when the final struggle came for imperial

234

power . . . this was the kind of thing they discussed, never dreaming it was understood.

One vital titbit of information explained why Yehonala, instead of staying with the Emperor at Jehol, had returned to the Summer Palace. I gathered that her four-year-old son, Tungchi, to whom she was devoted, was in Pekin, under the care of the Empress Consort Sakota – being heir to the throne, he was far too important to be entrusted to his own mother, who when all was said was only a concubine. This was something that Yehonala, for all her great hidden power, could do nothing about; she could only keep as close to the child as possible, ready to defy protocol by stepping in if he was in any danger, or if the likes of Sang or Prince I tried to get their hands on him. It might come to bloody palace revolution yet, and possession of the infant would be vital – quite apart from her being his doting mama. In the meantime, she could only wait and trust to Sakota, who was her cousin and bosom pal, they having been apprentice concubines together before Sakota was made Empress. (If it seems odd that Yehonala, the Emperor's favourite, hadn't managed to grab the consortship, the answer was that his mother, the canny old Dowager, had spotted her for a driving woman, and had decided that Sakota, an unambitious and indolent nonentity, would make a more manageable Empress. The two cousins had no jealousy, by the way; Sakota didn't mind being Number Two in bed, and Yehonala preferred the harlot's power to the Imperial title.)

It wasn't canny, hearing all these state secrets and knowing that the speakers regarded me as no more sensate than the chairs they sat on; I wondered if any spy had ever been so fortunately placed before. The irony was that it was of no practical use; with the eunuchs forever on the prowl, and guards within call, I might as well have been in a dungeon. But at least my own position seemed secure enough, so long as I betrayed no understanding; the really dangerous times were when Yehonala and I were in bed together, and her attention close upon me; her confounded playful poodle-talk unnerved me, for as you'll guess if you've ever listened to a woman scratching a kitten's belly, it consisted mostly of dam-fool questions which it took presence of mind not to answer.

"So ugly . . . so ugly," she would whisper, lying on my chest and brushing her unbound hair across my face. "So ugly as to be almost magnificent . . . aren't you? So misshapen and ungraceful, great lumpy muscles . . . you're very strong, aren't you? Strong and stupid, with teeth like a horse. Open . . . let me see them. Open, I say . . . Gods, do you have to be shown everything? Ugh, I don't want to look at them! Horrible . . . I wonder what your barbarian women are like? Are they repulsive, too? You'll find them so, after this, won't you . . . after the incomparable Yi Concubine? I must look like a goddess to you . . . do I look like a goddess? Is it possible you might prefer female barbarians, I wonder? I mean, great apes like each other . . . but you may never see your barbarian women-apes again . . . not if I keep you. I might, when my son rules, and I'm all-powerful. Would you like that? I could send you now to Jehol, before your friends come . . . or I could give you back to them. No, I don't want to lose you yet . . . and how unhappy you'd be, without me . . . wouldn't you? You must think you're in heaven, poor barbarian. If only you could speak . . . why can't you speak . . . properly, I mean? Suppose you could, what would you say to me? Would you make love to me with words, like the poets? Do you know what poetry is, even? Could you write a poem in praise of my beauty . . . in butterfly words fluttering crooked up and down the page of my heart? Jung Lu wrote me a poem once, comparing me to a new moon, which was not very original . . . What would you compare me to, d'you think? Oh, you're hopeless! You couldn't love with words . . . you know only one way, don't you? . . . like a great, greedy beast . . . like this . . . no, greedy beast, not like that! Be still . . . like *this* . . . slowly, you see? . . . this is the Fourteenth Gossamer Caress, did you know? There are more than twenty of them, and the last, the Supreme Delirium, can be experienced only once, for during it the lover dies, they say . . . let us be content with the Fourteenth . . . for the moment . . . then we'll try the Fifteenth, shall we . . .?"

It's desperate work, listening to that kind of drivel with a straight face, never showing a glimmer of comprehension, in constant fear lest a blink of surprise, to say nothing of an

236

ecstatic shriek in the wrong language, means certain and hideous death. For I had no illusions about this sweet young thing – if she so much as suspected I understood, the wire jacket would be the least of it; the more I knew of her, the more I became aware of what I said some time ago, that she was a compound of five of the Deadly Sins – greed, gluttony, lust, pride, and anger, with ruthlessness, cruelty, and treachery thrown in; it was fatally easy to forget it, gazing on that lovely face, and embracing that wonderful body, or listening to her chaffing Little An, or joking like a mischievous schoolgirl with her ladies – for she had a great sense of fun, and true playfulness, and yet in spite of all that, there's only one word to describe her: she was a monster.

For one thing, she really enjoyed cruelty, and as an authority in the bullying line myself, I don't speak lightly. Ranavalona of Madagascar has always headed my list of atrocious females, but she was raving mad, and did her abominations almost offhand, without emotion. Yehonala was anything but mad, and if her cruelties seem trivial beside those of my Malagassy Moonbeam, she still inflicted them with the relish of a true sadist. She had a servant following her about with a case of canes and switches, and when anyone displeased her, down came the breeches and lay on with a will, farrier-sergeant. When two of her eunuchs caught some crows and released them with firecrackers tied to their legs so that the birds were blown to bits in mid-air, Yehonala had the culprits' backsides cut to bloody pulp with bamboo whips, watching the infliction of the full hundred strokes with smiling enjoyment. You may say they deserved a drubbing, but you didn't see it.

Even crueller, I thought, was her treatment of a maid called Willow, who offended in some trivial way. Yehonala ordered another maid to start slapping Willow's face, and when she didn't do it hard enough, made Willow slap her back. In the end she had the two little chits thrashing each other in tears, while she laughed and clapped her hands. Add that it was she who constantly urged the slaughter of prisoners, and sent the suicide cords to unfortunate commanders, and I'd say the cruelty case is proved; for ruthlessness and treachery I'd refer you only to her first conversation in my presence.

As to the Deadly Sins – I saw her in a towering rage only once, with the bird-blowing eunuchs, but I'm told that her anger was legendary, and could be berserk in its fury. She wasn't a glutton in the ordinary sense, but her pleasure in food was voluptuous, especially in dainties like sugared seeds of various kinds, and every kind of confectionery, which seemed to have no effect on her figure. She enjoyed opium, but thought no one else should have it; she also took snuff, from a hollowed-out pearl with a ruby stopper, and was the prettiest sneezer you ever did see, giving tiny little "cheef!" noises and wrinkling her nose. She was uncommon greedy for precious things, which was astonishing since she had everything a woman could conceivably want; yet she gloated over her jewellery and clothing in a way that was positively indecent, and I doubt (from her conversation) if enough money could have been minted to satisfy her. Hand in hand with her delight in clothing, her transparent robes, her pearl capes, her enormous sleeves, her thousand pairs of shoes, the jewels which she would fondle as though they were alive, went her vanity, which was all-consuming – and she had every reason for it. As to her lust . . . don't ask me, how would I know?

Perhaps, on consideration, I'm wrong to call her a monster – unless it's monstrous to indulge an unbridled appetite without regard for anyone or anything. Yes, I think that's right; *I* do, and I'm a monster. With Yehonala, everything was extreme; whatever she did was done with every fibre of her, and enjoyed with sensual intensity – whether it was nibbling a sugared walnut, or half-killing a partner in bed, or flaunting a new dress, or having an offender flogged nearly to death, or watching the sun go down over the Fragrant Hills, or ruling an empire . . . she would squeeze the last drop of savour out of it, and lick her fingers afterwards. If you could have seen her even walking, with that quick, gliding stride, or pinning one of her five hundred jade butterfly brooches to her dress, or playing "The Eight Fairies Travel Across the Sea" game with her ladies, or spraying glycerine on her face to fix her cosmetics – always the same concentration, the same implacable zeal to do it exactly right, the same ambition for perfection. No wonder she became mistress of all China – or that the Emperor died of her mattress gymnastics. Ten years? It's a marvel he lasted ten days.

I append these details because, since she became one of the great women of history,* an eye-witness account may be of some interest; perhaps it'll help some clever biographer to plumb the mystery of her character. I can't; I knew her as a lover, you see, and Dick Burton assures me I'm a hopeless nympholeptic, which sounds good fun. She ravished my senses, right enough, and scared me to death – which, by the way, is true of the only three women (apart from Elspeth) whom I've truly loved: Lola, Lakshmibai, and Yehonala. An empress, a queen, and the greatest courtesan of her time; I dare say I'm just a snob.

However, my little character-sketch will have explained my growing anxiety in case she discovered that she was nourishing a Chinese-speaking British viper in her gorgeous bosom. For every day increased that risk . . . and still Elgin didn't move. The British and French army seemed to have put down roots at Tang-chao, a mere ten miles from Pekin; I couldn't fathom Grant's intentions, with winter coming on, his lines of communication gaping for a hundred miles behind him to the coast, his force still outnumbered at least four to one – if I'd had command of the remaining Tartar cavalry I'd have had him and his army and his bull fiddle bottled on the Peiho *yet*. The reason, according to Little An, was that the Big Barbarian was scared the prisoners would be murdered if he moved; knowing Elgin, I was sure there must be more to it; in fact, he and Grant were just "makking siccar", as my wife would say, counting on the very error which I heard Little An making to Yehonala.

"We shall have warning if they move," says he. "The big guns will sound, the order for the deaths of the barbarian prisoners can be dispatched, and we shall have ample time to retire to Jehol, leaving Sang and Prince I and Sushun and the rest of the reptiles to meet the wrath of the Big Barbarian.

*See Appendix II.

239

Hang-ki has charge of Pa-hsia-li and the other; they can be removed quietly and executed by the jacket whenever you wish. Unless," he glanced moodily at me, "you will be wise and put that thing away." Meeting his eye, I smiled amiably and nodded. "What in the name of Yen-lo are you going to do with him, Orchid Lady?"

"Take him to Jehol," says she. "Why not?"

"Gods! To Jehol – and play the harlot with him while . . . while the Son of Heaven is dying in the next room?"

"Well, I can hardly play the harlot with the Emperor, in his condition, can I? And you know me, Little An – I have to be playing the harlot with someone, or so you keep telling me."

"Will you jest, at such a time?" he shrilled. "Oh, little empress, if you have no shame, at least have sense! Prince Kung and the Empress Dowager are lodged only a mile away – in the Ewen-ming-ewen! Suppose word reached them of this beast's presence? Suppose Sang gets to hear of it? At the moment when you have the prize all but in your grasp – oh, why do I waste time, talking to a lovely idol with an ivory head? How will you hide him in Jehol, or on the road? It's a full day's journey!"

"He can travel with the eunuchs. It may be that I'll keep him as one, eventually. Perhaps make him chief – in place of you. At least he won't deafen me with impertinence. By the way, we'll travel to Jehol by night. Have the horse-litters and cavalry escort standing by from tomorrow; the barbarians may come soon now."

By gad, I hadn't liked the sound of that. Of course she was just joking – teasing Little An. Wasn't she? One thing was sure, she wasn't getting me to Jehol – when those guns sounded, I'd make a run for it, somehow. If I could give my watchdogs the slip, after dark – even if I didn't get out of the Summer Palace, there were acres of woodland to lie up in . . . I might even get clear away, and be in time to reach Grant and have him send a flying column slap into the city to rescue Parkes and the others . . . Probyn or Fane would be in and out before the Chinks knew they'd been. Aye, but I mustn't run the slightest risk of capture myself – the thought of being dragged back, helpless, to face her fury (they can't stand being jilted, these autocratic bitches) and Little An's malice . . .

240

"What's the matter with the filthy brute? He looks as though he'd seen a spirit!" It was Little An's harsh squeal, and I realised with a thrill of fear that he was staring at me. How I didn't start round in guilty panic, God knows; I forced myself to sit still – we were in the long ivory saloon of her pavilion, An standing beside her chair while she ate her supper of peaches sliced in honey and wine; myself on a stool about ten feet away. A few of her ladies were playing Go at the other end, laughing and chattering softly. Out of the corner of my eye I could see Yehonala had turned to look at me, laying down her spoon. I took a deep breath, pressed my hands to my stomach, and belched gently. She laughed.

"Fried bread dragons. Or love-pangs for his Orchid – eh, Little An?" She returned to her peaches.

"Perhaps." To my consternation he walked towards me slowly, and I gave him my idiot smile as he paused before me, a thoughtful frown on his pudgy face. "Do you know, Orchid Lady," says he, watching me, "I have sometimes wondered if this . . . this stallion of yours . . . is as senseless as he seems. Once or twice . . . just now, for instance . . . I've wondered if he doesn't understand every word we say."

It was like a douche of cold water, but I daren't drop my eyes. I could only blink, without interest, and hope the thunder of my heart wasn't audible.

"What?" Her spoon tinkled into the dish. "Oh, what old wool! Barbarians don't speak our language, stupid!"

"Pa-hsia-li does. Like a school-master." His little eyes were bright with suspicion. "So will others. Perhaps this one."

"And never a word out of him in days? Or any sign of sense? Nonsense! What makes you think so – apart from malice?"

He continued to stare at me. "A look . . . an expression. A sense." He shrugged. "I may be wrong . . . but if I'm not, the tale of your pleasuring him will be the least he can tell." His eyes narrowed, and I knew what was coming – and began a cavernous yawn to cover the reaction which I knew he was going to startle out of me. Sure enough:

"Look at his thumb!" he squeaked.

Now, I defy anyone in my position not to twitch his thumb,

241

or whatever extremity is mentioned – unless he has set his muscles and begun to yawn, which is a fine suppressor of the guilty start. Hutton, old Pam's Treasury gun-slinger, taught me that one. I saw the disappointment on Little An's face, and looked at him serenely.

"If you are right," says Yehonala, "then he understands us now."

I glanced at her, reasonably enough, since she'd spoken – and felt sick. She was frowning uncertainly, upright in her chair; she beckoned abruptly, so I got up and went over, meeting her stare with polite interest. After a moment:

"Do you understand me?' says she sharply, and I smiled hopefully as her eyes stayed steady on mine. Then she pointed at her feet, so I knelt upright in front of her, my face just below the level of her own, about two feet away. She continued to watch me intently, that lovely oval mask expressionless, and then said quietly:

"I don't know, An . . . but we must be sure. It's a pity. Take the sabre from the wall yonder . . . quietly. When I say 'Begin' . . . strike."

If it was a bluff, it was bound to work. Even Hope Grant or Rudi Starnberg wouldn't have been able to repress a flicker when she spoke the fatal word, and my nerves weren't in the same parish as theirs. I didn't hear Little An move behind me, but I knew he'd be there, quietly poising that razor-sharp blade, waiting. I could only kneel patiently, praying the sweat wasn't starting from my brow, meeting her cold gaze with smiling inquiry as I would have done if I'd been innocent, letting my smile fade uncertainly as she didn't respond. I strove not to gulp, to look easy, knowing it was no go – unless I could think of something I was bound to flinch at the word. In desperation, I lowered my eyes, searching for inspiration . . . finally letting my glance stray to her bust; she was wearing one of those tight silk Manchoo dresses that button at the throat and are open to the breast-bone, leaving a gap through which appetising curves of Eve's puddings are to be seen; I stared with rapt interest, moving my head slightly for a better view, moistened my lips, and blew gently at the opening. She flinched, and I glanced up with an insolent suggestive twitch of the brow to let her see how my

242

thoughts were running; there was a shadow of doubt in the dark eyes, so I returned to my leering contemplation of her bouncers with a contented sigh, leaning a little closer and blowing again, a longer sustained breeze this time . . .

"Begin," says she softly, and I continued to blow soft and steady, without a tremor, for I knew it was a bluff, and that Little An, far from holding a sabre over my head, was still ten feet away, watching. If you want to play double-dares with Flashy, don't do it when there's a polished walnut cabinet reflecting the room behind him.

"Idiot!" snaps Yehonala, and snatching up her spoon she flung it at An's head. "He doesn't understand a word! You're a snivelling old woman . . . and a spiteful little worm! Now get out, and leave us alone."

By George, I was glad to see the brute go; he'd had my innards in a rare turmoil for a few minutes, and I knew that now his suspicions were aroused he'd watch me like a lynx. Even in the small hours, when Yehonala had played us both out, I was still too nervous to go to sleep for fear I babbled in Chinese – and next day, to my consternation, I was confined to my room, with the door locked and a Mongol trooper of the Imperial Guards cavalry on sentry, which had never happened before. I glimpsed him when they brought my dinner – a hulking, shaven-headed rascal in a mail coat and yellow sleeves. I demanded in English to be let out, and they slammed the door on me without a word. I ate little dinner, I can tell you, pacing up and down my room with its high, impossibly tiny windows, asking myself if An had been poisoning her mind with suspicions, but as the day wore on my anxieties changed colour – something strange was doing in the Summer Palace. There was distant bustle in Yehonala's pavilion, voices raised and feet hurrying; outside in the garden, towards evening, there were unmistakable noises of horses going past, and a peremptory voice in Chinese: "I know the litters are there, but the third one's empty – no cushions or rugs! Why not?" An apologetic mumble, and then: "Well, get them! And stay with the grooms. If anyone wanders off, he'll walk to Jehol in a cangue!"

So she was going! Was Grant moving at last, then? But there hadn't been a single cannon-shot, ours or the Chinese;

243

he couldn't be advancing on Pekin without some hysterical Tartar touching off a field piece, surely? Tang-chao was less than a dozen miles away – the sound of firing would carry easily . . . but the afternoon light was fading; it wasn't possible he was coming today, Yehonala's people must have had a false alarm – and then, far-off, there was the brazen whisper of a Manchoo trumpet, and a drum of approaching hoof-beats, a single rider pounding across the sward, voices calling anxiously at the front of the house, and a hoarse cry of alarm:

"The barbarians! Fly for your lives! They are in the city – the streets run with blood! Everyone is dead, the Temple of Heaven is overthrown, the shops are closed!"

I swear it's what he said – and even the last part wasn't true. Not a single allied soldier was in Pekin, nor even a gun threatening its walls, the Manchoo army was watching in vain . . . but the barbarians were coming, all right. Grant had slipped his hounds without so much as a shout, our cavalry was sweeping in from the north (the last place they might have been expected), with the Frog infantry in support – everyone got lost in the dark and went blundering about famously, but that only added to the Chinese confusion. I knew nothing of that as I listened to the uproar in the pavilion . . . and now footsteps were padding to my door, it was thrown open, and a eunuch came in, threw me a cloak, and jerked his thumb. I slipped it over the loose tunic and trousers that were my only clothes, and followed him out, my Mongol guard looming behind me as we made our way to the ivory saloon.

The pavilion was in the throes of a flitting. The halls and passage-ways were cluttered with luggage, servants were staggering out under boxes and bundles, eunuchs fussed everywhere, maids were fluttering in silken confusion, and a stalwart young Manchoo Guards officer was barking orders and cuffing heads in an effort to bring them to order (I recognised the peremptory voice from the garden; although I didn't know it yet, this was Jung Lu, Yehonala's old flame and now Imperial Guards commander). Only in the ivory saloon was there comparative peace, with Yehonala looking uncommon fetching in a magnificent snow-leopard robe with

244

a gigantic collar, sitting at ease while Little An fussed about her, and half a dozen of her ladies waited in a respectful semi-circle at the far end, all dressed for the road. She indicated that I should stand by her table, and the Mongol fell in beside me, breathing garlic.

"Why don't they come?" Little An was squeaking; his face was bright with sweat. "If their soldiers are north of the city, we may be cut off here! How could we escape their devil-cavalry, who speed like flying dragons? Should we not send another messenger, Orchid? What can be keeping them?"

Yehonala stifled a yawn. "The Empress Dowager will have mislaid her eyebrow tweezers. Stop fussing, Little An – the barbarians are intent on Pekin; they won't come here. Even if they did, Jung Lu has men on the road to bring word."

Little An glanced round as though he expected to see Elgin climbing in the window, and stooped to whisper. "And if Sang should come? Have you thought of that? We know who he's after, don't we? Suppose he were to come with riders – what case are we in to resist him, with only a handful of Guards?"

"Sang has enough to do with the barbarians, fool! Besides, he wouldn't dare lay hands on the Empress . . . or on him." But I saw the silver nails were drumming gently on the arm of her chair.

"You think there's anything that madman would not dare?" An shrilled. "I tell you, Orchid Lady – the barbarians can have Pekin for him, so long as he can get his claws on –"

"That will do, Eunuch An-te-hai." The lovely voice had a dangerous edge. "You're alarming my ladies, which is bad for their digestions. Another word, and you'll stand on that table and repeat a hundred times: 'I beg the ladies' pardon for my unmannerly cowardice, and humbly entreat the Empress of the Western Palace to sentence me to a hundred lashes on my fat little bottom'. And she'll do it, too."

That sent her ladies into great giggles, and Little An fell sullenly silent. The noises of exodus were dying away in the pavilion; a door slammed, and then there was silence. I strained my ears – if our fellows were north of the city. they couldn't be more than five miles away. Yehonala was right;

245

they wouldn't bother with the Summer Palace until Pekin was secure, but if I could make a break, perhaps when we set off . . . it would be dark . . .

Brisk footsteps sounded, and the young Guards Commander strode in, halting smartly and bowing his pagoda helmet to his waist. "The Prince Kung and the Lady Dowager have decided to remain, Concubine Yi, but the others will be here in a few minutes."

"What *can* have happened to those tweezers?" says Yehonala. "And probably the sleeping pantaloons, too. Ah, well. Are the litters ready, Colonel Jung?"

"Three horse palanquins in the court, Orchid, with the carriage for your ladies." He was breathing hard. "I've sent the servants' carts ahead, so that they won't delay us, and had all the gates locked. It will be necessary to reach the court by the garden passage –" he pointed to the narrow arch at the far end of the room, where the ladies stood "– and from the court the Avenue of Dawn Enchantment is walled as far as the Jehol road, where I have a troop waiting." He paused for breath, and Little An cried:

"Why these precautions? Are the barbarians so close?"

Jung ignored him, speaking direct to Yehonala. He was a good-looking lad, in a dense, resolute sort of way; Guards officers much the same the world over, I suppose.

"Not the barbarians, Orchid . . . no. My rider at the Anting Gate has not reported. But it would be best to leave quickly, as soon as the Empress arrives. There may be . . . some danger in delay."

Little An absolutely farted in agitation and was beginning to squeal, but Yehonala cut in. "Be quiet! What is it, Jung?"

"Perhaps nothing." He hesitated. "I stationed my sergeant on the Pekin road, half-way. His horse came in just now – without a rider." There was silence for a moment, then:

"Sang!" shrills Little An. "I knew it! What did I say? Lady, there is no time to lose! We must go at once! We must–"

"Without my son?" She was on her feet. "Jung – go and meet them. Bring them yourself – bring them, Jung, you understand?"

He saluted and strode out, and Yehonala turned to the

246

palpitating An and said quietly: "Every shadow is not Prince Sang, Little An. Even sergeants fall off their horses sometimes. No, be silent. Whatever has happened, your bleatings will do nothing to help." She adjusted her fur collar. "It's cold. Lady Willow, have them put the screen across the window."

As her woman pattered to obey, she paced the floor slowly, humming to herself. Outside the sound of Jung's hoof-beats had faded, and we waited in the stillness, the air heavy with suspense. She may have found it cold, but I was sweating – whatever the possible danger, I reckoned Jung was a good judge, and he'd been a sight more worried than he let on. Little An was visibly bursting with silent terrors, in which Sang presumably had the lead role. Well, that was one I could do without . . . if he bowled in, I could see a pretty little scene ensuing when he recognised one of his star prisoners. Suppose I broke for it now . . . a bolt for the door, downstairs and into the garden . . .? My skin roughened at the thought . . . the Mongol was at my elbow, stinking to high heaven, never taking his eyes off me –

"Ho-hum, cheer up, Little An," says Yehonala, pausing in her walk, and prodding him playfully in the stomach. "You need some exercise, my lad. I know – where's my cup and ball?"

It was lying on the table beside me, a priceless little toy of solid gold stem with a jade cup, and a gold chain attaching to the ball, which was a black pearl. She was expert in its use, but Little An was a hopeless duffer, and it was a standing joke with her to make him sweat away at it, fumbling and squealing, while her ladies went into fits.

I picked it up and handed it to her.

Very well, I was off-guard, preoccupied with the thought of bolting for safety, and my action was purely automatic – so much so, that she had actually taken it, with a little smile at me, and it was only the horrified realisation dawning on my own face that made her stare. Without that, my blunder might have passed unnoticed, or I might have bluffed it out . . . but now her eyes were blazing, Little An was shrieking – and I lunged headlong for the door, slipped on a rug on the polished floor, and came down with a crash that shook

247

the building. The Mongol was on me before I could roll away, snarling like a bear, his great hands reaching for my throat; I thumped him once, and then like a clever lad he had his knife-point under my chin, climbing off me nimbly and bringing me up like a hooked fish, his free hand locked in my collar. He shot a glance at Yehonala, and asked for instructions.

"Kill him! Kill him!" squealed Little An. "He's a spy – a barbarian spy!" A brilliant thought struck him. "Gods! He was Sang's prisoner! He's a spy of Sang's! He –"

"Put him yonder," says Yehonala, and the Mongol thrust me down in her chair, taking his stand behind it with his knife prodding the angle of my neck and shoulder – it beats handcuffs any day.

"Why?" yelps Little An. "Kill him now! Aiee, Orchid, why do you hesitate? He has heard all – he knows! He must die at once, before the Empress comes! Please, Orchid! Kill him – quickly!"

She came to stand in front of me, moving without haste, and save for the black ice of her eyes there wasn't a trace of expression on the beautiful oval face framed in the fur collar – even in that hellish moment I couldn't help thinking what an absolute peach she was. She flicked the golden toy in her hand, and the black pearl fell into the cup with a sharp click.

"You speak and understand Chinese?" It was a cold whisper, and since there was no point in denial, I nodded. Ignoring An, who was gibbering for my blood, she clicked the ball into its socket again, and said the last thing I'd have expected.

"You must have nerves like steel chains. Last night . . . you knew what I had told Little An, but you didn't flinch by a hair's breadth."

"I'm a soldier, Empress of the Western Palace." I was trying not to croak with terror, for I knew that if there was any hope at all, it rested on a cool, offhand bearing – try it next time a Mongol's honing his knife on your jugular. "My name's Colonel – Banner Chief – Flashman, and I'm chief of intelligence to Lord Elgin, whom you call the Big Barbarian –"

248

"He's a spy!" shrieks An. "He admits it! Kill him! Give the order, Orchid Lady!"

"Why did you never speak before?" Her voice could never sound harsh, but it was fit to freeze your ears. "Why did you lie and deceive, by silence? Are you a spy?"

"Of course he is! He said so! He –"

"No, I was a prisoner of Prince Sang's, taken by treachery. When you found me, I was gagged and unable to speak. By the time I was released, I had heard so much that to have admitted my knowledge would have meant certain death." I frowned, gave my lip a gentle chew, and then looked her in the eye, speaking soft like a man striving valiantly to conceal his emotion – you know, a kind of ruptured Galahad. "I had no wish to die . . . not when I had found a new reason for living."

For a second she didn't take the drift – and then, d'you know, she absolutely blushed, and for the only time in our acquaintance she couldn't meet my eye.

"He lies!" screamed Little An, God bless him. "Orchid, he has the tongue of a snake! The lying barbarian dog! Will you let him insult you, this beast? Kill him! Think what he knows! Think what he's *done!*" Keep it up, Little An, thinks I, and you'll talk me out of this yet. She met my eye again, cold as a clam.

"You think you will live now?" She flicked her cup and ball again – and missed.

"Why should you kill me . . . when I can serve you better alive? What I've overheard is in no way dangerous to you . . . or to your son; on the contrary." I knew I mustn't babble in panic, but maintain a calm, measured delivery, head up, jaw firm, eyes steady, bowels dissolving. "Tomorrow the British army will be in Pekin, seeking a treaty – not with Prince Sang, or Prince I, or Sushun, but as you said yourself, 'with an Emperor acceptable to the barbarians'. Since it's likely that the present Emperor will die, I can think of no more acceptable successor than your own son . . . guided by those who love him and seek the good of China. So I'll tell Lord Elgin – and he'll believe me. He will also see it for himself. And believe me, Empress – if you want a friend, you'll find none better than the Big Barbarian. Except one."

249

By jove, it was manly stuff – and true, for that matter. How she was taking it, I couldn't tell, for her face was as mask-like as ever. Little An wasn't buying; he'd picked his line, a singularly unattractive one, and was sticking to it. The Mongol I wasn't sure about, but he wasn't a voting shareholder. I sat bursting with concealed funk; should I say more . . .? Yehonala flicked her cup again, and this time the ball snapped home with such finality that like a fool I came out with the first thing that entered my head.

"Of course, you'd want to stop the death warrants for Pa-hsia-li and the others. Lord Elgin would never forgive . . ." I stopped dead, appalled at the thought that I was voicing a threat – and an even more frightful thought occurred: suppose Parkes was dead already? Oh, Jesus what had I said? Yehonala's reply left me in no doubt.

"He would never forgive Prince Sang, you mean."

"Yes, yes!" cries An eagerly. "That is the way! Don't listen to this liar, Orchid! Kill him and have done! He's a spy, who'll take every word to the Big Barbarian, lying and poisoning him against us! What do they care for China? They hate us, mutinous slaves!" He turned on her, hissing. "And he would defame you . . . oh, he won't tell them just what he's heard! He'll invent foul slanders, abominations, mocking your honour –"

The temptation to bellow him down with indignant denials was strong, but I knew it wouldn't do with this icy beauty's eye on me, and her mouth tightening as she listened. I waited until he ran out of venom, and sighed.

"There speaks the jealous eunuch," says I, and gave her just a hint of my wistful Flashy smile. "What can he know, Orchid Lady?"

Those were my bolts shot, diplomatic and romantic, and if they didn't hold . . . I could try shooting feet first out of the chair and diving for the door, but I rather fancied the expert at my back would be ready for that. I waited, while she clicked her infernal toy again, and then she turned abruptly away, signing Little An to follow her out of earshot. At the end of the room her ladies stood agog, twittering at this sensation. While she and An conferred, my watchdog and I fell into conversation.

"Lift the point a little, soldier, will you?"

"Shut up, pig."

Whether our friendship would have ripened, or what conclusion Yehonala and An would have reached, I can only guess, for it was at that moment that we were interrupted. One second all was still, and then there was a confused tumult from the garden, a babble of voices with a man shouting and women crying out closer at hand; distant yells and the sound of approaching hoof-beats; feet running in the house itself, and then the door was flung open and a tiny boy rushed into the room. He was the complete little mandarin, button hat and dragon robe and all, and at the sight of Yehonala he screamed with delight and raced towards her, arms out – only to stop abruptly and make a very slow, deep bow which was never completed, for she had swept him up, kissing him, crying out, and hugging him to her cheek. Then there were women in the room, three of them – a tall, bonny Manchoo girl with scared eyes, in a sable hat and cloak, and two other ladies, one of them squealing in alarm. From the fact that everyone in the room except Yehonala and my Mongol (trust him) dropped to their knees and knocked head, I knew this could only be the Empress Sakota, and the little boy, who was demanding shrilly to be let down so that he could show Yehonala his new watch with the little bell (the damnedest things stick in your memory) must be the heir to the throne, Tungchi.

They were all crying out at once, but before any sense could be made of it there was a yell and a clang of steel from the front of the house, a stentorian voice roaring to knock the bastard down but not to kill him, and noises to suggest that this was being done, not without difficulty. Then the Empress Sakota went into hysterics, covering her ears and shrilling wildly, her ladies stood appalled and helpless until Yehonala slapped her soundly, pushing her towards her own ladies who bore her in a screaming scrimmage to the end of the room. One of Sakota's females swooned, the other was sobbing that the Prince General was here . . . and booted feet were striding up the passage, the half-open door was thrown back to the wall, and General Sang-kol-in-sen stood on the threshold.

251

It had happened more quickly than it takes to tell. I doubt if a minute had elapsed since the Mongol told me to shut up – and now for a second the room was still as death, except for the subdued sobbing of the Empress, and the little prince's shrill voice:

"See – when I push it, it rings! It rings!" He pulled at Yehonala's sleeve. "See, mama – it rings!"

She had set him down, but now she picked him up again and handed him to Little An, who had turned a pale green, but took the boy and was turning away at Yehonala's quiet word when Sang roared "Wait!" and advanced a couple of paces into the room. He was in full fig of tin belly and mailed legs, with a fur cloak hanging from his shoulders, his dragon helmet under one arm and his shaven skull gleaming like a moon. Two wiry Tartar troopers were at his back, and I think it was the sight of them that made my Mongol withdraw his knife and step clear of my chair, his hand resting on his sabre-hilt. I sat still; I'm nobody's fool.

Yehonala stood perfectly still in the centre of the room, facing Sang who had halted about ten feet away. His basilisk stare moved from Little An to her, and he gave her a curt nod.

"All harmony, Yi Concubine. I have –"

"All harmony, Lord Sang," says she quietly, "but you forget her Imperial Highness is in the room."

He grunted, and ducked his head towards the distant women. "Her Imperial Highness's pardon. My business is with his Highness the Son of the Son of Heaven. His sacred presence is required in Pekin. The Prince I commands it."

"His Highness is going to Jehol," says she. "The Emperor commands it."

Her tone rather than the words made his face crimson, and I saw the cords of his bull neck stiffen in anger, but instead of howling, as usual, he gave a contemptuous snort.

"You have a vermilion decree, swaying the wide world? No? Then we waste time. I'll take his Highness. I have an escort."

"Chief Eunuch," says she, "take his Highness down to the court . . . at once." She stood as stately calm as ever, but I

252

caught the shake in her voice, and so did Sang, for he laughed again.

"Stand still, bladder! Don't be a fool, Yi Concubine. Your Imperial Guards hero is down there with a broken head, and this fellow'll take my orders!" He jerked a thumb at my Mongol, glanced in our direction, and noticed me for the first time. For a moment he frowned, and then his eyes dilated and his mouth gaped, which didn't improve his appearance one bit. "That!" he bawled. "By death, what is it doing here?"

"He is a Banner Chief of the barbarian army!" she retorted. "A staff officer of the Big Barbarian himself –"

"I know what he is! I asked how he came here!" His glare fell on Little An, half-hidden behind Yehonala and clinging to the small prince as though he were a lifebelt. "You – capon! Is this some of your work? No, you scum, you never do anything but at her bidding!" He thrust out his jaw at Yehonala. "Well? What is an enemy prisoner doing in the Yi Concubine's pavilion?"

"I am not answerable to you!" Her voice trembled with anger. "Now get out of my house! And knock your head as you go, you low-born Mongol!"

He actually fell back a pace, and then he seemed to swell, towering above her with both mailed hands raised, mouthing like a maniac. My guard took a pace forward, but Sang mastered himself, glaring from one to other of us, and his dirty mind must have come to the right conclusion, for suddenly he gave a snarling grin. "Ah! I begin to see! Well . . . it's no matter. We'll put the foreign filth where he belongs – in the Board of Punishments! And you," he shouted at Yehonala, "can answer to the Supreme Tribunal . . . and bring your own silk cord with you, traitress!" He gestured to his men. "Take his Imperial Highness – and that *fan-qui* rubbish!"

One of the Tartars stepped towards Yehonala, none too brisk, and she turned and snatched the boy from Little An, pulling him close to her side. She was quivering like a deer, but her eyes were blazing.

"Dare! Dare to touch him, you stable scum, and you'll die for it! For treason and sacrilege! The Emperor will –"

253

"On the word of a faithless whore?" jeers Sang, and thrust the Tartar brutally forward. "Fetch him, fool!"

The Tartar took another step, Little An screamed and blundered bravely forward, arms windmilling, to bar his way, and Yehonala swung the prince up in her arms, turned to run in sudden panic, realised it was hopeless, and turned again, helpless. The Tartar flung Little An aside, the ladies behind wailed in terror, and Yehonala flung out a hand to ward off the Tartar, crying out.

"Help me! Stop them! Help me!" And, by God, she was calling to *me*.

Well, you know what follows when a beautiful young woman, threatened by brutal enemies, turns to me in a frenzy of entreaty, hand outstretched and eyes imploring; if she's lucky I may roar for the bobbies as I slide over the sill. But this was different, for while they'd been trading insults I'd been calculating like sin, and I knew how it must be, even before she hollered for help – if Sang prevailed, I was dead meat; if I turned up trumps, Yehonala would see me right; if Sang thought he could rule out the Mongol, he was wrong, for the brute was not only an Imperial Guardsman worth two Tartars any day, he had a mishandled chief to avenge, and the sight of Yehonala threatened had been causing him to bristle like a chivalrous gorilla. It was his size that determined me, and the fact that there wasn't a sill to slide over, anyway. It was now or never: I leaped from my chair, crimson with fear, and roared:

"Sang-kol-in-sen! That lady and her child are under the protection of Her Majesty's Government! Molest them at your peril! I speak for Lord Elgin and the British Army, so . . . so back off, d'you see?" And for good measure I added: "You dirty dog, you!"

It stopped 'em dead in sheer amazement, Dick Dauntless facing the stricken heathen, and I wished Elspeth could have seen me just then – or perhaps, considering what Yehonala looked like, better not. There was a breathless pause, and then Sang went literally mad with rage, howling and lugging out his sword. I yelped and sprang away, turning for the sabre which I knew was on the wall, since Yehonala had indicated it to An last night – and the damned thing wasn't there! Sang's blade whirled in a glittering arc, and I hurled myself aside, bellowing, as it shattered a table in my rear. There was the sabre, three yards along – I leaped and snatched it from the wall, whirling to meet another furious cut, roaring to the Mongol to get on parade, and breaking ground as Sang came after me, frothing like a pi-dog. On clear floor I fell on guard, parrying two cuts to take his measure, and my heart leaped as I realised I'd been right in one vital hope – he couldn't use a sabre to save himself. He was a blind, furious lasher, so I exposed my flank, took the cut on the forte, waited his lurching recovery, and ran him through the left arm. (I ain't Guillaume Danet, you understand, but Sang's swordplay would have broken the troop-sergeant's heart.)

I needn't have fretted about the Mongol. One Tartar was down, with his guts on the rug, and the other was in desperate retreat, with my lad coming in foot and hand. I had a brief glimpse of the room – wailing women stampeding for the archway passage leading to the court; Little An carrying the prince and herding them like a fat collie; Yehonala standing half-way, watching us, clutching her fur to her neck – and then Sang was on me again, spraying gore and hewing like a woodman; oh, he was game. Right, you swine, thinks I, this'll read well in the *Morning Post*, and I went in to kill him. I'd have done it, too, but the cowardly bastard got behind a table, roaring for help; Yehonala suddenly cried out, and I stole a glance behind – there were fur caps and swords in the doorway, with the Mongol charging them. More of Sang's riders, three at the least, but the Mongol was holding them in the narrow entrance; useful chap he was.

"Die hard, Attila!" I roared to encourage him, took a last cut at Sang, and turned to race along the room. Yehonala was at the archway, glancing back anxiously while Little An, who seemed to have got shot of the prince to one of the women, pleaded with her to make haste. I seconded that as I ran, for I wanted no one hindering my line of retreat: "Get out, woman! Run for it! We'll stand 'em off!" By which I meant that the Mongol would, but just as I came level with him, moving smoothly, the mob in the doorway forced him back, and I must turn to cover his flank.

He'd done for the original two, but had taken a couple of cuts in the process, one an ugly gash on the face that was running like a tap. There were four new swords against us, and as the Mongol reeled I could only ply the Maltese Cross for my very life (that's the Afghan's last resort, an up-down-across pattern that no opponent can get by until you fall down exhausted, which happens after about ten seconds, in my condition). Then he recovered, and we retreated shoulder to shoulder for the arch, while Sang came steaming up, with shouts and great action, damning 'em for sluggards but keeping his distance.

That Mongol was a complete hand. I've never seen a faster big man, and with his tremendous reach he could have given my old chum de Gautet a few minutes' trouble. He fought left-handed, with a short sword in his right, and didn't mind at all taking a cut in a good cause; he stopped one with his bare shoulder, grunted, and chopped like lightning – and there was a head trundling away across the polished floor while the Mongol bayed triumphantly, and the three other Tartars checked aghast and reviewed the position, with Sang going demented.

We were under the arch and into the passage, and since there was room for only one I considerately went first, while Genghiz turned and dared the foemen to come on, clashing his hilts against his mailed chest and howling with laughter. He seemed in such spirits that I left him to it, flying along the passage and round the corner, and not so much as a mouse-hole to hide in, so I must career down the stairs and into the starlit dark of the walled court.

Two horse-palkis were clattering out and away along an avenue of high impenetrable hedges; one remained, and Yehonala was drawing aside its curtain, preparing to climb in but looking back anxiously – for me, I like to think, for she gave a little cry as I appeared. Little An was trying to climb aboard the lead horse and making sad work of it, squealing oaths and slipping under its neck; I heaved him up bodily – it was like handling a mattress full of blancmange – and slapped the beast with the flat of my sabre. It started forward, and as the palki came by Yehonala had the curtain raised; she said nothing, but stretched out her hand; I caught it for a second, and she smiled; then the palki was past, and I got a foot on the shaft and swung aboard the rear horse and we were away, the palki swaying like a hammock between the two beasts. As we lumbered down the avenue, I looked back; the court was empty under the stars, which suggested that my Mongol was still at profitable labour – and if you cry out on me for a deserter, so I am, and you can spare your sympathy for his opponents.

The avenue ran straight for half a mile, and we picked up a good pace. With the panic of action over I was suddenly reeling tired, and trembling at the thought of the risks I'd run; the temptation to sink forward on the horse's mane, sobbing with relief, mastered me for a moment, and then I thought, sit up, you fool, you're still in the wood. The avenue was curving now, and the hedge had thinned to a border of bushes; two furlongs ahead there were lanterns burning, and the helmets of horsemen – Jung Lu's troop waiting on the Jehol road. Time to go, so I swung my leg over, gripped my sabre, and hopped down. The palki faded into the night, there were faint shouts from the gate, and the lanterns were moving up the avenue to meet it.[40]

Why did I slip my cable when I'd just won the gratitude of a powerful and beautiful woman who was half-crazy about me to start with? Well, I'll tell you: gratitude's a funny thing; do a favour, and often as not you've made an enemy, or at best a grudging friend. Folk hate to feel obliged. And in Yehonala's case, how long would it have been before she remembered how much dangerous knowledge I had of her and her ambitions, and the debt had dwindled into insignificance, with Little An putting in his twopenn'orth of hate?

Perhaps I misjudge her; perhaps she could feel gratitude with the same intensity she gave to her vice, but I doubt it. Gratitude feeds best on love, and the only love she had for me was an insatiable appetite for jolly roger. I, on the other hand, was perfectly ready for a change from Chink-meat – and yet, even now I can feel a stopping of the heart when I see in memory that lovely pale oval mask suspended in the blackness of the palki, smiling at me, and the slim fingers brushing for a moment across mine. Oh, she had a magic, and it's with me still; when I saw her again, forty years later,

257

I was gulping like a boy. That was during the Boxer nonsense, when she was "Old Buddha", still with China helpless in those tiny silver talons. She'd hardly changed – a little plumper in the face, more heavily-painted, but the eye was as bright as a girl's, and the voice – when I heard those soft, singing tones the years fell away, and I was in the Summer Palace, on a sunlit lawn, watching that perfect profile against the dark leaves, listening to the bells across the lake . . . She didn't recognise the big, silver-whiskered grog-faced ruffian among the diplomatic riff-raff, and I didn't make myself known. We spoke for only a moment; I remember she talked of Western dancing as two people holding hands and jumping all over the room, and then she gave a little sigh and said: "We should have thought it a very . . . *tame* amusement, in my young day . . ." I wonder if she did recognise me?

Anyway, wild horses wouldn't have got me to Jehol; my one thought was the army and safety, so I put the Pole Star just abaft my left shoulder and set off on my last quiet stroll through the Summer Palace; I was close by the boundary, well clear of Sang and his scoundrels – supposing the Mongol hadn't slaughtered them all, with luck – and knew that an hour's easy march should bring me in reach of the Pekin road; there I'd take stock and cast about for our fellows. Mind you, looking back, I was uncommon reckless, for heaven knew what Imps might be loose about the night; but it seemed so quiet and serene under the starlight, with the breeze soft in the branches and long cypress shadows reaching across the lawns, the distant glimmer of a lake, the twinkle of light from a pavilion half-hidden in the groves . . . I remember thinking as I walked, you'll never find such peace again; you'll forget the blood and terror in which you came to it and came away, and remember only the starlit garden . . . her place . . . and call it heaven. As I moved silently up the last slope, I looked back, and there it lay, fairyland on earth, the last Elysium, stretching away in the dawn dark, seen through the misty vision of her face.

It struck me that there might be some good portable loot in the Ewen-ming-ewen, and never a better chance, with the Empress's suite cleared out in haste, and everyone else either fled or occupied with events around Pekin; it wasn't much out of my way, so I slipped swiftly through the trees until I saw the great gold Hall of Audience ahead, and scouted through the bushes for a look-see. And d'you know what – the plundering Froggy bastards had got there first! I heard their racket ahead and couldn't make out who it might be, for our folk couldn't be so close, surely . . . then I tripped over a dead eunuch, and saw there were about a dozen of 'em, still figures sprawled on the sward towards the great gate; one poor fat sod was clutching a huge ornamental snickersnee of carved ivory, and another had a little lady's bow and golden arrows. And they'd tried to defend their treasure house against European infantry . . .[41]

The hall entrance was lit by flickering lanterns, and people were hurrying in and out; there were marching feet down by the gate, and then I heard: *"Halte! Sac a terre!"* and I whooped for joy and ran across the lawn shouting.

There was a young lieutenant posting pickets around the building, and when I'd made myself known he was in a rare frenzy, and I must see his captain, for I was the first prisoner they'd seen, death of his life, and where were the others, l'Abbé and M. Gommelle, and see, mon capitaine, un colonel Anglais, quel phénomène, avec un glaive et les pantalons Chines. I answered his questions as best I could, and learned that they were the advance guard of a French regiment sent to secure the northern approach to the city – and what was this place? Le Palais Estival, le residence impérial, ma foi! Ici, Corporal Fromage, and listen to this! Pardon? Oh, yes, there were British cavalry about somewhere, but in the dark, who knew? Now, if I would excuse him . . .

I sat on a rocket-box, dog tired, eating bread and issue wine, watching an endless stream of chattering, yelling Frog infantry swarming out of the Hall of Audience, weighed down with bolts of silk, bundles of shimmering dragon robes, jade vases, clocks, jewelled watches, pictures, everything they could lay hands on. Some were wearing women's dresses and hats; I remember one roaring bearded sergeant, with a magnificent cloth of gold gown kilted up above his red breeches, dancing a can-can as his mates yelled and clapped; another was skimming plumed picture hats up in the air like

259

a juggler's plates; my little lieutenant had a cashmere shawl embroidered with tiny gems about his shoulders, and the major was casting a connoisseur's eye over a fine gilt-framed painting and exclaiming that it was a Petitot, as ever was. There were enormous piles of loot growing in the court-yard – silks here, clocks there, paintings over yonder, vases farther on . . . very orderly in their plundering were our Gallic allies, but what would you? When grandpapa has followed Napoleon, you know how such things should be done, so the French army loot by numbers, with a shrewd eye to quality, while the indiscriminate British will lift (or smash) anything that comes in their way, just for the fun of it.

It was sunrise, and the Frogs were exclaiming over the sight of the Hall of Audience gleaming in the first rays, shading their eyes and running off for a better look, when I managed to collar a mule and set off at a nice amble down the Pekin road. The French were camped everywhere, but only a mile along I struck a troop of Dragoons boiling their dixies by the roadside. No, we weren't in Pekin yet, and Grant intended to force a capitulation by wheeling up his guns to the Anting Gate and putting his finger on the trigger, so to speak; so the campaign was over. I commandeered a horse, and a few minutes later was trotting in to the grounds of a fine temple where advance head-quarters had been set up, and the first thing I saw was Elgin still in his night-shirt, the rising sun gilding his pate, munching a bun and waving a bottle of beer at a big map on an easel, with Hope Grant and the staff ringed round him.

There was a tremendous yell when I hove in view, and a tumult of questions as I slid from the saddle, and fellows slapping me on the back and shouting: "The prisoners are safe!" and hurrahing, and Elgin came bustling to shake my hand, crying:

"Flashman, my dear chap! We'd given you up for dead! Thank God you're safe! My dear fellow, wherever have you been? This is capital! My boy, are you hurt? Have those villains ill-used you?"

I couldn't answer, because all of a sudden I felt very weak and wanted to blub. I think it was the kind words – the first I'd heard in ever so long, although it was barely three weeks

260

– and the English voices and everyone looking so cheery and glad to see me, and the anxious glower on Elgin's bulldog face at the thought that I'd been mistreated, and just the knowledge that I was home. Then someone whistled, exclaiming, and they were all staring at the sabre which I'd hung from my saddle, dried blood all over the blade – Sang's blood, and that struck me as ever so funny, for some reason, and I'd have laughed if I'd had the energy. But I just stood mum and choking while they cried out and shouted questions and rejoiced, until Hope Grant shouldered them all aside, pretty rough, even Elgin, and pushed me down on to a stool, and put a cup of tea in my hand, and stood with his hand round my shoulders, not saying a word. Then I blubbed.

❀ Survival apart, the great thing in intelligence work is knowing how to report. Well, you saw that at the start of this memoir, when I danced truth's gossamer tight-rope before Parkes at Canton. The principal aim, remember, is to win the greatest possible credit to yourself, which calls not only for the exclusion of anything that might damage you, but also for the judicious understatement of those things which tell in your favour, if any; brush 'em aside, never boast, let appearances speak for themselves. This was revealed to me at the age of nineteen, when I woke in Jalallabad hospital to find myself a hero – provided I lay still and made the right responses. Then, you must convince your chiefs that what you're telling 'em is important, which ain't difficult, since they want to believe you, having chiefs of their own to satisfy; make as much mystery of your methods as you can; hint what a thoroughgoing ruffian you can be in a good cause, but never forget that innocence shines brighter than any virtue ("Flashman? Extraordinary fellow – kicks 'em in the crotch with the heart of a child"); remember that silence frequently passes for shrewdness, and that while *suppressio veri* is a damned good servant, *suggestio falsi* is a perilous master. Selah.

I stuck to these principles in making my verbal report to Elgin that afternoon – and for once they were almost completely wasted. This was because the first words I'd uttered, after gulping Grant's tea, were to tell him that there was a vermilion death sentence on Parkes and the other prisoners; this caused such a sensation that, once I'd told all I knew about it (which wasn't much; I didn't know even where they were confined) I was forgotten in the uproar of activity, with diplomatic threats being sent into Pekin, and Probyn ordered to stand by with a flying squadron. And

262

when I sat down with Elgin later, and gave him my word-of-mouth, it was plain that the fate of our people was the only thing on his mind, reasonably enough; my account of the secret intrigues of the Imperial court (which I thought a pretty fair coup) interested him hardly at all.

It cramped my style, which, as I've indicated, tends to be bluff and laconic, making little of such hardships as binding, caging, and starvation. "Oh, they knocked me about a bit, you know," is my line, but he wasn't having it. He wanted every detail of my treatment, and damn the politics; so he got it, including a fictitious account of how they'd hammered me senseless before dragging me, gasping defiance, to audience with the Emperor, so that I didn't remember much about it (that seemed the best way out of that embarrassing episode). I needn't have fretted; Elgin was still grinding his teeth over Sang's threatening me with death by the thousand cuts, and clenching his fist at the butchery of Nolan.

My account of captivity in the Summer Palace, which I'd planned as my pièce de résistance, fell flat as your hat. I gave him the plain, unvarnished truth, too – omitting only the trifling detail that the Emperor's favourite concubine had been grinding me breathless every night. I believe in discretion and delicacy, you see – for one thing, you never know who'll run tattling to Elspeth. Anyway, I'd have thought my story sufficiently sensational as it was.

He received it almost impatiently, prime political stuff and all. I now realise that, even if he hadn't had the prisoners obsessing him, he still wouldn't have been much interested in all the tattle I'd eavesdropped between Yehonala and Little An – he was there to ratify a treaty and show the Chinese that we meant business; the last thing he wanted was entanglement in Manchoo politics, with himself acting as king-maker, or anything of that sort. He brightened briefly at my description of the set-to with Sang and his braves (which I kept modestly brief, knowing that my blood-stained sabre had already spoken more eloquently than I could), but when I'd done his first question was:

"Excepting Prince Sang's murderous attack, was no violence offered to you at the Summer Palace? None at all? No rigorous confinement or ill-usage?"

"Hardly, my lord," says I, and just for devilment I added: "The Yi Concubine's ladies did throw apples at me, on one occasion."

"Good God!" cries he. "Apples?" He stared at me. "In play, you mean?"

"I believe it was in a spirit of mischief, my lord. They were quite small apples."

"Small apples? I'll be damned," he muttered, and thought hard for a moment, frowning at the scenery and then at me.

"Did you obtain any inkling of the . . . purpose for which you were . . . kept at the house of this . . . Yi Concubine, did you say?"

"I gathered she had never seen a barbarian before," says I gravely. "She seemed to regard me as a curiosity."

"Damned impertinence!" says he, but I noticed his pate had gone slightly pink. "What sort of a woman is she? In her person, I mean."

I reflected judiciously. "Ravishing is the word that best describes her, my lord. Quite ravishing . . . in the oriental style."

"Oh! I see." He digested this. "And her character? Strong? Retiring? Amiable, perhaps? I take it she's an educated woman?"

"Not amiable, precisely." I shook my head. "Strong-willed, certainly. Exacting, purposeful . . . immensely energetic. I should say she was extremely well-educated, my lord."

At this point he noticed that his young secretary, who'd been recording my report, was agog with hopeful interest, so he concluded rather abruptly by saying I'd done extremely well, congratulated me on my safe return, told the secretary to make a fair copy for me to sign, and dismissed me, shooting me a last perplexed look; that business about being pelted with apples by harem beauties had unsettled him, I could see. He wasn't alone, either; outside I found the young pen-pusher blinking at me enviously, obviously wishing that he, too, could be regarded as a curiosity by ravishing orientals.

"I say!" says he. "The Summer Palace must be a jolly place!"

"Damned jolly," says I. "Did you get it all down?"

264

"I say! Oh, yes, every word! It was frightfully interesting, you know – not at all like most reports." He peered at his notes through steamy spectacles. "Ah, yes . . . what's a concubine?"

"Harlequin's lady-love in the pantomime . . . no, don't put that down, you young juggins! A concubine is a Chinese nobleman's personal whore."

"I say! How d'you spell it?"

I told him – and what he told others in his turn I don't care to think, but just to show you how rumours run and reputations are made, Desborough of the Artillery swore to me later that he'd heard one of his gunners telling his chum that there was no daht abaht it, Flash 'Arry 'ad got isself took prisoner a-purpose, see, 'cos 'e was beloved by this yeller bint, the Empress o' China, an' 'im an' Sam Collinson, wot was jealous, 'ad fought a bloody duel over 'er, an' Flash 'Arry touched the barstid in five places, strite up, an' then cut 'is bleedin' 'ead orf, see?

Strange how close fiction can come to truth, ain't it? The oddest thing of all was that the part of the yarn which did gain some acceptance, among quite sensible people, too, was that I'd deliberately allowed myself to be captured, as a clever way of getting into the enemy's head-quarters. Folk'll believe anything, especially if they've invented it themselves. Anyway, you can see why I don't count my report to Elgin entirely wasted.

Later that day he and Grant and our senior commanders went to the Ewen-ming-ewen, officially to view the splendours, but in fact to make sure that the Frogs didn't pick it clean before our army got its share. I was on hand, and absolutely heard Montauban protesting volubly that no looting whatever had taken place – this with his rascals still streaming out of the Hall of Audience with everything but the floor-tiles, and the piles of spoil filling the great courtyard. Some of our early-comers, I noticed, were already among the plunderers; a party of Sikh cavalry were offering magnificent bolts of coloured silk to the later arrivals at two dollars a time, and the Frogs, who'd had the best of it, were doing a fine trade in jade tablets, watches, jewelled masks, furs, ornamental weapons, enamels, toys, and robes, and finding

265

no lack of takers. The yard was like a tremendous gaudy market, for loot from the other buildings near at hand was being brought in as well, and fellows were bargaining away what they couldn't carry.

Elgin watched in bleak disgust, with Montauban hopping at his elbow crying, ah, but this is merely to make the inventory, is it not, so that all can be divided fairly among the allies; milor' might rest assured that every item would be accounted for, so that all should benefit.

"What a splendid place it has been," says Elgin sadly, standing in the entrance to the great golden hall. "And now, desolation." The floor was covered with broken shards of glass and jade and porcelain, broken cabinetwork and torn hangings, and gangs of Frogs and Chink villagers and our own early birds were swarming everywhere after the last pickings, the vast hollow chamber echoing to their yells of triumph and disappointment, the smashing of furniture and pottery that was too big to carry, the oaths and laughter and quarrelling. "No credit to our vaunted civilisation, gentlemen," says Elgin, and everyone looked sober, except Montauban, who sulked.

"Can't stop it," says Hope Grant, casting a bright professional eye and tugging his whisker. "Soldier's privilege. Time immemorial." He glanced at me. "Remember Lucknow?"

"It is the waste that offends!" cries Elgin. "I daresay this place contained a million yesterday; how much would it fetch now? Fifty thousand? Bah! Plunder is one thing, but sheer wanton destruction . . ." He shook his head angrily.

Wolseley, consulting a notebook, said that of course this was only a fraction of the Summer Palace, which was of vast extent, no doubt packed with stuff . . . Flashman probably knew it best of anybody, at which they all fell silent and looked to me; you never in your life saw so many beady eyes. Just for a second I had a vision of that pretty pavilion by the lake, and Yehonala's white hand placing a delicate ivory fairy-piece on the game board just so, the silver nails reflected in the polished jade, her ladies' silken sleeves rustling – and felt a sudden anger and revulsion – but what was the odds, when they'd find it anyway? And why not, after all? We'd

266

won. The irony was that if the Manchoos had kept their word on the treaty to begin with, or even compromised a fortnight ago, we'd never have been near the place.

I said there were hundreds of buildings, palaces and temples and so forth, spread over many miles of parkland; that the Ewen, where we stood, was probably the biggest, since it contained the Imperial apartments, but that the rest was pretty fine, too.

"Good spot o' boodle, though, what?" says someone; I said I supposed there'd be enough to go round.

At this there was great debate about the need for prize agents who would select prime pieces for each army, the rest going for individual spoil. Grant said he would have all the British share sold and paid out to the troops as prize money on the spot, rather than wait for government adjudication which (although he didn't say so) would have meant cut shares at the end of the day. Some ass said that was unauthorised; Grant said he didn't give a dam, he was doing it anyway.

"Who took Pekin?" says he. "Commons committee? No such thing. Our fellows. Very good. Wrath o' the gods? I'll stand bail." He did it, too.

Wolseley, who was a dab artist, was in a fidget to be exercising his pencil, so after the seniors had departed I strolled with him among the buildings, and we watched the looters gutting the place – as Elgin had observed, and I knew from India, they destroyed fifty times what they took away. "See how they enjoy destruction!" says Joe, sketching for dear life while I smoked and studied. "It's a marvellous thing, the effect of plunder on soldiers. I suppose they feel real power for once in their wretched lives – not the power to kill, they know all about that, it's just brute force against a body – but the greater power to destroy a creation of the mind, something they know they could never make. Look at that! Just look at 'em, will you?"

He was pointing up at a gallery where a mob of White-chapel scruff had found huge boxes of the most delicate yellow eggshell porcelain, priceless pieces varying in size from vases four feet high to the tiniest tea-cups, each wrapped carefully in fine tissue. They were throwing 'em down from the balcony in a golden shower, to smash on the floor in explosions of a million glittering fragments so light that they drifted like a snow-mist through the hall. Those below ran laughing among them, scattering them and making them swirl like golden smoke, yelling to the chaps above to throw down more, which they did until the whole place seemed to be filled with it.

"Can't draw that," grumbles Joe. "Hang it all, Turner himself couldn't catch that colour! Odd, ain't it – that's quite lovely, too."

We watched another gang, British, French, and Sikhs, man-handling an enormous vase, twenty feet if it was an inch, all inlaid with dazzling mosaic work, to the top of a flight of steps, poising it with a "One-two-three-and-AWAY!" and hurrahing like mad as it smashed with an explosion like artillery, scattering gleaming shards everywhere. And at the same time there were quiet coves going about methodically examining a jade bowl here and an enamel tablet there, consulting and appraising and dropping 'em in their knap-sacks – you know that porcelain statuette on the mantel, or the pretty screen with dragons on it that Aunt Sophie's so proud of? That's what they were picking up, while alongside 'em Patsy Hooligan was kicking a door in because he couldn't be bothered to try the handle, and Pierre Maquereau was grimacing at himself in a Sèvres mirror and taking the butt to his own reflection, and Yussef Beg was carving up an oil painting with his bayonet, and Joe Tomkins was painting a moustache on an ivory Venus, haw-hawing while Jock MacHaggis used it as an Aunt Sally, and the little Chinaman from down the road – oh, don't forget him – was squealing with glee as he ripped up cloth-of-gold cushions and capered among the feathers.

And through it all went the quiet strollers, like Joe and me, and the tall fair fellow in the Sapper coat whom we found in a room that had once contained hundreds of jewelled timepieces and mechanical toys, and was now ankle-deep in glittering rubble. He had found an item undamaged, and was grinning delightedly over it.

"I really must have this!" cries he. "She will be delighted with it, don't you think? Such exquisite craftsmanship!" He sighed fondly. "What pleasure to look at a gift for a dear

268

one at home, and think of the joy with which it will be received."

It was one of the little chiming watches, enamelled and inlaid with diamonds; he held it up for Joe and me to look at, exclaiming at the clear tone of the bell.

"See, mama – it rings!" thinks I to myself – dear God, had that been only yesterday? She would be safe in Jehol now, with her dying Emperor and the little son through whom she hoped to rule China. What would she think, when she came back to her beloved Summer Palace?

We complimented the fair chap on his good taste. I'd never seen him before, but I knew him well later on. He was Chinese Gordon.

The three of us took a turn in the gardens, and watched a group of enthusiasts digging up shrubs and flowers and sticking them in jade vases filched from the rooms. "I can see these taking splendidly in Suffolk!" cries one. "I say, Jim, if only we can keep 'em alive, what a capital rockery we shall have!" Give him the transport, he'd have had the blasted trees up.

Suddenly I stopped short at the sight of a round doorway in the third palace; it was the one, scarred now with shot-holes. We went in, and the ante-room that had been hung with the Son of Heaven's quilted dragon robes was bare as a cupboard, and not a trace of the musk with which Little An had sprayed me; no wonder, since the soldiery had been pissing on the floor. But here was the little corridor to the Chamber of Divine Repose; the great golden door hung half off its hinges, its precious mouldings stripped away and the handle hacked off. The tortoiseshell plaques of the concubines were scattered about, some of them broken; Gordon turned one over. "What can these be – tokens in some sort of game, d'you suppose?" I said I was fairly sure he was right.

My heart was beating faster as I followed the others into the room; I didn't really want to see it, but I looked about anyway. The filthy pictures and implements of perversion had gone (trust the French), the mattress of the great bed had been dragged from the alcove and hacked to shreds, its purple silks torn, the gold pillows ripped open. But it was the shattered hole in the dressing-table mirror that made me wince; that was where her lovely reflection had looked out at me, while she painted carefully at her lower lip; that broken stool had supported the wonderful body, with one perfect leg thrust out to the side, the silver toes brushing the carpet. Yet even amid that wreckage, while the others gaped and speculated foolishly about whose room it had been, there was a fierce secret joy about remembering. How the others would have stared if they'd known; Gordon would probably have burst into tears.

I didn't know which was her tortoiseshell plaque, but I took one anyway, slipping it into my pocket with the jewellery and gold I'd picked up on our walk – though none of it compared with the black jade chessmen I collared in the Birthday Garden a couple of days later; no one else would even look at 'em, which showed judgment, since the experts will tell you that black jade doesn't exist. I don't mind; all I know is that while Lucknow paid for Gandamack Lodge, those chessmen bought me the place on Berkeley Square. But I still have the tortoiseshell plaque; Elspeth stands her bedside teapot on it.[42]

*　　*　　*

"The prisoners are safe!" someone had hollered when I first rode into Elgin's headquarters, supposing that my appearance heralded the return of the others. They weren't, and it didn't although hopes ran high when Loch and Parkes turned up a day later; they'd been released *fifteen minutes* before their vermilion death warrant arrived at the Board of Punishments. Whether Yehonala or the mandarin who had special charge of them, Hang-ki, had held it back, or whether they were just plain lucky, we never discovered. They'd had a bad time: Parkes had escaped with binding and hammering, but Loch had been dungeoned and shackled and put to the iron collar, and from what he'd seen he suspected that some of the others had been tortured to death. Whether Elgin had any earlier suspicion of this I can't say; I think he may have, from the way he questioned me about my treatment. In any event, his one thought now was to get them out.

Grant had already positioned his guns against the Anting

Gate, and the word went to Prince Kung, the Emperor's brother and regent, that unless Pekin surrendered and the prisoners were released, the bombardment would begin. And *still* the Chinese put off the inevitable, with futile messages and maddening delays, while Elgin aged ten years under the mortal fear that if he *did* start shooting, the prisoners would be goners for certain . . . so he must wait, and hope, and question Parkes and Loch and me again and again about our treatment, and what we thought might be happening to the others.

I'd escaped on the Sunday; Parkes and Loch arrived on the Monday; it was Friday before eight Sikhs and three Frenchmen were set free, and when Elgin had talked to them he came out grey-faced and told Grant that he was to open fire the following noon. At the eleventh hour Kung surrendered – and the following night the first bodies came out.

They came on carts after dark, four of them, two British, two Sikh, and had to be examined by torchlight; when the lids came off the coffins there were cries of horror and disbelief, and one or two of the younger fellows turned away, physically sick; after that no one said a word, except to whisper: "Christ . . . that's Anderson!" or "That's Mahomed Bux – my *daffadar!*" or "That's De Normann . . . is it?" Elgin stopped at each coffin in turn, with a face like stone; then he said harshly to replace the lids, and stood turning his hat in his hands, staring before him, and I saw him biting his lips and the tears shining in the torchlight. Then he walked quickly away, without a word.

The other bodies came two days later; they had been used in the same fashion, fourteen of them, and if Elgin had given the word, our army would have slaughtered every man in Pekin.

Now, I've never aimed to horrify you for horrifying's sake, or revelled in gory detail with the excuse that I'm just being a faithful historian. But I'm bound to tell you what the Chinese had done, if you are to understand the sequel – and judge it, if you've a mind to.

The bodies were in quicklime, but it was still easy to see what had happened. I told you the Chinese tie their captives as tightly as possible, so that eventually the hands and feet

271

burst and mortify; some of our people had been bound for weeks, a few *au crapaudine* (hands and feet in the small of the back), some hung up, some with heavy chains; many had had their bonds soaked to make them tighter, others had been flogged. I'll add only that if, in a Chinese prison, you get the least cut or scratch . . . good-night; there's a special kind of maggot, by the million, and they eat you alive, agonisingly, sometimes for weeks. So you see, as I said earlier, there's nothing ingenious about Chinese torture; there don't need to be. They just rot you slowly to death, and the lucky ones are Brabazon and the little French padré, who were beheaded at Pah-li-chao, like Nolan.

"It is the uselessness of it that defeats me. If they had wanted to wring information from us, at least torture would be understandable. But this had no purpose. It was the wanton cruelty of men who enjoyed inflicting pain for its own sake, knowing that if retribution followed, it would not fall on them personally. I mean the Emperor, and Sang, and Prince I, and the like. For the Emperor certainly knew; De Normann's torture began in the royal apartments. Indeed they knew."

This was Harry Parkes, lean and pale but as stubbornly urbane as ever, although his drawl shook a bit when he told me how Loch, when he was sure he was going to die, had sung "Rule, Britannia" to let the others hear; and of Trooper Phipps, who'd kept everyone's spirits up with jokes when he was dying in agony; and Anderson, telling his *sowars* not to cry out, for the honour of the regiment; and old Daffadar Mahomed Bux, with no hands left, damning his torturers for giving him pork to eat. Even so, Parkes and Loch had more Christian forgiveness towards their captors than I care for; given my way, I'd have collared Sang and Prince I and the whole foul gang, and turned 'em over to the wives and daughters of our Afghan troopers, if I'd had to drag 'em the whole way to Peshawar to do it.[43]

What riled everyone was that the Chinks had been careful to surrender on terms *before* we'd seen the bodies, so there was no hope of the mandarins being punished as they deserved. How to make 'em pay – that was the question that ran through the army camped before Pekin, and Elgin sent

272

word to Kung that there'd be no talk of treaty-signing, or indeed any talk at all, until he'd decided how to avenge our people. Diplomatic claptrap, thinks I; we'll let the swine get away with it, as usual. I didn't know the Big Barbarian.

He took a day to think about it, brooding alone under the trees in the temple garden, wearing a face that kept us all at a distance, except Grant. He and Elgin talked for about an hour – at least Elgin did, while Grant listened and nodded and presently retired to his tent to put his bull fiddle through its paces something cruel. "That's his way of beating his wife," says Wolseley. "Summat's in the wind that he don't like – who's going to inquire, eh?" No one else volunteered, so during a pause in the cacophony I loafed in and found him staring at the manuscript on his music stand, with his pencil behind his ear. I asked what was up.

"Finished," says he. "Not right. Can't help it."

"What's finished and not right?"

"Quartet. Piano, violins, and 'cello." He grunted impatiently. "Journeyman work. Just to have to perform it. See what's amiss then."

"Oh, absolutely," says I. "It'll come right, I daresay, if you keep whistling it to yourself. But, general sahib . . . what's Elgin going to do?"

He turned those bright eyes and tufted brows on me, for about three minutes, and picked up his bull fiddle. "Man's in torment," says he. "Difficult." He began to saw away again, so I gave up and went back to the mess to report failure.

We weren't kept long in suspense. The last bodies came in next day, and after he'd seen them Elgin called an immediate meeting of all the leading men from both armies, with Baron Gros, the French envoy, sharing the table-top with him, and Parkes, Loch, and myself sitting by. He was wearing his frock-coat, which was a portent, since he was used to roll about in flannels and open neck, with a cricket belt and a handkerchief round his head. But he seemed easy enough, pouring a lemonade for Gros, asking if Montauban's cold were any better, making his opening statement in a quiet, measured way – just from his style, I was positive he'd memorised it carefully beforehand.

"It is necessary," says he without preamble, "to mark in a manner that cannot soon be forgotten, the punishment we are bound to award for the treachery and brutality which have characterised the Chinese Emperor's policy, and which have resulted in the cruel murder of so many officers and men. Of the Emperor's personal implication, and that of his leading mandarins, there can be no doubt. So, while the punishment must be apparent to the whole Chinese Empire, I am most anxious that it should fall, and be seen to fall, only on the Emperor and his chief nobles, who were fully aware of, and responsible for, these atrocious crimes."

He paused, looking round the table, and I wondered for a moment if he was going to propose hanging the pack of 'em, Emperor and all; the same thought may have been exercising Gros (a genial snail-eater who'd endeared himself to our troops by calling out: " 'Allo, camarades, cheer-o!" whenever they saluted him). He was wearing a worried frown, but Elgin's next words should have put his mind at rest.

"It is manifestly impossible to proceed directly against the persons of the culprits, even if we wished to, since they are beyond our reach. Considering the temper of the army – which, I confess, expresses my own feeling – that is perhaps as well. It remains to punish them by other means. Them and them alone."

He glanced at Gros, who came in nineteen to the dozen to say that milor' was bowling a perfect length, it leaped to the eye, the offenders must be made to account for their conduct unpardonable, and no nonsense. It remained only to determine a suitable method of expressing the just indignation of the Powers, and to –

"Precisely, monsieur le baron," says Elgin. "And I have so determined. After careful deliberation, I can see only one way to mark to the Chinese Empire, and to the whole world, our abhorrence of these wanton and cruel acts of treachery and bloodshed. I am therefore requesting the Commander-in-Chief –" he nodded towards Grant – "to take the requisite steps for the complete destruction of the Summer Palace."

My first thought was that I hadn't heard right; my second, what a perfectly nonsensical idea: someone murders twenty

274

people, so you plough up his garden. Others seemed to share my thoughts: Gros and Montauban were staring blank bewilderment, Parkes was looking thoughtfully at the sky, Hope Grant was pursing his lips, which in him was the equivalent of leaping up and beating his forehead; Loch's mouth was open. Gros was just drawing breath when Elgin went on:

"Before you respond, gentlemen, permit me to observe that this is no hasty decision. It is based on what seem to me to be compelling reasons." The bulldog face was expressionless, but he tapped a finger to emphasise each point. "Bear in mind that we have no quarrel with the people of China, who are in no way to blame; they do not suffer by this penalty. The Emperor and nobles suffer by the loss of their most precious possession; they suffer also in their pride because their punishment, and their sole guilt, are made plain for the world to see, and the Chinese people are made aware of their Emperor's shame. Nothing could show more clearly that he is not omnipotent, as he pretends; nothing could demonstrate so clearly our detestation of his perfidy and cruelty."

He sat with his hands flat on the table, waiting for the storm of protest which he guessed was coming from Gros, and perhaps as much from pique at not being consulted beforehand, as from genuine disapproval, the normally amiable little Frenchman weighed in like a good 'un.

"Milor'! I am astonished! It grieves me extremely to have to disagree with your lordship before these gentlemen assembled, but I cannot accept this . . . this extraordinary proposal! It . . . it . . . appears to me to have no relevance, this! It is . . . unthinkable." He took a deep breath. "I must beg your lordship to reconsider!"

"I have, monsieur le baron," says Elgin quietly. "With great care, I assure you."

"But . . . forgive me, milor', you appear to contradict yourself! You say we must punish the Emperor – with which I and all agree – but not the people of China! Yet you propose the destruction, the desecration of a . . . a national shrine of China, the repository of its ancient civilisation, its art, its culture, its genius, its learning!" He was in full Gallic spate

275

by now, all waving hands and eyebrows, bouncing in his chair. "What is this but an insult, of the most gross, to the very soul of China?"

"If it were that, I should not have proposed it," says Elgin. "The Summer Palace is not a shrine of any kind, unless to Imperial luxury and vanity. It is the Emperor's private pleasure park, and not one of the millions of ordinary Chinese has ever been inside it, or cares a straw for it and its treasures. If they think of it at all, it must be as a monument to human greed, built on extortion and suffering. China has bled to make that place, and China will not weep for its loss, believe me, monsieur le baron."

The fact that he said this as though he'd been reading the minutes of the last meeting, did nothing to cool Gros's indignation. He gasped for breath, and found it.

"And the treasures, then? Are they nothing? The irreplaceable works of art, the sublime craftsmanship, the priceless carvings and paintings and jewellery? Are they to be vandalised, to signal our abhorrence of the crime of a few guilty noblemen? Are we to punish their barbarism by an act infinitely more barbaric? By destroying a thing of infinite beauty, of incalculable value? It is . . . it is out of all proportion, milor'!"

"Out of proportion?" For the first time there was a touch of colour on Elgin's cheek, but his voice was even quieter than before. "That is a matter of opinion. A few moments ago you and I, monsieur le baron, looked on something which had been infinitely more beautiful, and of incalculably greater value than anything ever created by a Chinese architect: the body of a soldier of the Queen. His name was Ayub Khan. You saw what Chinese civilisation had done to him —"

"Milor', that is not just!" Gros was on his feet, white-faced. "You know very well I am as enraged as yourself at the atrocities committed upon our people! But I ask you, what can it profit your good soldier, or any other of those martyred, to take revenge in this fashion, by destroying . . . something with which they, and their deaths, had nothing to do?"

"Please, sir, take your seat again," says Elgin rising, "and with it my assurance that I intended no reflection on your humanity or your concern for our dead comrades." Didn't

276

you, though, thinks I. He waited until Gros had sat down again. "There is no way to profit, or adequately to avenge them. My purpose is to punish their murderers in a way that will best bring down their pride and publish their infamy. That is why I shall burn the Summer Palace, unless your excellency can suggest a suitable alternative."

Poor Gros stared at him helplessly, and waved his hands. "If it seems good to destroy some building – why, then, let it be the Board of Punishments, where the crimes were committed! What could be more fitting?"

"I've heard that suggestion," says Elgin dryly. "It emanated, I believe, from the Russian Mission at Pekin – to burn the Board and erect a suitable memorial on the site to Chinese perfidy. I can think of nothing better calculated to inflame hatred of our two countries among ordinary Chinese. I hesitate, of course, to conclude that that is why the Russians suggested it. You would say, monsieur le baron?"

"Only . . . only . . ." Gros shrugged in real distress. "Ah, milor', you think only of the effect on the Emperor and the others! But consider another effect – on the honour of our countries and ourselves! Think how such an act will be regarded in the world! It is not the Emperor of China who will be disgraced by what all civilised peoples must see as a . . . as a barbarism, grossier, incivilisé! Are we to bear the brand of Attila and Alaric, merely to punish the Emperor's vanity?" And possibly encouraged by the approving cries of his own folk, and the doubtful looks of some of ours, the silly ass put his great Frog foot right in it. "Ah, surely, milor', you of all men must be aware of what . . . of what public opinion . . ." Realising his gaffe, he broke off, shaking his head. "Ah, Dieu! The destruction of precious works of art is not well regarded!" he finished snappishly.

Even the other Frogs were trying to look elsewhere; Parkes, beside me, sighed and murmured something about "Gros by name and nature, what?" Well, everyone knew how Elgin's guvnor had stripped half Greece of statuary; even then Elgin Marbles was a slogan of outrage among Hellenic enthusiasts. The only person present who didn't seem to mind was Elgin himself. For the first time in days, he absolutely grinned.

"I had no notion," says he affably, "from the conduct of your troops at the Ewen-ming-ewen, that such a sentiment prevailed in France –"

"Milor'!" Montauban was wattling furiously, but Elgin didn't mind him.

"If stigma there be," he went on, talking straight to Gros, "I shall be content to bear it alone, if I must. It will be a small thing compared to the wound dealt to the pride and false glory of the creature who calls himself Emperor of China."

"And if it wounds him, as you hope," cries Gros. "If you so disgrace him in the eyes of his subjects, have you considered it may mean the downfall of the Manchoo dynasty?" He was on his feet again, all frosty dignity. Elgin rose with him, all John Bull.

"If I thought that, monsieur le baron," says he, "I should be in the Summer Palace this minute, with a torch and a bundle of straw. Alas, I fear it will have no such consequence."

Gros bowed stiffly. "Milor' Elgin, I must officially inform you that my government cannot associate itself with a policy which we must consider ill-advised, disproportionate, and – I have to say it, deeply as I deplore the necessity . . . uncivilised." He looked Elgin in the eye. "Monsieur, it is cruel."

"Yes, sir," says Elgin quietly. "It's meant to be."

When the French had stalked off, Elgin sat down and passed a hand across his forehead; suddenly he looked very tired. "Aye, weel," says he heavily, "a stoot he'rt tae a stae brae – eh, Loch? Now, Grant, which troops shall do the work?"

They settled on Michel's division, the destruction to begin two days hence. Loch was instructed to write the letter of information to Prince Kung, and the proclamation for general distribution; I was interested that neither referred to the deaths of our people, but only to the Emperor's treachery and bad faith – that, officially, was why the Summer Palace was to be destroyed, to show "that no individual, however exalted, could escape the responsibility and punishment which must always follow acts of falsehood and deceit."

"Here endeth the lesson," says Parkes to me. "He means to rub it into the Emperor, rather."

"The Emperor don't know a dam' thing about it," says I. "The fellow's an idiot – probably a dead idiot, by now."

"You don't really care for this, do you?" says he, eyeing me.

"Me?" I shook my head. "Tain't my house and flower-beds."

He laughed. "I don't like it, much, myself. My suggestion was for a thumping fine, and the surrender to our justice of the actual murderers – the jailers and tormentors who did the work, and in particular one gross brute who took the keenest satisfaction in pulling my hair out by the roots. H.E. pointed out, correctly, that a fine would inevitably fall on the populace, and that the jailers were merely doing what they were bidden by fiends like Sang. Also, that they probably wouldn't be handed over – they'd send us a batch of condemned convicts, and who would know the difference?" He looked to where Elgin was sitting, hands in pockets, talking to Grant. "In fact, he's dead right. This will accomplish what he wants to do."

"Teach the Emperor a lesson, you mean?" says I, not greatly interested.

"Oh, no. He's teaching China. The word will go to the ends of the Empire – how the barbarians came, and smashed the chalice, and went away. And for the first time all China will realise that they're not the world's core, that their Emperor is not God, and that the dream they've lived in for thousands of years, is just . . . a dream. Gros was right – it'll bring down the Manchoos, no error; not today, perhaps not for years, but at last. The mystery that binds China will go up in smoke with the Summer Palace, you see. And just by the way – China will break no more treaties; not in our time."

I thought about Yehonala, and wondered if he was right. As it turned out, he was, almost; China was quiet for forty years, until she roused the Boxers against us. And now the Manchoos are gone, and who'll deny that it was the fire that Elgin kindled that made China's millions think thoughts they'd never thought before?

279

He called me over presently, and asked – not ordered, mark you, but asked, which wasn't his usual style – if I'd mind going with Michel as guide, so that no buildings were missed. "You know the Summer Palace better, I daresay, than any European living," says he. "Had that occurred to you?" It hadn't, as it happened. "But the duty's not distasteful to you, Flashman?" I said I didn't mind.

Grant had gone off, and we were alone by the table in the temple garden. He gave me a keen look, and then fell to examining the peeled skin on the back of his hand, smiling a little.

"I seem to sense some disapproval in my staff," says he, "but since I dislike embarrassment almost as much as I dislike contradiction, I have borne it in silence. A chief of intelligence, however, has an obligation to be forthright. Do you agree with Gros?"

Once on a day I'd have cried no, my lord, you're entirely right, my lord, burn the bugger hull and sticks, my lord, like a good little toady. But it's better fun to tell the truth, when it can't hurt, and is bound to cause devilment. So I said:

"No, my lord. I'm sure your decision is correct." I waited until he was looking at me to see that I meant it, and then added: "But in your position, I'd not burn the Summer Palace."

He stared at me, frowning. "I don't understand, Flashman. You think it right . . . but you wouldn't do it? What can you mean?"

"I mean I wouldn't dare, my lord." I do love to stir 'em up; oh, I'll fry in hell for it. "You see, Gros is right in one thing: it'll get a dam' bad press. And I'd not care to have *Punch* labelling me Harry the Hun."

His jaw jerked at that, and for a moment I thought he was going to explode. Then he gave a jarring laugh. "By God," says he, "you're an uncomfortable man! Well, you're honest, at least. Which is more than can be said for the French, who have already looted the place, but take care to escape the odium for its destruction. Ha! And while crying 'Philistine!' they and the other Powers will be happy enough to enjoy the trade benefits and safe commerce which our salutary action will have ensured." He folded his arms, leaning back,

280

and gave me a bleak look. "Harry the Hun, indeed. They'll have no need to coin a nickname for me; the Chinese have done it for them, have they not?"

The Big Barbarian, he was thinking; he knew what to expect, but it had rattled him to have me state it so bluntly – which is why I'd done it, of course. Yet he wasn't altogether displeased; I wondered if he wasn't glad, in a way, to be bearing the blame alone. He was odd fish, was Elgin. He was no vandal, certainly; indeed, bar Wolseley, he was probably the most sincere lover of the arts in the army – not that I'm an authority, you understand; give me Rubens and you can keep the rest. So how could he bring himself to destroy so much that was rare and beautiful and valuable? I'll tell you. He was avenging our dead with cold-blooded fury, striking at their murderers (the Emperor, Sang, Prince I, and – although he didn't know it – Yehonala, who probably shaped Imperial policy more than all the rest) in the way he knew would hurt them most. For he was right there; he knew the Chinese mind; he was hitting 'em where they lived – and putting the fear of God into China, too.

But I suspect he had another reason, which he may not have admitted to himself: I believe that the Summer Palace *offended* Elgin; that the thought of so much luxury and extravagance for the pleasure of a privileged, selfish few, while the coolie millions paid for it and lived in squalor, was too much for his Scotch stomach. Odd notions for a belted earl, you think? Well, perhaps I'm wrong.[44]

Tragedy usually has a fair element of farce about it, and this was seen next day when the mass funeral of our dead took place at the Russian Cemetery, outside Pekin. As Elgin observed, the French had a wonderful time, making speeches in bad taste and following their usual practice of firing the final volleys *into* the grave and not over it. Chinese observers were heard to remark that this was to make sure the corpses were dead. There were Protestant, Roman, and Greek priests officiating together, which looked odd enough, but the sight I wouldn't have missed was Hope Grant taking part in Papist rituals, sprinkling holy water at Montauban's request, and plainly enjoying it as much as John Knox in a music hall.

We began to burn the Summer Palace the day after. Michel's division marched up to the Ewen-ming-ewen gate, where they were split into parties, furnished with crowbars, sledges, axes, and combustibles, and despatched under their officers to chosen spots in the four great gardens – the Enclosed and Beautiful, the Golden and Brilliant, the Birthday, and the Fragrant Hills. I rode round to the Birthday Garden entrance, because I had no great desire to view the whole splendid panorama again from the Ewen slope before the fires were lighted. It was a glorious day; there wasn't a soul to be seen, and the park seemed to glow in the sunlight, the great beds of flowers and avenues of shrubs had never been so brilliant, or the lawns so green; a little breeze was ruffling the waters of the lake and stirring the leaves in the woods; her pavilion gleamed white among its trees, the birds were singing and the deer posing in the sunshine, and there was such a perfume on the warm air as you might breathe in paradise. From a long way off I caught the first drift of wood-smoke.

Then there were distant voices, and the soft tramp of feet, and someone calling the step, sounding closer, and the stamp as they halted, and the clatter of crowbars and hammers being grounded. And a voice sings out: "Which 'un fust, sir?" and "Over there, sarn't!" and "Right you are, lads! This way!" and the first smash of timber.

I'm a bad man. I've done most wickedness, and I'd do it again, for the pleasure it gave me. I've hurt, and done spite, and amused myself most viciously, often at the expense of others, and I don't feel regret enough to keep me awake of nights. I guess, if drink and the devil were in me, I could ruin a Summer Palace in my own way, rampaging and whooping and hollering and breaking windows and heaving vases downstairs for the joy of hearing 'em smash, and stuffing my pockets with whatever I could lay hands on, like the fellows Wolseley and I watched at the Ewen. I'd certainly have to be drunk – but, yes, I know my nature; I'd do it, and revel in the doing, until I got fed up, or my eye lit on a woman.

But I couldn't do it as it was done that day – methodically, carefully, almost by numbers, with a gang to each house, all ticked on the list, and smash goes the door under the axes, and in tramp the carriers to remove the best pieces, and the hammermen to smash the rest with sledges, and the sappers to knock out a few beams and windows for draught, and set the oily rags and straw just so, and "Give us one o' your fusees, corporal . . . right . . . fall in outside!" And then on to the next house, while behind the flames lick up, blistering the enamels, cracking the porcelain, charring the polished wood, blackening the bright paint, smouldering the silks and rugs, crackling under the eaves. Next to the wreck of a human body, nothing looks so foul as a pretty house in its setting, when the smoke eddies from the roof, and the glare shines in the windows, and the air shakes with the heat.

That was how it was done, by word of command, one place after another, tramp-tramp-tramp, smash-smash-smash, burn-burn-burn, by men who didn't talk much, or swear, or laugh – that was the uncanny thing. British soldiers can make a jest of anything, including their own deaths; but no one joked in the Summer Palace. They went about it sour-tempered, grudging; I'd say they were heartsick, or just plain dull and morose. I remember one North Country voice saying it seemed a reet shame to spoil that many pretty things, but the only other note of protest came in a great set-to when some woods caught fire, and a red-faced fellow comes roaring:

"What the hell are you about, sir? Your orders are to burn buildings! That's good timber – fine trees, damnation take you! Are you a madman, or what?" And the reply: "No, sir, I'm not! But in case it's escaped your notice, bloody trees are made of bloody wood, you know, which commonly burns when exposed to bloody fire, and d'you expect me to race about catching all the bloody sparks?"

Now the curious thing about this was that one of the speakers was Major-General Sir John Michel, and the other a private soldier, gentleman-ranker, and they cussed each other blind, with no thought of discipline – and no reprisals, either. It was a strange day, that.

Later I remember the rending sound of roofs caving in, and the great rush of flames, the red glare of fire on bare chests and sweat-grimed faces, the harsh crackling and the foul stench as choking smoke drifted across the lawns, blotting out the lakes and flowers, the weary shouts and hoarse commands as the gangs moved on to the next little white jewel among the trees.

I've said I couldn't have done it – which is to say I wouldn't, for choice, but could if I had to, just as I've packed Dahomey slaves when needful. The Summer Palace was just about as sickly as that, but I watched, for curiosity, and because there was nothing else to do – Michel's men seemed to find the houses without my assistance. And it was curiosity that took me up the Ewen slope, towards evening, to look back on the great pall of smoke, many miles in extent, covering the country to the distant hills, with ugly patches of flame behind it, and here and there a break where you could see a blazing building, or a smouldering ruin, or a patch of burning forest, or virgin parkland, or a pool of dull grey water that had been a shining lake, or even a white palace, untouched amid the green. It looked pretty much like hell.

I'm not saying Elgin was wrong; it achieved what he wanted, without his having to break down a door or smash a window or set a match. That's the great thing about policy, and why the world is such an infernal place: the man who makes the policy don't have to carry it out, and the man who carries it out ain't responsible for the policy. Which is how our folk were tortured to death and the Summer Palace was burned. Mind you, if that wasn't the case, precious little would ever get done.

But didn't a tear mist my eye, or a lump rise in my throat; didn't I turn away at last with a manly sob? Well, no. Yes, as the chap remarked, it was a shame so many pretty things were spoiled – but I'm no great admirer of *objets d'art*, myself; they just bring out the worst in connoisseurs and female students. But even you, Flashman, surely to God, must have been moved at the destruction of so much beauty, in a spot where you had spent so many idyllic hours? Well, again, no. You see, I don't live there; I'm here, in Berkeley Square, and when I want to visit the Summer Palace, I can close my eyes, and there it is, and so is she.

284

❀ It burned for almost a week, with a vast pillar of smoke a mile high in the windless air, like some great brooding genie from a bottle, spreading his pall across the countryside; Pekin was a city in twilight, its people awestricken to silence. To them it was incredible, yet there it was, and they saw it, and believed at last. If we hadn't burned it, but had merely occupied Pekin for a season and gone away again, I don't doubt that in no time the Manchoo propagandists would have convinced the population that we'd never been there at all. But with the Summer Palace in flames they couldn't doubt the truth – the barbarians had won, the Son of Heaven had been humbled to the dust, and there was the funeral pyre to prove it.

As some callous scoundrel remarked – and it may have been me, by the sound of it – at least *The Times* couldn't complain that Elgin hadn't avenged their correspondent properly; poor young Bowlby having been one of the Emperor's victims, you see. That smoke spread, metaphorically, all over the world, and some called Elgin a Visigoth, and others said he'd done the right thing, but one of the warmest debates was over exactly what he *had* done. Most folk still believe that one great palace building was burned; in fact, there were more than two hundred destroyed, to my knowledge, with most of their contents and great areas of woodland and garden. Some, like Loch, have softened it as best they can by claiming that many buildings and much treasure escaped, that some palaces were only half-burned(!), that few manuscripts were lost, and that the damage was less than it looked. The plain truth is that the great Summer Palace, eight miles by ten, was a charred ruin, and if Lloyds had been faced with the bill they'd have shut up shop and fled the country.

285

The lesson was driven home with the usual Horse Guards pomp when the convention was signed a few days later, Kung having had to agree to everything we demanded, including £100,000 for the families of our dead. Elgin, looking like Pickwick strayed into an Aladdin pantomime, was toted through the streets of Pekin in an enormous palanquin by liveried Chinese, with our troops lining the route for three miles to the Hall of Ceremonies, the band playing the National Anthem, an escort of infantry and cavalry hundreds strong, and the senior men mounted in full fig, wearing that curious ceremonial expression of solemn intensity, as though they were trying not to fart. I can't be doing with Hyde Park soldiering; it looks so dam' ridiculous, when anyone can see with half an eye that it costs more time and trouble and expense than fighting a war, and the jacks-in-office and hangers-on who take part plainly think it's a whole heap more important. I'd abolish the Tin Bellies *and* Trooping the Colour, if I had my way. But that's by the by; the public love it, and there's no question it awed the Chinese; they gazed at Elgin in stricken silence, and knocked head as he went by.

The treaty was signed with tremendous ceremony, before a great concourse of mandarins in dragon robes, and ourselves in dress uniforms, Elgin looking damned disinheriting and poor little Prince Kung plainly scared out of his wits by Beato's camera, which he seemed to think was some kind of gun. (The picture never came out, either.) It was infernally dull and went on for hours, both sides loathing each other with icy politeness, and the only possibility of fun was when Parkes, that imperturbable diplomat, spotted the chap who'd pulled his hair, standing among the Chinese dignitaries, and I believe would have gone for him then and there, if Loch, the spoilsport, hadn't restrained him.[45] (Parkes got his revenge, though; he had Prince I turned out of his splendid palace, and bagged it for the new British Embassy.)

And then, quite suddenly, it was all over. Elgin had his piece of paper, with red seals and yellow ribbon; China and Britain were sworn to eternal friendship; our traders were free to deluge the market with pulse, grain, sulphur, saltpetre, cash, opium (ha-ha!), brimstone, and even spelter;

286

there were a few hundred new graves along the Peiho (Moyes at Tang-ku and Nolan at Pah-li-chao among them); the Summer Palace was a smoking ruin; in Jehol a dainty silver finger-nail was poised to pin the Chinese Empire; and I was going down-river on *Coromandel*, with Elgin's kindly note of appreciation in my pocket, a black jade chess set in my valise, and a few memories in mind.

So often it's like that, when the most vivid chapters end; the storm of war and action hurtles you along in blood and thunder, seeking vainly for a hold to cling to, and then the wind drops, and in a moment you're at peace and dog-tired, with your back to a gun-wheel at Gwalior, or closing your eyes in a corner seat of the Deadwood Stage, or drinking tea contentedly with an old Kirghiz bandit in a serai on the Golden Road, or sitting alone with the President of the United States at the end of a great war, listening to him softly whistling "Dixie".

So it was now – for that's my China story done, save for one curious little postscript – and I could loaf at the rail, looking forward to a tranquil voyage home to Elspeth and a gentleman's life, far away from mist and mud and rice-paddy and dry-dung smells and Tiger soldiers and silk banners and nightmare Bannermen and belching ornamental cannon and crazy Taipings and even crazier Yankees and fire-crackers and yellow faces . . . no, I wouldn't even miss the gigantic bandit women and jolly Hong Kong boaters and beauteous dragon queens . . . not too much, anyway.

Possibly those three were in my mind, though, a few weeks later, as I sat in Dutranquoy's bar in Singapore, where the mail had dropped me, idly wondering how I'd kill the fortnight before the P. & O. Cape ship sailed for Home – for I was shot if I was going by that infernal Suez route. At any rate, something awoke a memory of the voluptuous Madam Sabba, with whom I'd wrestled so enjoyably on my last visit there, until she'd spoiled sport by whistling up the hatchet-men – heavens, that had been more than fifteen years ago. Still, I doubted if Singapore had gone Baptist in the meantime, so I took a palki across the river and up through Chinatown to the pleasant residential area which I remembered, where the big houses stood back in their gardens, with paper lanterns glimmering on the dark drives and burly Sikh porters bowing at the front door. Very genteel resorts they were; no trollops on view or anything of that sort; you had a capital dinner and caught the waiter's eye, and he drummed up the flashtail discreetly.

I demanded to be taken to the best place, and it looked A1, with a big dimly-lit club dining-room where silent bearers waited on the tables, and two smart hostesses went the rounds to see that all was in order. One of them was a stately ivory who might have been Sabba's daughter; I considered her carefully as I ate my duck curry with a bottle of bubbly, but then I noticed the other one, at the far end of the room, and changed my mind. She was white and fair and excellently set up, and I felt an almighty urge to try some civilised goods for a change; I heard her soft laughter as she paused by a table where half-a-dozen planters were eating; then she passed on to a solitary diner, a blond-bearded young stalwart in good linen with a clipper-captain look to him, and I wondered if he was on the same lay as myself, for she stood in talk for quite five minutes, while I consumed a jealous soufflé. But then she turned away and swayed to my corner, smiling graciously and asking if everything was to my satisfaction.

"It will be directly," says I, rising gallantly, "if you'll condescend to join me in a bottle of fizz." I was setting a chair when I heard her gasp; she was staring as though I were Marley's ghost. Hold on, thinks I, my new whiskers are grown enough to be presentable, surely – and then I almost dropped the chair, for it was Phoebe Carpenter, pillar of the Church and wholesaler of firearms to the Taiping rebels.

"Colonel Flashman!" cries she. "Oh, dear!"

"Mrs Carpenter!" cries I. "Good God!"

She swayed, eyes closed, and sat down abruptly, gulping and staring at me wide-eyed as I resumed my seat. "Oh, what a start you gave me!"

"That's what I said, up the Pearl River," says I. "Well, well, I never! Here, take a glass . . . and do tell me how the Reverend Josiah is keeping. Missionary society doing well, is it?"

"Oh, dear!" she whispers, trembling violently, which im-

288

proved an already delightful appearance. I hadn't known her because the Phoebe I remembered had borne her beauty in matronly modesty, innocent of rouge and fairly swathed in muslin; this was a most artistic translation, red-lipped and polished, with her gold ringlets piled behind her head and her udders threatening to leap with agitation from a low-cut gown of black satin which I doubted had come from the last sale of work. She drank, her teeth chattering.

"What must you think?" says she, speaking low, and taking a quick slant to see that no one was listening.

"Well," says I cheerily, "I think you're wanted in Hong Kong, for gun-running, which should get you about five years if anyone were inconsiderate enough to mention it to the Singapore traps. I also think that would be a crying shame –"

"You wouldn't betray me?" she whimpers faintly.

"You betrayed me, dear Phoebe," says I gently, and laid my hand on hers. "But of course I wouldn't –"

"You might!" says she, starting to weep.

"Nonsense, child! Why ever on earth should I?"

"For . . . for . . . re-revenge!" She stared piteously, like a blue-eyed fawn, her bosom heaving. "I . . . we . . . deceived you most shamefully! Oh, dear, what am I to do?"

"Have some bubbly," says I soothingly, "and rest assured I have no thoughts of revenge. Compensation, perhaps . . ."

"Comp-compensation?" She blinked miserably. "But I have no substance . . . I couldn't afford . . ."

"My dear Mrs Carpenter," says I, squeezing her hand, "you have absolutely capital substance, and you know perfectly well I don't mean money. Now . . . I'm sure Josiah has told you all about Susannah and the Elders. Well, I'm not feeling exactly elderly, but . . . oh, Susannah!" I beamed at her, and she blinked again, dabbed her nose and looked at me thoughtfully, still heaving a bit but settling down and accepting another ration of fizz.

"I'm by no means sure that they would send me to prison!" says she, unexpectedly, pouting. "After all, it was a very good cause!"

"It was a dam' bad cause," says I, "and if you think they won't shove you in clink, just ask dear Josiah."

"I can't! He has abandoned me!"

"You don't mean it!" I was astonished. "He must be mad. You mean he just up and left you? Here?"

"Can you suppose I would accept employment in a restaurant if I were still a clergyman's wife? Well, I am still his wife," she admitted, taking another sip, "but he has deserted me and gone to Sumatra."

"Has he, though? Missionary work or piracy? Well, that's bad luck to be sure. But you'll soon get another chap, you know, with your looks," I reassured her. "Well, take tonight, for example. Why, before I even recognised you, I was most entirely fetched –"

"Oh, say you will not inform on me!" She leaned forward, all entreaty. "You see, I have a most fortunate situation here, and am in hope to save sufficient to go back to . . . to England . . . to Middle Wallop and my dear parents . . . at the rectory . . ."

"I knew it must be a rectory. Middle Wallop, eh?"

"When I think of it," says she, biting her lip, "compared to . . ." She gestured at the room pathetically.

". . . compared to beating copra in the women's compound with all those smelly Chinese sluts? Absolutely. Well, now, Phoebe, tempus is fugiting – when does your shop shut, and where shall we . . . ah . . .?"

"We close in an hour. I live in the house," says she, looking at the table, and shot me a reproachful pout – my, she was a little stunner. "You do very wrong to compel me. If you were a gentleman . . ."

"I'd shop you like a worthy citizen. If you were a lady, you wouldn't hocus fellows into running guns. So we're well suited – and I ain't compelling you one bit; you're all for it." I gave her a wink and a squeeze. "Now, then, where can I spend the next hour? Got a billiard table, have you? Capital. Just pass me the word when you've got the dishes washed – oh, and see we have a couple of bottles, iced, upstairs, will you? Come on, goose – we'll have the jolliest time, you know!"

She gave her head a little toss, going pink, and glanced at me slantendicular. "And you promise faithfully not to tell . . . anything? Oh, if only I could be sure!"

"Well, you can't. Oh, come . . . why should I peach on a

290

little darling like you, eh?" As we stood up, close together, I squeezed the satin unseen, and her mouth opened on a little gasp. "See? Two hours from now, you won't care."

I ambled down to the empty billiard room, in prime fettle, calling "Kya-hai!" and ordering up another bottle of bubbly. I tickled the pills until it arrived, and then wandered, glass in hand, to the verandah to look out into the tropic dark; it had started to rain with great force, as it does in Singapore, straight down in stair-rods, battering the leaves and gurgling in the monsoon ditch, bringing that heavy, earthy smell that is the East. I stood reflecting in great content: homeward bound, champagne, good Burma cheroot, and lissom little Phoebe under starter's orders. What more could a happy warrior ask? After the second glass I tried a few combination shots, but my eye wasn't in any longer, and after a while I left off, yawning and wishing impatiently that Phoebe would hurry the mateys along, beginning to feel sleepy as well as monstrous randy.

The door opened abruptly and a chap stuck his head in, rain glistening on his hat and cape. He gave me a cheery nod.

"Evenin', sport. Seen Joss about, have you?"

"Joss?"

"The guv'nor. You know, Carpenter. Or maybe you don't know. Ne'er mind, I daresay he's upstairs." He was withdrawing.

"Hold on! D'you mean . . . the Rev. Josiah Carpenter?"

"The one and only," says he, grinning. "Our esteemed proprietor."

I gaped at him. "Proprietor? You mean he *owns* this place? He's not . . . in Sumatra?"

"Well, he wasn't this afternoon. I say, are you all right?"

"But Mrs Carpenter distinctly . . . told me . . ."

"Oh, she's about, is she? Good, I'll see her. Chin-chin."

The door slammed, leaving me standing bewildered – and angry. What was the little bitch playing at? She'd said . . . hold on . . . she had said . . . I turned sharply at a step on the verandah, lurching heavily against the table and catching hold to steady myself.

The big blond-bearded chap who'd been in the restaurant

291

was standing in the open screen; he was wearing a pilot-cap now, and there seemed to be another fellow in a sou'wester, just behind him in the shadows . . . why was I so dizzy all of a sudden?

"Hollo," says the blond chap, and his glance went to the bottle and glass on the side-table. He grinned at me. "Enjoying your drink?"

[With words apparently failing their
author for once, the eighth packet
of the Flashman Papers ends here.]

APPENDIX I:

The Taiping Rebellion

The Taiping Rebellion was the worst civil war in history, and the second bloodiest war of any kind, being exceeded in casualties only by the Second World War, with its estimated 60 million dead. How many died during the fourteen years of the Taiping Rising can only be guessed; the lowest estimate is 20 million, but 30 million is considered more probable (three times the total for the First World War). When it is remembered that the Taiping struggle was fought largely with small arms and only primitive artillery, some idea may be gained of the scale of the land fighting, with its attendant horrors of massacre and starvation. Again, the word "battle" nowadays is frequently applied to struggles lasting over months (Ypres, Stalingrad, etc). Using the more traditional sense of the term, which covers only days, it can be said that the bloodiest battle ever fought on earth was the Third Battle of Nanking in 1864, when in three days the dead exceeded a hundred thousand.

So far as his account goes, up to the summer of 1860, Flashman gives an accurate, if necessarily condensed version of the Taiping movement and its astonishing leader, the Cantonese clerk Hung Hsiu-chuan, who fell into a trance after failing his civil service examinations, saw visions of Heaven, and became inspired to overthrow the Manchus, cast the idols out of China, and establish the Taiping Tienkwo, the Heavenly Dynasty of Perfect Peace, based on his own notions of Christianity. He is said to have been much influenced by a missionary tract, "Good Words to Admonish the Age".

That Hung was a leader of extraordinary magnetism is not to be doubted, and he was materially assisted by the corruption and decadence of Manchu government; China was ripe for revolution. At first his small movement concentrated on attacking idolatry, but with the persecution of the sect for heresy, magic, and conspiracy, his crusade developed into guerrilla warfare, and the first rising in Kwangsi in 1850 spread into other provinces. With able generals. such as Loyal Prince Lee, the Taiping armies fought with increasing success; their organisation and discipline far outmatched the Imperials, and after the capture of Nanking in 1853 they threatened Pekin and controlled more than a third of China, establishing capitals in provinces which they had devastated. Flashman saw them when they were at their peak and might still have accomplished their revolution, but the seeds of defeat were already apparent. For all their zeal and military discipline, the Taipings were poor social organisers and administrators; their rule was oppressive and haphazard, and they failed to attract either foreign support (although their apparent Christianity gained them some European sympathy at first) or the Chinese middle and upper classes. They also suffered from internal feuds and the degeneration of the once inspirational Hung, who after 1853 went into almost complete seclusion with his women and mystical meditations. Strategically, the Taipings made the mistake of never securing a major port through which they might have made contact with the outside world, and failing to concentrate their thrust at Pekin, the seat of Imperial power.

After the events of 1860, their decline was rapid. Tseng Kuo-fan organised the Imperial reconquest, aided by the Ever-Victorious Army under Ward and Gordon, and after Hung's suicide by poison in June 1864, Nanking fell, and the greatest rebellion ever seen in the world was over; six hundred towns had been destroyed, whole provinces devastated, billions of pounds worth of property lost, and countless millions were dead, including all the rebel leaders. Loyal Prince Lee and Hung Jen-kan were both executed in 1864. Other notable Wangs were:

The East King (Tung Wang), Yang Hsiu-ching, a charcoal burner who became a shrewd and ruthless general; also known as God's Holy Ghost. He was murdered in 1856 by

The North King (Pei Wang), Wei Chiang-hui, pawnbroker, who in turn was executed with twenty thousand followers by the Heavenly King in 1856.

294

The West King (Si Wang), and the *South King* (Nan Wang) were both killed in action in 1852.

Apart from these early Wangs ("The Princes of the Four Quarters") the principal leaders included the young and formidable General Chen Yu-cheng, who with Lee raised the siege of Nanking, and died in 1862; the redoubtable Shih Ta-kai, also known as the Assistant King (I Wang), executed in 1863; Hung Jen-ta (Fu Wang), elder brother of the Heavenly King, executed 1864; the Ying Wang (Heroic King), executed 1862; and most pathetic of all, Tien Kuei, the Junior Lord (Hung Fu), son of the Heavenly King, executed by the Imperialists in 1864; he was fifteen.

Among eye-witnesses of the Taipings, none is more interesting than Augustus Lindley, an intensely partisan young Englishman who defended them as moderates, contended that the Heavenly King had been elected, not merely self-declared, denied that his claim of relationship to Christ was meant to be taken literally, and defined as "anti-Taiping" all Britons of the Elgin school, the opium interests, missionaries, Roman Catholics, and merchants generally. He paints an attractive picture of Loyal Prince Lee, whom he met (and shared his indignation at being repulsed from Shanghai), and is a mine of detail about Taipingdom. He is at variance, however, with other contemporary writers, the most extreme of whom describe the Taipings as enslavers, destroyers of trade, living on loot, etc.* At this distance they look, as Flashman says, like a worthy movement gone wrong; in fairness, it has to be said that they included some sincere reformers, even among local commanders, and in some areas at least brought lower taxation and tried to encourage trade and agriculture.

As to the havoc they wrought, the one point on which most authorities seem to agree is that the Imperialist forces were worse. Jen Yu-wen described the carnage when the Taipings took Nanking (with 30,000 Bannermen wiped out and thousands of women burned, drowned, and cut down)

---

*H. B. Morse, an eminently fair authority, is blunt: "The Taiping Government is not known to have organised any form of civil administration, even in Nanking. Levying of taxes was simplicity itself: it took everything in sight." (*International Relations*).

as the first and last Taiping massacre; considering the scale of bloodshed in the war, it is difficult to accept this.

There is a considerable modern literature on the subject, and Chinese scholars have devoted close study to the writings and philosophy of the movement. (See Lindley, *Ti-ping Tien-kwoh*, 1866; Lewis B. Browning, *A Visit to the Taipings in 1854* (in *Eastern Experiences*, 1871); Franz Michael, *The Taiping Rebellion*, vol. i, 1966; Jen Yu-wen, *The Taiping Revolutionary Movement*, 1973; J. C. Cheng, *Chinese Sources for the Taiping Rebellion*, 1963; H. W. Gordon, *Events in the Life of Charles George Gordon*, 1886; Walter Scott (publisher), *Life of General Gordon*, 1885; Morse; Wilson, Blakiston; Forrest; Scarth; Cahill.)

APPENDIX II:

The Orchid

Yehonala, later Empress Tzu-hsi (1834–1908), known variously as the Orchid, Imperial Yi Concubine, Empress of the Western Palace, and latterly, Old Buddha, was the effective ruler of China for half a century. The daughter of a Manchu captain of the 8th Banner Corps, she was seventeen when she and her cousin, Sakota, were chosen with 26 other Manchu beauties as concubines for the young Emperor Hsien Feng, and although Sakota became Empress Consort, Yehonala quickly established herself as the Imperial favourite. When she bore the Emperor's only son in 1856 her hold over the ailing, weakly monarch, and on political power, became greatly strengthened, with fateful results for China. For the young concubine, although well educated by Manchu standards, was ignorant of the world outside; she was also an extreme reactionary, inflexibly autocratic, and highly aggressive in diplomacy. She appears to have been a prime mover in China's resistance policy during the Arrow War and Elgin expedition, forbidding trade, putting prices on British heads, sending suicide orders to unlucky commanders, inspiring the death warrants, and urging opposition to the barbarians at all costs. ("My anger is about to strike and exterminate them without mercy," Daniel Varè quotes her. "I command all my subjects to hunt them down like wild beasts.") At the same time, with the Emperor's health failing, she was entering on a political struggle to ensure her son's succession and her own survival.

Flashman's account of her scheming in September 1860 is uncorroborated, but there is no doubt that she was already deep in palace plotting, and in the year that followed her courage, ruthlessness, and genius for intrigue were tested by events which resemble sensational fiction rather than sober fact. For the Emperor did not die quickly, as expected; he lingered for a year at Jehol, and in that time Yehonala suffered an almost fatal setback. Reports of her affair with Jung Lu, who was said to be her lover, reached the Emperor, and she was forbidden the royal presence; worse still, when a council of regency was appointed by the Emperor's decree on the day before his death in August 1861, its leaders were her bitterest enemies, Prince I, Sushun, and Prince Cheng;* Yehonala herself was excluded.

That should have been the end of her, but her enemies had overlooked one small but vital point. The edict of regency, signed by the Emperor, had not been sealed with the dynastic seal – Yehonala had purloined it. And at a time when it was essential for the reins of power to be seized in Pekin, Prince I and the other regents were bound by court protocol to remain with the royal corpse at Jehol, and then accompany it, in slow ceremonial procession, to the capital. Not so Yehonala and the Empress Sakota, whose duty it was to go ahead to Pekin and meet the coffin on its arrival.

Prince I and Sushun, well aware of Yehonala's popularity with the troops, and fearing what might happen if she reached Pekin first, arranged to have her and Sakota ambushed and murdered on the journey. But the faithful Jung Lu learned of the plot and set off from Jehol by night, overtook the royal ladies on the road, escaped the ambush, and brought them safely to the capital, where Yehonala lost no time in raising support; Sakota, as usual, was content to stay in the background. Thus when Prince I and the regents finally arrived with the cortege they were welcomed by an urbane Yi Concubine who thanked them graciously, dismissed them from the regency, and had them arrested in the name of the new Emperor (whose decrees proved to be properly sealed).

The regents, charged with responsibility for the recent war and (a fine effrontery on her part) with treacherously capturing Loch and Parkes, were sentenced to be tortured to death, but this was commuted to suicide by the silk cord for Princes I and Cheng, and beheading for Sushun. Jung Lu was rewarded with the viceroyalty of a province and control of the army; Yehonala and Sakota assumed the titles of

*But not Sang-kol-in-sen, who had been stripped of his title and command after the fall of Pekin in October, 1860.

Empress of the Western and Eastern Palace respectively,* and from that moment the former concubine never relaxed her grip on imperial power. When her son, the new Emperor, died in 1873, she engineered the succession for her infant nephew, but when he reached manhood and showed reformist tendencies she had him interned and wielded supreme authority until her death.

Yehonala Tzu-hsi was the world's last great absolute queen, and may be compared to Catherine the Great and the first Elizabeth. For the ills her country suffered through her resistance policy and refusal to accept change, she may fairly be blamed; against that, she kept the world at bay from China until the end of the century, when economic decline, war with Japan, and the Boxer Rising (which she exploited against the foreign powers) completed the undermining of imperial rule. Soon after her death China was a republic; whether it would have profited from earlier revolution, earlier reform, and earlier acceptance of the outside world, no one can say.

In its details, Flashman's portrait of Yehonala is a faithful one; her beauty and charm were legendary, as were her less admirable qualities, and his account of her lifestyle is confirmed elsewhere, even to such trivia as her favourite food, clothes, jewellery, and board-games. How just he is in his sweeping assessment of her character is a matter for conjecture; as her biographer Sergeant observes, contemporary writers, depending on their viewpoint, show her almost as two different women, "one a monster of iniquity, the other a lovable genius". There is ample evidence that she was vain, greedy, cruel, and autocratic, but less that she was as callous, ruthless, and promiscuous as Flashman suggests. Opinions differ sharply about her private morals; she was for years concubine to a depraved monarch, and rumours of her immorality were persistent (but she did not lack malicious enemies); apart from Jung Lu, her lovers were said to include a later Chief Eunuch, Li Lien Ying ("Cobbler's Wax"), her confirmed favourite, who may not have been a eunuch at all

*Flashman is plainly mistaken in assigning this title to Yehonala in 1860.

– the American artist, Katherine Carl, described him as tall, thin, and "Savonarola-like", with elegant manners and a pleasant voice. There is virtually no personal evidence for her early life; most of the memoirs refer to her later years, when the picture is of a sprightly, domineering old lady of unshakeable will, immense vanity, high intelligence, and winning charm when she chose to exert it; obviously a once great beauty, and retaining to the end her silvery voice and flashing smile. (See Philip W. Sergeant, *The Great Empress Dowager of China*, 1910; Daniel Varè, *The Last of the Empresses*, 1936; E. Backhouse and J. O. P. Bland, *China Under the Empress Dowager*, 1910, and *Annals of the Court of Pekin*; Princess Der Ling (Te Ling), afterwards Mrs T. C. White, lady-in-waiting to the Dowager Empress, *Two Years in the Forbidden City*, 1924, and *Old Buddha*; Charlotte Haldane, *The Last Great Empress of China*, 1965; J. and M. Porteous, "An Explanatory Account of the Chinese Ladies", pamphlet, Dublin, 1888. For the political intrigues of 1861, see Morse, *International Relations*.)

APPENDIX III:

The Doctor of Letters of the Hanlin Academy

One of the most touching, and illuminating, documents of the China War is a diary covering the last few weeks before Elgin's army reached Pekin. It was kept by a Doctor of Letters and member of the Hanlin Academy, living in the capital, and is an invaluable record of the crisis as seen by an educated, middle-class Chinese. He calls it "a record of grief incurable"; the time of national catastrophe was also, for him, one of personal tragedy because, while the barbarians were closing on Pekin, the doctor's aged mother was dying, and the diary is a moving record of his personal anxieties set against the background of great events. The diary has another value: it shows the power which the Yi Concubine Yehonala exerted on the dying Emperor and his court, and the extent to which she was responsible for the bitter resistance to the Allies' demands.

"In the moon of the Ken Shen Year (August)", writes the doctor, "rumours began to circulate that the barbarians had already reached Taku (Forts)." There was "alarm and uneasiness" in Pekin, but no flight as yet. "His Majesty was seriously ill, and it was known that he wished to leave for the north, but the Imperial Concubine Yi . . . dissuaded him and assured him that the barbarians would never enter the city." After news of the defeat at Taku, however, people began to leave, and as the news became progressively worse, the exodus became one of thousands.

The doctor now turns to his own immediate troubles: his mother's medicine, the preparation of her coffin, its appearance, and its cost – which, he reflects, would have been much greater if he had not had the foresight to buy the wood years earlier and keep it in store. "This comforted me not a little."

His next entry is divided between national affairs and the progress being made on the coffin. There are "rumours that

Pekin would be bombarded on the 27th [sic], so that every-one was escaping who could. On the 27th we put on the second coating of lacquer. On that day our troops captured the barbarian leader Pa-hsia-li (Parkes) with eight others, and they were imprisoned in the Board of Punishments." He notes that the Emperor was preparing to leave, but the Imperial Concubine Yi persuaded some of the high officials to memorialise him to remain. All officials were now sending their families and valuables out of the city.

His mother's death was clearly approaching, so the cere-monial robes were prepared. His mother thought the coverlet was too heavy, so one of silk was substituted, but she thought that too luxurious. "Her parents-in-law," she pointed out, "had not had grave-wrappings of such valuable stuff." Mean-while, in "the battle at Chi Hua Gate" (which presumably means Pah-li-chao), "the Mongol cavalry broke, and many were trampled to death in the general rout."

And now "the Princes and Ministers besought the Concu-bine Yi to induce His Majesty to leave . . . His Majesty was only too anxious to start at once . . . (but she) persuaded the two Grand Secretaries to memorialise against his doing so, and . . . a decree was issued stating that in no circum-stances would the Emperor leave the capital."

Another battle was reported the next day (September 22; this was either a false rumour, or more probably the Allies mopping up after Pah-li-chao), and the Emperor, "attended by his concubines, the Princes, Ministers and Dukes [sic], and all the officers of the household, left the city in desperate rout and disorder unspeakable". In fact, the doctor notes, the barbarians were still some way off, and the court was at the Summer Palace, so there was nothing to fear.

"Up to the last the Yi Concubine begged him to remain . . . as his presence could not fail to awe the barbarians, and thus to exert a protecting influence for the good of the city and people. How, she said, could the barbarians be expected to spare the city if the Sacred Chariot had fled, leaving unprotected the tutelary shrines and the altars of the gods?"

Shortly after this, the doctor's mother died, "abandoning her most undutiful son . . . her death lies at my door, because of my ignorance of medicine." He was worried about having

302

her buried, in case the barbarians should desecrate her grave, but finally had her buried in a temple. A few days later he notes briefly "vast columns of smoke seen rising to the north-west".

"When the Yi Concubine heard of the . . . surrender, she implored the Emperor to reopen hostilities." But His Majesty was dangerously ill, "so our revenge must be postponed for the time being".

He was not a Doctor of Letters for nothing, for in short space he conjures up a most moving and vivid picture: of life and death going on in a small house in Pekin while the captains and the kings make history; of his concern for the indomitable old lady reproving his extravagance while the Imperial Army crumbles; of his touching self-reproach at her death and his admiration for the fiery Yi Concubine vainly urging resistance for the honour of China; of his fears for his mother's grave while the Summer Palace is burning. And perhaps the strongest impression he leaves is that if the men of Pekin had matched the spirit of the women, Lord Elgin would have bought his treaty dear. (For the Doctor's diary, see Backhouse and Bland.)

Glossary

bahadur	title of honour (Hindustani)
bandobast	organisation (Hind.)
cangue	wooden punishment collar
chandoo	high quality prepared opium
chin-chin	good-bye; conversation (Chinese)
chow-chow water	dangerous cross-currents
daffadar	cavalry commander of ten (Indian Army)
fan-qui	foreigner
Ghazi	fanatic
harka	force of Bedouin cavalry
Hong	association of Chinese merchants
impi	Zulu regiment
indaba	business, affair (lit., council. Swahili)
jemadar	under-officer
kampilan	slender-bladed cleaver (Malay)
Kya-hai!	summons to waiter or bearer (lit. "What is!" Hind.)
lorcha	Chinese-rigged river ship
naik	corporal (Indian Army)
rissaldar	cavalry troop commander
samshu	rice spirit
Sat-sree-akal	Sikh greeting, sometimes used as a slogan
Sawney	Scotsman
sgian dhu	black knife of Scottish Highlanders
shabash	bravo! (Hind.)
sing-song	Chinese music-hall

snotty	midshipman (Royal Navy)
sowar	trooper (Indian Army)
syce	groom (Hind.)
taipan	head of a business (lit. great man, boss)
tanguin	Malagassy poison
tutti-putti	broken (*tutti-putti zamin*, broken ground. Hind.)
Wang	king, prince
yamen	official residence, office.

NOTES

1. Flashman is usually vague about dates, but from internal evidence (see p. 35) it is clear that the ten days were March 1–11, 1860. It is not known why he was on transit through Hong Kong at this time; approximately eighteen months earlier, in the autumn of 1858, he was definitely in India, preparing to return to England at the end of his service in the Indian Mutiny, which earned him a V.C. and knighthood (see *Flashman in the Great Game*), but the present narrative makes it plain that this return did not take place, and that during 1859 he was engaged in further foreign service. What this was a later packet of the Papers may explain, but there is some reason to suppose that it was connected with China, since up to the end of 1858 he had never visited that country, yet at the beginning of the present memoir he writes of it with apparent familiarity, and displays some fluency in Chinese, a language not mentioned in his earlier reminiscences. There is a possible alternative for 1859, far-fetched though it may seem: one reference in his earlier writings suggests an acquaintance with John Brown, the American abolitionist, whose celebrated raid on Harper's Ferry took place in October, 1859, and since Flashman had been at one time an agent (albeit an unwilling one) of the Underground Railroad, it is not impossible that the missing eighteen months were partly spent in the United States – although in what capacity it would be rash to speculate.   p.9

2. A reasonable summary of Anglo-Chinese relations up to 1860, including the Arrow War of 1856. For details of the Palmerston–Cobden debate (February 26, 1857), see Division IV of J. Ewing Ritchie's *Life and Times of Viscount Palmerston*.   p.18

3. Flashman, of course, had no scruples about the opium trade, but the mere fact that he mentioned morality to Mrs Carpenter is some reflection of the opposition that was growing against the opium interests. China had legalised the traffic for the first time under the 1858 Treaty of Tientsin; the opium lobby brazenly claimed that this was voluntary; Sir Thomas Wade, a leading China expert, said the concession had been "extorted", and Lord Elgin postponed the relevant clause rather than force China's hand. In fact, the Chinese recognised that there was nothing they could do about it; "the present generation of smokers must and will have opium," their commissioner told Elgin, a fact recognised by such experienced observers as the missionary Alexander Williamson, who called for abolition by Britain, but admitted that it would make little difference to the Chinese, who would get their drug anyway (Williamson knew the figures, and that it was not uncommon for a labourer to smoke 80 cash worth of opium

a day out of his wage of 120 cash (2½p.)). This argument was fastened on by the opium lobby, whose line is echoed by Mrs Carpenter; what is surprising is that even old China hands like John Scarth could assert that the drug was smoked as a sedative rather than as a narcotic. An excellent summary of the subject is J. Spencer Hill's *Maitland Prize*-winning essay of 1882, *The Indo-Chinese Opium Trade* (1884); Hill came to the subject strongly prejudiced against the anti-opium lobby, but his investigations changed his mind. (See also John Scarth, *Twelve Years in China* (1860); Alexander Williamson, *Travels in North China* (1870); H. B. Morse, *The Trade and Administration of the Chinese Empire*, 1908.) p.22

4. Unless there were two Jack Fishers, midshipmen on the China Station in 1860, Flashman's young acquaintance can only have been John Arbuthnot ("Jackie") Fisher, later admiral of the fleet, Baron Fisher of Kilverstone, godfather of the Dreadnought battleship, and the foremost name in the Royal Navy since Nelson. Just as Wolseley (see Note 6) may be called the architect of the modern British Army, so Fisher with his "big-gun" turbine ships gave the Royal Navy command of the seas in the first half of the present century. He entered the navy when he was thirteen, and served during the Crimea before going to the China Station in 1859, where he took part in the capture of Canton and the attack on Taku Forts. He was in Chinese waters in the spring of 1860, and still a midshipman although acting-lieutenant, a rank not confirmed until the end of the year. Since Flashman certainly knew Fisher in later life, it is surprising that he does not identify him at their first meeting; on the other hand, his brief description sounds very like the young "Bulldog Jackie". p.33

5. Chinese secret societies, tongs and triads (the Heaven and Earth Association, the Dagger Men, and others) had various recognition signals; three fingers round a cup was that of the White Lilies. (See Scarth.) p.35

6. Garnet Joseph Wolseley (1833–1913), "the model of a modern major-general", was one of Britain's most important soldiers. He won no distinction as a commander in a great war, but his record in the so-called "little wars" – indeed, the variety and success of his service generally – is probably unique in the history of arms. An Anglo-Irishman, he followed his own maxim that if a young officer wants to do well he should try to get himself killed; Wolseley tried really hard, first in the Burma War, when he was badly wounded leading the attack on an enemy stockade; in the Crimea, where he was twice wounded, losing an eye; in the Indian Mutiny, where he served in the relief and siege of Lucknow, being five times mentioned in despatches; in the China War of 1860; in Canada, where in his first independent command he put down the Red River Rebellion without a casualty; in Africa, where he won a lightning campaign against King Koffee of Ashanti, and captured Cetewayo, the Zulu leader; in Egypt, where he beat Arabi Pasha at Tel-el-Kebir and took Cairo; in the Sudan, where he reached Khartoum just too late to rescue Gordon, his old friend of the Crimea and China. He was made a viscount, and later field marshal.

But Wolseley's real importance was as a military reformer and creator of the modern British Army; having seen and suffered under a traditional regime which, while largely successful, had hardly changed in centuries, and being a confirmed champion of the private soldier, he foresaw the need for change in a rapidly changing military world. He had seen the first "modern war" in the struggle between the American States (where he met Lee and Stonewall Jackson), and his reforms and reorganisations, bitterly opposed at the time, prepared the British Army for a new era of warfare; his influence, largely forgotten, is on the Army still. He was (as Gilbert and Grossmith recognised when they caricatured him in "The Pirates of Penzance") a man of many talents; a trained draughtsman and surveyor, he sketched and painted well, and wrote several books, including most notably *The Soldier's Pocket Book*, a life of Marlborough, a novel, and his reminiscences of the China campaign.

Flashman shows him briefly as a young staff-officer, before the full flowering of the quick temper and impatient efficiency which were to make the expression "All Sir Garnet" synonymous with the modern "Right on!" Wolseley always wanted the best; typically, he chose for one campaign a man who had beaten him in competition. Disraeli passed an illuminating judgment on him: "Wolseley is an egotist and a braggart. So was Nelson." (See his *Narrative of the War with China in 1860* (1862), and *Story of a Soldier's Life* (1903); Sir John Fortescue, *History of the British Army*, vol XIII, (1930); Dictionary of National Biography.   p.46

7. Since Flashman probably knew more eminent fighting men – including the great names of the Crimea, Mutiny, U.S. Civil War, and Afghan and American frontiers, to say nothing of his various native foemen – than any other observer of his day, his opinion of James Hope Grant (1808–75) has to be taken seriously. The record seems to bear him out; Grant's active service in India and China is chiefly remarkable for the amount of time he spent in hand-to-hand combat, to which he brought an iron constitution and an apparently total disregard for his own safety. "To die is nothing," he once explained, "it's only going from one room to another." It was in outpost work and the leadership of flying cavalry columns that his talent lay, although his one major command (China, 1860) was conducted with efficiency, despite his being to some extent at the mercy of his diplomats (Fortescue is scathing on this). Flashman's character sketch and physical description are sound; he makes the important point that the terrible fighter and stern disciplinarian was an unusually gentle and kindly man, whose consuming interest was music – Grant was a gifted 'cellist and composer, and indeed owed an early advancement to the fact that his commanding general was a keen violinist who wanted a 'cello player as brigade-major. Despite his sketchy education, Grant was something of a military innovator; he is credited with introducing regular manoeuvres and the war game, and it is interesting that Wolseley, the most intellectual of soldiers, should say: "If I have attained any measure of military prosperity, my gratitude is due to one man, and that man is Sir Hope Grant." (See Sir Hope Grant and Major Knollys,

Incidents in the China War; Fortescue; D.N.B.) p.47

8. The Hon. F. W. A. Bruce was at 46 a diplomat of considerable experience, having served in South America, Egypt, Hong Kong (as colonial secretary), Newfoundland (as governor), and in China, first as secretary to his brother, and from 1858 as superintendent of trade and envoy extraordinary to the Chinese Empire. p.50

9. The Inn of Mutual Prosperity was fairly typical, to judge from the experience of that sturdy missionary, the Rev. Alexander Williamson, who stayed in similar establishments while ranging North China on behalf of the National Bible Society of Scotland. He and John Scarth (their works are cited in Note 3) are lively and informative sources for China at this time, and their observations of the social scene, customs, manners, recreations, costume, food, crime, punishment, etc., accord closely with Flashman's. Mr Williamson has a keen eye for detail and a fine sweeping style; thus the Chinese are "ignorant, conceited and supercilious" and regard Europeans as a fierce, mentally deficient, semi-tamed breed "to be placated like dogs, or as wilful children." He is scathing on Chinese morals: "Secret dens of hideous licentiousness exist in every city", and on the great roads "all disguise is thrown off." Scarth takes a particular delight in minutiae, and is good with the telling phrase: professional mourners he describes as "howling for hire". They and many foreign writers confirm Flashman's strong impression of the Chinese conviction of superiority over all other races, whom they regarded as having tributary status. p.85

10. Professional bandits, pirates, and members of the triad secret societies occasionally joined the Taipings, as did other rebels against the Manchu regime, only to fall away because of the revolutionaries' strict social and religious discipline, and because regular crime paid better. Some of the bandits continued as auxiliaries, among them at least two female brigand leaders, one of whom was called Szu-Zhan.

It was an offshoot of the triads, the Small Sword Society, which took Shanghai in 1853, a conquest which Flashman mistakenly attributes to the Taipings (see p.50). In fact, the Small Swords claimed association with the rebels, but the Taipings repudiated them "because of their immoral habits and vicious propensities", and so missed the opportunity of gaining a major port. (See H. B. Morse, *The International Relations of the Chinese Empire*, vol i, 1910.) p.89

11. Flashman's account of the formidable Taiping army is in accord with other contemporary descriptions, so far as armaments, uniforms, organisation, battle tactics, black flags, etc., are concerned. (See especially Augustus Lindley, and the other sources listed in Appendix I). But one eminent military man disagreed with him about the rebels' discipline: Wolseley, who visited Nanking a year later, thought the Taipings "an undrilled, undisciplined rabble" whose strength lay in the fact that the Imperial army was even worse. Even so, Wolseley had a deep admiration for the Chinese, whom he saw as "the coming rulers of the world." His vision of Armageddon was China versus the United States – "fast becoming the greatest power of the world. Thank heaven, they speak English." (Wolseley, *The Story of a Soldier's Life*, 1903). p.90

309

12. One revolution is probably very much like another, and readers of Flashman's narrative will no doubt detect resemblances between Taipingdom and Communist China a few decades ago. The Taipings were, of course, a socialist movement (at the risk of attracting thunderous denunciation, it may be said that certain aspects of Soviet life today awake more echoes of Tsarist Russia than a modern Russian might care to admit). This is not the place to labour the point; sufficient to say that the pronouncements of the Heavenly King seem to have been received with the same kind of reverence later accorded to the thoughts of Chairman Mao. (Dr Sun-yat-sen, the father of the Chinese Republic, may be seen as an interesting link between the Kingdom of Heavenly Peace and modern China; he was the nephew (one historian says the son) of a Taiping rebel, and in his early days described himself as "the new Hung Hsiu-chuan" who would expel the Manchus.)
p.101
13. Flashman's description of Loyal Prince Lee (Li-Hsiu-ch'eng), Chung Wang and Taiping commander-in-chief, requires some qualification. Whatever Flashman may have thought (and he seems to have been in some doubt), Lee was certainly not mad. A former charcoal burner who had joined the Taipings as a private soldier, the Chung Wang was the best of the rebel generals, and many authorities believe that had he had sole control of the movement, the revolution would have succeeded. An intelligent, enlightened, and (at least by Taiping standards) humane soldier, Lee had a sincere belief in the Taiping mission, and in the bond of Christianity which he supposed should exist between the Taipings and the foreign powers; in the latter he was to be bitterly disappointed. He was said to be egotistical and jealous (particularly of Hung Jen-kan, the Taiping Prime Minister), but the impression left by Lindley is of a courteous, capable, and thoroughly rational man. He also seems to have been a good administrator, unlike most of his fellow-generals. Flashman's physical description is close to Lindley's. (See Lindley and Appendix I.)   p.103
14. Flashman's description of Nanking and what he saw there is so detailed that it really requires foot-noting throughout. To save space, it should be said that everything which he saw and heard in the city can be verified from other sources, principally Thomas W. Blakiston's *Five Months on the Yangtze*, 1862, which contains, among much other information, R. J. Forrest's account of a progress through the city almost identical to Flashman's. Forrest corroborates virtually everything, from the street scenes, the ante-rooms of the Heavenly King's palace, and social conditions, to the furnishings and life-style in the homes of the Taiping leaders. Flashman's personal adventures are, of course, another matter, but for the rest, from the Taiping soldier with his attendant urchins to the bottles of Coward's mixed pickles in Jen-kan's living-room, the author can be accepted as an accurate reporter. (See also Wolseley, *Story of a Soldier's Life*, and other works cited in these notes.)   p.105
15. The character and personality of Hung Hsiu-chuan, inspirer and leader of the Taiping Rebellion, remain a mystery which Chinese scholars are still working hard to solve, chiefly by examination of the writings

310

attributed to him. Obviously he was one of these rare, unfathomable folk with the gift of communicating religious zeal and inspiring devotion in a way which is hardly understood even by those who know them intimately. Hung's case is complicated by the fact that he was, by any normal standards, quite mad, and his condition seems to have deteriorated with time. Although almost a recluse at Nanking, he was seen by visitors on occasion; he is described as being about five feet five inches tall, well-built and inclining to stoutness, with a handsome, rather round face, sandy beard, black hair, and piercing dark eyes. He was said to be physically very strong, with a forceful personality. At the time of his meeting with Flashman he was 47 years old.

The details of that meeting, while obviously uncorroborated, are by no means inconsistent with other evidence. Hung's time seems to have been devoted entirely to mystical speculation, writing pronouncements and decrees, and his numerous harem. The vision he described to Flashman is the one which he proclaimed after waking from his original trance; the recitation of his concubine tallies closely with an exhortation which is to be found in Taiping literature. (See Appendix I.)   p.121

16. Hung Jen-kan (1822–64), Kan Wang (Shield King), Prime Minister and Genëralissimo of the Taipings, is the most interesting and enigmatic of the revolutionary leaders. A cousin of the Heavenly King's, he studied with him at a Baptist mission in Canton (where he, too, failed his civil service exams), and became one of his first disciples, but was thought too young to join the revolution at its outset. In 1854, after working at a Protestant mission in Hong Kong, he tried to reach Nanking, but failed, and spent another four years in the colony with the London Missionary Society. In 1859 he succeeded in reaching Nanking, and within a year had become second only to his cousin in the revolutionary hierarchy. Favouritism aside, this meteoric rise can be attributed only to Jen-kan's native talent, and the advantage which worldly education had given him over the largely uneducated Taiping Wangs. With the deterioration of the Heavenly King, Jen-kan, with Lee, became the real head of the movement, and one can only speculate why they did not combine more effectively. Jen-kan was a strong man of vision and faith, and one of the few Taiping leaders with a real knowledge of affairs and the world outside China; he spoke English fluently, and like Lee wanted to improve Taiping relations with the European powers; he also wished to inculcate orthodox Protestant Christianity.

Jen-kan was a stout, genial, outgoing personality, and from all accounts as pleasant as Flashman makes him sound. He seems to have been alone among the Taipings in genuinely detesting war (the quotation about a war of extermination is authentic), had a deep admiration of British education and institutions, and in his personal behaviour and tastes was perhaps closer to the West than the East; he certainly appears to have had a realistic grasp of foreign attitudes to China, particularly where trade was concerned. Flashman and Forrest agree on his manner and lifestyle; unlike the luxurious generals, he enjoyed a simple, rather untidy existence in his cluttered

311

study, kept no harem, often ate European food, and ignored (as did many of the Wangs) the Taiping prejudice against alcohol. (See Blakiston, Forrest, and Appendix I.) p.126

17. That there was rivalry between Lee and Jen-kan is not only possible but likely, in view of the latter's sudden ascendancy, but only Flashman suggests that it was carried as far as this. There must always be doubt about what was happening behind the scenes at this critical stage in Taiping fortunes, but while Flashman's story is plausible, and not inconsistent with later events, and while some mystery attaches to Jen-kan's role within the movement, it is only right to say that no other writer has suggested that the prime minister was actively plotting the general's downfall. p.133

18. The expression "the almighty dollar", which now refers to American currency, was applied to the Chinese dollar in the last century. p.134

19. Flashman does more justice than is usually shown to Frederick Townsend Ward (1831–1862). The American soldier of fortune was unlucky in being succeeded in command of the Ever-Victorious Army of mercenaries by one of the great heroes of the Victorian age, Major-General Charles George ("Chinese") Gordon, who not only crushed the Taiping Rebellion but achieved immortality by his defence of Khartoum two decades later; it was the kind of fame that overshadowed all but his most eminent contemporaries, and Ward's part in the China wars was quite eclipsed. It remains that Ward did found the Ever-Victorious Army, and after initial reverses, won several victories, in the course of which he forged the weapon which Gordon was to wield so brilliantly. No doubt Ward's reputation suffered from his unpopularity with the foreign consulates in China, particularly the British, who resented his recruitment of the soldiers and sailors who were at one time the backbone of his force; it was also feared that his activities might endanger British neutrality. Ward's biographer, Cahill, is reasonably indignant at the scant credit which the American has received in comparison to Gordon, but seems to spoil his case by overstatement; to say that Ward was "a military genius who helped change the history of China" may be defensible, but to call him Gordon's superior as an organiser, strategist, and diplomat, and "unquestionably the greatest foreign soldier who fought in the Taiping Rebellion", is perhaps to exaggerate.

Flashman's account of Ward seems fairly accurate as far as the facts of his career go. A native of Salem, Mass., he was a mate on merchant ships when he was only 16, and had military experience in Central America, Mexico, and the Crimea with the French forces (he spoke French, but not Chinese). He came to China, apparently with romantic notions of joining the Taipings; there is no record of his ever having run guns or opium, but in the spring of 1860 he was mate of a Yangtse steamship, and fought a successful action against pirates when his vessel grounded. He was later mate of an Imperial gunboat in Gough's flotilla, before forming his own private army to defend Shanghai for the Manchus; in this he was financed by China merchants including Yang ("Takee") Fang, whose daughter he married. Flashman's account of Ward's initial battles is entirely accurate; after his second defeat at Chingpu, and the loss of Sungkiang which followed, he went to France to recuperate, returning to China and fighting with growing success (but not without controversy) until his death: he was killed leading an attack on Tse-kee, on September 21, 1862. Then came Gordon, to inherit his army, and at least one of his gestures: it is a small thing, but while it is Gordon who is remembered as the general who led his men into battle carrying only a cane, the practice seems to have originated with Ward.

He was a small man, active and wiry, with intense dark eyes and a mild, pleasant manner. Little is known of his personality except that he was cheerful and amiable, but he must have had a remarkable gift of leadership, if only to hold his little army together through its early reverses, especially the first assault on Sungkiang, when his entire force arrived in action in an advanced state of intoxication. It may well be that he was as genially eccentric as Flashman suggests; by his own account, he did once fall overboard while pursuing a butterfly, and it is a matter of record that he was carried to the second attack on Chingpu, with his five wounds heavily bandaged, in a sedan chair. (See *Yankee Adventurer*, by Holger Cahill, 1930; *The Ever-Victorious Army*, by Andrew Wilson, 1868; *With Gordon in China*, by Thomas Lyster, 1891; *History of China*, vol iii, by D. C. Boulger, 1884; *Gordon in China*, by S. Mossman, 1875.)

The man in the Norfolk jacket, described by Flashman, was probably Henry Burgevine (1836–65), Ward's lieutenant, who briefly commanded the Ever-Victorious Army in the interval between Ward's death and Gordon's appointment. An explosive eccentric from the American South, Burgevine had served in the Crimea, and changed sides several times during the Taiping Rebellion. He lost the command of the E.V.A. after assaulting an official for withholding his troops' pay, went over to the rebels, subsequently deserted and rejoined Gordon (with whom he seems to have been on good terms), tried to change sides again, but was arrested and subsequently met his death by drowning in mysterious circumstances.   p.143

20. French travellers to Soochow, including priests and missionaries, had assured Lee of a warm welcome in Shanghai, and since he set great store by the Christian bond between Taipings and Europeans, he advanced on the city in high hopes of a peaceful occupation, only to be thunderstruck when he was opposed. A rumour later arose that Roman Catholic priests, who detested the Taiping religion, had encouraged his advance in the hope that he and his army would be destroyed.   p.145

21. Admiral Hope's failure to force a passage at the Taku Forts on June 25, 1859, is a forgotten imperial incident; it was also probably the first occasion on which British and American servicemen fought side by side, if unofficially. Hope's gunboats came under heavy bombardment from the Chinese batteries, and one, the *Plover*, lost thirty-one out of her crew of forty, her commander was killed, the admiral was wounded, and the remaining nine seamen were fighting their guns against hopeless odds. It was too much for the elderly Commodore Josiah Tattnall, watching from the neutral deck of his U.S. Navy

steamer *Toeywhan*; as a young midshipman he had fought against the British in the War of 1812; now, disregarding his country's non-belligerent status, he took a boat in under fire and offered Hope his help. Hope accepted, and Tattnall's launch brought out the British wounded; only later did he discover several of his men black with powder smoke. "What have you been doing, you rascals?" he asked, and received the reply: "Beg pardon, sir, but they were a bit short-handed with the bow gun." The old commodore made no excuses, for himself or his men, in reporting the incident to Washington. "Blood," he wrote, "is thicker than water." (See A. Hilliard Armitage, *The Storming of the Taku Forts*, 1896.)

Hope's failure at Taku met with less sympathy from the London correspondent of the New York *Daily News*, Karl Marx. Reporting the subsequent debate in Parliament, he wrote: "The whole debate in both Houses on the China war evaporated in grotesque compliments showered . . . on the head of Admiral Hope for having so gloriously buried the British forces in the mud." (see Edgar Holt, *The Opium Wars in China*, 1964). Marx was a trenchant commentator on Chinese affairs; he it was who likened the dissolution of the Manchu Empire to that of a mummy in a hermetically-sealed coffin brought into contact with the open air.   p.147

22.   Last night among his fellow roughs,
             He jested, quaff'd and swore;
             A drunken private of the Buffs,
             Who never look'd before.
             Today, beneath his foeman's frown,
             He stands in Elgin's place,
             Ambassador from Britain's crown
             And type of all her race.

Flashman had witnessed one of the most dramatic moments of the China War, and its most famous heroism, when Moyes, "the drunken private of the Buffs", who had been captured along with an Irish sergeant of the 44th and some coolies (one version says Sikhs), flatly refused to kow-tow to his Chinese captors, and was cut down in cold blood. Yet but for Sir Francis Doyle's poem the incident might hardly have been heard of; today it is largely forgotten, and the facts behind it are difficult to trace. The story rests on the sergeant's authority, and there seems no reason to doubt him, or Flashman – or for that matter, Doyle's poem, which only errs (possibly deliberately) in presenting Moyes as a young Kentish country boy, when in fact he was a fairly disreputable Scot, old enough, it is said, to have been broken from the rank of colour sergeant for insubordination – which seems characteristic. Not much more is known of Moyes, whose presence in the Buffs (the East Kent Regiment) was presumably a matter of chance. A rumour that he died of drink in captivity seems to have no foundation; he was in the hands of the Chinese for barely one day, and the sergeant's account, which Doyle obviously accepted, is consistent with the experience of later prisoners.

It is just possible that Doyle, who was Matthew Arnold's successor as Professor of Poetry at Oxford, had the Moyes story from a most

314

authoritative source – Lord Elgin himself. They had been contemporaries at Eton and Christ Church, where both took Firsts in Classics in 1832, belonged to the small circle of Gladstone's intimates (Doyle was his best man), and may have met again after Elgin's return to Britain in 1861. p.155

23. The hoot of the tawny owl, the *chat huant*, was a recognition signal among the peasant guerrilla fighters of Britanny ("les Chouans") who remained loyal to the crown in the French Revolution. Probably only Flashman, hearing the words at such a critical moment, would have known (or bothered to note) that the speaker was presumably a Breton. p.156

24. According to British Army custom, the most smartly turned out member of a guard was (and possibly still is) excused guard duty, and given the light task of orderly to the guard. This is known as "taking the stick", possibly because the orderly would carry a cane rather than a weapon. The practice of carrying the guard on to parade was still occasionally seen in India in the editor's time, forty years ago. p.160

25. It is fairly rare for Flashman to show much regard for "politicals", but the three with whom he was to work on the Pekin expedition seem to have been exceptions. They were, in fact, an impressive trio. *James Bruce*, 8th Earl of Elgin (1811–63) was Britain's most accomplished foreign envoy in the middle years of the century, and served with distinction as governor of Jamaica, governor-general of both Canada and India, and on missions to China and Japan. His great diplomatic service was to prevent annexation of Canada to the U.S., and negotiate the Reciprocity Treaty of 1854, which he was accused of floating through the American Senate on "oceans of champagne". *Harry Parkes*, former Canton commissioner and Elgin's interpreter, was to spend his life in the Orient, and make a name in both China and Japan; small, wiry, tenacious, and a glutton both for work and punishment, he had an adventurous career, distinguished by his ability to survive attempts on his life. He was the first foreigner ever received in private audience by the Mikado. *Henry Loch* (1827–1900), as Flashman indicates, already had a highly active service career behind him, belied by his gentle disposition and scholarly appearance; he was to write the standard work on the Pekin expedition, and was subsequently governor of the Cape, of Victoria, Australia, and of the Isle of Man, where he had the unusual distinction of having part of the sea-front named after him. (See James Bruce, *Extracts from the Letters of James, Earl of Elgin . . . 1847–62* (1864); G. Wrong, *The Earl of Elgin* (1905); Theodore Waldron, editor, *Letters and Journals of James, 8th Earl of Elgin* (1872); Henry (Lord) Loch, *Personal Narrative of . . . Lord Elgin's Second Embassy to China, 1860* (1869); S. Lane-Poole, *Sir Harry Parkes in China,* (1901); Samuel Eliot Morison, *Oxford History of the American People*, vol ii, 1972). p.163

26. An opinion Elgin was to revise before the campaign was over. British opinion of the French was, as usual, highly critical, but on the march Elgin noted that the French soldiers were better improvisers than the British, and adapted well to the conditions. "Our soldiers do little for themselves, and their necessities are so great, that we move but slowly.

315

The French work in all sorts of ways for the army. The contrast is, I must say, very striking." (Elgin, *Letters and Journals*.) p.165

27. The fight between Tom Sayers, the Pimlico bricklayer, and John Camel Heenan, U.S.A., for the equivalent of the modern world heavy-weight title, had taken place at Farnborough in April and ended in a draw after 60 rounds, by which time neither man was fit to continue. The exchanges had been so brutal that there was an outcry, and the new Marquess of Queensberry rules were introduced a few years later. This was the last bare-knuckle prize fight in England.
p.166

28. Flashman is right in supposing that the regimental march of the Buffs is attributed to Handel, but almost certainly wrong in saying that it was played on the march to Pekin: the Buffs had been left behind to guard the Taku Forts, while the 60th were left at Sinho, and the 44th sent as reinforcements to Shanghai, thus reducing the army to a more manageable size. As to the Handel attribution, there is no conclusive proof that he wrote the march, although the Buffs' tradition is strong on the point; the suggestion is that the composer had an affection for the regiment, with its distinguished record of Continental service, and perhaps also because it had its origins in the old trained bands of London, his adopted home. (See Fortescue, vol. XIII; Walter Wood, *The Romance of Regimental Marches*.) p.168

29. Flashman gives a condensed but accurate account of the march to Pekin, which finally took 44 days to complete. For fuller accounts see Loch; Wolseley; Grant and Knollys; Rev. R. J. L. McGhee, *How We Got to Pekin* (1862); R. Swinhoe (Hope Grant's interpreter), *Narrative of the North China Campaign* (1861); D. Bonner-Smith and E. W. R. Lumley (Navy Records Society), *The Second China War*, 1944; Robert Fortune, *Yedo to Pekin* (1863). p.168

30. It is not often that the editor finds it necessary to supplement Flashman's narrative with any important matter, but the present glaring omission has to be filled. Having devoted almost half his narrative to his mission to Nanking, and his efforts to prevent the Taipings taking Shanghai, the author now blandly forgets all about the matter; of course, it is quite characteristic that he should no longer have cared whether Shanghai fell or not, since he was safely away from it, but one would have expected at least a line about the outcome, especially since Elgin had just drawn it to his attention. For the Manchu request for British help against the Taipings was prompted by the news from Shanghai, where Loyal Prince Lee's forces had been repulsed by British marines and Sikhs on August 18–21. It was not a major action, although the Taipings suffered some casualties; Lee's reaction appears to have been one of bewildered disappointment at being rejected by fellow-Christians. His failure seemed to do him no harm in the Taiping hierarchy. p.169

31. Flashman may not have persuaded General Sir John Michel to part immediately with *Dr Thorne*, the new best-seller by Anthony Trollope, since it is known that Lord Elgin was reading it some months later. It and Darwin's *Origin of Species*, published the previous year, were his lordship's relaxation during his China mission. p.170

316

32. Flashman was remembering the murder in 1841, in similar circumstances, of Sir William McNaghten, British Envoy to Kabul, at the hands of the followers of Akbar Khan. (See *Flashman*.)　　p.184

33. The events of September 18, when the Chinese tried to ambush the allied force at Five-li Point, and took several prisoners in violation of the truce, are corroborated by the authorities cited in Note 29, especially Loch, who with Parkes was captured by Sang-kol-in-sen himself. Loch, like Flashman, paints a most unpleasant picture of the warlord, who worked himself into a fury, storming and yelling abuse at his prisoners while his guards beat them, forced them to kneel, and rubbed Loch's face in the dirt; he called Parkes a liar, accused him of trying to humiliate the Emperor and of preparing a treacherous attack on the Chinese forces, and added "that he would teach us what it was to speak to high officers of the Celestial Empire in the manner in which they had been addressed yesterday" (i.e. at the Tang-chao meeting with Prince I). It was after this that Loch and the others were taken to the Board of Punishments. (See Loch.) Screaming at barbarians seems to have been common among the mandarins when their superiority was in question; Sang flew into a passion at the suggestion that Queen Victoria was the equal of the Emperor. Incidentally, Flashman is the only authority that Sang was responsible for Private Moyes' murder, but it is interesting that the tirade directed at the Tang-ku prisoners is identical with one delivered by Sang on another occasion.

"Sam Collinson" was something of a mascot to the British troops, probably because of his name. He was certainly a resolute if unskilful opponent. Physically, he was powerful, with a face described as "broad, humorous, savage, strong, and crafty." (See the portrait by Beato, *Illustrated London News*, vol. xxxviii, p.357).　　p.185

34. Flashman's account of events at Pah-li-chao Bridge might seem incredible if it did not conform so closely to known facts. The mandarin commanding the bridge was twice wounded during the battle, and ordered the execution of Brabazon and the Abbé de Luc in revenge; both were beheaded on the parapet of the bridge, although there is no record, outside Flashman, of the death of Nolan. The Chinese authorities later said that the two had died from natural causes, but unofficial Chinese sources agreed that the mandarin beheaded them in reprisal; this was confirmed by the Russian Mission, whose intelligence service was excellent. Months later, the graves were identified by Chinese, and two headless skeletons were found, along with scraps of cloth from artillery trousers and a piece of silk consistent with French ecclesiastical clothing. (See Loch.)

The battle, in which the French suffered the heavier casualties among the allies, followed the course briefly described by Flashman: the Chinese forces were routed, and driven to within six miles of Pekin. It was the last action of the campaign. Montauban, the French commander, was ennobled as Count Palikao.　　p.196

35. Shaw's only "Western", *The Shewing-Up of Blanco Posnet*, was first staged in 1909.　　p.196

36. Such is the power of propaganda, that at Sinho the Imperial troops

317

thought the British infantry were kow-towing when their front rank
assumed the kneeling firing position. p.202
37. The Emperor Hsien Feng, Son of Heaven, Complete Abundance,
Solitary Prince, Celestial Emperor, Lord of the Middle Kingdom,
etc., was 29 at this time, and dying of dropsy and debauchery. As with
many other oriental princes, care had been taken to deprave him early
in life; his tutor in vice had been his assistant secretary Sushun, and
he appears to have been completely in thrall to his favourite concubine,
Yehonala. At one time he had been a fine gymnast, and even when
his health was breaking down he retained a stately, dignified bearing. He was "simple of face", with a small mouth, and wore a little
moustache.

Flashman's observation of the Imperial throne room in the Forbidden City is accurate, as are his later descriptions of the Emperor's
private apartments in the Summer Palace.

It was customary to address his majesty with the words: "Your
slave, kneeling . . ." His decrees, written in vermilion ink, began:
"Swaying the wide world, we . . ." Protocol demanded that he should
always face south, and nobles invariably stood in his presence, even
when eating. (See Appendix II.) p.205
38. Many travellers visited the old Summer Palace and marvelled; it has
been described by several of Flashman's army comrades, although
none of them had the opportunity to study it as closely as he did, but
it was obviously a place that had to be seen to be believed. It was a
wonder on two counts: for the priceless treasures it contained, and as
the supreme example of landscape gardening – for every inch of its
extensive grounds, its lakes, and woods, and hills, was said to have
been built by craftsmen to the most careful design, some of it over
centuries. (See McGhee, Wolseley, Loch, Swinhoe, and volumes
xxxvii and xxxviii, *Illustrated London News*, 1860, 1861.) p.227
39. One of Yehonala's six-inch block shoes, fringed with pearls, is said to
have fetched £25,000 after being looted in the Boxer Rising. p.227
40. Flashman is clear about the date of Yehonala's departure: the night
of October 6–7. At first sight there is an inconsistency here, since
other records established that the Emperor and his suite, *including
Yehonala*, left for Jehol on September 22, the day after Flashman's
audience with the Emperor. The explanation is provided in Flashman's
narrative: Yehonala did leave on the 22nd, and returned two days
later (Flashman states that he did not see her for two days after their
first meeting, and writes elsewhere that she made a flying visit to Jehol
"early in my captivity"). Others of the court also remained at Pekin
until the last minute; the Empress Dowager and Prince Kung narrowly
escaped the French advance on the Ewen-ming-ewen. p.257
41. About twenty badly-armed eunuchs made a valiant effort to stop the
French vanguard, and were shot down. (See Wolseley.) p.259
42. The looting of the Ewen-ming-ewen by the French, the subsequent
visit by Elgin (whose reaction Flashman reports correctly), the generals' conference about dividing the spoil, the participation of British
troops and Chinese villagers, the wanton destruction of anything too
big to carry, etc., are all confirmed in other accounts; most of the

318

eye-witnesses express sadness, disgust, or horror, but (with the exception of a few, notably Elgin and Grant) seem to have taken their share. Wolseley, who watched the proceedings with an artist's eye, has interesting reflections on the psychology of looting – which, incidentally, is not a subject to be pronounced on by those who have never had the opportunity. (See Wolseley, Swinhoe, Wrong, McGhee.)

Flashman's black jade chess set may well have been a priceless rarity, even if it was probably a black variety of jadeite rather than nephrite. The very existence of "black jade" has been denied (see *Encyclopedia Britannica*, Eleventh Edition), but there are references to it in Chinese literature, and some black jade carvings are said to be extant, including a knife of the Early Chou Dynasty (1122–722 B.C.) illustrated in S. C. Nott's *Chinese Jade* (1936). p.270

43. On the treatment of the prisoners and the return of the bodies, Flashman is scrupulously exact. (See Loch and others, with the depositions of Daffadar Jawalla Singh and Sowars Khan Singh and Bugel Singh, all of Fane's Horse.) p.272

44. Whether Flashman is right in his examination of Elgin's motives, he has at least set out clearly the chain of events which led to the decision to burn the Summer Palace, and the arguments which were advanced for and against at the time. And he has done this so fully that there is little to add. Whether Elgin was justified of his act of calculated vandalism is a question which may be set as an interesting historical exercise, but not in the hope of receiving a satisfactory answer. Such matters are simply not to be judged at a distance. It is abominable to destroy priceless works of art; against that, Elgin was faced with the necessity of making a gesture which would not only have the effect of punishment but of inculcating a lesson, and of securing future peace and security so far as he could see; his time and means were limited. His critics cannot merely say he was wrong; they must say what else he could have done, and they must show that it would have been equally effective.

It is also necessary to bear in mind the personality of the man himself, and to put aside the idea that the burning was an act of mindless imperial barbarism (of course, it can be cited as a splendid example of just that, for the purpose of debate, provided all the facts of the case are not deployed). Mindless, it certainly was not. James Bruce was no unthinking vandal; far from it, he was almost the last man to do such a thing. It is not possible to say that he felt no primitive desire for revenge; if he did, he had cause, but not enough to cloud the judgment of an experienced and responsible statesman who was also a sensitive and decent man. Elgin was enlightened beyond his day (his words on imperialism, treatment of foreign races, and his country's high-handedness, spoken at his first interview with Flashman, are to be found in his writings); to some of his contemporaries (though to fewer than modern revisionists seem to realise) he may have seemed almost heretical. He knew, too, that in judging his act, the world would not forget the Elgin Marbles acquired by his father. It took a brave man to burn the Summer Palace. He hated doing it;

319

he does not mention it in letters to his wife, and there is a gap in his correspondence from October 14 to 26, when he notes that he has not been keeping his journal lately. But, knowing the circumstances as only he could know them, he did at Pekin what he thought best, and it worked. Whether the end justified the means is a matter of opinion. Barbaric is a fair word to apply to the deed; it is not, paradoxically, a fair word to apply to the Big Barbarian.

The reactions of his subordinates are interesting. Loch plainly felt guilty about it. McGhee regretted it, but thought it necessary. Wolseley, the artist and art collector, was saddened by it; he had strong views on looting, and paid for his share, although he is said to have been given a Petitot picture by a French officer. The impenetrable Hope Grant refused any share of loot, but insisted that his troops should receive their proper entitlement (which came to about £4 a head). Gordon wrote of pillaging and destroying "in a vandal-like manner"; it was "wretchedly demoralising work". But he noted succinctly: "Although I have not as much as many, I have done well." Since his loot included furs, jade, enamel, and part of a throne, he obviously had. But whatever their opinion of the burning, most of the British felt that the French had got the best of the loot, although Wolseley may have been nearer the truth when he estimated that the Chinese villagers had plundered more than the British and French combined.   p.281

45. Flashman disagrees here with Loch, who says that this incident, when Parkes unexpectedly came face to face with his tormentor, the President of the Board of Punishments, took place three days earlier, on October 21.